A TANTALIZING LESSON

"When a woman leaps like a frightened doe each time a man comes near her, she needs to be thoroughly kissed so she will know what to expect," Cale murmured as he combed his fingers through her silken hair. "Passion is one of the greatest pleasures a man and woman can experience. I want to teach you not to be so apprehensive about it . . ."

Mikyla braced her hand on his chest to hold him at bay. "And how much is this lesson going to cost me?" she questioned suspiciously.

A wry smile rippled across his full lips. "You can pay whatever you think the lesson is worth."

"Don't be surprised if you receive *nothing* for your instruction," Mikyla said just before his mouth took possession of hers.

It would have been so much easier to cope with her emotions if Cale hadn't been so amazingly gentle. His hands and lips were everywhere at once, discovering each curve and swell, learning each sensitive point with tender care. Mikyla gulped for breath only to find that Cale had stripped the air from her lungs. Like a drowning swimmer, she clung to him, knowing she was clutching at danger, not safety. There was nothing safe about this sensuous rake. He was as dangerous as a man could be . . .

STORMFIRE

CAROL FINCH

ZEBRA BOOKS
KENSINGTON PUBLISHING CORP.

ZEBRA BOOKS

are published by

Kensington Publishing Corp.
475 Park Avenue South
New York, NY 10016

First printing: May, 1989

Printed in the United States of America

This book is dedicated to my family for their patience and support. To my husband Ed, to my children Christie, Jill, and Kurt. Love you . . .

And to Jack and Martha White for letting me borrow "Sundance" for this romp through the pages of history. Many thanks!

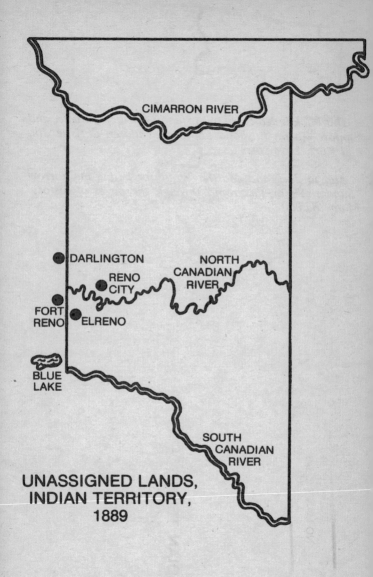

CIMARRON RIVER

DARLINGTON

RENO
CITY

NORTH
CANADIAN
RIVER

FORT
RENO

ELRENO

BLUE
LAKE

SOUTH
CANADIAN
RIVER

UNASSIGNED LANDS,
INDIAN TERRITORY,
1889

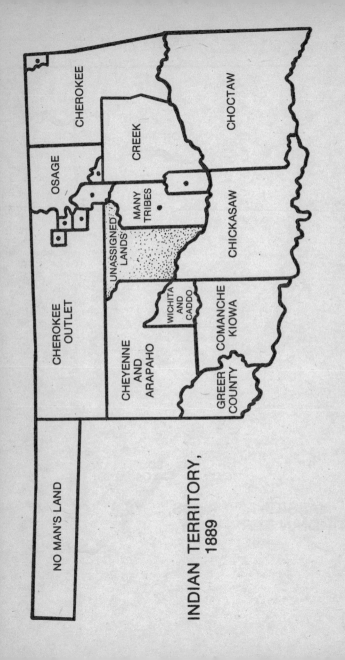

INDIAN TERRITORY, 1889

Part I

Follow a shadow, it still flies you;
Seem to fly it, it will pursue;
So court a mistress who denies you;
Let her alone, she will court you.
                    —Ben Jonson

Chapter 1

Indian Territory, April 1889

A mass of black clouds hung so heavily in the sky they seemed to scrape the sprawling prairie. Above the low-hanging clouds, piling upward like hundreds of threatening, doubled fists, were the rumbling thunderheads that were notorious for wreaking havoc in Indian Territory. The boiling storm swallowed the sun, flinging dark shadows across the green sea of undulating grass. Occasional shafts of sunlight splintered from the perimeters of the thunderheads, leaving them looking as if they were rimmed with silver. And then just as suddenly, the brilliant light evaporated, burying the prairie in foreboding shadows.

A streak of lightning shot toward the ground, as if some vengeful warrior had plunged his spear into the earth in warning of impending doom. The piercing shaft of light from the heavens was punctuated by a ferocious crack of thunder that left the earth trembling in apprehension of what was to come. The cold southwesterly wind swept through the trees and grass, trumpeting the approach of another spring storm.

Cale Brolin involuntarily flinched when an oversize raindrop slapped him on the cheek. Another white-hot thunderbolt ripped through the ominous clouds and Cale felt a snake of apprehension slithering down his spine. Cale detested storms, especially the turbulent, cyclonic kind that raged across the rolling plains, bringing death and destruction. They reminded him of the tragic incident that had occurred three years earlier—almost to the day. He did not consider himself a coward. Indeed, Cale usually took adversity in stride. But nothing got under his skin faster or more effectively than the appearance of a thunderbolt, especially when he knew how devastating and deadly . . .

Wrenching the dreadful thought from his mind, Cale tipped back his hat to stare skyward. His keen silver-gray eyes monitored the swift movement of the storm. Random lightning bolts blared against the backdrop of gloomy clouds, causing the unpleasant memories to erupt all over again. Cale tried to forget what he didn't want to remember, but the storm activated the sequence of events that had mushroomed into catastrophe.

As if it were only yesterday, Cale could visualize the tragic scene, relive each nerve-shattering emotion. Muttering, Cale squeezed his eyes shut, but he could still see the blinding flash of piercing white light, hear the deafening explosion and the blood-curdling almost inhuman scream—his own.

Long black lashes swept down to block out the tormenting vision from the past. But those horrifying memories still had the power to haunt him, to make his blood run cold. Resolutely, Cale gathered his composure and swung from the saddle. Moving with swift efficiency, Cale staked his string of horses in the gently sloping valley to wait out the storm. A man on horseback was a sitting duck during a violent thunderstorm, Cale reminded himself grimly. He had viewed firsthand what it was like to become a human lightning rod. Cale cursed the instinctive shudder that sizzled through him as that fateful night rose in his mind like a tormenting apparition.

Crouching, Cale stared across the wide expanse of the prairie. A man was every kind of fool if he didn't observe caution during storms. Cale pulled down his Stetson to fend against the sharp stab of wind-blown raindrops and heaved a frustrated sigh. He had hoped to reach his camp before the storm unleashed its fury . . .

Between the brilliant flashes of silver and the explosive

thunder Cale detected the sound of galloping hooves. His narrowed gaze scanned the rolling hills to locate the source of the sound. His dark brows jackknifed when a rider appeared like a lone ship sailing in a sea of waving grass.

"Damned fool," he scowled as he crouched lower. But his gaze never wavered from the magnificent stallion that seemed to sprout wings and fly across the storm-tossed prairie. A flaxen mane and tail trailed in the wind, contrasted by the deep red sheen of the stallion's muscular body.

Cale prided himself in being a connoisseur of horse flesh. He made his living selling mules, cattle, and horses in Indian and New Mexico Territory. Even at a distance Cale recognized a good horse when he saw one. It annoyed him to see this reckless rider risking his life and his valuable animal by defying the storm.

While Cale was cursing the man's stupidity, the hat that camouflaged the rider's features caught in the wind and tumbled, end over end, across the ground. Another mane undulated in the breeze like a silver-gold banner. It was a female dressed in a man's shirt and breeches! That stupid witch. She was going to get herself killed just like . . .

Cale felt the thought ricochet through his mind and evolve into an eerie sensation that riveted down his backbone. Frustrated emotion brought him immediately to his feet, even while common sense was screaming for him to stay put. His hand snaked out to grasp his mount's reins.

"Damned fool woman," Cale snorted. As the strawberry roan gelding, unnerved by the rumbling thunder, skitted sideways, Cale leaped to his back in a single bound. Frowning, Cale aimed himself toward the idiotic female who obviously didn't have enough sense to take shelter from the rain.

When a thunderclap resounded directly overhead, Cale watched in amazement as the powerful stallion reared on his hind legs and thrashed the air. His shrill whinny stabbed the damp air and he bolted off like Pegasus, the mythical winged stallion.

Cale was certain the stupid twit had lost control of her

steed. She was clinging to the stallion's neck as he raced against the wind and won! With a sharp bark to his mount, Cale pursued the rider, straining to close the distance between them. But the roan, swift of hoof, resembled a plodding nag in comparison. The blood-red stallion took off as if Cale were standing still!

Mikyla Lassiter glanced over her shoulder to survey the man who was slapping his steed to catch up with her, and with little success. Obviously, the man had read one too many chivalrous knight novels and was picturing himself as the gallant warrior who saved damsels from distress. It wasn't the first time Miki's wild rides had been misinterpreted as runaway flights. Once the men in the Boomer camp realized that she was an accomplished equestrian and that Sundance was unrivaled, they merely boasted her talents and praised her stallion, but it was apparent that the man who galloped behind her was not among the settlers in the Boomer camp. If he were, he would have known he didn't stand a chance against Sundance.

Smiling to herself, Mikyla tugged on the reins, commanding Sundance to slow his breakneck pace. But before she could bring herself back to an upright position in the saddle and offer any sort of greeting to the stranger, a steely arm hooked around her waist. Mikyla was uprooted from the saddle like a tree upended by a cyclone.

A startled yelp burst from her lips as she was left dangling in midair. Before she could protest being rescued while in perfect control of her steed, she was planted on the man's lap. His arm slanted diagonally across her like a vise grip, forcing the air from her lungs and pressing all too familiarly against her breasts.

The words that flocked to the tip of her tongue washed away when the sky opened to pour buckets of rain down upon them. And while Mikyla was sputtering to voice a protest and wiping the torrents of rain from her eyes, Cale yanked on his steed's reins. The laboring animal came to a skidding halt. Mikyla's head was thrown forward and she slammed back against Cale's rock-hard chest.

The man was a maniac, Miki decided. He had stripped her

14

from the saddle, deposited her on his lap, and then he very nearly flung her head from her shoulders. But before she could tell him what she thought of his rough abuse, he stepped from the stirrup, dragging her with him as if she were a rag doll. Her feet had barely touched the ground before Cale shoved her facedown, leaving her to mutter a curse into the grass. When Mikyla attempted to bolt to her feet, Cale sprawled on top of her, knocking another string of curses back into the damp grass.

"What do you think you're doing?" Mikyla asked.

Had she misjudged the man's intentions? Naive fool, she shouted at herself. All this time she presumed he was trying to save her from her wild ride, but now she was left to wonder if it was molestation he had in mind. He was already closer to her than any man had ever been, and the big galloot was squashing her flat!

Lightning darted from the bleak sky and struck a nearby cottonwood tree. Cale's body went rigid. Lord, that was all too close! If this dim-witted female had still been on her horse she would probably have been frying alive at this very moment, just like . . .

"What I'm doing is saving your foolish neck, dammit!" Cale growled in belated response, shifting his weight upon her to ensure that she remained on the ground. Not that she didn't deserve to be flat as a pancake, curse her!

Mikyla bowed her neck and swiveled her head around to acquaint Cale with her look of icy disdain. "Dammit, yourself! I did *not* need saving," she spewed at him, her blue eyes blazing. "I was in complete control of my horse. And if I hadn't pulled back on the reins you never would have caught up with me."

The smell of the burning tree set fuse to Cale's temper, one that usually was attached to a long wick. His soggy arm shot past her upturned nose, directing her attention to the curl of smoke that drifted from the trees on Cheyenne-Arapaho Creek.

"I was saving you from the lightning, you little idiot!" he snapped just as hatefully. "Have you ever seen anyone struck down?" Cale didn't wait for her to reply. He was caught up in the terrifying scene that flashed across his mind's eye. "Well, by God, I have! And you don't want me to describe how you would look if you had been cremated in a split second."

Mikyla twisted in the wet ground to glare at the grass, remaining silent while the thunder resounded like the roll of a huge bass drum. She had been foolish to race back to the Boomer camp during the storm, she reflected pensively. But she feared being caught by the cavalry patrols while she was trespassing in the Unassigned Lands. She shouldn't have sneaked inside the boundaries that would soon open to settlers, but curiosity had gotten the best of her and she was looking for just the right place to stake her claim and . . .

"Well? Have you nothing to say for yourself?" Cale scowled irritably. "Hasn't anyone ever told you how dangerous it is to be poised atop a horse during a thunderstorm? And what the hell are you doing out here in the first place? This part of the territory is only open to those who carry a government license, little lady. I'm willing to bet you don't have one!"

Mikyla was not accustomed to being raked over the coals as if she were a naughty child. "Has anyone ever told you to mind your own business, mister?" she sniffed sarcastically.

She wormed sideways to unseat the big brute who was still squashing her into the ground. A pained grimace claimed her muddy features as Cale's ivory-handled Colt .45 accidentally jabbed her in the ribs, infuriating her all over again. Her attempt to wriggle free was getting her nowhere. Damn, she might as well have been lying beneath a boulder.

"Curse it, get off me. You must weigh two hundred pounds," Mikyla muttered scornfully.

"Two hundred and twenty-five, if you must know," he growled at the back of her head.

What a sassy little thing she was, Cale decided. He had saved the chit's life and she had not shown a smidgen of gratitude. Hell, he should have let her take her chances with the storm.

Mikyla thought he would surely remove himself and grant her space to breathe after he read her the riot act. But Cale kept her pinned to the cold, wet ground for what seemed

16

forever. It was humiliating enough to be shoved in the grass and held there indefinitely. But it was doubly embarrassing to feel this stranger's sinewy body molded so intimately to her backside. Mikyla was not accustomed to lying beneath a man. In fact, in all her twenty-one years she couldn't recall being this close to one, and she was unsettled by their suggestive position. Her only consolation was that she wasn't on her back, facing him. That surely would have been worse, she reckoned.

As Mikyla grappled with that thought, she became aware of Cale's breathing, as if it was a part of her. She could feel his whipcord muscles grinding into her soft contours, feel the long, taut tendons of his thigh wedged between her legs to keep her spread-eagled on the ground. The warmth of his solid flesh scorched through her damp clothes, making her far too aware of things about this man she would have preferred to ignore.

She could have sworn an hour had elapsed while the rain pelleted down upon them and thunder clapped above them like an audience applauding Mother Nature's spectacular fireworks display. And still her self-appointed guardian angel lay atop her. Time was inching by at a snail's pace, and her annoyance was compounded by the awkwardly uncomfortable situation of lying with a man she didn't even know.

Drumming her fingers on the ground, Mikyla impatiently waited for Cale to declare that conditions were no longer favorable for lightning bolts to fry her alive. She detested the fact that she was spending her time pondering the man who had snatched her from her stallion's back and threw her facedown in the muddy grass. Confound it, if he ever let her up she was going to squash *him* flat and see how *he* liked it!

Chapter 2

Cale's irritation and apprehension ebbed when the storm rumbled past them, leaving only the cold, drenching rains. Once the danger had passed he became vividly aware of the woman beneath him. Until that moment, he had been too engulfed in painful memories to give her much consideration. He had been far too busy yanking her from the saddle and pushing her to the ground to pay much attention to her face. And even now, he couldn't see past the mop of silver-gold hair that capped her head. When she had turned to fling her sassy remarks there were so many renegade strands falling over her face that Cale had been unable to tell much about the chit. For all he knew, her face might have been her chaperone, one that would frighten the daylights out of a *thunderstorm*.

The faintest hint of a smile touched Cale's lips when he realized how ridiculous they would look to anyone who happened upon them. "What's your name, honey?" he queried as he eased down beside her and levered himself up on an elbow.

The casual endearment rubbed Mikyla the wrong way. As if everything about him hadn't already, she thought with a disgusted sniff. "I am not your honey," she snapped curtly. Mikyla pushed herself from the ground and twisted to sit up beside him, then tossed her wild mane of hair over her shoulder and glowered at this man lounging beside her. "The name is Mikyla Lassiter. *Miss* Lassiter to you," she added on

19

a sour note.

Cale considered himself an excellent judge of horse flesh and he wasn't a novice with women either. He had changed women as often as he changed bed linen and he had seen his fair share of females. But this feisty minx was second to none. She had generous curves and swells in all the right places. The soaking rain caused her shirt and breeches to cling to her shapely form, as if the cloth had been stitched directly to her skin. Cale hadn't meant to rake her so thoroughly, but his roving eyes were helping themselves to an uninhibited tour, not missing the slightest detail. The taut peaks of her breasts pressed wantonly against the wet fabric of her shirt. The trim-fitting breeches hugged her small waist and curvaceous hips so exquisitely that Cale had difficulty breathing.

His wandering gaze finally worked its way back from her shapely legs and up to the generous swell of her bosom. He found himself wishing he hadn't been so preoccupied with the storm while he held this lovely bundle to the ground. When he got around to lifting his appreciative gaze to her face, he found himself staring into the most incredible pair of blue eyes he could ever remember seeing. They reminded him of the sky at dawn, just as the sun flung its bright light over the horizon. Surrounding those lovely azure pools were long curly lashes. The pouring rain had washed away the splotches of mud, exposing her creamy complexion and her soft, pouting lips—the kind that invited kisses. Her delicate, refined features captivated him. And for another long, fanciful moment, Cale ran a measuring eye over her curvaceous figure, indulging his lusty thoughts. Damn, she was gorgeous! If he had known he was lying atop such a bewitching beauty he definitely would have . . .

Mikyla had seen that leer too many times on men's faces not to recognize the direction Cale's thoughts had taken. Her features puckered in a scornful frown. Men! Was that all they ever thought about when they ventured near a woman? None of them could carry on a civil conversation without imagining how a woman would look in the altogether! This bold stranger was ogling her as if he were the rat and she was he cheese. He portrayed his role superbly, rat that he was!

Although Mikyla was glaring furiously at Cale she couldn't determine if he had interpreted her look of irritation. His head had tilted and his eyes were shielded by the wide brim of his felt hat, which was drooping from the excessive water that had pounded upon it.

"I'll thank you not to be so obvious in what you're thinking," Mikyla sniffed distastefully.

Against her will, her gaze slid down to inspect her companion. He had shoulders like a bull. Her curious eyes drifted on to survey the broad expanse of his chest, which had been molded against her only minutes before. The top two buttons of his green chambray shirt were missing. Most likely because of the excessive strain of their wild ride and nasty dismount, she supposed. A dark matting of hair shadowed the golden muscles. Mikyla could not help but gawk at the arousing sight. The stranger looked so large and powerfully built that it was impossible not to notice him.

Continuing her visual observation, her eyes measured his tapered waist and narrow hips. Long, muscular legs—one bent, the other outstretched—captured her undivided attention. He reminded her of a mountain just sitting there—all rock-hard flesh that had been carved into one of the most well-sculptured physiques she had ever seen. There was not an inch of flab on his body, at least not that she could see. And since his damp clothes fit like an extra set of skin, Mikyla doubted he could have concealed any unnecessary bulges. Although she hated to admit it, the stranger was incredibly well constructed—like a bronze figure placed on display in a museum for all to admire.

The past few weeks, Mikyla had been introduced to hordes of available young men, handsome ones and plain ones, but none of them had piqued her feminine interest as quickly and thoroughly as . . . Mikyla winced as if she had been stabbed from behind. For heaven's sake, she didn't even know the man's name and he had been lying on top of her for at least half an hour.

"*Now* who's staring, *Miss* Lassiter?" Cale taunted in a deep husky voice that vibrated on Mikyla's skin.

His thumb nudged the limp hat away from his forehead, exposing raven hair and revealing twinkling silver-gray eyes that were rimmed with thick black lashes. A rakish smile pursed his sensuous lips and carved deep lines in his tanned face.

It seemed the good Lord had gathered all the distinct, striking features He had created and plastered them all on this rogue. The stranger had it all—the noble profile, the physique of a Roman god, the ruggedly handsome visage.

The impact of that penetrating silver stare made Mikyla flinch as if she had been stung by a wasp. She swore he could stare right through her to pluck out her secretive speculations about him. Mikyla blushed up to her perfectly arched brows. She felt as if she had been caught window-peeking, which indeed she most certainly had been!

Composing herself, Mikyla tilted a proud chin. "Would you mind telling me who I'm staring at?" she requested. Although she tried to remain aloof, she found it necessary to bite back the beginning of a sheepish smile.

Cale felt an odd warmth trickle through him when Mikyla peeked up at him through a veil of rain-kissed eyelashes. Her smile cast a radiant glow on an otherwise gloomy afternoon. He would have unfolded himself from the ground to make a formal bow if he hadn't been forced to relinquish this particular view of her arresting assets. But then, Cale seriously doubted she would be less appealing from *any* angle.

"Cale Brolin," he drawled in belated response.

A wry grin dangled from the corner of his full lips. Damned if I can keep my eyes from mapping the luscious terrain of her body, Cale thought to himself. Everything about Mikyla drew his gaze and held it—the cupid's bow of her lips, the lustrous whites of her eyes that encircled those dazzling, sky-blue pools, the exquisite texture of her skin, that enticing body beneath those clinging clothes . . .

Disapproval was stamped on Mikyla's features. She had noticed the all-consuming path his eyes had taken when they strayed from her face. Yes, she had been ogled by a various sundry of men, but there was something very potent about e way Cale scrutinized her. His probing gaze sent a fleet of goosebumps cruising across her skin. It was as if those perceptive silver-gray eyes had unfolded invisible tentacles that reached to glide over her flesh . . .

Miki mentally pinched herself for permitting her thoughts to detour down such sordid avenues. But when Cale looked at her as if he were touching her, she could almost feel his exploring caress. Hastily, she glanced away and sought to distract him, as well as herself. If she wasn't careful, things could get completely out of hand.

Pasting on a reckless smile, Mikyla gestured a slim finger to the east. "What brings you to the boundaries of Oklahoma country? Are you planning to participate in the Land Run like the rest of us?" Her voice was a bit strained, but it was the best she could do, considering the disturbing effect this rogue was having on her.

Like a rousing lion, Cale pushed himself into an upright position on the ground. Judging by her question, Cale presumed this daring lass was one of the hopeful settlers who had gathered along the four borders of the Unassigned Lands to make the Run for one hundred sixty acres of free homesteads. For weeks, Indian Territory had been clogged with camps of settlers who awaited the first Land Run into the heart of Indian country. There were more people than a man could shake a stick at, and Cale resented the intrusion. This virgin prairie was all that was left of the wild frontier and the government was about to give it away to land-hungry homesteaders.

"No, I have no desire to enter this madcap race. I am licensed to sell horses and mules to the forts, Indian agencies, and stage lines in the territory," he explained. "In truth, I consider the Boomer camps an unsightly intrusion on what was once a peaceful countryside."

Cale couldn't help himself. He reached over to brush away the renegade strands of hair that clung to Mikyla's cheeks. His fingertips skimmed her satiny skin, finding it as soft and exquisite as he had anticipated.

Mikyla jerked away from his inquiring touch and flung him a reproachful glare. Although she had never been

23

lightning struck, she was beginning to imagine how it felt—if Cale's electrifying touch was any indication of what she might expect. The sizzling sensation leaped through her entire body, grounding her to the damp prairie.

"You are much too bold, Mr. Brolin," she scolded, hating her violent reaction to a perfect stranger. There was no reason why his touch should affect her so!

"Cale," he corrected. The resonance of his voice was soft and husky and altogether seductive. "And I've been told that before."

"Obviously, you neglected to take the constructive criticism to heart . . ."

Miki stared at him in utter disbelief when he pushed his soggy Stetson from his raven head and moved toward her with slow deliberation. Sweet mercy! He was going to kiss her. It was written all over his craggy features. They had only met and he was attempting to take outrageous privileges. That scoundrel. Did he think she owed him some display of affection just because he might have saved her from being struck down by a lightning bolt? She was grateful, but not *that* grateful!

With an indignant squeal, Miki jumped up as if she had been sitting on a scorpion. But Cale came uncoiled like a striking snake. When he snared her arm, her momentum took her backward instead of upward. She landed with a splat in the oozing mud and Cale came down more suddenly than *he* intended, and with a lot less dignity. He found himself lying on top of Mikyla . . . again . . .

Miki had earlier contemplated how uncomfortable her predicament would have been if she were facing Cale while he was sprawled on top of her. Now she knew! The feel of his sinewy body meshing intimately against hers caused her to gasp in astonished outrage. She could feel his searing imprint on her wet skin, feel the broad-muscled width of his chest crushing into her breasts. He was astride her, his thigh crowding her hips, his hard length swallowing every inch of her naive body.

Wide blue eyes focused on Cale's ruggedly handsome features . . . until she fell into those liquid silver pools that could helplessly entrance a woman. His stunning eyes were smiling down at her, not in a threatening sort of way, but in a provocative manner that brought all her senses to life. She could feel his whipcord muscles flexing and relaxing against her. She could see those bronzed cheeks and sensuous lips at close range. She could inhale the masculine scent of him and she was sorely wishing she would have been struck deaf, dumb, and blind. Lord, she didn't want to cope with what she was feeling and thinking!

A quiet smile rippled across his lips, which were now only a few breathless inches away from her soft mouth. "I only intended to kiss you, Ky." He had immediately overstepped formality and selected a nickname, which he uttered so huskily that Mikyla melted into a puddle. "I want to appease my male curiosity. It's as simple as that. No harm intended . . ."

His dark face tilted slightly, reassessing her. Lord, she had the most kissable mouth ever planted on a female face, he mused appreciatively. His eyes slid over her soft, trembling lips long before he took them under his. The brush of his mouth was light and inquiring, as if he were testing his reaction to her. Seemingly satisfied that this would not be an unpleasant encounter, Cale deepened the kiss. His tongue traced the gentle curve of her lips and then probed deeper to investigate the sweet taste of her. His fingers speared into her unruly hair, tilting her face to his. His steel-hard body seemed to absorb her and he relaxed above her as they lay thigh-to-thigh, chest-to-chest, sharing what was supposed to have been a simple kiss.

Suddenly the steady patter of rain drowned beneath the erratic beat of Mikyla's heart. Her pulse was leapfrogging through her bloodstream and she swore butterflies were rioting in her stomach. This was not supposed to be happening, Mikyla thought shakily. No other man had ever caused her to come unglued when he kissed her!

His mouth moved expertly over hers, stripping her breath and then giving it back the split second before she feared she would drown in the taste and feel of him. Cale Brolin had robbed her of her defenses, leaving not one inch of her innocent body unaffected. He wasn't offering a kiss; he was adding an entirely new dimension to the word!

It was just as Cale suspected. Those cupid's-bow lips were made to be kissed. They were as soft as rose petals and tasted like sweet, addicting wine. Cale felt a tremor of desire ripple through him when he helped himself to another sample of her intoxicating kiss. He would be content to spend the remainder of the afternoon discovering more about this luscious angel. It had only been a matter of days since he had held a woman in his arms, but the way Miki affected him, one would think he had been deprived of affection for an eternity!

As simple as that? Cale's quiet words echoed through Mikyla's mind. What she was feeling surely wasn't simple. It was highly complicated and nerve-shattering. Her integrity was being subjected to a temptation that rivaled nothing in her limited experience. Her body was being assaulted by sensations that were strange and unfamiliar. It wasn't just the suggestive promise in his kisses, but also the tantalizing way Cale pressed against her that rattled her and made her feel so wildly feminine.

A riptide of emotions channeled through her. Mikyla was ashamed of herself for enjoying this romantic encounter and she was baffled by the feeling that uncoiled inside her. In the past, Mikyla had kept herself aloof and remote from men, enjoying their courting, but keeping her emotions respectably distanced.

For more than a year, she had been driven by a dream, one so strong and compelling that she had refused all romantic involvement. But this man had so distracted her, that for the life of her, Mikyla couldn't remember what purpose compelled her or why it was so all-fired important. Cale Brolin kissed her and she forgot who she was and what she wanted.

Mikyla was lost in a world of erotic sensations until Cale's wandering hands migrated over the swells of her breast to tease the throbbing peak. His bold caress jolted her to her senses. With an indignant gasp, Mikyla whacked him across the cheek, slapping Cale back to *his* senses. *The nerve of this man!* she silently fumed. What did he think she was, some eager harlot who gave herself to a total stranger just for the thrill of it all?

"Are you quite finished?" Miki snapped contemptuously. "You said you only desired a simple kiss, one you didn't even deserve in the first place." Her breasts heaved as she inhaled an agitated breath. "I will not tolerate your roaming hands. As a matter of fact, I wasn't all that crazy about your kiss. If you hadn't been squashing me flat I wouldn't even have given in to *that!*"

Mikyla didn't know why she felt the need to insult him. Perhaps it was to protect her wounded pride, she mused. She was thoroughly ashamed of her behavior. The kiss had been truly overwhelming, to be sure, but Mikyla would have died before she admitted that to him. When a man knocked the props out from under a woman she didn't come right out and tell him so. It would be like aiding and abetting the enemy!

Cale chuckled good-naturedly as he rolled away to sit cross-legged. Mikyla reminded him of a wet cat—hissing, spewing, and clawing her way out of danger. But she was also irresistibly lovely when she was all fire and flying fur. A sly smile surfaced on his lips as he inspected the welt on his cheek. That hellcat had lied about their kiss. He had felt her body respond, and knew she had enjoyed their embrace as much as he had, but she was too proud and stubborn to admit it.

"Sorry, Ky, I just got a little carried away," he confessed, but his tone was far from apologetic. Leisurely, he reached back to retrieve his soggy Stetson and set it cock-eyed on his head. "Had I known how inexperienced you were with men I would have proceeded at a much slower pace."

If Mikyla could have gotten her hands on his Colt .45 she would have shot him on the spot! How dare he ridicule her inexperience. To hear this rake talk one would have thought it a criminal offense to be a virgin.

"The name is still *Miss* Lassiter!" she spumed huffily as she vaulted to her feet. "And my inexperience is none of your business."

Mikyla stood with feet askance and arms akimbo. Her

eyes burned a hot blue flame that would have fried a normal man to a crisp. It infuriated her that she was still suffering the aftereffects of their embrace while Cale had turned off his emotions the moment he sat up. Damn, how did he do that? No doubt he had taken so many women in his arms that it was second nature to him, as reflexive as the batting of an eyelash. It was humiliating to be the only one who emerged from the riveting encounter with a pulse rate of two hundred beats per minute! Dammit, he could have at least *looked* a little ruffled by what had transpired between them!

Silver eyes made a languid ascent from the tip of her muddy boots, across the tempting curve of her hips, along the alluring swells of her bosom, up to the livid hue of her features. Mmm . . . the view was indeed spectacular, no matter what the angle, Cale mused pensively. Shrugging off her contemptuous glare, Cale rose from the ground to confront her.

Mikyla's jaw sagged on its hinges when Cale unfolded himself and *kept* unfolding himself. My Lord, he towered over her like a giant cottonwood tree, standing at least a head and a half taller than she. Indeed, Mikyla would have required a step ladder if she ever hoped to stare him squarely in the eye instead of focusing on that incredibly masculine chest.

While she was begrudgingly admiring his well-sculptured physique and the arousing way his rain-soaked clothes displayed the bunching muscles and taut tendons, Cale's arm stole around her waist. "You've challenged me, Ky," he murmured as he lifted her off the ground. "You leave me no choice but to redeem myself." A wry smile caressed his lips. "I am a good kisser . . . at least that was what I had been told until you came along to disclaim my abilities . . ."

He wasn't good, he was superb, Mikyla thought dizzily. His warm lips rolled over hers, savoring and devouring her all in the same moment. He had done it again. He had kissed the breath out of her and sent her heart racing like her winged stallion. His darting tongue inflamed her with a need she didn't want to experience. His competent hands held her against him, setting fires that even the dowsing rain couldn't

28

extinguish. Mikyla couldn't logically explain why Cale Brolin turned her emotions inside out with that sexy voice of his, with kisses that ignited flames of desire. He just did, as plain and simple as that!

When Cale finally had the decency to set her to her feet, her legs folded up like an accordion. Embarrassment stained her cheeks when Cale arched an amused brow and slipped a supporting arm around her to steady her wobbly knees. While Miki was fighting to recompose herself, Cale's shoulders were shaking with silent laughter. He had discovered a way to control this spitfire. She was not accustomed to romantic encounters and decomposed each time he dared to touch her. If he wanted to silence her outbursts all he had to do was kiss her. Not that he would complain about that! It was a rewarding technique that offered titillating benefits.

"Come along, Ky. Let's see if we can round up our runaway horses," he managed to say without snickering in self-satisfaction.

Mikyla jerked away from his grasp and elevated a proud chin. It infuriated her that Cale knew how strongly he affected her. "I can retrieve my own horse, thank you very much," she told him brusquely. "You have done quite enough already."

Cale regarded her from beneath the drooping brim of his hat. Amusement twinkled like stars in those silver eyes. "The second kiss was much better, wasn't it?" he asked with a smile. "A good deal more potent than the first. Indeed, one might even say it knocked you to your knees."

Mikyla stood there gaping at his unmitigated gall. She was totally exasperated, so much so that she had difficulty putting words to tongue. Her mouth kept opening and closing like a damper on a chimney. Dammit, she didn't want to discuss what his kisses did to her knees or any other part of her anatomy. She didn't even want to *think* about them!

Deciding not to dignify his remark, Miki spun around to expel a piercing whistle that could have roused the dead and did, in fact, penetrate Cale's eardrums.

Cale cupped his ears with his hands to block out the blare. The thought of such a loud, manly whistle exploding from this feisty little imp's lips provoked him to laughter. "What the devil do you expect to accomplish with that, Ky? If that was meant to be a signal for the cavalry to appear on the ridge . . ." His mocking voice trailed off when, lo and behold, the magnificent blood-red stallion with the flaxen mane and tail came galloping out of nowhere to answer his mistress's call.

A triumphant smile pursed Miki's lips as she glanced sideways to see Cale's jaw swinging on its hinges. "I don't need the cavalry, Mr. Brolin, only Sundance." Her smile broadened into a taunting grin that complemented her enchanting features. "And just how do you intend to retrieve *your* horse?"

Cale wasn't certain which distracted him most, this gorgeous firebrand or the powerful steed that was thundering toward them. Separately, Mikyla and Sundance were eye-catching. Together they were awe-inspiring. Cale watched in mute amazement while Miki ambled forward to meet her devoted stallion. His eyes swung from the provocative sway of her hips to the sleek, muscular steed that skidded to a halt in front of her.

And for a moment, Cale swore Mikyla had shut him out of her thoughts. Her admiring gaze was fixed on the stallion that lowered his broad head to await the gentle touch of her hand. Quiet words of adoration tumbled from Mikyla's lips as she brushed her hand over Sundance's velvet muzzle. The steed, like a loving puppy, nuzzled against her shoulder. Cale swore the animal would have hugged her had he been able. They were like two dear friends, each filled with undeniable respect for the other, who shared a special bond of closeness. Cale felt as if he were intruding on a private moment, sensing Mikyla's strong attachment for this spectacular stallion and Sundance's unquestionable devotion to Mikyla.

When Cale sauntered forward, Sundance laid back his ears and shied away, eyeing the intruder warily. Cautiously, Cale extended his hand to sketch the powerful muscles on the stallion's neck. With an indignant snort the stallion pranced sideways, refusing Cale's touch. Throwing his proud head, Sundance shifted his weight, as if he meant to kick. His wild eyes were fixed on Cale, sending him a keep-your-distance glance. Cale wisely chose to retreat.

"Sundance is particular about his friends," Mikyla chortled, wedging past Cale to take her place beside her steed. "He isn't too fond of men."

"Neither is his mistress," Cale speculated, flashing her a wry smile. "Or is it that neither of you likes *me* in particular?"

"Like Sundance, I would probably like you better, Mr. Brolin, if you would observe a respectable distance," she replied with a meaningful glance.

Cale let the matter drop and focused his attention on the powerful stallion. "Where did you get this magnificent animal?" he questioned curiously. "I've seen my share of Thoroughbreds, but this one is truly a prize. He is built to run and he does it with such lithe grace that he hardly seems to be expending any energy."

The unexpected compliment caused Miki to smile involuntarily. Her attention shifted to Sundance, giving him another affectionate pat. "My father bought him for me as a colt before we moved to Kansas," she elaborated. "Sundance was a scrawny little thing and he didn't look to be worth his ration of oats. He was all legs. But with daily exercise and plenty of nourishment he has developed into a remarkable steed. I have been approached by a number of men who would give most anything to buy him and make use of his speed during the Land Run."

Cale didn't doubt that for a minute. He had sold several swift mounts to homesteaders who camped along the boundaries of the Unassigned Land. Horses were going for as much as five hundred dollars to those who could afford them. Indeed, he had made a tidy sum selling extra horses to anxious settlers. Sundance would bring top price if Mikyla decided to auction him off.

While Cale was lost in pensive deliberation, Mikyla swung into the saddle. There was a hint of reluctance in the way she offered her hand. "Do you wish to search for your mount or does he answer to a whistle?"

Even if the strawberry roan could have read written messages, Cale wouldn't have refused the opportunity of sitting behind this shapely bundle. Mikyla sorely wished she hadn't been so generous when Cale slid onto the stallion's back. His sinewy body molded itself to her backside, evoking a chain reaction of sensations that left Mikyla wondering when and where they would end. The brush of his muscular flesh made her maddeningly aware of him behind her. She was too easily disturbed by his virile body, by the soft draft of breath against her neck.

When Cale settled his hands on her waist to steady himself in the saddle, Mikyla could swear lightning had struck her. Even Sundance shifted uneasily. Mikyla leaned down to comfort the fidgety steed, but she wasn't certain which one of them needed reassurance. Cale had her so rattled she couldn't think straight.

Gulping nervously, Mikyla reined Sundance west. Keeping her eyes fixed on the horizon, Mikyla asked herself how she had managed to get mixed up with a man who left her feeling as if she had accidentally backed up to a hot stove. She didn't have to see him behind her. She could *feel* him, and her pulse was very nearly beating her to death!

Chapter 3

A sly smile pursed Cale's lips as they rode through the drizzling rain. He could feel Mikyla tense when their bodies brushed familiarly against each other. She was awkward around men—a mite apprehensive, a mite mistrusting. Men flocked to her like birds migrating south for the winter, true, but she was wary of their intentions. Cale certainly had done nothing to reverse her low opinion of the male species, in fact, he had only reinforced her feelings.

Hoping to soothe her nervousness, Cale opened a safe topic of conversation . . . or so he thought. He was soon to realize that he had broached the wrong subject. "Are you and your family making the Run for a homestead or townsite?"

The question came from so close to her ear that Mikyla very nearly leaped out of her skin. Recovering, she cleared her throat and swallowed her thudding heart. "My father is interested in a townsite, but I have my sights set on a homestead. I want a hundred and sixty acres of thick grass and an abundance of water and shade trees. My dream is to raise a fine breed of horses—Sundance's offspring." A wistful smile softened the tension in her features as she recalled the site she had discovered during her afternoon ride.

"I presume you found it when you sneaked across the border to the Unassigned Lands that are soon to be known as Oklahoma country," Cale guessed. No wonder she was riding like a bat out of hell. If the cavalry patrol had caught her, she would have been severely reprimanded for crossing the line.

"Yes, I did," she informed him. "And when the cannons explode on April twenty-second, marking the beginning of the race to available homesteads, I know exactly where I intend to set my claim stake." Mikyla gestured a slim finger toward the dense canopy of trees that hugged the South Canadian River. "Just beyond the rise is a perfect place to establish a ranch. And with Sundance as my mount, I will be the first to arrive."

The determination in her voice drew Cale's skeptical frown. "I hope you won't be too disappointed if you have to settle for your second choice. Surely you realize there are families illegally camped inside the boundaries, hoping to elude the patrols and avoid this insane stampede of horses and wagons. Some will be routed, their camps burned and destroyed, but others will succeed in hiding. Don't be surprised if you arrive only to find some Sooner has already staked claim to your dream site."

The remarks sent Mikyla's spirits plunging. Her heart would break if she lost that precious claim to a sneaky Sooner. "I might become a Sooner myself if I thought I wouldn't get caught," she begrudgingly admitted. "I risked being captured once this afternoon and I won't take that chance again . . ."

Cale's previous remark about the Run and the tone in which he had conveyed it darted through her mind, causing her to frown curiously. Mikyla twisted in the saddle to spare him a quick glance. "I assume you don't approve of this Land Run, Mr. Brolin. Why is that?"

Cale retrieved the reins from her hands to direct her toward his campsite. "The theory of a Land Run might look good on paper," he contended. "But a run for *land* will be worse than the Forty-niners flocking to the California gold fields." Cale expelled a derisive snort. "I see the Run as an act of monumental human greed. Settlers are planning to make a frantic dash to grab up the two million acres of land promised to the Indians forevermore. Now the government has forced each Indian of each tribe to take an allotment of one hundred sixty acres and sacrifice what is left to the land-hungry Boomers who have been lobbying Congress for the past year. I won't be surprised to see settlers kill each other when a conflict arises over who places the first stake on a claim."

Cale grumbled under his breath. He could see it all now—mass chaos, shouting matches, gun fights. "Honesty is almost discouraged by the very fact that it is a *race* to the choice tracts of land. It encourages cheating, and these ever-broadening camps along the border invite swindlers and thieves."

The more he discussed it, the more annoyed he became that this foolish female was even considering throwing herself into harm's way. "You don't stand a chance against the ruthless cutthroats who covet prime land. A woman alone is easy prey," Cale told her gruffly. "If you know what's good for you, you will pack up and go back where you came from."

Mikyla's back went rigid with defiance. She was characteristically stubborn and her determination rose proportionate to the amount of resistance she encountered. It annoyed her that Cale thought to lecture her on what she should do with her life. It was hers, after all. Cale didn't know how important it was for her to establish her own home. She had dreamed of free land since President Harrison signed the proclamation. This was her opportunity to make a new beginning. She would no longer be forced to bear the burden of her father. The land would be hers and she could mold a new life from this virgin prairie.

"You are far too cynical to see the good that will come from this Land Run," she snapped in annoyance. "No doubt you perceive the settlers as an inconvenience that might eventually cut into your business of selling horses and mules to government agencies in the territory. But for those of us with nothing, it is the golden opportunity to fulfill our dreams. Settlers will build homes and put down roots. The Run can provide a future of prosperity. I think it is selfish of you to deny the unfortunate an opportunity they so desperately need."

Muttering under his breath, Cale pulled the stallion to a halt and dismounted near his campsite. The confounded female! She had stars in her eyes. She might see the good that could come from this ridiculous race for land, but she was a fool if she didn't acknowledge the problems the Run instigated. A woman racing all by herself, building a ranch all by herself? Hell, that was crazy! A woman's place was in a home, *after* it had been constructed and fences were strung around it.

Before Mikyla could protest, Cale yanked her from the saddle and held her at arm's length. "You are chasing rainbows, sweetheart," he growled at her. "Even if you manage to stake your dream site, claim jumpers will swarm like pesky hornets. They will make every attempt to steal your land out from under you. I hope you are handy with a rifle." His silver-gray eyes probed into hers. "Do you intend to shoot a man down in cold blood if he threatens to swipe your precious claim? And are you willing to get *yourself* killed because of a quarter section of sod?"

Mikyla hadn't considered the possibility. She had been too preoccupied with the race and the land she had selected for her ranch. But now that Cale had brought it to her attention she supposed she would be willing to do what was necessary to protect her claim.

When Mikyla glanced up into Cale's stern face she was stung by irritation. It wasn't the possibility of trouble that aggravated her. It was Cale's domineering attitude that ruffled her feathers. He was a total stranger and *he* was trying to tell *her* how to run her life. Men! They were all so certain of their superiority. Obviously, Cale was laboring under the ill-conceived philosophy that she was a woman, therefore, she was a fool. Wasn't that just like a man? He presumed, and quite arrogantly, that he could tell her what to do and she would obediently obey, just because *he* was a man and he thought men knew best.

Mikyla felt no obligation to pay heed to this cynical cowboy. The day she accepted his advice would be the day the Gulf of Mexico became a barren desert!

36

One by one, she pried his fingers from her forearms. "I came to race for a choice piece of land and that is exactly what I intend to do. I will take my chances with the tramps and thieves," she told him firmly.

Cale scowled under his breath. Women! Their brains were permanently frozen at thirteen years of age and they didn't have enough sense to accept good advice for what it was worth! This minx was defying him for pure spite. "Lady, you are so damned stubborn you'll wind up getting yourself killed," he snorted sarcastically.

"Thank you for insulting me," Mikyla muttered sourly.

An ornery grin claimed his bronzed features. "The pleasure was all mine," he drawled.

Her chin elevated to fling him a scornful glare. "Well, I hope you don't count tact and diplomacy among *your* virtues," she sniped. "I may be stubborn, but *you* are obnoxious!"

Cale didn't flinch when slapped with the insult. "At least I'm sensible," he declared proudly. "And you haven't got a prayer, honey. The opportunists are going to eat you alive."

The soft whinny of horses drew Mikyla's attention. She glared at the improvised corrals Cale had built to hold his herd. When she glanced up at the tall, swarthy man who ridiculed her intentions, her lips pursed in a mocking smile. It was apparent to Mikyla that the pot was calling the kettle black.

"It seems you are one of the opportunists who preys on hopeful settlers," she sniped. "Surely you don't expect me to believe you haven't contacted the citizens in Boomer camps and convinced them they stand a better chance riding your prize steeds instead of their lumbering plow horses."

Cale itched to wipe that taunting smirk over her beguiling features. He was too annoyed to defend himself, but knew if he had done so he would have found himself in the middle of a shouting match with this obstinate, and argumentative, daredevil female. After counting to ten, Cale grabbed Mikyla's arm and steered her toward his tent.

Hastily, he snatched up a set of dry clothes and shoved them at her. "Here, put these on. I should hate for you to catch your death of cold before you make the Run," he smirked, his tone implying he couldn't have cared less if she fell into a delirious fever.

As Cale wheeled to exit, Mikyla's taunt caught him flat-footed. "You *have* taken advantage of the wealthier settlers, haven't you? You condemn our intentions, but you are making the most of *your* opportunity. At five hundred dollars a head, I imagine you have turned a tidy profit."

Cale counted to ten again, twice. Slowly, he pivoted to face her intimidating smile. "Yes, I've sold horses to those greedy settlers. But it is you and your friends who are dreamers and fools," he scoffed. "I am a realist who takes what he gets without living on unattainable dreams."

His long, measured stride brought him back to loom over Mikyla. And he loomed so well, confound him. It was as if she had fallen under an ominous shadow.

"You talk of free land, but nothing is free, sweetheart," he scoffed cynically. "You will work and toil to carve a ranch in this wild country . . . *if* some vicious claim jumper doesn't shoot you in the back first! One third of the settlers who are lumped together in those Boomer camps will become discouraged because this land of milk and honey turns sour. Another third will stake claims with no other purpose than to turn around and sell them for profit. The remainder will manipulate and connive for wealth and political power."

His stormy silver eyes glided down her body in mockery. "I'm willing to bet the money I've made selling my horses to greedy homesteaders that you won't last six months. When the going gets tough, you'll sell out and go back where you belong. Your dream will come tumbling down around you. You'll ride off, whining and crying, wishing you had listened to my advice."

That arrogant, high-handed rake! If she had an axe she would have cut him down to size! "I'll take that bet," she replied, thrusting out a determined chin. "I know what I want and I intend to have it. I'll have my land and my ranch, one that's brimming with registered stock. I'll build a home no one can take away from me. Not this time!" Her voice was becoming higher and wilder by the second. "Because of my father we lost everything. He has squandered . . ." Mikyla clamped her mouth shut, cursing her careless outburst.

For a long moment Cale stood there, regarding her with his penetrating gaze, wondering why this young woman was so fiercely determined to construct a home in the heart of Indian Territory. What had her father done to provoke her bitterness? She seemed obsessed with making this confounded run for land, but how the devil could a woman alone erect a home and fences and protect her property? She couldn't, Cale predicted, not unless she could raise the funds to hire the manual labor needed to construct her dream. Judging by the willful expression stamped on Mikyla's features, Cale knew she would do everything to find a way— or die trying.

Forcing the semblance of a smile, Cale bent down to scoop up his own set of dry clothes. "I'll be sure to drop by your ranch in six months to see how you're managing," he declared, his tone dripping sarcasm. He paused momentarily, his eyes flickering over her rigid stance. "Do you also plan on marrying a stout, hard-working young man to handle the physical labor or had you intended to *hire* one of the unfortunates who lost the race or buckled beneath a claim jumper's threat?"

Furiously, Mikyla hurled the garments at him. Cale resembled a clothesline with the jeans and shirt draped on his broad shoulders, she thought. "You can mock me if you wish. But at least I have a dream," she spouted self-righteously. "I'm going to set down roots and make a home while you wander, hither and yon, making camp and then drifting wherever the wind takes you, Mr. Horse Trader! You may think I'm every kind of fool, but I think you are a rudderless idiot!"

Cale opened his mouth to counter her biting rejoinder and then compressed his lips until they very nearly split under the excessive pressure. "Fine, honey. You live your life *your* way and I'll stumble through mine," he growled. Mechanically, Cale collected the clothes that dangled from his arms and tossed them back at her. "One day you are going to realize land isn't the most important treasure to be had and you'll wish you had listened to me."

As he spun about, Mikyla glared flaming arrows at his

wide back. "And just what do you presume to be more precious than land and a home, Mr. Brolin?" she wanted to know.

Dammit, I am not going to argue with this hellcat anymore, Cale told himself firmly. *I wish I had never opened the subject of the Land Run.* It had only strung higher fences between them. Although Mikyla Lassiter was incredibly attractive and quick-witted, she was also obsessed with visions of grandeur. If she didn't know land and wealth didn't buy happiness, she would find out the hard way. Once her bubble burst and she came back to earth, maybe she would take a good long look at reality. Until then, Cale could talk until he was blue in the face and his pleas would fall on deaf ears.

"When you're dressed, come join me outside," he instructed, ignoring her question. "We'll have a bite to eat before you fly back to your cave to join the rest of the bats."

With that, Cale disappeared outside and Mikyla unclenched her fists, which were strangling the dry clothes Cale had offered her. The man had no tact, she concluded. And if that weren't enough, termites of cynicism had gnawed so deeply into his brain that it was about to collapse.

Cale had put her on the defensive with his cynical remarks, forcing her to retaliate. What did he care what happened to her? They were practically strangers. And it was obvious that they were cut from different scraps of wood. Cale Brolin was driftwood and she was an oak. He could ramble like a tumbleweed if he wished, but she was going to have a home, just like the one she had enjoyed when her mother was alive. It would be a warm, cozy home like the one that had sheltered her before her father . . .

Mikyla squelched the bitter memories that trickled from the corners of her mind. The Land Run of 1889 was going to be a new beginning. She was going to make a life for herself and she would have a home her father could never take away from her. And nothing Cale Brolin could say would deter her from her purpose!

* * *

By the time Cale had fed his horses and mules and peeled off his wet shirt, Mikyla reappeared. Her eyes landed on the sinewy shoulders and the dark matting of hair that dived into the band of his jeans. Damn, she did not need to admire this giant of a man while she was trying to hate him, but she had to admit he had a gorgeous body. Cale was definitely easy on a woman's eye and hard on her blood pressure.

A knowing smile tugged at the corner of Cale's mouth when he intercepted Mikyla's approving gaze. "Do you like what you see, Ky, even while you despise me and all I represent?" he teased mercilessly.

A hot blush began at the base of her neck and worked its way up to the roots of her silver-blond hair. "Actually, I am indifferent to what I see," she lied to save face.

Cale sauntered toward her, practically daring her to break and run. Stubborn as she was, Mikyla held her ground, cursing the fact that she had to look up to this mountain of brawn and muscle.

"The lady is also a liar," Cale stated with great conviction. His heated gaze flooded down his oversize shirt, sorely wishing *he* was wrapped around this minx instead of his garment.

His smug smile annoyed Mikyla to no end. Pride and anger joined hands to spur her response. And her rejoinder came in the form of a doubled fist, one that plowed into the relaxed muscles of his belly. Cale's breath came out in a pained grunt. When he instinctively doubled over, Mikyla clasped both hands and jerked them upward, catching Cale in the chin.

Cale, who had presumed this petite bundle of spirit was beneath vengeful violence, realized he had unleashed a spiteful she-cat. Mikyla Lassiter, in spite of her angelic beauty, possessed a hellish temper. Even though Cale had inadvertently bitten his tongue when Miki's fists collided with his chin, he came uncoiled with tigerish swiftness and pounced on his fleeing assailant. This wild-haired witch needed to be taught a few lessons in etiquette and he was just the man to instruct her!

When Cale's lean fingers bit into her arms, Mikyla's

abrupt squeal pierced the damp air. She was roughly yanked back against his heaving chest and engulfed in muscular arms that held her so tightly she could barely inhale a breath.

"Let me go, you big ape!" she snarled at him.

"Not until I repay you for attacking me," Cale breathed down her neck. "And when I do let you go, I hope the hell I never lay eyes on you again!"

Before Miki realized what he was about, Cale whipped her around and slammed her against his hard, unyielding contours. His mouth came crushing down on hers, bruising her lips, stripping the last ounce of breath from her collapsed lungs. His probing tongue forced her lips apart with demanding insistence. His adventurous hands roamed over her buttocks, learning her innocent body by touch.

Mikyla was so furious she was seeing Cale through a veil of red. Oh how she detested his superior strength, his ability to exploit her naïveté with men. She knew he was aware that she was virtually inexperienced with passion. And he delighted in humiliating her with his prowess, his male magnetism. But if he thought he could kiss her into humble submission he had grossly misjudged her. She wasn't aroused. She was downright outraged!

Suddenly, Cale released her from his powerful arms—like a hawk unclamping his claws and allowing its prey to take a fall. Mikyla braced herself when she felt the ground beneath her feet. Instinct took command. Like a striking snake she slapped the same cheek she had struck earlier that afternoon. But this time, to her utter disbelief, Cale slapped her back! That scoundrel! How dare he hit a woman!

In a burst of fury, Mikyla raised her arm to counter with another punishing blow. Cale's hand darted through the air to snag her wrist before she could wipe the ridiculing smile off his face.

"I wouldn't if I were you, honey," he warned in a rough growl.

As if she were a feed sack, Cale slung her over his shoulder and carried her to her stallion. When he had deposited her in her saddle, he stepped back to fling her a gloating grin.

"I would say it has been a pleasure meeting you, but it

hasn't," he smirked, delighting in watching the livid purple hue claim her lovely features. "I honestly think I would prefer to be run down by a horse. As a matter of fact . . ."

Cale's eyes widened in astonishment when Mikyla gouged her heels into Sundance's flanks. She intended to trample him, for crying out loud! Without wasting another moment in thought, Cale dived sideways, narrowly missing the horse's deadly hooves. After scraping himself off the ground he glowered poison arrows at Mikyla's departing back and silently wished her a one-way trip to hell.

Thoroughly frustrated, Cale kicked at the clump of grass beneath his feet, uprooting it from the spot. "Damn billy goat of a woman!" he scowled as he stomped over to retrieve his dry clothes. "Someone ought to take that minx over his knee and throttle her shapely backside!"

No wonder she wasn't married. The ornery little snip! There wasn't a man on God's green earth who could get along with that rambunctious bundle of temper and distorted ideals. From the moment they met, Cale had found himself on an emotional teeter-totter, one that had a fire blazing beneath it. It was obvious he and Ky brought out the worst in each other. They could agree on nothing.

Cale had encountered more than his share of women in his thirty-two years of rugged living. But none of them compared to that feisty hellion. Most women knew their place and accepted the fact that they were second to the male of the species. But not Mikyla Lassiter. She had a chip on her shoulder the size of the Rock of Gibraltar. She defied a man just for sport. She would challenge impossible odds rather than swallow one iota of her damnable pride.

Let her court catastrophe. Let her rush off in this insane race for land, riding at breakneck speed on the back of that devil stallion, Cale mused spitefully. Let her fend against the ruthless scoundrels who would prey on a woman all alone against the world. Let her buckle beneath the wild land and harsh elements. She didn't know beans about building a ranch and managing it, he predicted. One day he would ride across her precious claim and find her slinking around with her tail tucked between her legs—defeated, disenchanted.

Then she would see how unimportant her colossal pride was, how worthless her unattainable dream!

Cale stormed into his tent. While he shrugged on his clean shirt and wrestled his way out of his breeches, a specter rose to torment him. Cale cursed the lingering vision of flaming blue eyes and silver-gold hair that billowed about a shapely feminine form. Damn that headstrong woman. She had the power to arouse him, but she also tugged so viciously at the strings of his temper that he wanted to strangle her!

Out of the corner of his eye, Cale saw the tent flap rise. Hastily, he snatched up his breeches to cover himself as best he could. To his amazement, Mikyla peeked inside. Her face colored profusely when she found Cale holding his breeches in front of him, exposing bare hips and well-muscled legs. She kept shifting her weight like a leery rabbit that expected to be attacked from several directions at once.

Summoning her composure, Mikyla dragged her eyes off his lower torso and focused on those stormy gray eyes. "I came back to tell you what was on my mind . . ."

"Then by all means, unburden yourself," Cale suggested flippantly. "I doubt your female brain can endure the excessive weight."

Mikyla ignored his sarcasm and plowed on before she lost her nerve. "I don't expect you to understand how it feels to want something so badly you can taste it," she murmured. Her gaze dropped to the oversize shirt to toy with a button, and then she heaved a heavy sigh. "More than anything, I want a home to call my home, instead of living out of a peddler's wagon, drifting from town to town. I'm tired of constantly saying good-bye to new acquaintances, never having a true friend to confide in."

Mikyla expelled another tremulous breath and raised her eyes to Cale's somber face. "Is it so wrong to dream? To crave something you lost long before you were prepared to let go?" Her eyes misted with tears. "You told me to pack up and go back where I belong, but there is nothing there except bittersweet memories. All I have now is a dream. Sundance is going to help me get what I want, whether you think I need it or not."

Blinking back the tears that threatened to bleed down her cheeks, Mikyla focused on the wall of tent. "I'm truly sorry I hit you. It was most unladylike and unforgivable. I do appreciate your saving me from being lightning struck. Riding during a storm was another of my foolish mistakes." Her eyes darted momentarily to Cale and she tried very hard not to notice he was standing there without his breeches covering those long, masculine legs. "Good-bye, Mr. Brolin. I'm sure you will make a fortune selling your horses. They are good stock, well worth the price you demand for them. And if not for Sundance, I, too, would be begging for the fastest steed in your herd."

Pivoting, Mikyla lifted the tent flap to exit and then peered over her shoulder. A sheepish smile rippled across her soft mouth. "I may be inexperienced with men . . ." Mikyla bit at her bottom lip, wondering why she felt compelled to offer this compliment when it would very nearly kill her to voice it. "It begrudges me to say so . . . but you do kiss very well."

As quickly as she had appeared, so she vanished, leaving Cale clinging to his breeches and reevaluating his harsh opinion of Mikyla Lassiter. Blast that woman. Just when he had his heart set on disliking her, she had to go and say something nice.

Cale strode over to watch Mikyla gallop off into the sunset. When she disappeared from sight, his hand fell away from the flap, enclosing himself with his conflicting thoughts. Maybe he had been too hard on her, he thought in retrospect. After all, he shouldn't be sitting in judgment. And he had to give that spitfire credit. She was a very determined woman. But she was also on a collision course with trouble. A female alone, especially one as lovely and desirable as Mikyla, would never have an easy time of it.

If Mikyla were homely, men would shy away from her. But she was a far cry from that, Cale thought with a rakish smile. In fact, there was no other way to put it. That was one gorgeous female, fiery temper and all. Even when she looked her worst, her natural beauty intrigued him. She had looked ridiculous standing at the entrance of his tent. Her hair looked like a bird's nest and the clothes he had offered her hung on her shapely body like a feed sack. But there was no disguising that bewitching face, the living fire that flickered in her eyes, or that creamy smooth complexion that begged for caresses . . .

A faraway look captured Cale's craggy features as he thrust a leg into his breeches. He had the feeling he and that high-spirited minx would meet again, somewhere along the way. She had to be camped near the border of the Unassigned Lands. His dealings with settlers might eventually bring them face-to-face. And next time I won't be quite so domineering and overbearing, Cale promised himself faithfully. He would make an effort to be civil and polite.

Okay, so he had been terribly rough on Ky. But only because someone needed to bring her back in touch with the bitter truth, Cale rationalized. This crazed Land Run wasn't going to be a Sunday picnic. It was going to be a human stampede. If Miki didn't watch her step she could be run down, shot down—or worse. If she were aware of what she faced, she might have a fighting chance. A slim one, he mused cynically. But at least there was the remote possibility she might succeed.

Cale shook his raven head to shatter his wandering thoughts. He had never wasted much time pondering women. But even as he reminded himself of that fact, Mikyla's bewitching features leaped to mind. Cale could still feel her luscious body meshed to his. Her feminine scent still clung to his skin. The taste of her lips still lingered on his mouth . . .

Forget her, Cale told himself gruffly. He hadn't come to Indian Territory to drool over that fiery chit. He was here to sell his horses and mules. If he wanted female companionship there were dozens of women around who didn't respond to his kiss with a doubled fist. He should chalk this encounter up to experience and leave it at that. The last thing he wanted was to get involved with Mikyla's insane, obsessive crusade. Sooner or later she was going to realize she needed a man's help to mold her dream. No doubt, she would become desperate. She would latch onto a man, not

46

because she loved him, but because she *needed* him. And Cale Brolin was not the kind of man a woman could *use*.

And yet, while Cale was listing all Mikyla's failing graces—starting with stubborn and proceeding through arrogant and hot-tempered—he couldn't smother the warm flame that had begun to burn. It struck him as odd that he was intrigued by her shortcomings, challenged by her spirited nature. Perhaps he was simply fascinated that a woman would dare to create her own niche in a man's world.

Only that, Cale reassured himself. He had only taken note of her because she was attempting the impossible. He admired her spunk, but that certainly didn't mean he wanted to fall in love with an underdog! Hell, he didn't want to fall in love at all. He liked his life just fine the way it was. He didn't need complications. And Mikyla Lassiter would definitely be a complication. She could come into a man's life like a misdirected cyclone, turning his world upside down. Cale preferred to keep his world right-side-up and he didn't need the trouble Mikyla could cause a man.

After delivering himself that self-inspiring lecture, Cale retrieved dry kindling from beneath the tarp and built a campfire. But as he munched his meal, he found his thoughts drifting back to enormous blue eyes and hair that was spun with threads of silver and gold. Damn, that woman had moved in and taken up residence in his head! But if Cale had any sense at all he would remember that there were some things that were better left alone. Mikyla Lassiter should be draped in a warning sign that read DANGER . . . HIGHLY EXPLOSIVE. Cale Brolin had no intention of going up in smoke!

Chapter 4

The sun dipped low on the horizon, garnishing the world in molten gold, flinging muted shadows over the gentle slope of the land. A flock of puffy clouds paraded across the darkening sky. In the distance, a myriad of campfires flickered like bronze stars twinkling in the haze of shadowed grass. The camp Mikyla referred to as home for the past month was situated beside a grove of cottonwood and cedar trees. As newcomers continued to arrive, the camp swelled out in all directions.

More than six thousand anxious settlers now populated the north, south, east, and west boundaries of Indian Territory, waiting for the day when the cannons and pistols discharged to signify the opening of Oklahoma country. But until the day of the nation's first Land Run, white canvas tents, prairie schooners, and camps dotted the countryside. Bonneted women, laboring over their Dutch ovens, stood silhouetted against the flickering amber flames. Small children chased in circles, laughing and squealing. Men repaired their wagons and buggies and fussed over their livestock in nervous anticipation. Many of the settlers had no intention of breaking the soil into farm ground. Some sought to locate in towns as laborers, carpenters, merchants, and professional men. They had come from all walks of life to homestead the nation's last frontier.

Mikyla was very much a part of this life of apprehensive waiting. And yet, in a way, she was different. Although every citizen shared her hopes and dreams, she wondered how many of them, which of the families she counted as friends, would become disenchanted and leave their claims as Cale prophesied. His harsh appraisal of the Land Run stabbed holes in Mikyla's dream, leaving her to ponder what lay ahead.

A faint smile brimmed her lips when Cale's image materialized before her. Never had she met a man who could make her so furious one moment and then kiss her senseless the next. He was plain-spoken, overpowering, opinionated . . . undeniably handsome . . . And dammit, even his rough, demanding kiss had melted her knees.

Mikyla had left his camp in an explosion of angry outrage. She had attempted to run him into the ground. But after she had ridden all of a tenth of a mile, her conscience began to haunt her and she felt obliged to return to apologize. Maybe the fact that Cale was right about her was what had put her in such a snit. Maybe she *was* too obsessed with her dreams. But what else did she have to inspire her if not the possibility of a bright future? She certainly wasn't content to linger in the past, dwelling on painful memories that resembled a nightmare.

Heaving a tired sigh, Mikyla nudged Sundance toward one of the many Boomer camps that sprawled across Indian Territory. Within an hour she would again be one of the bonneted women, her face flushed from the heat of the campfire, milling among the other hopeful settlers who shared her hopes and aspirations. And her father would . . .

Mikyla forced back the dreary thought and weaved her way toward the dilapidated tent and battered peddler's wagon. After Sundance had been brushed down and fed a generous ration of grain, Mikyla slipped into the tent to change into her calico gown. Her father was nowhere to be found, but Mikyla wasn't surprised. She suspected he was where he always was by this hour of the day.

"Miki?" Greta Ericcson called softly. "Are you dere?"

The sound of Greta's heavy Swedish accent or that of her husband, Dag, always brought a smile to Mikyla's lips. The Ericcsons made speaking sound like music. It added new dimension to the English language. Eager to greet a friendly face, Mikyla tugged at the tent flap to allow the tall blond woman to enter.

"You've been exercising your stallion again, yah?" Greta questioned. When Mikyla nodded affirmatively, Greta expelled a sigh. "Ah, vhat my Dag wouldn't give for a horse like yours! But he did buy a sleek mare dis morning from a nice young man who came through camp."

Mikyla wondered if that "nice young man" had been Cale Brolin. In Greta's opinion, most everyone was nice, except for the riffraff whom she distastefully referred to as "vicked." Mikyla's thoughts circled back to Greta's previous remark and she frowned cynically. No doubt that "nice young man" was making a killing when he sold his herd of horses to the Ericcsons and the other settlers.

Greta shifted uncomfortably from one foot to the other. "I think you should round up your father," she murmured awkwardly. "He's been down by de creek since you left dis afternoon." A bright smile crinkled her face as she turned to a more pleasant subject. "And tonight, I vould like you to meet a nice gentleman vith whom I vas visiting dis morning. I told him all about you."

A wary expression sank into Mikyla's exquisite features. Greta was a dear woman, but she had her heart set on playing matchmaker. Greta considered it outrageous that Miki was twenty-one years old and yet unmarried. Thus far, Greta had matched Mikyla with at least ten eligible bachelors, all of whom were polite, gracious, but exceedingly dull. They couldn't hold a candle to Cale . . . Miki chided herself for allowing herself to make the comparison. She was not about to stack any of her beaux up against Cale Brolin. That was utterly ridiculous. Any romantic inclination she might have toward Cale—*might* have had, mind you—were so remote that Mikyla didn't even want to waste time considering them.

Cale set fire to her temper so quickly one would have thought he was a human torch. Mikyla had struck out at him with only the slightest provocation. The man just naturally put her on the defensive and they disagreed on every subject.

He embarrassed her, he taunted her, he argued with her, and he stood for everything Mikyla detested. They had absolutely nothing in common. He was worldly and she was innocent. And damn him for mocking her inexperience! That in itself was enough to make her realize they were as different as dawn and midnight.

Oh, why was she rehashing their volatile arguments, their stinging insults? Cale Brolin should have been out of sight and out of mind. Mikyla did not intend to exhaust herself thinking about that infuriating man.

"Vell?" Greta demanded impatiently. "Vill you yoin Bradley Chapman for an after-dinner stroll, Miki?"

"I would be happy to meet him," Mikyla assured Greta. A diversion was just what she needed. Keeping company with another man would dissolve any lingering thoughts of that arrogant, domineering Cale Brolin, she reckoned.

After Greta swept out of the tent, Mikyla tied her floppy-brimmed bonnet in place and ventured outside. Because of the rain, the campfires had been waterproofed with layers of buffalo chips. The faint odor of burning chips hung in the damp air and Mikyla cut her way through the poignant darkness to seek out her father.

What had Emet gambled away this time, she wondered bitterly. His wagon? His peddler's wares? Mikyla breathed a dispirited sigh. Since her mother died, Emet Lassiter had sought solace in liquor bottles and at gambling halls. Liquor was supposed to be illegal in Indian Territory, but it was difficult to enforce the law. There were not enough marshals and military troops to patrol the area that was congested with settlers. Emet never seemed to be without a drink when he wanted one.

Once her family had owned a farm in the Ozarks, a quaint cabin in the hills. Her father, in order to supplement their farm, had provided a traveling mercantile store for the settlers whose homes were far from town. Emet's business had flourished and the Lassiters lacked for nothing. Mikyla had been sent off to live with her spinster aunt in St. Louis and had received her formal education there. When a letter arrived informing Mikyla that her mother was gravely ill, she returned home immediately. Those last days had torn her emotions into ragged pieces and they had totally devastated Emet.

Mikyla brushed away the tears that sprung to her eyes as she weaved through the underbrush toward the creek. Losing her mother had been a crushing blow to Mikyla, but Emet had never recovered from his loss. He carried Michelle's memory like a haunting burden. He seemed determined to punish himself for being unable to save his wife, even if it would have required a miracle to spare her. Emet no longer had a purpose for living. He went through the paces but nothing satisfied him. He was restless and lonely and he looked for compassion in bottles, preoccupation in a deck of cards.

Fleeing the tormenting reminders of the home Michelle had furnished with love, Emet had insisted that he and Mikyla migrate to the flat plains of Kansas. Emet claimed he was tired of seeing the sun through the congested canopy of trees that clogged the Ozark Mountains. When Mikyla protested the move, Emet became angry and trotted off to ease his frustration with liquor. Two days later, looking like a creature that had emerged from a swamp, Emet returned to the cabin. He informed Mikyla that they had no choice but to move away. He had gambled away the farm in a poker game. To this day, Mikyla wasn't certain if Emet meant to lose or if he had been drinking so heavily that some conniving gambler had taken full advantage of him.

With little more than a wagonload of peddler's goods and the yearling colt Mikyla had fallen in love with on sight, the Lassiters trekked through the Ozark hills, across the eastern corner of Indian Territory, and on to the sprawling flats of western Kansas. The land was so unlike the towering hills and deep valleys of the Ozarks. But that was what Emet wanted—a direct contrast to the life he had known.

For more than two years, Mikyla had been forced to drift from town to town. The profit Emet made in peddling his goods was usually squandered in liquor and gambling. What little money they saved was won when Mikyla raced her magnificent stallion against men who thought wagering against a foolish young woman was easy gain.

Mikyla hoarded the money she had made, spending only what was necessary to survive. When news came that the Boomers were petitioning the government to open Indian Territory for settlement, Mikyla had insisted they join the gathering homesteaders. Reluctantly, Emet had agreed, but he declared that he would stake a townsite and set up a permanent mercantile store. He wanted nothing to do with breaking ground for farming and ranching as he had done in the Ozarks. Since Mikyla was of age to claim her own homestead, she informed her father of her intentions. Of course, Emet mocked her childish dream. But Mikyla was determined to see it through, knowing her father would eventually gamble away his town lot and become penniless again. At least his name would not be listed on the deed to *her* claim, Mikyla consoled herself. No one was going to take her land from her. Never, ever again!

Her wandering thoughts dispersed when a peal of laughter rang through the trees. Mikyla focused her attention on the campfires that lay beside the stream. The community of white tents that hugged the creek was that of gamblers and riffraff who had also come to the territory to seek their fortune and prey on others. There were thieves, pickpockets, and an assortment of swindlers—just as Cale had declared. Some of the varmints had even stooped to drawing maps of choice locations, a territory most of them had yet to see. But the overanxious settlers paid good money for worthless maps, hoping to get the jump on their neighbors.

Mikyla tried to overlook these scoundrels but Cale had brought them to her attention, forcing her to consider the dangers they presented. But Mikyla wasn't afraid of them, not when she carried a Colt and a dagger for protection. She had learned to use the weapons as well as any man.

What infuriated Mikyla most was that her father rubbed shoulders with these scalawags. But nothing she said seemed to faze Emet. He wandered down to the creek to drink and gamble each time it met his whim. It had become Mikyla's lot to fetch Emet home each time he strayed.

Mikyla spied her father sitting among a congregation of

gamblers—the brethren of the green cloth, as they were referred to by respectable citizens. Her blue eyes narrowed in annoyance, wondering how much Emet had lost this time. As she moved deliberately toward her father, one of the men at the tables latched onto her arm. Mikyla looked down her nose into a smiling face that was blessed with handsome features. Although the blond-haired man seemed pleasant enough, Mikyla was prepared to dislike him because of the company he kept.

"My dear, I fear you have ventured in where angels fear to tread," Morgan Hagerty informed her. His green eyes drifted at will, liking what he saw.

Mikyla brushed his hand from her arm, as one would shake off a pesky insect. "I am well aware of the risks involved," she told him coolly. "But I have come to fetch my father home before you and the other cardsharps bleed him dry."

Morgan's thick brows rose in silent admiration as Mikyla squared her shoulders. She cut through the sound of clanking bottles and rattling chips to march toward the poker game in progress. Without ado, she grabbed Emet's arm, practically yanking him off his seat.

"Hey! Wait just a damned minute!" one of the gamblers complained. "Emet owes me six bits."

"I'm sure you will be paid in due time," Mikyla snapped insolently. "My father is going home and . . ." Her left hand emerged from the pocket of her gown, revealing the pistol that was aimed at the man's inflated chest. "If you are wise, you won't make a scene. It might well be your last . . ."

Although the comments were meant only for the men at Emet's table, Morgan was watching and listening in wry amusement. My, the lady would probably square off against Satan himself if he dared to cross her, he decided.

Mikyla had dealt with several of these gamblers when she came to fetch her father. Most of them let her pass without incident, but tonight was different. The older man with wiry brown hair wasn't satisfied with a verbal I-owe-you. His pistol appeared from beneath the table to meet Mikyla's challenge.

The click of a third Colt .45, the one belonging to the newcomer, Morgan Hagerty, broke the silence. "The lady promised to assume the debt. Leave it at that." His voice was cold, holding a chilly warning of impending doom.

The gambler wilted onto his wooden crate when he found himself staring at two pistols that were aimed at his chest. "I'll be around tomorrow to collect my debt, Miss Lassiter," he informed her in a more civil tone.

Morgan retrieved a gold piece from his vest pocket and tossed it to the man. "Now you have no reason to trouble Miss Lassiter with your petty debts."

When Mikyla shuffled her father to his wobbly legs, Morgan grabbed him around the waist to propel him forward. Mikyla appraised the well-dressed gambler. He looked more sophisticated than most of his associates, but Mikyla quickly reminded herself that clothes didn't make a man.

"I will see that you are repaid when I put Papa to bed," she assured him, casting him a glance of wary trepidation.

Morgan's eyes made another deliberate sweep of her tantalizing figure. He had seen her bewitching features beneath the camouflaging bonnet and he had been immediately intrigued by this feisty female who had dared to enter the gambler's den. Most decent women wouldn't have gone near the creek, but obviously Miss Lassiter dared to do what she pleased and what she deemed had to be done.

"There is no need to repay me. It's worth more than one coin to keep company with such an attractive young lady," he murmured provocatively. "I will always be happy to assist you." Touching the tip of his black hat, Morgan graced her with a charming smile. "The name is Morgan Hagerty. You can summon me whenever you wish . . ."

Mikyla tensed. Morgan seemed cordial enough, but she didn't trust his motives. If he was mingling with the swarm of gamblers and thieves, he couldn't be much better than those vagrants.

"Where are we going, Miki?" Emet slurred, blinking like an awakened owl.

"The same place we go every night at this time," Mikyla

56

grumbled resentfully.

Emet's head rolled loosely on his shoulders. He could hear Mikyla's voice but damned if he knew for certain where he was. "That's nice . . ." he droned before his eyes slammed shut, blocking out the spinning gray haze.

Mikyla's eyes soared heavenward and then she focused on the handsome gambler. "If you think to flatter me with your eloquence, Mr. Hagerty, you are wasting your breath. I do not condone my father's ritual of gambling and drinking himself insane. Nor do I associate with men who make their living by robbing others at card tables."

His amused laughter rumbled in the air. "You are delightful, my dear. A refreshing change from the kind of women I usually chance to meet."

"How many kinds are there?" Mikyla inquired with a taunting smile. "Two? Those who will and those who won't? I think you can predict into which category I fall." Grimacing, Mikyla hoisted her staggering father over a fallen tree. "If you presume ours to be a long and lasting acquaintance, I expect you to observe the limitations of our relationship."

Another peal of laughter bubbled in his chest. "I have been here a mere two days and already I have heard the stories of the brave and daring Miss Lassiter who retrieves her father from the gaming tables. At first I thought my comrades had invented a legendary heroine. But I can see for myself that you are everything the rumors suggest . . . and more . . ."

"I am touched by your flowering compliments," Mikyla sniffed, her tone implying she was nothing of the kind.

"I can tell," Morgan snickered as he braced himself to catch Emet, who was stumbling over his own two feet.

The moment Mikyla and Morgan tossed Emet on his cot, she immediately exited from the tent. The last thing she wanted was to be closeted with this charismatic gambler. If she needed assistance there would be none forthcoming, for Emet was snoring the moment his head hit the pillow. He barely recalled being uprooted from his wooden crate and shuffled back to camp. He would never have awakened if Mikyla needed him.

"Have you eaten supper?" Morgan questioned as he studied the enticing bundle of spirit with masculine appreciation.

"I'm dining with the Ericcsons," she informed him. "And afterward I am meeting a *nice* young man who doesn't waste his time in poker games."

Morgan shrugged off the subtle jibe like a duck fluffing beads of water off his feathers. "Perhaps tomorrow then?"

Her head jerked up to stare straight into Morgan's green eyes, which glistened amusement and male speculation. "Have I not made myself clear, Mr. Hagerty?"

Morgan tittered softly. "Oh, I understand you perfectly, my dear Mikyla. But you will learn that I am a very determined man." He took a bold step forward. His hand cupped her chin, tilting her face to his seductive smile. "I am accustomed to getting what I want. Make no mistake, you fascinate me. I intend for us to see a great deal of each other."

His hand was soft and smooth, a direct contrast to Cale's rugged, calloused fingertips. It assured her that Morgan had spent more time shuffling cards than breaking a sweat in manual labor. Perhaps Cale didn't possess refined features and refined manners, but of the two, Mikyla would prefer Cale's touch any old day . . .

I most certainly don't want Cale's touch, either, Mikyla shouted at herself. Blast it, she had vowed not to compare other men to that pesky Cale Brolin. And here she was doing it, despite her firm resolve.

"Mikyla! Ve are ready to take supper. Come yoin us," Greta interrupted, casting Morgan a condescending glare.

Knowing he would get nowhere with Greta Ericcson hovering around this lovely lass like a mother hen, Morgan backed away. With a slight bow, he flashed Mikyla a rakish smile.

"Until we meet again, my dear . . ."

Frowning pensively, Mikyla watched the expensively dressed gambler swagger away. There was a certain charm about Morgan Hagerty, but Mikyla couldn't quite bring herself to trust him. He was a man and therefore he was dangerous. This one was literally a card-carrying gambler.

Mikyla was certain Morgan was never without his own marked deck. His kind meant trouble. Like all of them, she reminded herself cynically.

Exhaling an annoyed breath, Mikyla pivoted on her heels and followed Greta. Damn men everywhere. They were nothing but headaches. Her father was drinking and gambling his life away. Morgan wasted his life, depending on the fall of the cards and his abilities with sleight-of-hand tricks. And Cale Brolin . . . Dammit, she wasn't even going to give that man another thought. The shiftless horse trader wasn't her kind, either!

Besides, there were more important things on her mind than men. Her funds were running short again. Rumor had it that weekly horse races were held at Fort Reno for the enjoyment of the officers and settlers. And Sundance would be among the contestants, Mikyla promised herself. All the prize money and side wagers she could win from men like Morgan Hagerty would be employed to buy supplies and lumber for her ranch—the one she was going to stake in the Run, whether or not Cale Brolin thought it was a foolish dream that would never collide with reality.

Mikyla broke stride when she realized she was no better than Morgan Hagerty. She was willing to bet on Sundance. Wasn't that gambling? Her shoulder lifted in a shrug. No, that was vastly different, she rationalized. She was staking her reputation and Sundance's on the race. That wasn't exactly betting. It was defending one's honor and credibility. If she proclaimed that her stallion could outdistance any horse in the territory and someone argued the point, they could *pay* for doubting her word. That wasn't gambling. That was surviving the best way she knew how. And it wasn't easy when Emet drank the profits like a thirsty fish and gambled away his possessions as if he were made of money!

Chapter 5

While Dag and Greta Ericcson journeyed to Darlington, the Indian agency and commissary that lay to the north, Mikyla offered to keep a watchful eye on their three children. After filling the youngsters' heads with Ozark tales of the Lady of the Valley and the Lost Louisiana Mine, Mikyla instigated several games of tag for a group of children in the Boomer camp.

Greta returned late that afternoon with her own supplies, and those the Ericcsons had picked up for Mikyla. When Greta had rounded up her children and left Miki to herself, she felt oddly restless. Her father was God only knew where . . . and she needed something to occupy her. Her eyes fell to the neat stack of clothes lying at the foot of her cot—garments Cale had lent her during the storm. Should she return the apparel or save herself considerable distress by avoiding the man? If she knew what was good for her, she would take a wide berth around Cale Brolin. Mikyla had come to recognize trouble at a glance, and Cale was definitely trouble.

Again her gaze strayed to the garments and she chewed indecisively on her bottom lip. It would be impolite to borrow Cale's clothes without returning them, she reminded herself. Hounded by mixed emotions, Mikyla scooped up the garments and went to fetch Sundance.

Most likely, Cale wouldn't be in his camp. He was probably out selling his horses at outlandish prices to the eager settlers who awaited the Run. It would be a simple matter for her to deposit the clothes in Cale's tent and return to the Boomer camp without confronting the ornery but charismatic Cale Brolin.

Mikyla wasn't sure if she was disappointed or relieved that Cale was nowhere to be found when she arrived at the site. The campfire was blazing, but there was no one around to attend it. Perhaps Cale had ambled to the creek to bathe, she speculated. He had probably stripped from his clothes and . . .

Squeezing back the thought, Mikyla dismounted. She didn't even want to imagine how Cale would look, standing in midstream, naked as the day he was born. She had seen far too much of him during their first encounter.

Drawing herself up to a proud stature, Mikyla strode toward Cale's canvas home billowing in the brisk spring wind, then ducked beneath the waving flap. She stared at the meager furnishings of Cale's home, which could be folded and relocated in a matter of minutes. There were very few personal possessions that could tell her about the man she had met the previous week, the man who kept creeping into the corners of her mind. Miki kept telling herself she disliked the overbearing cowboy, but she could not control the forbidden tingle his image aroused.

Her eyes fell to the crumpled shirt draped over the folding chair. Mikyla ran her hand over the fabric that had absorbed Cale's masculine fragrance and her senses were suddenly alive with memories of this man who could kiss her witless and then make her so furious she itched to club him over the head. He had her swinging on an emotional pendulum, constantly gliding from anger to forbidden desire.

"I didn't realize snooping was among your numerous faults" came the low husky voice that crackled with amusement.

Mikyla jumped straight up and reversed direction in midair. She came down to see Cale's awesomely masculine frame fill the entrance of the tent. "I . . . I wasn't snooping," she defended.

She quickly dropped the shirt she had been absently fondling so Cale wouldn't know she had been hugging the aromatic garment to her body. It was a foolish gesture that suggested she was romantically attracted to the man who wore the shirt. That was ridiculous, of course, Mikyla reassured herself. Cale Brolin didn't mean a thing to her.

"I was simply returning the clothes I had borrowed." Her slim finger indicated the neat pile of garments she had washed with a great deal more care than she used when laundering her own apparel. But she wasn't about to divulge that information to Cale!

Twinkling eyes watched his discarded shirt flutter to the chair behind this curvaceous blonde. "Thank you for your consideration. Even if you were snooping," he tacked on with a teasing grin.

Flinging her nose up in the air, Mikyla attempted to sail out of the tent, but she was forced to brush against Cale's sinewy body, which he refused to remove from the exit. Shock waves undulated down her spine and her senses were swamped by the musky scent of him, by his muscular, six-foot-four-inch frame, and by his blatant masculinity.

Lord, what was there about this man that rattled her so? It was unsettling to be near him and Mikyla found herself reacting defensively, as if she needed to protect herself. But from whom? Mikyla wasn't sure whom she mistrusted most—Cale or herself.

Cale scrutinized the saucy blonde, marveling at how quickly his blood pressure soared when she was within reach. Miki walked in and filled up his world and he was suddenly aware of nothing but those lustrous blue eyes and those kissable cupid's-bow lips.

There were at least one hundred reasons why he should shoo this sassy minx on her way, but at the moment Cale couldn't conjure up even one of them. And Cale knew, even before he crept to his tent to see her hugging his shirt, he didn't want her to rush off. She intrigued him. But it was only a temporary fascination, Cale assured himself confidently. There were very few women who could hold his attention for any length of time—not even this gorgeous, tantalizing firebrand.

"Since you didn't stay for supper when last we met, the invitation is still open," Cale heard himself say in a husky whisper. "Will you join me?"

Mikyla inched past Cale, rankled that her body exploded in spontaneous combustion each time it came into contact with his. "I can't," she breathed shakily. "It's almost dark and I . . ."

"You can't or you won't?" Cale prodded, carefully gauging her reaction to their closeness. "Is it that you are afraid of me, Ky?"

Mikyla sidestepped to allow herself breathing room. Thrusting out her chin, she glared clouds on his sunny smile. Confound the man. Why did he delight in putting her on immediate defense? "You don't frighten me," she assured him more firmly than necessary.

"I think the lady offers too strong a reaction," he rasped.

Cale moved with lithe grace, erasing the narrow distance that separated them. He was close, *too* close. Mikyla could actually *feel* the aura of sensuality that exuded from him. It was like standing beside a blazing stove and absorbing its warmth. His masculine aroma fogged her senses, paralyzing her brain. Even her hands were clammy, for heaven's sake, and her tongue had wrapped itself in knots and her knees clanked together like cymbals. What was the matter with her? She had never suffered such a violent reaction to any other man? Why did this brawny giant affect her so?

"Convince me that you aren't afraid of me," Cale challenged, holding her wide-eyed gaze.

He edged even closer, assessing the cupid's-bow curve of her lips. His raven head was poised above hers and Mikyla was suffering from oxygen deprivation. Breathing was virtually impossible when Cale suffocated her with his nearness. When his arm stole around her waist to bend her into his hard contours, Mikyla melted like an overheated candle.

His mouth took skillful possession of hers, reminding Miki how very little she had known about kissing until Cale

Brolin had instructed her. He probably knew more about seduction than she could hope to learn in a lifetime. He could erode a woman's defenses and leave her craving things she had never even known existed, making her wonder if anything could satisfy this wild, all-consuming longing. His masculine warmth engulfed her, bringing a strange contentment. His lips moved languidly over hers and Miki found herself thinking she belonged in his protective arms, even though she knew nothing could have been further from the truth.

When Cale slowly withdrew, Mikyla's body was left to tingle and sway back toward his solid strength. Her lashes fluttered upward to see Cale's lips pursed in a triumphant smile, which jolted Mikyla to her senses . . . or at least what was left of them.

Mikyla held herself erect. While she still had the strength to make an honorable retreat, she ordered her legs to carry her away from temptation.

"Thank you for the use of your clothes in my hour of need," Mikyla bleated like a lamb that had been startled by a prowling wolf. Damn, she hated herself for sounding so rattled! "I must decline your invitation for supper." She shot him a suspicious glance. "If I stayed I might find myself the main course."

While Mikyla wobbled off on rubberized legs, Cale propped himself against the corral, crossing his arms and legs in front of him. He was mesmerized by the graceful sway of her hips, wrapped in trim-fitting jeans. He was fascinated by her feminine poise and the uncanny way she kept herself distant and aloof, even after she had unwillingly melted against him the previous moment. Cale couldn't recall another woman denying him what he wanted quite as effectively as this shapely sprite. Women usually flocked to Cale with little more than an encouraging smile and, even more often, without his invitation. But Mikyla was determined to ignore the sparks that flew when they kissed.

Although she dressed like a man, there was a lot of woman lurking beneath those boots and jeans. Cale had always loved a challenge, whether it be a wild mustang or a contrary woman. And Miki Lassiter held both challenge and a lure.

When Mikyla trotted off on Sundance, Cale patiently waited for her to draw the stallion to a halt, for he was limping noticeably on his front leg. Cale knew Mikyla wouldn't risk injuring her steed when she needed him to run this ridiculous race for land. As she climbed down to inspect the steed's hoof, Cale strode over to offer assistance.

"Let me have a look," he insisted, moving her out of the way before she could lift the injured leg.

Mikyla's frown denoted the extent of her concern. "What's the matter with him? He was fine when I rode into camp."

"Sundance must have picked up a rock in the 'frog' of his hoof," Cale diagnosed. "I wouldn't advise riding him until he has time to mend. You might permanently damage a tendon if he is forced to favor his good leg."

"But what am I supposed to do?" she groaned in dismay. "I can't very well walk back to camp before dark."

Cale gestured toward the corral, which was brimming with horses. "If you are afraid to stay the night with me and permit Sundance the rest he needs, you can take one of my mounts and let me doctor the stallion."

Afraid to stay? The comment caused Mikyla to bristle in indignation. Leave Sundance with this wily horse trader? Why, Cale would probably have her stallion sold before she could return to retrieve him!

Without waiting to hear her decision, Cale unfastened the girth, removed the saddle, and led the limping steed toward the hitching post he had constructed. Mikyla glared at Cale's broad-muscled back and wrestled with her dilemma. Damn, of all the times for Sundance to come up lame!

She voiced her concern when Cale had completed hitching up Sundance.

"Where do you intend to sleep if I should decide to stay?" she wanted to know.

"I intend to sleep where I usually sleep," he informed her blandly. "In my tent, on my bed . . . in the buff." He turned from his task of rubbing a poultice on Sundance's leg to flash Mikyla a roguish smile. "But I think you'll find me to be a

66

reasonably generous man. I don't mind sharing my bed with you."

Mikyla's mouth dropped open to her collarbone. "I'd rather die!" she assured him in no uncertain terms.

Cale's shoulders lifted in a nonchalant shrug. "I can live with that." His suddenly disinterested gaze flickered over her assets, but he pretended to be undisturbed by the tantalizing picture she presented. "Don't make the mistake of thinking I would be disappointed if you left. Virgins aren't my style. I prefer *women,* not sassy tomboys who don't know the first thing about satisfying a man."

Mikyla would have stormed over to slap him silly if she thought she could get away with it. "And indiscriminate philanderers aren't *my* type," she snapped back.

One thick brow arched over his laughing silver eyes. "What is *your* type?" he questioned on a snicker. "A mealy-mouthed weakling you can order about, one who wouldn't make any physically exhausting demands on you?"

Mikyla clenched her fists so tightly that her nails dug into the palms of her hands. Oh, how she would love to place a stranglehold on his arrogant neck! "If I ever do succumb, I expect my lover to at least be a member of the human species!" She hurled the insult at him, along with a glare that silently requested a random lightning bolt strike him on the seat of his breeches!

Grinning in amusement, Cale surveyed the outraged flush that stained her exquisite face. "You wouldn't be implying that I'm inhuman, would you, honey?"

"Don't call me 'honey,'" she demanded tersely. "And yes, that is exactly what I am suggesting, you oversize wolf!"

Her remark provoked Cale's sudden burst of laughter. My, but Miki was a saucy little firebrand. She gave as good as she got. Cale liked that. A woman with spunk was more of a challenge than the run-of-the-mill beauties who melted in a man's arms.

"And I am not about to leave Sundance here with you, either," she added, drawing Cale from his contemplative deliberations.

"You think I would sell your stallion to prevent you from

running this ridiculous race for homesteads—even if I would be doing you the greatest favor one person could do for another," he smirked in speculation.

"I don't need you or anyone else deciding what is best for me," Mikyla sniffed. "I am my own person."

Cale chuckled at her explosive tone. "Amen to that, sweetheart. But it's still a pity *your person* is going to be trampled beyond recognition when you risk your lovely neck in this crazy race."

"I am perfectly capable of taking care of myself. I have been doing so for quite some time now," she told him tartly. "I don't need you to do my thinking or make my decisions."

"But you have yet to realize that when free land becomes a man's passion he will fight harder for a few hundred dollars worth of land than he will for ten thousand dollars in cash," Cale snorted disconcertedly. "When I was in Darlington two days ago, there were more settlers and wagons clogging the dirt streets than there were Indians and tepees surrounding the agency! And with settlers come opportunists." His steel-hard eyes drilled into her with penetrating effectiveness. "And you, young lady, are not worldly enough to distinguish between those who *seek* opportunity and those who are pure, scheming *opportunists*. I am willing to bet my last dollar you will get yourself into trouble before this is all over!"

"Then it will be *my* problem," Mikyla reminded him sharply. "I do not need a self-appointed guardian wolf telling me what to do and what *not* to do. You are so pessimistic that you project your own faults on everyone else," Mikyla insisted as she raked him with scornful mockery. "There are a lot of good, honest people in the world . . ."

"And most of them are residing somewhere else," Cale scoffed. "I've even heard it rumored that syndicates from as far away as New York are scrambling about, trying to defraud settlers of prime townsites and homesteads."

"The people in Indian Territory are not all swindlers and thieves," Mikyla defended hotly. "I live in a camp with thousands of decent citizens."

"And I would imagine they all wear a pistol strapped on

each hip to protect themselves," Cale guessed as he glanced meaningfully at the Colt .45 that dangled from Mikyla's waist.

There *were* criminals in their midsts, Mikyla silently admitted, hating it when Cale was right. But there were still a good many respectable settlers.

Deciding it best to drop the subject before their debate became a shouting match, Mikyla pivoted to survey the situation in Cale's tent. She may have been forced to stay because of Sundance's injury, but she wasn't about to become a midnight snack for this wolf.

A mischievous smile bordered Cale's lips when Miki stalked off to investigate his tent further. While she was rustling around inside the canvas, Cale extracted the rock he had purposely wedged in the stallion's hoof.

It was a devious tactic, and Cale chided himself for all of a half-second. But this standoffish minx had bewitched him. Cale delighted in getting her dander up, watching her face flush with embarrassment and irritation. He couldn't bypass the opportunity of taunting her, of thrusting her into awkward situations. It would be pure joy to watch her squirm when she was forced to share sleeping quarters with a man.

After Cale put Sundance into the corral to recover from his feigned injury, he sauntered to the campfire to check the stew that had been simmering all afternoon. When Mikyla emerged from the tent, she cast Cale a cautious glance and then plopped down on the blanket he had spread beside the fire.

"You really don't trust me, do you, Ky?" Cale questioned abruptly, watching her fidget like a caged cat.

Mikyla darted him a hasty glance before she accepted the plate he had prepared for her. A disappointed frown tarnished her features. "Stew?" she muttered when she stared at her meal. "I was hoping for your heart . . . *fried.*"

Cale overlooked the jibe. "I asked you a question and I'm awaiting an answer."

"I trust *gentlemen,*" she stipulated. "But I refuse to classify you in that category."

69

His silver eyes glistened in the firelight. "Ah, yes, I believe you said I was a member of the canine species. A wolf, to be specific," he murmured in that low, husky voice that always sent a skein of goose bumps gliding across her skin.

Mikyla chose to ignore both his glance and the seductive voice that would undoubtedly reduce a lesser woman to a rippling puddle. "At first I suspected you of being a wolf," she confessed. "But the more I think on it, I would say you tend more toward the fish family."

Cale's amused gaze flickered down his torso. "I beg to differ, my dear. I feel no compulsive need to spend most of my time in water. And these garments do not conceal scales and fins." An ornery grin stretched across his lips. "If you like, I can disrobe and allow you to see for yourself whether I am wrapped in skin or scales . . ."

Mikyla felt the blush rise in her cheeks when Cale unfastened his belt. "That won't be necessary. Human sharks and barracudas probably don't possess scales."

"I have been called many things, including a wolf," he admitted, chuckling good-naturedly. "But I cannot remember a lady labeling me a fish. To be honest, I think I prefer to be called a wolf . . . if you feel obliged to call me anything at all."

Mikyla munched on her meal, wondering why she felt this odd need to insult Cale every chance she got. Was it because she felt inferior in his presence? Was she trying to cut him down to size? To strike out in defense . . .

"Enjoying your supper?" Cale queried, leaning closer than necessary.

Her plate teetered in her hands when she realized she should have been paying close attention to her predator rather than trying to understand her feelings. He was only inches away, his entrancing gaze lingering on her lips.

Mikyla shoved the half-empty plate into his stomach and scrambled to her knees. She had intended to gain her feet, but Cale's restraining grasp would permit her to go no farther.

"Sit down, Ky," Cale requested, his voice like a soft caress. "If you are going to brave this Run in the midst of thousands of men, we need to quell your instinctive need of darting away from those of the male persuasion." Using her arm as a tow rope, Cale brought the wary blonde down beside him on the quilt. "You are too fidgety for your own good. Every time I come within close range you jump like a startled grasshopper."

Mikyla found herself on her back with Cale's sensuous form hovering over her. "And I suppose after a few quick lessons from *Master* Brolin, I will be able to fend against the most roguish of rogues," she smirked into his craggy features.

"If I want to teach a nervous mare to hold her ground, I flap feed sacks at her until she can stand still without coming unglued," he murmured as he combed his fingers through the lustrous tendrils of spun silver and gold. "When a woman leaps like a frightened doe each time a man comes near her, she needs to be thoroughly kissed so she will know what to expect." His lips were poised over hers and she could feel the warm draft of his breath caressing her cheek. "Passion is one of the greatest pleasures a man and woman can experience. I want to teach you not to be so apprehensive about it . . ."

Mikyla braced her hand on his chest to hold him at bay when his raven head made a slow, deliberate descent toward hers. "And how much is this lesson going to cost me?" she questioned suspiciously.

A wry smile rippled across his full lips. "You can pay whatever you think the lesson is worth . . ."

"Don't be surprised if you receive *nothing* for your instruction," Mikyla had just enough time to say before his mouth took possession of hers.

It would have been so much easier to cope with her emotions if Cale had roughly assaulted her. But he was so amazingly gentle that Mikyla feared she would melt in his hands. His lips courted hers like a bee hovering on a flower. His practiced hands lightly traced the curve of her thigh and hips before venturing upward. Mikyla swore Cale had worked magic on her naive body. Somehow he had removed every bone without performing surgery. She wasn't sure she could have unfolded herself from the blanket if she wanted to. She could only have *flowed* from one place to another like a stream of water trickling across the ground.

When his adventurous caresses scaled her ribs to glide over the peaks of her breasts, Mikyla flinched. His touch set her innocent body to quaking with apprehension and desire. Mikyla didn't like what she was feeling. It put sinful thoughts in her head and left her aching to satisfy her curiosity about this strange physical phenomena she was experiencing.

His hands and lips were everywhere at once, discovering each curve and swell, learning each sensitive point. Mikyla gulped for breath, only to find Cale had stripped the air from her lungs. Like a drowning swimmer, she clung to him, knowing she was clutching at danger, not safety. There was nothing safe about this sensuous rake. He was as dangerous as they came.

Cale had only intended to tease this naïve imp into awareness of what transpired between a man and a woman. But suddenly Cale was all too conscious of this gorgeous but leery creature. He found himself wanting the pleasure he had shared with countless other women. But when Miki returned his kiss with such inventive innocence, Cale knew passion would never be the same as it had been with his experienced lovers. This curvaceous pixie was the image of pure, untutored desire. She didn't even know what he expected from her but she merely responded to the odd sensations that encompassed her. Cale didn't want to teach her how to deal with men, only to instruct her on how to satisfy one man— *himself.*

Now was that crazy? he asked himself as he savored her sweet lips. *Permanent* wasn't even in his vocabulary! And yet he found himself speculating on what it would be like to live out his life with this firebrand, teaching her the joys of lovemaking.

Of course it was crazy, Cale assured himself. He had no intention of getting involved with Miki Lassiter. He was only amusing himself, taking pleasure where he found it, just as he always had. Once he had seduced her he would be only too happy to send her on her way without giving her a second thought. Besides, she was going to get herself into trouble and he had enough troubles of his own without entangling himself with this daring minx.

When his roaming hand dived beneath her shirt to make sizzling contact with her bare flesh, Mikyla wormed away. "I think I have had enough education for one night," she chirped. "We mustn't overload this thimble of a brain that men deem a woman to possess."

Cale chuckled at her squeaky attempt at sarcasm. In Cale's estimation, there were scores of dim-witted females—but this quick-tongued termagant wasn't one of them.

Before Miki could make her break for freedom, Cale pressed her back to the quilt. "The first lesson isn't complete until we have tested your progress," he insisted, his voice ragged with the side effects of passion. "If I can kiss you without your coming apart at the seams you'll pass the beginners' course with flying colors . . ."

Mikyla could see her reflection in those flickering pools of silver. She could feel Cale's muscular leg lying suggestively across her thighs, feel his broad chest crushing her throbbing breasts. And then he was kissing her and she could feel nothing but one delicious sensation after another converging upon her. How could she feel as if she were sailing on pinioned wings when she was pressed beneath Cale's heavy weight? It was the paradox of passion, she decided as she unwillingly surrendered to his devouring kiss.

When Mikyla returned his passionate kiss, Cale swore someone had sneaked up to build a fire beneath him. He hadn't expected this volatile reaction. They had kissed several times since they met, and each embrace had been as wild and explosive as the first. It wasn't supposed to be like this, Cale knew that for a fact. He was experienced with women and he wasn't supposed to be reacting like a young lad who was standing on the threshold of desire for the first time in his life! And he also knew he wasn't going to be satisfied until he possessed this enigmatic bundle of spirit and femininity.

Withdrawing, Cale studied her kiss-swollen lips and those enormous blue eyes that had darkened with desire. While

Mikyla unfolded herself to rearrange the clothes that had tangled about her, Cale stretched out on the blanket to survey her from all angles. This sweet witch was going to join him in bed and they were going to learn all there was to know about each other, he decided. He had always avoided virgins, but this one was far too tempting to resist. Besides, she needed to be taught a few things about men and there was nothing better than firsthand experience.

Smiling in roguish anticipation, Cale climbed to his feet to strut into the tent behind Mikyla. Mmm . . . it was going to be a most enchanting evening. Cale pulled up short when he entered the tent to find a rope strung from one supporting pole to the other. A sheet had been draped over the rope, dividing the room in half. *His* and *hers,* no doubt. Cale's cot had been relocated in one corner and a pallet had been prepared in the other corner.

"What the hell is this?" he snorted, wondering why he even bothered with the question. He knew exactly what *this* was. It was a division line that might as well have been a stone wall. The implication was just as concrete.

One dainty finger indicated the cot. "That is the bed where you always sleep. And this is my pallet," she informed her bug-eyed companion. Mikyla flashed him a sassy smile. "I'm sure you are accustomed to having your way with women. But kissing lessons are as far as this tête-à-tête is going to go. I intend to ride out in the morning with my virtue intact. If you force yourself on me, I will have no choice but to render you useless to any woman. I'm sure that would spoil your greatest ambition in life—populating the continent all by yourself."

Cale gaped at the saucy chit. "You'd shoot me?" he croaked in disbelief.

An ornery smile rippled across her lips. "In a minute," she assured him firmly. "If you dare to cross the boundary line, you won't walk away on your own accord."

She really wasn't giving in, Cale grumbled in annoyance. Damn that minx. He knew he had aroused her sleeping passions. And yet she refused to allow them the pleasures they could give each other. And to make matters worse, she was prepared to defend her own honor. Knowing this resourceful vixen could ride as well as any man led Cale to believe that she could fire a pistol like a sharpshooter.

Well, perhaps it was for the best, the logical side of his brain told his disappointed male instincts. He didn't really want to get involved with Miki Lassiter. He had attempted to seduce her and he had failed. If he were smart, he would leave well enough alone.

Cale dropped into a mocking bow. "Have it your way, my dear. I'm sure you usually do. But if you turn out to be a dried-up old spinster, you have no one to blame but yourself."

"It has to be better than becoming a man's plaything, one that is recklessly used and cruelly discarded," Mikyla defended huffily. "Passion is not just something people shrug in and out of like a shirt!"

Cale burst into snickers as he strode along the improvised dividing wall to plop down on his cot. "Since when did you become such an expert on love? As near as I can tell, tonight was your first experience with anything remotely close to passion."

"I consider myself a quick learner," Mikyla muttered as she sank down on her pallet. She glared at the sheet that separated her from the infuriating man who knew just what to say to stoke the fires of her temper. "I know what I *don't* want. A tumble in the grass with a man like you could, at best, appease animal lust. That has nothing to do with loving and caring. There is no mutual affection or respect and . . ."

"And I wish I hadn't asked!" Cale groaned, covering his ears. "Spare me the lecture, sweetheart. At the moment, I can't think of one good reason why I would want to join you on your pallet. You wouldn't know the first thing about pleasing a man."

His resentful tone of voice relieved Mikyla's anxieties. She had fully intended to build walls between them, dividers invisible as well as sheets hanging from ropes! She was not going to get mixed up with this shrewd horse trader. Mikyla had no need of steamy affairs such as he offered. She had her dream. In a week, Cale would have drifted off to parts unknown and she wasn't going to care!

The rustle of clothing jostled Mikyla from her silent reverie. "What are you doing over there?"

"Stripping from my shirt," he teased wickedly. Another rustle of fabric broke the tense silence. "And now I'm shedding my breeches. I'm wearing nothing but a smile. Shall I show you?"

Mikyla's face flushed crimson red. "I don't want to see! Can't you sleep in your underwear for just one night!" She was becoming frantic.

"Nope" came his reply, crackling with barely contained amusement. "I prefer to sleep in the raw, even if there is no one with whom to share my nakedness."

Her face registered seven more shades of red. If Cale dared to stroll to her side of the tent, she was not about to be caught looking at him. She would stare at the canvas wall, purposely ignoring him. "You are perverted, Cale Brolin," she gritted out as she flounced on her pallet.

"Why? Just because I sleep in the nude?" he chuckled as he laid his arms over the sheet wall to stare down at Mikyla, whose face was mashed into her pallet. "If the good Lord wanted men to sleep in underwear they would have been born with a pair."

Braving a glance, Mikyla peered up at the tousled raven hair and bare shoulders that rose above the flimsy dividing wall. The lantern that blazed on Cale's side of the tent cast his masculine silhouette against the bed linen that hung over the rope. Although Mikyla couldn't see specifics, she was stung with the impression that Cale was solid muscle. The thought caused her cheeks to pulsate with even more color. If Cale was trying to embarrass her to death, he had very nearly accomplished his goal.

"Can't we just go to sleep?" she groaned miserably. "I don't wish to discuss your nakedness."

"For one of your kisses, I'll crawl into my corner and promise not to pester you for the remainder of the night," he bartered with a mischievous smile.

Mikyla stared at his grin, knowing things could only get worse if she didn't patronize the scoundrel. Resigning herself to the fact that she would have to endure another soul-shattering round of sensations to pacify this dragon, Mikyla came to her feet. Keeping her eyes on his smiling face, Mikyla approached the dividing wall with the same caution a hunter would stalk a starving lion.

One thick brow rose to a teasing angle. "Now *that* is progress. Two hours ago you would have crashed through the tent to avoid me."

His taunt inspired Mikyla to counter his orneriness. He wanted a good-night kiss, did he? Well, she would present him with a blazing kiss that even a blizzard couldn't cool. There was only one way to deal with a man like Cale Brolin, Mikyla assured herself. A woman had to prove to him that she was immune to his charms. She would inflame him with her kiss and then she would walk away unaffected. Cale would realize he had met his match and that he was wasting his time trying to seduce her.

Following that practical theory, Mikyla wrapped her arms around his neck and pressed wantonly against the sheet that separated them. Employing the techniques Cale had taught her, Mikyla plied him with a burning kiss that could melt an iceberg.

Now it was Cale's turn to wonder if he had met a woman *he* couldn't handle. Mikyla was breathing a fire into him that left him boiling with desire, the kind that couldn't be appeased until passion had run its full course.

And then, as pretty as you please, Mikyla removed herself from his close proximity. "Good night, Cale. I trust you will sleep well."

When she sank back on her pallet, her eyes fell to the bulge in the sheet that hadn't been there the moment before. Her gaze drifted to Cale's craggy face and then descended to the sheet. "Is it possible for a man to sleep facedown, in your . . . condition?" Mikyla could have kicked herself for allowing her curiosity to find its way to her tongue!

Cale's face cracked in a devilish grin. "Would you like to come watch me try, my curious little imp?"

A chuckle burst from Cale's lips when Mikyla buried her head in her pillow like a frightened ostrich. He was laughing at her and she was thoroughly humiliated! Good heavens, she was receiving far more education than she had anticipated. Cale Brolin had her doing and saying things she wouldn't have believed possible. He had made her acutely aware of the differences between a man and a woman, and Miki realized she was tracking through dangerous territory. The thought of sleeping in the same tent with a naked man had her blushing all over again.

"I think we are both discovering more about each other than is safe." Cale's hoarse voice came from the opposite corner of the now darkened tent. "Sundance should be well enough to travel by morning without suffering complications. I suggest you ride out of here." There was a long pause and the silence crackled with invisible sparks. "Don't come back to my camp unless you expect us to share more than the same tent, Ky. You are a temptation I cannot continue to ignore. I won't be so lenient with you if there is a next time . . ."

Mikyla gulped down her heart after it had climbed the ladder of her ribs to lodge in her throat. How was she supposed to sleep after Cale's suggestive proclamation? She wasn't, she realized as the hours crept by at a snail's pace. And as soon as the first streaks of dawn splintered across the dark sky, Mikyla was up and gone. She tried to hold Sundance to a walk, afraid she would aggravate his injury. But it was difficult not to gallop away when she felt the need to put miles between her and Cale Brolin. Her attraction to him truly frightened her. There had been a time when she would have been outraged by his insinuation. And now, God help her, she found herself wanting to know more about the man, to experience the wonders of lovemaking. And what disturbed her most was that she wanted no other man to teach her!

Cale watched Mikyla's early-morning flight until she disappeared over the rise. He, too, had lain awake, grappling with his feelings. He had been rejected, humiliated, and aroused. All three emotions were struggling to dominate his

78

thoughts. But no matter how he rationalized the incident, he came away wanting Miki Lassiter in his bed. She challenged him, excited him.

Find yourself a female who won't complicate your life, Cale chided himself gruffly. *Just because you want that feisty minx doesn't mean you have to have her. Indeed, you are much better off without her.* Cale inhaled a deep breath and slowly expelled it. Common sense and caution should be observed when dealing with that lovely blonde. She came with strings attached—the kind that could tie a man's heart in knots. Cale was going to keep his distance. He had played with fire twice and he had been singed. There wasn't going to be a third time.

He had surely seen the last of Mikyla. But it was unnerving to know there was a woman in the territory who could arouse him against his will—as well as her own. They ignited fires in each other, fires that could blaze out of control. But Cale was not going to get involved. He was footloose and fancy-free, and he was going to stay that way. If he wanted a woman's affection he didn't have to look far to find it. Miki Lassiter wasn't the kind of woman who understood fleeting affairs. Hell, she understood very little about the male of the species. If she needed further education she could consult someone else. As a matter of fact, he was going to forget that shapely blonde with the wide blue eyes even existed. Why, by evening he probably wouldn't even remember her name.

Chewing on that positive thought, Cale saddled his steed. By dark, he wouldn't remember the way Miki's lips melted like warm honey on his lips, the way her soft contours blended so perfectly into his. He wouldn't recall the fresh clean scent of her hair, the impish way she smiled . . .

Cale shook away the tantalizing vision he had unwittingly created. He was going at this all wrong, he realized. If he wanted to forget Ky, he had to list all her annoying characteristics. That shouldn't be too difficult. The lady had scores of them!

Chapter 6

Cale approached the fort that was situated on high ground overlooking the vast, sweeping basin of the North Canadian River. It was a bright spring day that could boost the lowest spirits. The landscape of lush green grass swayed serenely beneath a cloudless sky. The myriad of homestead camps was all that marred the sprawling prairie and Cale glared at the tents with more contempt than he had felt in previous weeks.

Since the day he had unhorsed Mikyla Lassiter during the electrical storm he had been vaguely discontent. Since the night she had slept in his tent he had been blatantly restless. He kept seeing that bewitching face dancing in the evening shadows. He had witnessed the same dazzling color of her eyes each time he gazed skyward. And each time he took a sip of any sort of beverage nothing quenched his thirst quite as thoroughly and completely as her innocent but intoxicating kiss.

Yes, it was a ridiculous fascination, Cale had lectured himself daily. But even after five hectic days of commuting between the Cheyenne-Arapaho Agency at Darlington and the stage stations that were scattered throughout Indian Territory, Cale couldn't get that fiery minx off his mind.

He could almost feel her supple body against his. He could feel her lips melting beneath his inquiring kiss. He could see her charging at him with that magnificent blood-red stallion. She was there, garbed in his oversize shirt, looking so small and vulnerable that he ached to draw her into his protective arms. She was standing on the opposite of her makeshift wall, tempting him to the limits of his self-control . . .

Cale gave himself an inward shake. He intended to spend the day at Fort Reno, enjoying Major Brock Terrel's hospitality, engaging in the competitive sport of horse racing, and admiring Emily Terrel's stunning beauty.

A faint smile bordered Cale's lips when the attractive redhead popped to mind. Before Brock had been commissioned at Fort Reno, Cale and Emily had been on the friendliest of terms. Quiet laughter rumbled in his throat as he glanced back to check the long string of mules and horses that were following behind him. *Friendly?* That was a rather modest description of his affair with Emily.

The commander's daughter had caught Cale's eye the first time he rode north from his family's vast ranch in Texas. Cale had come to deliver livestock to the military posts and he had found himself doing far more than business. Emily hadn't been the least bit bashful about her intentions toward him. Indeed, she was the one who propositioned Cale! He hadn't had any intention of settling down, but he had been willing to sample Emily's affection each time he happened to the fort to sell his mules and horses. But Emily had marriage in mind and the instant Brock Terrel arrived on the scene she latched on to him.

The fact that Cale had been intimate with Brock's wife put a strain on the relationship—at least on Cale's part. Brock was obviously unaware of their passionate affair. Which was a damned good thing, Cale reminded himself. It would have made the situation impossible since Brock was the officer in charge of purchasing military livestock and also delegated the duty of overseeing the lease of Indian land to Texas cattlemen. Cale's family had grazed more than a thousand head of livestock on the vacant Indian reserves. The tribes were anxious for the profit derived from leasing their reserve land and the Brolins were elated to pasture their animals on the plush prairies.

Cale's perceptive gray eyes focused on the immaculate fort in the distance. Yes, he was fortunate that Brock knew nothing about Emily's fling. If he had, there was sure to be animosity. Brock would never have allowed Cale to graze or sell a single head of beef in the area. And Cale also doubted that Brock would have bought even one of his mules or horses for the military post. As a matter of fact, Cale's business would have been in bad shape all the way around if Brock learned that his wife knew Cale Brolin a helluva lot better than Brock did!

Cale didn't consider himself a ladykiller, but neither was he blind. He knew Emily still carried a torch for him. He had kept his distance from her for Brock's sake. Yet, there had been one or two occasions when he wished he hadn't been Emily's former lover. She had played up to him, leaving Cale squirming in his skin. And if Brock ever learned that Cale and Emily . . .

Cale flung aside the apprehensive thought. He and Brock were friends, not close friends, but compatible business associates. Cale didn't want to see their relationship spoiled because of a careless fling with a woman. The whole lot of females could cause a man a peck of trouble. Women were flighty, emotional creatures . . . Except for Mikyla Lassiter, who was stubborn beyond compare, fiery as a torch, hardheaded as a bull, sassier than a spoiled child . . . Cale continued to list all of her annoying faults for no other reason than to reassure himself that he didn't give a whit about her.

Oh, he had battled the inner war of common sense against desire more times than he cared to count. And yes, his eyes scanned the various camps he had visited to sell his extra horses, hoping to catch sight of her silver-gold head and snapping blue eyes. But male pride prevented him from turning Indian Territory upside down to locate her. Besides, that minx probably had a string of men constantly following behind her. She wouldn't last long in Oklahoma Country, he predicted. Some claim jumper would inevitably force her off her land or she would find herself an able-bodied husband whom she could order about like her slave. And if she lost her precious claim she would probably stoop to turning her feminine wiles on a man who had managed to hold on to his property. As determined as Mikyla Lassiter was, she would find a way to get what she wanted, unless some ruthless varmint killed her first . . .

"Well, well, if it isn't Cale Brolin." Brock Terrel stood with feet askance, his arms folded over his chest. "I wondered if you had sold all your horses to the swarm of settlers and found yourself short of the order to be filled at Fort Reno."

A lazy smile captured Cale's craggy features. With lithe grace he swung from the saddle. "I just happen to have a few head for the cavalry," Cale chuckled, his arm sweeping the air to indicate the long procession of sturdy stock.

Brock clasped his hands behind his back and strode down the parade of horses. Abruptly, he paused to clamp his fingers around a dun gelding's mouth. After checking the horse's teeth, he glanced teasingly at Cale. "You didn't pull this nag's incisors to lead me to believe he's a four-year-old, did you, Brolin?"

Cale dragged his hat from his rumpled raven hair and placed it over his heart. "I'm honest as the day is long, Major. I wouldn't cheat you. The dun lost his teeth the natural way. I don't practice equestrian dentistry."

The Army made it a policy to purchase horses between the ages of four and seven years old. There were some horse traders who stooped to pulling teeth to sell a young colt. Cale, however, was not one of them. He prided himself on his reputation. If he claimed a colt to be five years old, that was the exact age of the animal. Any adept horse trader could look a horse in the mouth and determine, by the number and the smoothness of the animal's teeth, how old it was or if it had been served a diet of lush grass or prickly bushes. Cale's stock was top quality, bred by registered studs and raised on thick pastures. Brock knew that, but he delighted in taunting Cale just the same.

Nodding mutely, Brock assessed the herd and then pivoted to face Cale. "You don't happen to have a steed in this string that can outrun that strawberry roan of yours, do you?"

Brock was a fierce competitor when it came to racing. It annoyed him that he had never once defeated Cale on the

Fort Reno track. Nothing would have pleased Brock more than to outrun Cale on one of his own horses.

"You're an excellent judge of horse flesh," Cale snickered lightheartedly. "Do you see a steed in the string that you think could leave my strawberry roan choking in dust?"

Brock thoughtfully rubbed his chin as he paced back and forth assessing the horses. His eyes narrowed on a big, muscular palomino that equaled the size of Cale's mount. "The palomino is long and lean and well-muscled. He *looks* like he has the stamina to run."

Cale stifled an amused grin when Brock ran a deliberate hand over the horse's rump and then strode around to the other end to pry open its mouth and calculate its age.

"If you want him he's yours . . . for a reasonable price," Cale stipulated.

Brock nodded agreeably. "One hundred dollars seems fair," he bartered in a businesslike tone.

An incredulous laugh burst from Cale's lips. "I could get six hundred for this one from those land-hungry settlers. Why would I want to sacrifice that palomino to a man who will inevitably cheat me out of this whole damned string of horses?"

Brock's dark eyes narrowed on Cale. "You're a hard man, Brolin. Two hundred fifty dollars. That's my final offer. And I'll throw in one of Emily's home-cooked meals."

"Sold, even if you practically stole my prize mount out from under me," Cale chuckled.

After Cale and Brock haggled over the price of the rest of the horses and mules, they ambled toward the racetrack to survey their competition. Cale broke stride when he saw the powerful blood-red stallion with the flaxen mane and tail. A wordless scowl exploded from his lips as he scanned the area in search of the stallion's ornery mistress. A conglomeration of Indians, gamblers, and soldiers were huddled in a circle near the starting gate. Cale didn't have to be a genius to guess who was the focal point of the group. No doubt, Mikyla was in the thick of things, preying on men who would bet against her ability to endure a grueling race in which all of her challengers were men. Dammit, was that woman ever out of her element?

"It looks as if the crowd is involved in heavy betting," Brock observed with a wry smile. "Are you staking your entire profit on this race, Brolin?"

"I'm taking only one side bet," Cale growled, his disposition turning as sour as a lemon. Damn, when he got his hands on that daring sprite he was going to shake the stuffing out of her for wedging herself into a sporting event that should have been off limits to women!

While Brock walked off to retrieve a saddle for his newly purchased palomino, Cale shoved bodies aside to seek out the owner of the blond hair that was sparkling in the sunshine. And there she was, decked out in her trim-fitting breeches that displayed her curvaceous figure, damn her! She seemed to have no interest in feminine fashion. Miki was not the least bit concerned with what was in vogue, only what was practical for her outrageous behavior.

Glaring at Mikyla's shapely backside, Cale snaked out a hand and clamped his fingers around her forearm. Mikyla found herself whisked from the circle with incredible speed. She had been snatched away in midsentence and there was no circulation in her arm. Cale was crushing that particular appendage in his death grip.

Cale thrust his face into hers, his silver eyes blazing. "What the sweet loving hell do you thinking you're doing?" he scowled into her shocked expression.

On every occasion, when Mikyla had confronted Cale Brolin, she felt as if she were standing in the shadow of a towering mountain, just like the ones she had left behind in the Ozarks. A woman couldn't see over him, around him, or through him. Cale filled up her world and blocked her view. That in itself was enough to stoke the fires of her explosive temper. But what really galled her was that the mere sight of this brawny rogue set her pulse to thumping like a jackrabbit bounding across a meadow.

"Not that it is any of your business," she pointed out. "But I am planning on winning enough money to tide me over for the next few months *and* to build Sundance's reputation as a stud for future race horses."

"Not to mention attracting a various assortment of scoundrels who will be hounding you all the way back to camp to relieve you of your winnings . . . *if* you don't break your damned fool neck first!" Cale spewed into her flushed face.

"I am not a novice on the racetrack," she spouted, her blue eyes flashing as she glared up into his chiseled features.

"Obviously not," Cale scoffed derisively. "You were wheeling and dealing with the best of them when I snatched you away." When he realized how fiercely he was gripping her arm he eased his grasp. But his voice was still heavily laden with sarcasm. "Forgive me for assuming you to be a lady. You, my lovely Miss Lassiter, are a misfit who has yet to learn her place. And, by God, it is *not* in the midst of gamblers."

Oh, how Cale itched to clamp his fingers around her neck and shake her until her teeth rattled. Damn her! She was openly inviting trouble!

It did Mikyla's heart good to see smoke rolling from Cale's ears. Usually he was the one who had her temper boiling like a steam engine. One decliate brow rose sharply and an impish smile glided across her lips.

"Are you, by chance, racing your gelding, Mr. Brolin?" she inquired, her voice crackling with a challenge. The dare struck the raw nerve that was attached to Cale's male pride. "Would you like to put a small wager on which one of us is the better rider and which of us owns the better horse?"

Cale muttered a quiet string of curses as he peeled several bills from his fist and waved them under her pert nose. "It just so happens I *am* racing, sweetheart." The endearment sounded suspiciously like a curse. And, at the moment, that was exactly how he meant it. "I'll take your bet. If I win, you pack up and get the hell out of here. If you win . . ." Cale flicked his wrist, allowing Mikyla to calculate the generous wad of cash. "All this money is yours."

Mikyla's eyes popped when she estimated the handsome sum Cale was dangling in front of her. If she won, she would have more than enough cash to sustain her for six months. With the other wagers she had made before Cale had dragged her aside, she could survive another few months. The temptation was too great to ignore.

"You've got yourself a bet," she proclaimed, punctuating her words with a decisive nod.

"I rather thought I did," Cale muttered disdainfully.

Damned woman! When she lost the race he would personally escort her to the Kansas border and nudge her on her way. This gorgeous little firebrand was way out of her league. If she didn't watch her step she would either be trampled during the race or she would lose her life to a thief who wanted her purse of coins.

Hadn't anyone ever told Mikyla that a woman's place was at home, cooking and cleaning. Her place was *not* at a racetrack, wagering against professional gamblers! Blast it, where was her father? Didn't he exert any control over this female daredevil?

When Cale stomped off to fetch his strawberry roan gelding, Mikyla elbowed her way back into the betting circle, determined to make the most of opportunity. She would show that cocky cowboy who had the best horse in all of Indian Territory! Just let him eat humble pie. She hoped he choked on it!

Mikyla swung onto Sundance's back and leaned down to give him his customary pep talk before the race. There was a great deal of money riding on this race and Mikyla intended to win it. She desperately needed the cash—money her father couldn't gamble away, money to pay expenses and purchase building materials for her dream site.

When Cale eased the strawberry roan up beside Sundance, Miki spared him a quick glance. Cale reminded her of a statue. His face was as hard as granite. His finely tuned muscles were poised in grim anticipation.

Although there was a large field of contestants Mikyla couldn't see past Cale Brolin. This was her one opportunity to redeem her pride after he had ripped it to shreds. Well, perhaps she was naive and inexperienced with men, she admitted. But she could ride as well as any man. Cale Brolin was about to observe her resourcefulness and expertise firsthand.

A haughty smile bordered her lips as she eased Sundance toward the starting gate. Cale didn't know how Sundance responded to abrupt sounds—noises such as the clap of thunder or the crack of a shotgun that would signal the onset of this race. Sundance was swift, but he exploded into lightning speed when startled by loud noises. And *that* was going to make all the difference, Mikyla assured herself confidently. She couldn't wait to see the look on Cale's face when he was defeated by a woman.

While Mikyla was smiling smugly, Cale was grinning in self-satisfaction. Just who did that minx think had won every race he had ever entered at Fort Reno? Cale had yet to give the strawberry roan his head. But today, Cale intended to hold nothing back. The roan would gobble up the dirt on the racetrack like a lion devouring a feast. Mikyla Lassiter's monumental pride was going to shatter in a thousand pieces when she finished second to Cale.

It was a shame she didn't realize that losing was the best thing that could happen to her. She had no business in this wild, untamed land. She was easy prey to men who lusted after her pretty face and shapely figure, men who made their living betting races and risking fortunes on poker hands.

Yes, indeed, Cale was actually doing her a favor by defeating her and sending her away before the Land Run. A woman should not be making a run for property or placing wagers on a horse race.

The chatter of the crowd died into silence when one of the uniformed officers stepped onto the platform. Mikyla didn't glance at the soldier who raised his pistol into the air. Her attention was fixed on the track. Her nerves were taut with anticipation. She could feel Sundance's bulging muscles beneath her, feel the tension in his sleek, powerful body. This stallion knew what she expected of him and she knew he would never willingly let her down.

Cale felt a flood of excitement gush through his veins. The steady thud of his heart had accelerated to a gallop. He leaned against the roan, awaiting the crack of the pistol. He could envision this race, one that had more to do with *pride* than *prizes*. When the other horses began to wear down, the roan would reach his peak, Cale predicted. The roan would surge past the pack, leaving Mikyla choking in his dust. Cale could hardly wait to see the expression on her face when she had to admit she had lost.

A sharp crack of the Winchester pistol sent the horses lunging onto the track. The thunder of hooves clattered against the ground and echoed in Mikyla's ears as she curled down against Sundance's neck, urging him to maintain his swift speed. He had bounded from the starting gate like an exploding cannonball, leaving his competition half a length behind him. A wild roar erupted from the crowd as Mikyla, her unbound hair waving in the breeze like the flaxen mane and tail of her stallion, took the undisputed lead.

Cale gritted his teeth and slapped his gelding on the rump. He was determined to follow at Sundance's heels until the stallion tired and the roan could lope into the lead. A hasty glance over his shoulder found Brock's newly purchased palomino less than half a length behind him.

The harsh frown on Brock's face and the menacing set of his jaw startled Cale. He knew Brock Terrel had always been a fierce competitor, but never had the major looked so thirsty for victory. However, Cale didn't waste much time analyzing Brock's reasons for wanting to win this race. His thoughts and his eyes swept back to the magnificent stallion that flew around the track as if he had sprouted a pair of wings. Cale glared at Mikyla's back, biding his time until Sundance began to labor and the powerful roan proved his endurance.

And then it came, the slow, gradual erosion of distance that separated them. The roan was pacing in his swiftest speed while Sundance was beginning to show signs of tiring. The stallion was pressing himself, forcing his gait.

Cale would have allowed himself a gloating smile, but he was too intent on *hatching* his eggs before he counted his chickens. First, he planned to win this race and *then* he would never allow Mikyla to live down her defeat.

Mikyla caught sight of the roan's head moving into the perimeters of her vision, matching Sundance stride for stride. She focused intently on the finish line, calculating the distance to victory. Just as Cale's mount pulled neck and neck, Mikyla leaned close to the stallion's ear. The barking command resembled the abrupt crack of the pistol and the steed responded accordingly.

Like a bolt out of the blue, the stallion sailed away, causing Cale's jaw to drop off its hinges. If he hadn't seen it with his own eyes he never would have believed it! The blood-red stallion with the sharply contrasting mane and tail surged ahead of the roan as if the gelding were standing still.

Cale expelled a few curses as he crossed the finish line two lengths behind Mikyla. And Brock Terrel let loose with a string of expletives when he loped in one length behind Cale.

A roar of applause erupted from the crowd as Mikyla trotted Sundance around the arena, allowing the lathered steed to recover from his exertion. While Mikyla was basking in the limelight Cale swung his gelding through the gate and out of sight. He needed a moment to compose himself after losing to that feisty witch and her devil stallion. Damn, Cale had been so certain of the roan's abilities. But it was apparent that he had sorely misjudged Sundance's stamina and Miki's expertise. That horse would run himself into the ground if Mikyla demanded it!

Infuriated that he had finished a humiliating third, Brock Terrel paced his palomino back to the throng of bettors who were exchanging money. Swinging down, Brock glared enviously at the muscular stallion Mikyla was riding.

"I'd give anything to have that horse," Brock muttered aloud.

A low chuckle resounded in Morgan Hagerty's chest when he overheard the major's words. Morgan had just arrived at the fort, but the moment he spied Mikyla, with her glorious head of hair, approaching the winner's circle, he had aimed himself toward her. His appreciative gaze clung to Mikyla's alluring assets as she pranced her stallion around the track.

"And I'd give a king's ransom for that horse's mistress," he openly confessed.

Brock swiveled his head around to see the awestruck expression on the gambler's face. Following Morgan's gaze, Brock surveyed the woman who was in the process of dismounting. Brock had been far too obsessed with defeating Cale to give much thought to the woman. But now that he considered it, Brock found it amusing that Cale Brolin had been outdistanced by this petite female. That should get Cale's goat, Brock mused with a mischievous smile.

When Brock jerked the palomino toward the stables, Morgan ambled over to offer his congratulations to Mikyla. But Morgan would not have been in such a cheerful mood if he had paid the slightest attention to the man who had finished second. Cale Brolin had come and gone without Morgan noticing him. Yet the day was rapidly approaching when Morgan would confront Cale face-to-face. It had been three years since Morgan had seen Cale. But what was between him and his archrival was like a recurring wound, one that even time and separation couldn't heal. Morgan had sworn he would never forget what Cale had done to him—and he hadn't! Indeed, those bitter memories poisoned Morgan's blood and provoked a hatred that was beyond any hope of reconciliation.

After collecting her winnings, Mikyla surveyed the crowd. But to her dismay, the raven-haired giant had faded into oblivion. That scoundrel, she fumed. He had no intention of paying his debt. Although Mikyla had made a killing at the racetrack, she had anxiously awaited the opportunity of facing the conquered Cale Brolin. That would have been victory in itself.

Hounded by a cluster of men who threw generous bids at her, Mikyla vocalized a firm, unequivocal *no* to any and all offers. She wasn't selling Sundance for all the gold in the federal treasury. But there were a few persistent men who continued to toss tenders and temptations in her face.

"The lady said no!" Morgan's clipped tone brought momentary silence.

Mikyla spun around, not particularly thrilled to find Morgan portraying her champion. As much as she hated to admit it, she would have preferred to see Cale looming behind her.

Morgan's hand folded around her elbow, steering her away from the swarm of men who coveted her winnings, her stallion, and the lady herself. "I think it wise for me to escort you back to camp, my dear," he murmured as his eyes slid down her form-fitting breeches and shirt.

"Ah, now you are sending the fox to protect the goose," Mikyla chortled as she wormed free of his hand.

His shoulder lifted in a lackadaisical shrug. "From your point of view, I suppose you consider that an appropriate comparison." A wry smile pursed his lips as he raked her with careful scrutiny. "But in my estimation, you have become one of us. You just *gambled* on your stallion," he pointed out.

Her nose tilted to a self-righteous angle as she led Sundance past the officers' quarters. "There is a vast difference between putting one's money where one's mouth is and risking cash on a questionable poker hand. I only wager on what I perceive as a sure thing. And that is exactly what Sundance is. I protest the making and losing of fortunes at the card table."

Morgan didn't want to debate this fiery nymph. There were far more pleasurable things on his mind. Morgan was not in the habit of moving at such a slow, cautious pace with women, but with this defensive beauty he knew it would be the only effective tactic.

"Whatever you say, Mikyla," he patronized with a charismatic smile. "I did not come here to argue with you. I also give my word as a gentleman . . ." When her head jerked up to contradict him, Morgan broke into a wide grin. "As much the gentleman as you deem a gambler to be . . ." he stipulated for the sake of debate, "I have no intention of separating you from your money. I only wish to see you and

93

your winnings safely back to camp."

Why was she so mistrusting of Morgan? He had shown himself to be courteous and respectful in her presence. In fact, he was much more the gentleman than the exasperating Cale Brolin who had slinked off without paying his debts, that sneaky rat!

Reluctantly nodding her consent, Mikyla allowed Morgan to accompany her back to camp. She didn't notice the sly smile that pursed Morgan's lips as he swung into his saddle. If she had, she would have demanded to know what he was thinking. Morgan was scheming, plotting the events that would eventually get him what he wanted—the fascinating, challenging Mikyla Lassiter.

Morgan was bedeviled by Mikyla's undaunted spirit and unrivaled beauty. Yes, there were ways to maneuver this proud creature into his bed. Morgan had learned the value of patience. Endless hours at gaming tables in various saloons in dozens of towns had taught him that patience and perseverence were valuable trump cards. When a man wanted something badly enough, he had to bide his time and consider all the possibilities. And Morgan wanted Mikyla— at least until he tired of her. She would make a most delightful distraction for the months ahead.

As they trotted east, engaging in idle conversation, Mikyla kept glancing behind her. Cale had bitterly disappointed her. She never expected him to welch on their bet. Where was that raven-haired devil? And, blast it, why was she stung by this insane urge to see him again, and not just from the desire to collect her winnings? What compelling spell had Cale spun about her?

Heaving a frustrated sigh, Mikyla tried to concentrate on Morgan's conversation. But her thoughts kept straying to the brawny giant who had somehow managed to take control of her being. She could rattle off at least a dozen sensible reasons why she should avoid Cale Brolin. And yet she yearned to be with him. Even their arguments stimulated her. Wasn't that ridiculous, Mikyla asked herself. She and Cale had nothing in common and they never would. She felt a strange physical attraction for him, but it would pass,

Mikyla reassured herself. For heaven's sake, it wasn't as if there weren't hundreds of available men in the territory. If she wanted male companionship it was easy to find. So why was she drawn to that insufferable Cale Brolin who taunted and tormented her for the mere pleasure of it? Mikyla hoped one day soon she could puzzle out the answer.

Chapter 7

Cale vigorously brushed down his gelding, but his thoughts were on that curvaceous bundle of femininity who kept crossing his path. And knowing they would inevitably meet again, knowing he had to pay his bet, only infuriated Cale further.

After Cale had composed himself, prepared to face that minx's taunts, he had led the roan back to the racetrack. But Mikyla was nowhere to be found. Cale had questioned one of the bystanders, who informed him that the young lady had left the fort with another man. And *that* had annoyed Cale, even though he hadn't wanted to admit it to himself. Since he had prepared himself to eat crow, he might have charged off after her. But damned if he were about to be humiliated in front of one of Mikyla's endless rabble of male admirers!

Deciding to wait until Mikyla came to him, Cale had veered toward the stables at Fort Reno to pamper the roan who had finished a mortifying second. But busying himself with his task had not proved one hundred percent effective in taking Mikyla off Cale's mind. Over and over again, he kept seeing that blue-eyed witch who shrieked incantations at her stallion, gracing Sundance with magical powers . . .

The thought caused Cale's back to stiffen. *Loud, abrupt, noises!* So that was the secret to Sundance's phenomenal bursts of speed. It all came back to Cale with vivid clarity. The crack of thunder. The startling bark of a pistol. The sharp cry so close to the stallion's ear . . . Dammit, if he had known that stallion had been trained to respond to sharp noises, he would have demanded that the race begin with the drop of a flag! Confound that witch, she had purposely trained Sundance to jump when he heard abrupt signals.

Most horse trainers labored to ensure that their horses didn't bolt and run at loud sounds. The last thing a cowboy or cavalryman wanted was a horse that would practically leap out from under him when thunder boomed or rifles discharged around him. But that was Mikyla's secret weapon. She knew what to expect from Sundance. She knew exactly how he would respond, how he would react. She was always prepared for his powerful lunges, and she made use of his bursts of energy. Damn, if he had been paying closer attention to the stallion instead of that distracting blond-haired hellion . . .

"Well, you outran me again, damn you," Brock scowled as he stomped out of the stall. "I should have known better than to waste money buying a horse from Brolin stock. If the palomino was as fast as your roan you would have been riding him yourself."

Cale nodded mutely and continued to devote his attention to the gelding. It served as a practical preoccupation while he was cursing that shapely silver-blonde who could make confetti of a man's pride.

"I'd give my eye teeth for the stallion that spunky female was riding," Brock went on to say as he handed the saddle and bridle to the lowly corporal who had spent the day wading in manure. "Just once I would like to beat you at something. My only consolation is that it was a woman who left you dawdling in the homestretch."

Cale inwardly flinched at the jibe, but his expression remained indifferent. Leisurely, he turned to study Brock, who was still grinning in ornery satisfaction. "I respect your competitive spirit, Brock," he said smoothly. "But I cannot imagine how you can gloat when *you* finished third to a female."

Brock snorted derisively. "You had to spoil my day by bringing that to my attention, didn't you, Brolin? And just when I was enjoying watching you be defeated, even if I wasn't the one to do it."

"As long as that blood-red stallion is in Indian Territory, neither one of us stands a chance," Cale remarked as he focused on his chore.

Brock expelled a heavy sigh. "I don't think you realize how much I want to beat you at *anything,*" he burst out and then quickly recomposed himself.

A perplexed frown plowed Cale's brow. His head swiveled around to regard Brock who stood with his fists clenched at his sides. A peace treaty smile slid across Cale's lips. "Why don't you beat me to the house and inform Emily you have invited me to dinner," he half-teased the flustered major. "And don't take the race so seriously. It is supposed to be all in fun, remember?"

Brock's rigid shoulders sagged and he broke into a sheepish grin. "I guess I was behaving childishly," he admitted. "And I will indeed alert Emily to your coming." Doing an about-face, Brock exited the barn, flinging his last remark over his shoulder. "But one of these days, Brolin, you won't find me running a distant second behind you."

Cale's measured gaze drifted down Brock's departing back. What devil was hounding Brock? He certainly didn't seem his old relaxed self. Cale shrugged away the worrisome thought. Hell, the poor man had to contend with thousands of land-hungry settlers who swarmed the territory. Brock was probably meeting himself coming and going in his attempt to patrol the borders of the Unassigned Lands. And to make an intolerable situation unbearable, Brock had to pacify the Indian tribes who were none too happy to see hordes of homesteaders tromping on their pastures and trailing through their land as if they owned the whole damned place. And of course, there were the railroad executives who constantly requested assistance when they laid their tracks through unfriendly territory. The railroad was eager to join Kansas with Texas and they often employed the services of the cavalry to scout out the most practical routes.

Drifting in thought, Cale aimed himself toward the

Terrels' spacious living quarters. Yes, there were plenty of reasons why Brock might be on edge. His life was undoubtedly hectic at the moment. Brock was often called upon to quell disturbances between the five civilized tribes in the territory. Crazy Snake had organized his own government and set up his own light horse cavalry to rebel against the appointed Creek leaders in the eastern sectors of the area. Brock was up to his neck in worries, that was for sure. There weren't enough soldiers to chase down Crazy Snake, contain the flood of settlers, and pacify the tribes who wanted to be paid for the damages incurred by careless homesteaders who were taking advantage by grazing their livestock wherever they pleased . . .

"Cale! How wonderful to see you again!" Emily Terrel gushed as she burst through the door to greet Cale on the stoop.

Cale glanced up in time to become the recipient of an overzealous hug and an enthusiastic kiss on the lips. He winced uncomfortably when her soft breasts brushed wantonly against his chest. Pushing the vivacious redhead to a respectable distance, Cale shot forth a glance to determine if Brock was watching Emily's blatant show of affection. He was.

God, this wasn't what Cale needed on top of a perfectly miserable day. Brock was already in a huff because he had paid good money for a losing horse and wound up in third place. Cale had no intention of instigating friction between himself and Major Terrel. But Emily was behaving as if she were trying to make her husband jealous. What was she up to, Cale wondered suspiciously.

Strategically positioning himself a safe distance away, Cale dropped into his chair. But Emily maneuvered into the adjacent seat and reached under the table to clamp her hand on Cale's thigh. He very nearly strangled on his meal! It was difficult to carry on a normal conversation with Brock while the man's wife was groping under the table, making overt suggestions with her hands. Dammit, had the woman lost her mind?

Cale fended Emily off as best he could, but the situation

worsened when one of Brock's men rapped on the door. After a quiet conference, Brock glanced back at his wife and his guest.

"I have a pressing matter to attend," he grumbled. "I will return as quickly as possible."

The moment Brock closed the door behind him, Emily rose from her chair to retrieve the apple pie. "Your favorite, if memory serves," she purred softly.

Emily set a generous portion under Cale's nose and then, to his utter astonishment, she set *herself* in his lap! Cale's wide eyes swung to the door, frantically praying Brock hadn't been lingering on the porch and inadvertently glanced through the window.

"For God's sake, are you itching to have me placed in front of a firing squad?" Cale muttered, his voice sour enough to curdle milk. "Brock wouldn't appreciate seeing you planted in my lap as if we were . . ."

Unabashed, Emily slipped her arms around Cale's broad shoulders, adoring the feel of rippling muscles beneath her fingertips. "I doubt Brock would notice," she murmured absently. "He's become a different man these past six months. Even if he discovered we were once lovers I doubt it would faze him."

When Emily inched ever closer, Cale turned the other cheek before she dared to kiss him right on the mouth. "Brock has a lot on his mind," he defended. "And I for one have no intention of compounding his problems. Now will you please get off me! You are married and your husband is my business associate!"

Emily didn't budge and Cale couldn't rise without upending the table. She had wedged her legs under the edge of the round table and Cale was trapped. "You know I'm a passionate woman, Cale," she cooed as her lips skimmed his cheek.

As if he had to be reminded! There had been a time when Cale only had to look as if he wanted a kiss and Emily had made certain he was showered with scores of them.

"I need to be loved and loved regularly. But Brock is so . . . well, he's so preoccupied, and, you know . . ."

Cale rolled his eyes toward the ceiling. If Brock burst through the door while Emily was pouring her heart out and sitting in a lap that didn't belong to her husband, they were in serious trouble!

"Seeing you again brings tantalizing memories to mind," Emily whispered as her hands speared into Cale's jet-black hair. "I would have married you in a minute. But a woman can't wait forever. You were the one I . . ."

"Emily, don't . . ." Cale demanded sternly. "We can't go back and I can't . . ."

"Ah, but you can—and most skillfully," she interrupted with a provocative smile. "That is something a woman never forgets—the tenderness, the . . ."

Cale clamped a hand over her mouth and glared daggers at her comely face. There was a time when this seductive redhead could instantly arouse him. But now she was off limits and, besides, another face kept stealing into Cale's thoughts. He had been unwillingly comparing Mikyla to Emily since the moment he set foot in the house. Emily was indeed a passionate woman, but Mikyla, with all her obvious faults, challenged and intrigued him as no other woman had. Cale wasn't sure if he wanted Mikyla just because she was so unapproachable or because of something deeper, something . . .

Eager lips settled on Cale's mouth, demanding his undivided attention. Although Cale was in the process of prying his clinging vine loose, it didn't look that way from Brock's view. He had just sailed by the window when Cale's hands had clutched Emily's arms. Silently cursing, Brock halted in front of the door and rewound his unraveled composure. It took every ounce of self-restraint to assume a casual air. After jiggling the doorknob to announce his entrance, Brock appeared. Although his manner was nonchalant, he was inwardly fuming. Dammit, it seemed he couldn't best Cale Brolin anywhere, on the racetrack or in his own home. Would he always find himself playing second fiddle to this wealthy Texas rancher? Brock couldn't help himself. He envied everything about Cale—his abilities, his money, his way with women.

The moment Emily heard the creak of the door, she leaped to her feet and flounced down in her own chair. With shaky fork in hand, Emily gobbled her pie. She was just touching her napkin to her lips when Brock strode up to the table.

Meanwhile, Cale was staring at his plate, asking himself why the devil he had even bothered to climb out of bed this morning. He would have been a helluva lot better off if he had kept his feet off the floor. His two offending appendages had traipsed from one disaster into another.

"Em makes a delicious apple pie," Brock commented as he methodically set his hat upon its rack and eased into his seat. "Surely you aren't going to turn *that* down, Brolin."

Wary silver eyes lanced off Brock's smart blue uniform before refocusing on the untouched slice of pie. There was an underlying meaning in Brock's remark and Cale had detected the slight hint of sarcasm. He would have bet every penny of profit he had made on his horses that Brock had seen Emily perched in Cale's chair while he was still occupying it. But Brock was an officer and a gentleman and it was beneath him to burst out in accusation, Cale reminded himself.

Since the day was already in shambles, Cale unfolded himself from his seat and bowed stiffly to his hostess. His eyes slid to Brock. "I have two other stops to make before I return to camp," he announced, his voice void of the emotional conflict he was experiencing. "I'll be in touch . . ."

Cale wished he had selected a more suitable parting remark. The words that flocked to his tongue suggested things he desperately wanted to avoid. There wasn't going to be any more touching! At least not where Emily Terrel was concerned. Cale wasn't going to get within ten feet of that woman, tempting and appealing though she was. No woman was worth losing a friend and a business association that was bringing him steady profit.

The moment the door eased shut behind him, Cale half collapsed against the outer wall of the whitewashed house. Dammit, had Emily lost her mind? Surely she didn't think he was going to dally with her when he and Brock were reasonably good friends! Hell's bells, a man should avoid all women like the plague.

But just as Cale resolved to swear off women, a pair of twinkling blue eyes appeared to torment him. Cale felt the quick rise of frustration intermingling with unfulfilled desire. Why was he drawn to this feisty blond she-cat? She could make a woman who was undeniably lovely and passionate seem a dim shadow in comparison. Emily Terrel knew how to please a man and Mikyla Lassiter didn't have a clue. Emily was open and eager while Mikyla was distant and unapproachable. There was not one logical reason why Cale should be wasting a moment's contemplation on that quick-witted, sharp-tongued hellcat. But dammit, he was wearing himself out trying *not* to think about the way her lips lifted in an impish smile, the way her eyes burned hot blue flames when she was provoked to anger, the way her naive body roused to his exploring caress . . .

Cale clamped a tight grip on himself and stalked toward the stables to retrieve his mount. And there was another rub, Cale scowled under his breath. He couldn't even swing onto his strawberry roan gelding and gloat over a victory, for Mikyla had wounded his pride by defeating him on the racetrack. It rankled him that he had spent most of his life breeding and racing horses, only to be bested by a fiery female who stood no more than five feet tall in her bare feet! She was a tiny little thing, but she couldn't have squashed his pride any flatter if she had tipped the scales at three hundred pounds!

Blast it, he was doing it again. He was allowing that high-spirited minx to dominate his thoughts. What he and Mikyla Lassiter had in common were the very things that would drive wedges between them and keep them there, Cale reminded himself fiercely. They didn't see eye-to-eye on any subject and they never would. She was trying to carve her niche in a man's world, but she didn't think like a man or behave like a man. Who ever heard of a woman entering a horse race, for crying out loud! Why couldn't she garb herself in a dress and sit among the spectators like females were supposed to do? Mikyla should take a few pointers from Emily Terrel. Then she would realize that what a man wanted and needed from a woman was not competition and argument.

Why am I even giving that spitfire a second thought? Cale asked himself crossly. She defied everything he had ever wanted or expected from a woman. And realizing that, Cale couldn't fathom why he was still attracted to that fiery witch. He must be losing his mind. There was no other explanation.

Totally frustrated by the internal war that hounded his thoughts and emotions, Cale thundered back off to tend to his business. He was not going to let himself get involved with that exasperating woman, not today, not next week, not next month.

Cale felt ever so much better after he had this heart-to-heart talk with himself. Mikyla Lassiter was off his mind for good. She meant nothing to him. They were as compatible as a mongoose and a cobra. They had disliked each other on sight, and it had been downhill from that first day. And when Cale concluded his business in Indian Territory he was going to hightail it back to Texas to pleasure himself with a variety of women, all of whom knew what a man needed and wanted. Why should he care what happened to Mikyla-muleheaded-Lassiter? He didn't. She could sit here and rot in Indian Territory. Cale didn't give a damn.

Chapter 8

Dressed in one of her simple everyday gowns, her face hidden beneath the floppy-brimmed bonnet, Mikyla climbed onto Sundance's back. Although the patrols were defending the borders of the Unassigned Lands more carefully than in previous weeks, Mikyla was tempted to steal off to her dream site. She had committed the fertile bottom land that lay beside the South Canadian River to memory. But just once before the Run she would love to stare across the plush pastures that would one day be hers. And they would be hers, she thought determinedly, even if Cale Brolin thought her to be utterly mad for even considering staking a claim.

Yet, the sight of several Sooners being dragged from their hiding places along the creeks and rivers discouraged Mikyla from sneaking into the territory again. The patrols were cracking down on offenders and she did not relish the thought of being one of them.

Heaving a restless sigh, Mikyla nudged Sundance in the flanks. Even if she didn't have the opportunity to visit the site she had selected for herself, she was determined to escape the Boomer camp. She and her father had engaged in a trenchant argument and Mikyla needed time to regain control of her temper.

Emet had been selling worthless maps to unsuspecting new arrivals in camp. The maps sorely misrepresented the region of the Unassigned Lands and anyone who followed them would be totally confused. Mikyla ought to know. After all, she had crept inside the boundaries to have a look for herself! The maps Emet was selling resembled none of the landscape she had ever seen.

It seemed to Mikyla that her father was becoming more corrupt with each passing day. He was drinking, gambling, and conniving to acquire money to support his vices. When Mikyla had brought that fact to Emet's attention he had become indignant. He had railed at her for lecturing her own father. And then he had the nerve to demand that she forget her foolish dream of a ranch. Emet expected her to aid him in securing a townsite. He demanded that she ride Sundance and stake a city lot with *his* name on it! When Mikyla adamantly refused, Emet had stormed off and Mikyla had saddled Sundance.

Damnation, her father was beginning to sound like Cale Brolin, she mused resentfully. But she knew exactly what her father had in mind. Emet wanted Mikyla to tend the store he planned to erect while he was drinking and gambling away their profit. Well, she was not going to be a party to his plans. Emet might have been her father, but he had changed so drastically the past few years that Mikyla barely recognized him. And she certainly didn't respect him. He didn't deserve an ounce of consideration, not when he had no regard for anyone else, not even himself.

Frustrated, Mikyla urged Sundance to a faster clip, hoping to outrun her problems with her father. The feel of the wind whipping about her face revived her spirits. If she had Sundance she would be able to stake her claim and raise a breed of horses that would bring top dollar. All she needed was the opportunity. And the Land Run was her only chance. Once she established her ranch she might be able to help her father turn his life around. But things would never run smoothly unless she was in control and Emet was forced to come to *her*.

Mikyla was jostled from her troubled deliberation when she glanced up to see the lone tent perched on the sprawling meadow. She hadn't meant to ride this direction and for the life of her she didn't know why she had. Cale had delivered an ultimatum after their last encounter and she had not forgotten what he implied.

Suddenly, a wry smile surfaced on her lips. Perhaps it *was* time to pay Cale Brolin a visit, threat or no threat. Mikyla was confident she could handle Cale. She had escaped their last tête-à-tête unscathed, hadn't she? Today seemed to be a day for battles. Her father had already set fuse to her temper so she might as well put it to good use. Besides, Cale had yet to settle his debt after the horse race at Fort Reno. And she might even let Cale off easy if he consented to escort her to her dream site. Since he was licensed to journey inside the boundary she could accompany him. The opportunity to view her claim was worth every cent Cale owed her.

With those thoughts buzzing through her mind, Mikyla reined toward Cale's tent. When she drew near, she spied Cale milling among his herd of horses. He had already roped and hobbled four mares and had secured them to the hitching post. Cale was in the process of singling out another steed when Mikyla pulled Sundance to a halt beside the large corral.

The ease with which Cale swung his lasso, the sensuous way his shirt strained across his shoulders drew her admiration.

Mikyla didn't want to be fascinated by this brawny giant, but she was. She found herself comparing Cale to the suitors Greta had dragged to her tent for inspection. After sizing up each beau, Mikyla kept visualizing the lazy smile that played across Cale's craggy face. She could see his raven hair lying carelessly across his forehead. She remembered the way his silver eyes shined like mercury when they flooded possessively over her. She recalled the long, muscular columns of his legs, *bare* legs she had gawked at the night she returned to apologize for her temper tantrum. She remembered the sparks that flew the night she shared his tent.

She could hear his deep voice and his commanding words, words that constantly beseeched her to leave the territory before she got herself into trouble. Since her father had gambled away their home in the Ozarks, there was nowhere else to go, Mikyla mused remorsefully. For more years than she cared to count, home had been a peddler's wagon and a rickety tent. She didn't have a choice. All she had was a dream, one that she fully intended to bring to reality. Cale was not going to deter her from her purpose and Emet wasn't going to snatch her home out from under her ever again . . .

"Did you come to gloat over your recent victory, to collect your bet . . . or both?" Cale queried, rousing her from her silent reverie.

Mikyla's thick lashes swept up to see Cale closing the distance between them with masculine grace. He moved like a powerful mountain lion, the kind that prowled the wooded Ozarks. Each step was a deliberate stalk. Each long, lithe stride left the impression of controlled vitality and layers of rippling muscles.

There was something in the way he moved that stirred her, intrigued her. There was something in the way he cocked his head to smile up at her that sent shock waves rolling down her spine. That aura of rough sensuality captivated Miki, even when she didn't want to notice anything about Cale Brolin.

Blast it, the man had done nothing but intimidate her and taunt her, she hastily reminded herself. So why was she compelled to him? Why did she stare at him, marveling at the hard, masculine contours? Why did she vividly recall the way those full lips drifted over hers in the whisper of a kiss, making her yearn for a dozen more just like it? How could she feel these wild, unexplainable tingles when she swore she wanted nothing to do with him?

No man had ever affected her quite like this. Her heart leaped each time her eyes traveled over his virile torso. Her breathing became altered when Cale dared to stand too close, to touch what had been unchartered territory until she encountered Cale . . .

"Cat got your tongue, honey?" Cale drawled as he regarded the shapely bundle of calico from beneath the brim of his hat.

Mikyla couldn't see his eyes, but somehow she knew they were twinkling with that Brolin brand of mischief. It annoyed her that he persisted in using that endearment when she had specifically ordered him not to. Before she could formulate a suitable taunt, Cale's lean fingers curled around her waist, drawing her from the saddle.

Cale could take a simple gesture and transform it into a provocative assault. His rugged face tilted as he brought her slowly downward, his eyes probing and assessing, carefully gauging her reaction to his intense gaze and his masterful touch.

Mikyla felt her heart leapfrog as if it meant to pop out of her chest when Cale brought her body into familiar contact with his. She felt the steel-hard muscles of his chest brushing against her hips, her abdomen . . . and then, her breasts. He had seen to it that his sinewy flesh had caressed hers during her slow, tantalizing descent, had forced her to note all the distinct differences between a man and a woman when he slid her innocent body down the full length of his masculine frame.

She trembled in response to his arousing tactics and Cale felt her body quake as his lean flesh molded itself to her feminine curves. He had seen the flicker of emotion in those wide blue eyes. And sometime between his last lecture to himself on keeping his distance from the argumentative, stubborn misfit and the first moment he touched her, Cale forgot he had planned to avoid her.

He had only intended to taunt her, to reinforce the wall between them. He had formulated remarks, planning to tease her about that ridiculous bonnet that capped her silver-blond hair, to mock her innocence and inexperience. But his deliberate attempt to rattle her had backfired. His technique had made them all too aware of each other and Cale could see the emotion glistening in her liquid blue eyes.

Beneath Mikyla's defensive shell was a warm, responsive woman who didn't understand what she was feeling or why. Her slumbering passions had been stirred but never fully aroused. With the right man this wary hellcat could blossom into a loving, passionate woman. The only problem was that a man required a chisel to crack that thick wall of stubbornness and mistrust that encased her heart. Not that he cared to try, Cale quickly reminded himself. He wasn't getting involved. He was only amusing himself, meeting the challenge this spitfire presented.

As Cale set Mikyla to her feet, she gasped in surprise. Mikyla had observed the physical changes in a man when he was aroused. But it was an altogether different matter to feel his bold manhood pressing intimately against her thigh.

Cale almost laughed out loud when he noticed the stunned expression on her exquisite features. "It's a normal reaction. We discussed it during your first lesson on the birds and bees," he murmured, his voice more disturbed than he would have preferred.

He had promised himself he wasn't going to get entangled with this troublesome witch. And he wasn't, of course. He had already made up his mind. So what if she aroused him, he thought with a mental shrug. Any man would have responded to their titillating physical contact. It was a perfectly natural response and it didn't mean a thing.

"You know you are hard on a man's blood pressure, Ky, not to mention what you do to the other parts of his male anatomy. It's a simple masculine response, provoked by close contact with *any* attractive female." Did he sound casual enough? Cale certainly hoped so. He was feeling a little shaky on the inside and certainly didn't want her to know *that*.

Mikyla's back was as rigid as the corner post of a fence. Her delicate jaw tilted to that defiant angle Cale had come to know all too well. "I did not come here to discuss your overactive glands," Mikyla squeaked, her voice two octaves higher than normal. "I . . ."

Cale couldn't resist the temptation. Her pouting pink lips lured him closer. Not that he was interested, mind you. He was only retesting his reaction, to ensure that this was a simple matter of lust, no more, no less.

Her feminine fragrance drew him like a moth to a flame. Suddenly, Cale found himself wanting to lose himself in the warm, compelling fire. His arms stole around the small indentation of her waist, bringing her back into familiar contact with his solid length. Lord, she was so soft and enticing, he mused with a contented sigh. Kissing her was a

112

foretaste of heaven—like drifting on a fluffy cloud . . .

Mikyla stiffened, determined not to respond to Cale's amorous embrace. But his kiss was so incredibly tender that she simply couldn't control her body's involuntary reaction. His sensuous lips drifted across hers, tracing their generous curve. Mikyla felt as if she were sinking into the dewy soft grass at dawn, basking in warm spring sunshine that spread its golden fingertips over every inch of her flesh.

As if they belonged there, her slender arms crept to his broad shoulders. Her lashes fluttered down to block out the world. But even with her eyes closed Mikyla could see those ruggedly handsome features, distinct and deeply tanned, capable of crinkling in amusement or turning to stone depending on his mood.

Her heart tumbled around her chest like an acrobat and her breath stuck in her throat. Cale was draining her strength, slowly but surely. She felt like a limp rag doll supported by his strong arms. Desire unfurled deep inside her, like a delicate blossom unfolding to absorb a shower of sunbeams.

Her brain malfunctioned and instinct took command. Mikyla was kissing him back, inventing her own techniques and employing some of the tantalizing tactics Cale had taught her. She ached to return a portion of the pleasure she was experiencing. Timidly, her tongue flicked against his lips and he opened them to her, permitting her to explore the moist softness that drastically contrasted his rough-edged exterior. Her hands began to move on their own accord. Her fingers combed through the thick crop of raven hair and investigated the taut tendons of his neck. The peaks of her breasts throbbed against the corded muscles of his chest and she felt the rapid beat of his heart matching her thundering pulse.

When his hands migrated across her ribs to map the curve of her hips, Mikyla felt hot and tingly inside. She was beginning to ache in places she didn't realize existed. She was playing with fire and she knew it. But she couldn't have wrested herself from him, even if her life depended on it. Cale Brolin was the master of seduction. He knew just how to touch a woman, how to destroy her barriers of defense, how to make her crave the intimate, forbidden pleasure he could offer.

Cale swore he had gone up in flames when Mikyla melted in his arms. He wanted to crush her to him. He resented the hindering garments that separated them. Sweet mercy, what was the matter with him? He said he wasn't going to get involved with this headstrong vixen who defied femininity and yet was the very essence of it. And, by damned, he wasn't. Cale had made a vow and he was going to keep it!

Fighting the overwhelming battle of self-conquest, Cale dragged his lips from hers and inhaled a steadying breath. He didn't dare move for fear his betraying body would *advance* rather than *retreat*. For a long, agonizing moment, Cale waged war against the beast within him, struggling to regain a smidgen of composure. When he could trust himself to ambulate, he mentally ordered his reluctant legs to take a valiant step backward. But it was like fighting his way through a magnetic field that sought to pull him in the opposite direction.

Abruptly, Cale presented his back to Mikyla and stared at some distant point, seeing nothing, not even the two score of horses that blocked his vision. Cale didn't trust himself to speak for fear of sounding like a croaking bullfrog. And so he didn't. He just stood there, battling the primal needs that Mikyla had unleashed with her innocent kisses and caresses.

Cale thought *he* was having difficulty coping with his volatile reaction, but Mikyla was twice as flustered. She had her heart set on hating Cale. Indeed, she enjoyed driving spikes between them. But when he touched her with such amazing gentleness, the good lessons of sense she had been collecting these past twenty years simply vanished.

While Cale was facing west, standing like a marble monument, Mikyla wheeled around to peer east. They stood back to back for several tense minutes, each of them grappling with the supernatural phenomenon that engulfed them when they touched.

Finally, Cale was confident enough to speak without projecting the turmoil that raged within him. His head swiveled around to see Mikyla pointed in the opposite direction. Inhaling a deep breath Cale resumed his sentinel stance. "I would have come to repay my debt, but I didn't know which camp you were living in. There are so many of them, I figured it would take me a week to locate you," Cale commented and then mentally patted himself on the back for sounding so calm and casual . . . so *uninvolved*.

"It's the closest one to your campsite and I like kissing you . . ." Mikyla slammed her mouth shut so quickly she nearly bit her tongue in two. For pity's sake! Why did she keep blurting out such embarrassing confessions? Her blunder was like offering her mortal enemy a weapon and inviting him to use it on her!

The silence was so thick it could have been stirred with a wooden spoon.

"I warned you about coming back here," he rasped, fighting for hard-won composure. "I want to make love to you, Ky . . ."

Cale's words floated back to her in the whispering breeze. They swirled around her like a soul-shattering caress. Mikyla swore someone had nailed her feet to the ground. She knew she should bound onto her stallion's back and run for her life. But while better judgment was screaming at her to go, her heart bade her to stay.

It wasn't the anticipation of receiving her wager that had compelled her to Cale's camp, Mikyla finally admitted to herself. That was a flimsy excuse. It was the man himself who lured her. She had run from her father, angry and frustrated. And she had run *to* Cale. Greta's matchmaking hadn't eased the strange need Cale had awakened in her. Morgan Hagerty's persuasive charm hadn't replaced the illogical fascination for this complex man who kept her emotions brewing in a caldron of black magic.

But this was a purely physical attraction, Mikyla assured herself sensibly. She and Cale had no future together. He was a rolling stone and she was an immovable boulder. Cale thrived on his unbound freedom. He enjoyed drifting from place to place without chains to hold him. But Mikyla possessed an entirely different outlook on life. She longed to set stakes and build fences around her domain. She didn't feel the need to chase the sun, only to bask in its warmth while she sat in her own little corner of the world. Cale was restless. He yearned to wander, to appease his passion with any woman who caught his eye. He wasn't interested in forever, only in a brief passing moment before he moved on. But Mikyla wanted a dependable, responsible man or no man at all. She protected her heart as if it were made of twenty-four karat gold.

She well remembered how it hurt to lose someone she loved. Just look what had become of her father when Michelle died, Mikyla reminded herself. The loss had destroyed Emet. Would she be as thoroughly devastated if she lost the man she loved? Mikyla was afraid to allow her fascination with Cale to progress to such a deep state of emotion. She couldn't risk falling in love with him. She would only get hurt, and she refused to spend her life pining for a man who could turn and walk away from her when he grew tired of the scenery.

Mikyla was startled to find that Cale had swung onto his mount while she was cutting her way through a jungle of entangling thoughts. He was sitting above her, holding Sundance's reins. His leg was leisurely hooked over the pommel of the saddle and he was staring at her floppy bonnet with a disdainful frown.

"I hate that damned hat," he told her candidly. "You are far too attractive to have that thing tied beneath your chin. Take it off."

My but he had changed moods as quickly as the wind changed direction. It only served to remind Mikyla that she was out of her league. She was still stewing over her attraction to him and her reaction to his proposition. But Cale had shrugged off his impulsive suggestion and stepped into the stirrup, leaving her to sort out her emotions one at a time, only to find them converging on her.

Mikyla continued to stand there, staring up at him from beneath the brim of that silly bonnet, gaping at him as if he had tree limbs protruding from each side of his head. Cale leaned down to hook his arm around her. As if she were

116

feather-light, he plucked her off the ground and deposited her on her stallion's back. That accomplished, Cale untied her bonnet and stuffed it into his saddlebag.

"You are coming with me," he announced matter-of-factly. "I have to deliver some horses to the trading post at Caddo Jake's crossing."

"I don't think I should," Mikyla murmured awkwardly.

"You will when you see what I have to show you," Cale insisted as he reined his gelding west, leading the five mares he had selected from the herd.

While Mikyla sat in the saddle, engaged in a mental tug-of-war, Sundance filed obediently behind the string of steeds. The stallion's reflexive movement didn't annoy her, but the fact that Cale never looked back certainly did. He was behaving as if he expected her to follow him without question. He always tried to tell her what she ought to do and then naturally assumed she would heed his advice. Wasn't that just like a man, she fumed. He expected her to listen without protest and follow without complaint.

"This had better be spectacular," Mikyla begrudgingly ground out, glaring hot branding irons at his back.

Cale twisted in the saddle. His silver-gray eyes sketched her full breasts and trim waist. Damn, she was lovely, he mused with an approving smile. "Compared to you, Blue Lake rates a distant second," he heard himself say.

Quickly, Cale faced forward to chastise himself. He shouldn't have invited her with him in the first place and he never should have complimented her. She was probably receiving an overabundance of flattery from all her beaux in the Boomer camp. And why in the world had he made that outrageous declaration earlier, Cale asked himself incredulously. For a man who was determined to keep his distance from this minx, he was certainly saying and doing the strangest things!

But could an innocent journey to Blue Lake hurt? Mikyla would enjoy the scenery and the distraction and he could certainly use both himself. The only problem was, how could a man distract himself when he brought his distraction with him? *That was a stupid move,* Brolin, he scolded himself. He should have handed her the money to pay his wager and shooed her on her way while he went his.

Cale's offhanded compliment caused a becoming blush to color Mikyla's cheeks. Damn if she could understand this complicated man. One minute he propositioned her, the next instant he insulted her bonnet, and in the next breath he complimented her appearance. Was that why Cale intrigued her so, because he was so unpredictable, because he didn't cater to her the way Greta's handpicked string of eligible bachelors did?

Mikyla wrestled with those questions while she followed Cale over the rolling hills of Cheyenne and Arapaho country. From the high rise, Mikyla could see for miles across the green carpet of native grass and wildflowers. The low-lying creeks gleamed like silver in the sunlight and herds of cattle and horses dotted the majestic countryside. Mikyla didn't ask who owned the livestock that grazed the Indian reserves. She supposed it was one of the fabulously wealthy ranchers from Texas who leased the fertile prairie from the tribes. It had been common practice to rent the plush grassland and she imagined the ranchers who lost their leases because of the upcoming Land Run would have loved to relocate their herds in this rich valley that lay west of the Unassigned Lands.

Had she known Cale Brolin was one of those wealthy ranchers and these were his cattle and horses she would have tumbled out of the saddle. But Cale wasn't one to boast of his riches. He simply went about his business without mentioning that they were trekking across land that he and his family had leased five years earlier. In fact, Cale didn't want Mikyla to know that he was more than just a drifting cowboy who preferred open spaces to clumps of humanity. She had formed her opinion of Cale and he wasn't certain he wanted her to alter it. She could think what she wanted because he *definitely* wasn't going to become involved with her.

Cale's face puckered in a disgusted frown. How many times a day was he going to have to tell himself that until he firmly believed it? As many times as necessary, Cale lectured himself sternly. This was a harmless excursion to Blue Lake.

They would enjoy the afternoon and then they would go their own ways. Perhaps they could even part as casual acquaintances rather than bitter enemies, he mused wistfully. Why, they might even become friends. No, Cale quickly contradicted himself. Friends were individuals who shared the same opinion on a variety of issues. They enjoyed the same recreations. They engaged in light conversation and discussed problems in a calm, rational manner. He and Mikyla would never fit into that category. The best they could ever hope for was a tolerable *acquaintanceship*.

Clinging to that thought, Cale edged down the steep slope and descended into the plush valley near Blue Lake. But with all his lectures and resolutions he couldn't quite overcome the warm tide of pleasure that coursed through him when he contemplated the kiss Mikyla had bestowed on him earlier. It was out of character for her to respond with such wild abandon. She was usually so protective and defensive of her emotions. She refused to surrender to desire of the flesh. Miki could barely tolerate him, and she delighted in telling him so. But yet she had melted in his arms as if . . .

As if what? Cale growled under his breath. He didn't want to analyze that woman. Damnation, she was giving him fits even when she wasn't trying and he was working himself into a cold sweat, attempting to resist his illogical attraction.

He *did* hate her, Cale suddenly realized. He despised the inner turmoil she evoked in him. He detested having these private conversations with himself. Cale had been content and carefree until Mikyla had stumbled into his life. Now he was preoccupied and confused, hungering insanely for a woman he didn't even want. He knew Miki would be tripping on the borderline of catastrophe if she dared to make the Land Run. Cale didn't want to care if she found her dream crumbling around her. He wanted to say I-told-you-so. And yet, he wanted to protect her from the disappointment he was sure was inevitable.

But most of all, Cale didn't want to get mixed up with the feelings and emotions that were tied to this bewitching female. If he did, he would be every kind of fool. Mikyla Lassiter was not the sort of woman a man could cast aside after a reckless moment of passion. She was the most fascinating, complicated, enigmatic creature Cale had ever encountered. And if he looked too deeply, he might find himself inextricably entrapped.

Will you stop all this analytical nonsense, Cale muttered, giving himself a mental shake. He was going to spend a harmless afternoon at Blue Lake with a lovely woman. They were going to share the enchanting view, and that was the beginning and end of it. Afterward, Cale would take his horses to Caddo Jake's crossing and return to camp. It was that simple.

Cale slumped in his saddle. He had the sinking feeling that he would be an even bigger fool if he allowed himself to believe *any* excursion with Mikyla Lassiter could be labeled as innocent and uncomplicated. *Potentially dangerous would be nearer the mark,* he mused. Cale could only hope he was smart enough to recognize quicksand when he saw it and be wise enough not to wade into it.

There was no doubt about it, Cale again muttered under his breath. Miki Lassiter was definitely quicksand. But Cale, who prided himself on being logical and sensible, was going to keep his feet planted on solid ground!

Chapter 9

After weaving through the dense underbrush and dodging the maze of locust, cedar, and dogwood trees, Mikyla spied the spectacular natural lake. Her mouth dropped open in mute amazement. There before her lay crystal-clear water, surrounded by Mother Nature's fence of trees. Ageless cottonwoods bowed toward the sparkling water. Sun-dappled shadows danced along the sandy beach that rimmed the enticing pool.

It had been an eternity since Mikyla had had the privacy of a bath or even a swim. With thousands of settlers swarming around her, there had been little opportunity to indulge in such simple luxuries of life. But this beautiful lake offered a compelling invitation Mikyla could not resist and with a delighted squeal, she nudged Sundance into the water.

There were some horses who regarded water as a necessity for survival, never setting foot in it of their own free will. There were others that took to water like a duck. Sundance fell into the latter category. Without complaint he splashed through the lake and then stretched out to swim a wide circle.

A quiet smile slid across Cale's lips as he watched Miki slide from the saddle to catch hold of the stallion's tail. The steed paddled around the lake with his mistress gliding in his wake. Her delicious laughter mingled with the warble of the birds that serenaded them from the low-hanging branches. When Mikyla giggled like a carefree child and rattled in light

121

conversation, Cale swore she was speaking to another person, but it was Sundance who was the object of Mikyla's attention, not Cale. He was stung by the feeling that Mikyla had blocked him out of her world and that she could survive quite nicely with Sundance as her only companion.

Cale was aware of Mikyla's fond attachment for the magnificent stallion. But only now did he realize how greatly she valued this animal. Her eyes, sparkling like the sun-kissed waters of Blue Lake, were fixed upon the stallion. Still giggling, she released Sundance's tail and treaded water until he circled back to retrieve her. Mikyla reached up to loop her arms around the steed's neck. Her head rested against his wide jaw as he carried her drifting body with him. As if he were answering her quiet murmurings, Sundance whinnied and cut through the water like a giant swan, amusing both of them with their playful antics.

Another bubble of sheer happiness burst from Mikyla's lips as she pulled herself onto Sundance's back, chattering to him as if he were her childhood playmate. When Sundance found solid footing, he paused and flung back his proud head. As if she were taking his cue, Mikyla stood up on the saddle and tied her soggy skirts into a careless knot, leaving an arousing display of leg. Employing the stallion as a diving board, Mikyla plunged into the water. The steed pricked his ears and waited for his mistress to resurface. And, like a devoted puppy, he lunged forward to return to her heels.

The enchanting scene left Cale's senses reeling in pleasure. He had anticipated that Mikyla would enjoy the beauty of Blue Lake. But never in his wildest dream did he expect *he* would derive such satisfaction from watching her enjoy herself. She seemed so vibrant and alive, so delighted with the world and everything in it. Her laughter was sweet music to his ears. Her smile outshined the sun, giving her face a mystical inner radiance. And Cale, who had always considered himself a reasonably normal individual, was suddenly and ridiculously wishing he were a horse— Sundance in particular.

How he ached to see this gorgeous mermaid smiling up at him, to feel her arms gliding around his neck, to hear her

122

playful murmurs as they frolicked together in the lake. That damned horse was enjoying the affection of the one woman Cale had been unable to chase from his thoughts. He was jealous of a four-legged stallion, for heaven's sake! Mikyla adored that creature and it was obvious the two of them had participated in similar antics on numerous occasions. They were as at home in the water as on land, and they were so wrapped up in each other that Cale might as well have been a tree stump, for all they cared!

Cale expelled an envious snort. Didn't he deserve a "thank you very much" for leading Mikyla to this secluded wonderland? My God, it seemed she had shoved him completely out of her mind. Well, her actions pretty much said it all, he silently fumed. He was wrestling against an obsessive attraction to a woman who didn't care if he existed . . .

His resentful thoughts dissolved when Mikyla arched backward to bob on the water's surface. Her damp clothes accented the generous swells of her breasts and the luscious curve of her hips. Her flawless features were soft in repose— like an angel adrift on a silver-lined cloud.

The sight of her set Cale aflame, and all the water in Blue Lake couldn't extinguish the fire of frustrated desire. He wanted to scoop that bewitching dryad from the water and carry her to the sandy bank. He yearned to mold his eager hands to her appetizing body and discover each sensitive point of her flesh.

A groan of unholy torment bubbled in Cale's laboring chest. This was a mistake, he thought bleakly. He was sitting here wanting things Mikyla couldn't give him. He had allowed himself to see another facet of this bewitching imp's personality—the reckless, carefree side that contrasted with her willful determination. He was looking beneath that defensive armor to study her various moods, seeing her as she truly was.

When Mikyla called to Sundance to shield her while she peeled off her wet gown, Cale stopped breathing. He remained paralyzed with anticipation as the brown calico dress sailed through the air to land on the stallion's back.

And then to Cale's utter agony, her chemise dropped atop her discarded garments, settling on the saddle for safe-keeping.

Cale would have paid a fortune if Sundance could have made himself transparent at that particular moment. But the confounded horse continued to block a view that Cale suspected would, now and forevermore, form the dimensions of his dreams. He could only catch fleeting glimpses of bare skin as Mikyla glided to and fro, never daring to stray too far from the shield of the stallion's bulky frame. But Cale could imagine how Mikyla looked in the altogether. Hell, he had pictured her wearing nothing but a smile every time he stared at her. Her skin would be like exquisite satin, the color of melted honey. She would be soft and feminine . . .

Blast it, this wasn't helping matters, Cale scowled to himself. He was trying to keep his distance, to remain uninvolved. But he ached for that high-spirited nymph who was using her devoted stallion as a dressing screen. And like the idiot he was, Cale had confessed he wanted her. Didn't she realize how difficult it was for him to sit in the sand when his body was reaching out to her, longing for her?

A virgin, Cale groaned in torment. Cale had religiously avoided them all his life. And now he confronted the most inexperienced woman he had ever met and he was wanting her in the worst way. Didn't she know better than to strip naked in front of a man? It was one thing for him to peel off his clothes as he had done the night she shared his tent. But having *her* disrobe was an altogether different matter! What did she think he was made of? Solid rock?

Sundance turned his head when Mikyla burst to the surface and Cale was granted the view he craved. There, amid the rippling waves of silver that undulated in all directions, was an enchantress so delicately shaped and perfectly formed that Cale gasped to inhale a breath.

It was as if he were staring at this lovely creature through a tinted glass window. The clear water offered him an unlimited spectacle. Her breasts were full, their dusky peaks taut and inviting. Her shoulders were like ivory, studded with sparkling water droplets. Her hips were well-sculptured and her legs were firm and yet arrestingly feminine. Every enticing inch of her would have been an artist's dream. But Cale doubted even the masters could duplicate such loveliness on canvas. A one-dimensional portrait could not have captured such radiant, dynamic beauty.

The sight of this free-spirited pixie, her face alive with happiness, gliding across the water to explore the perimeters of Blue Lake, would be forever branded on Cale's mind. And when Sundance repositioned himself, stretching his broad neck in such a manner that deprived Cale of the titillating view, he could still see her. She was etched on his mind. Mikyla was breathtaking, unequaled in beauty and grace.

Since Cale had shown no inclination to join her for a swim, Mikyla had taken the risk of swimming without her cumbersome clothes. It had been ages since she and Sundance had wandered to an abandoned stream to bask in the sunshine. And now, with six thousand homesteaders, most of them men, choking the creeks, she hadn't dared to swim in the buff. But today had been too great a temptation. Mikyla reveled in diving into the clear depths. She marveled at the wondrous beauty of this secluded lake. The dense underbrush and canopy of trees protected this paradise and it was hers alone for a time, her private haven.

And maybe, deep down inside, beneath her protective armor, she wanted Cale to join her in this peaceful wonderland. She had defended her innocence against a swarm of men these past few months, but none of them had left Mikyla wondering how it would feel to abandon her inhibitions. She wanted Cale in ways that startled her. She was curious to know how it would feel to have his skillful hands upon her bare skin, to lose herself in the unexplored world of passion. Would Cale be a gentle lover? Would he treat her with respect or would he be more concerned with pleasuring himself? Would their encounter be special to him or would she be just another female on his extensive list of conquests?

Her eyes widened when she caught sight of the shiny black

hair and ruggedly handsome face that appeared just beyond Sundance's sturdy form. Cale's expression was so solemn, his gaze so intent that Mikyla felt shards of fire pricking her skin. No other man could look at her with such a potent stare, speak to her in a language that needed no words. Those glistening silver eyes, framed with thick black lashes, cast a spell that entranced her. The expression that rippled in the beguiling pools whispered intimate promises as they glided over her skin. Cale was suggesting things Mikyla knew nothing about, had never experienced. And to compound her frustration, this rough-edged rogue was the symbol of everything she wasn't—shiftless, worldly . . .

She would have continued to list their differences if her brain hadn't broken down. Mikyla nervously struggled to stay afloat, knowing she had treaded into dangerous waters long before she swam out into these bottomless depths. She couldn't have pried her eyes from Cale's craggy features to save her soul. And when he waded around in front of Sundance, Mikyla knew the waiting and wondering would soon be over. Cale wasn't going to permit her to continue her swim in privacy and she wasn't sure she wanted to.

Cale had shed his shirt and gun belt. He stood poised in water that lapped against his hips. Her eyes slid across the bronzed expanse of his bare chest, focusing on the dark matting of hair that extended down his belly. The bright spring sunlight flickered in the ruffled raven hair that framed his face and glowed like copper on his hard flesh. The muscles of his arms were taut with restraint, like a crouched lion that awaited the opportune moment to pounce on his prey. The tendons of his neck flexed as his all-consuming gaze devoured her, touching and affecting her just as surely as if he had reached out a hand to caress her.

He stood there smoldering in barely constrained desire, threatening to reduce himself into a cloud of steam. His body roused to the stunning sight that lay just beyond his grasp. He wanted this bedeviling minx more than he had ever wanted anything in his life. And yet, he didn't want to feel an attachment to this determined woman who defied her own destiny. But he had allowed himself to understand her many moods, to see her without her protective armor. On the outside, she was the essence of strong will and defiance, but on the inside, she was a dozen kinds of passions, aching for release. He had investigated the depths of her fierce pride and had witnessed the awakening of her feminine desires. He had been touched by her relentless spirit and awed by her adoration for her magnificent stallion. He knew of her obsession for land and a home of her own. He hadn't wanted to become involved. But dammit, he was! There was no talking himself out of it this time, not now, not when she was so temptingly close.

Cale was like a man poised on the edge of a towering cliff. He knew he should back away, but he was compelled ever closer to the perilous ledge. His conscience and his male instincts waged a devastating war within him. Common sense struggled to overcome needs that were as ancient as time itself. The emotional turmoil was tearing him to pieces, bit by excruciating bit. There was no noble restraint left. Now it was up to Mikyla to decide what happened next. Cale had depleted every ounce of gentlemanly reserve.

"Ky, if you don't swim to the far side of the lake and quickly . . ." His voice was raspy and his eyes blazed with the internal heat that was frying him alive. His big body shuddered as if besieged by an earthquake. "I'm not blaming you for tempting me, because I'm not even sure you know to what extent you arouse a man," he breathed roughly. "But neither can I hold myself responsible for what's going to happen . . . if you don't run for your life."

Mikyla couldn't breathe, not when her breath was frozen in her chest. Her body moved reflexively to stay afloat, but her movements took her closer instead of farther away. She could feel the fire, see the flames in his silver eyes. They were like white-hot wildfires, scorching her inside and out. She knew she was making a reckless mistake by drawing nearer. But, God help her, she wanted him in ways she was helpless to explain. She was lured by his male magnetism, by the mystique of passion.

Would he be rough and forceful when he took her in his arms? Or would he be as gentle and patient as he had been

127

when he kissed her? Would he treasure this encounter or would it be one of only many in his vast experiences with women? Mikyla had pondered these same questions before and she found them cropping up, again and again, even if she didn't have the nerve to put them to tongue. Like a fool, she found herself wanting to discover the answers, to end her curiosity about this man and his luring brand of passion.

Cale inwardly grimaced when the graceful mermaid swam toward him. The inquisitive and yet hesitant look in those dazzling blue eyes tore at his heart. She had placed the slightest bit of faith in him, trusting him to teach her the ways of love. And Cale knew, even before he extended his hand to trace her delicate features that he wouldn't, *couldn't* disappoint her, that he would die before he hurt this wary creature who was so unlike any other woman he had known.

"Ky, are you very sure?" he whispered as his eyes flooded over her curvaceous body, marveling at her beauty.

Mikyla's gaze locked with his. Consent was in her eyes. She was a mite reluctant and yet helpless to deny either of them the moment that had been inevitable since their first stormy encounter.

Cale would have waded through hell for this glimpse of heaven. He ached up to his eyebrows but he showed unbelievable restraint, a tender reserve he didn't even know he possessed. His hand wavered as he sketched the trim column of her neck and explored the silky slope of her shoulder. She was softer than he had even imagined—like the velvet petal of a rose.

His eyes remained fixed on those deep azure pools as his fingertips drifted down to graze the rigid bud of her breast. He watched the shock of his inquiring caresses register on her delicate features, felt her naive body tremble as his hand swirled around each taut peak.

As if he were approaching a wary dove who would take flight if she feared danger, Cale inched steadily closer. Her head tilted upward to monitor his movements, sending the waterfall of silver-blond hair cascading down her back. Her alluring fragrance invaded his nostrils, fogging his senses. His left hand cut through the water to settle on the satiny

128

curve of her hips, and he heard the quick intake of her breath. Or was it his? Cale couldn't be certain and he was not about to take the time to puzzle it out. He was standing next to a fire that was dangerously close to burning out of control. It no longer mattered how or why he had come to be there. He was reaching out to touch the feelings that had always been between them, to nourish the passion with tenderness, allowing it to blossom and grow.

Mikyla felt the fierce chain reaction skitting through her nerves and muscles as his hands weaved their skillful magic on her flesh. The flame of desire flickered in the very core of her being, leaping upward and outward until it had consumed her, body, mind, and soul. Her lips parted. They were bone-dry, as if she had been stranded on a sun-baked desert. His full, sensuous mouth was only a hairbreadth away. His silver eyes, surrounded by a fan of jet-black lashes, were boring into her, tempting her with wildly exciting promises.

"You are exquisite." Cale's warm breath whispered over her flushed cheek, allowing her to feel his soft words as well as hear them. "Incomparable . . . like a legendary goddess . . ."

His lips slanted across hers, grazing her mouth, while his hands scaled her ribs. His thumb flitted over the throbbing peaks of her breasts. His muscular thigh insinuated itself between her legs, teasing and arousing her. Mikyla could not contain the tiny gasp of pleasure that escaped her lips, nor could she control the shiver of desire that rippled through her. She was on fire—a trifle apprehensive but too entranced by his seductive magic to care what dangers awaited her.

"I don't want to hurt you, Ky," he murmured as his moist lips skimmed her shoulder. "I want to love you, to cherish you . . ."

A moan of surrender tripped from her tongue as she arched to make titillating contact with his hair-roughened skin. Mikyla felt and heard his tormented groan as he molded her naked flesh into his muscular contours. She wrapped herself around him like an entwining vine. She couldn't seem to get close enough to appease this strange, sizzling ache that burned like a bonfire. She returned his kiss with savage impatience. Mikyla wanted him with every fiber of her being. She was totally oblivious to all except the firm pressure of his hands, the addicting taste of his kiss. And still she couldn't press close enough, not even when every inch of her body was melded to his sleek, masculine torso.

Mikyla clung to him, her nails digging into the whipcord muscles of his back, her lips twisting and slanting to devour and savor him, all in the same moment. But even his flaming kiss was no longer enough to ease this maddening hunger that gnawed at her. She could feel his bold manliness against her hip and, instinctively, she moved to caress him with her trembling body.

"What madness is this?" Mikyla choked out, her eyes wide with confusion. "Cale, what is the matter with me? I feel so . . ." She couldn't find the appropriate words to translate the emotional turmoil that engulfed her.

Cale was adrift somewhere in a black abyss of sensual pleasure. He could hear her quaking voice but she might as well have been speaking in a foreign tongue. Her innocent movements were pure, sweet agony and he couldn't think past the whirlwind of sensations that were assaulting him from every direction.

He didn't know how and when he carried Mikyla to the warm sand that surrounded the crystal waters. All he knew was that he was there, bending over her, seeing the naive, desirable goddess who had concealed her passionate nature inside a defensive shell. This complicated creature of a thousand moods was wrapped into one incredibly lovely package and Cale couldn't resist her.

He didn't care that Mikyla was chasing her own rainbows, that they were too much alike and yet worlds apart in politics and philosophy and everything else. What *did* matter was that wild horses couldn't have dragged Cale away. He was lost and he didn't care if he ever regained his sanity *or* his sense of direction.

His body shuddered as he crouched above her, marveling at the way her wild hair drifted across the sand like a quilt of silver-gold, the way her kiss-swollen lips parted in anticipation of his kiss. He felt the muscular columns of his thigh contrasting the silky flesh of her legs, felt the warmth of her upon his probing fingertips.

Carefully, he came to her, drawing upon his last ounce of patience and tenderness. And then he was moving with her, setting the gentle cadence of love. His lips molded to hers, sharing the same ragged breath.

He was the living flame within her—the warm, pulsating fire that blended body and soul. He was both the possessor of passion and the possession of Mikyla's unselfish giving. Ironic, Cale mused dizzily. He could not take pleasure from this mystical nymph without giving a part of himself in return. And when Mikyla surrendered her innocence to him she melted the frozen barrens of his heart. She had touched him with her untutored passion, taking far more than he had intended to give . . .

Cale's thoughts scattered when the hauntingly sweet crescendo built into the wild rhapsody of passion. Splendorous sensations spilled over him like a raging river tumbling over its banks, running wild and aimless on a low-lying flood plain. He was a part of the flowing current, gliding with the flow, drowning in the depths of ecstasy.

Mikyla winced as he drove into her and then withdrew. But the initial pain lasted no more than an instant. Cale had aroused her until she was begging for him, until she would have endured even torture itself to satisfy the monstrous craving that overwhelmed her. She was shameless in her response, like a wild, uninhibited creature consumed by innate powers, reveling in a pleasure beyond bearing.

Time dissolved and the world flickered with brilliant white lights, as if it had suddenly exploded around her. Sensation upon wild, maddening sensation converged upon her, sweeping her up into the flames and then flinging her into sizzling darkness. And still her heart continued beating, pounding in her temples long after she swore she had died in the rapture of Cale's exquisite lovemaking.

And even now, while his heavy weight crushed into hers, while he drove into her without the slightest self-restraint, Mikyla could feel nothing but sweet, satisfying ecstasy. Her innocent body was his to command. Her soul had merged with his. She was arching involuntarily toward him, matching the magical rhythm of his lovemaking. She was reveling in a splendor that defied description.

The sensations were so incredibly contradictory, Mikyla thought dazedly. She was sinking into the sand and yet she was soaring like an eagle. She was wild and free and yet she was chained in the tight circle of Cale's arms. She was reaching past the darkness to grasp the shards of white-hot light, feeling the intense heat without experiencing burning pain. And just beyond the piercing beams that splintered through her body and soul was a universe of exquisite emotion, a paradise where sensation was, in itself, a unique dimension of life.

Mikyla held on to the only stable force in a careening world. She was afraid to let go, afraid she had dreamed it all . . .

Cale was numb with the aftereffects of pleasure. Even after passion surged from his body in massive shudders he couldn't will himself to move away. For what seemed eternity, he held Mikyla to him, wondering when the feelings would subside and he could think through the haze that clouded his mind. When he finally gathered enough strength to ease beside her, he collapsed on his back. Linking his fingers behind his head to form a pillow, he allowed the sun to burn into the length of his spent body. Gradually, his heart slowed its frantic pace and returned to a reasonably normal beat.

Although Cale couldn't muster enough energy to fill a thimble, Mikyla felt as if her spirit had been recharged. She wasn't drowsy in the aftermath of passion. She was bubbling with curiosity about the man who had introduced her, and most skillfully, to the sensual world of desire. He had indeed been a gentle, considerate lover, she mused with a contented sigh. Cale Brolin was the walking contradiction of unrivaled strength and tender passion.

Unabashed, she reached out to run her fingertips over the broad, powerful muscles of Cale's chest. An impish smile cut becoming dimples in her cheeks when Cale pried open one

132

heavily lidded eye to peer up at her. Blushing slightly, Mikyla continued her inquisitive investigation. Her hand mapped his bronzed flesh, delighting in the feel of masculine strength beneath her palms. He was like a Roman god, so well proportioned, so finely muscled, so virile . . .

Her hand brushed against the hard sheath of manhood and she jerked back, her face stained beet red. She hadn't meant to be so bold in her explorations.

Glancing up at Cale's handsome face, she regarded with embarrassed pleasure the roguish smile twitching his lips, lips that had only moments before migrated over her flesh, discovering each sensitive point . . . The thought burned through her. Mikyla didn't think she could turn a deeper shade of red, but she did.

"Feminine curiosity?" Cale teased wickedly. "I knew you weren't the shy, retiring type, but I never expected you to possess such inquisitiveness, minx."

The crunch of sand so close to his head drew Cale's eyes upward. There, with hooves dangerously close to his skull, stood Sundance. Cale swore the stallion was glaring jealously at him. It was as if he were silently warning Cale to get up and move away or risk being crushed by a thousand pounds of muscled horse flesh.

"Don't make any abrupt moves or sounds," Mikyla cautioned in a whisper.

Growling under his breath, Cale inched away to retrieve his breeches. But Sundance laid back his ears and lowered his head. Amusement bubbled from Mikyla's lips when Sundance herded *Cale* into the lake, staring at him as if he were a contrary calf that had strayed from the herd.

"Call off this damned horse," Cale snapped before he shot sideways to avoid the stallion's deadly hooves.

Mikyla dashed into the water, giggling all the while. But just as she slid onto the saddle to take the reins, Cale's gelding tromped into the lake to drink. In a gesture of male superiority, the ornery roan nipped Sundance on the rump. The stallion reacted with a quick kick. Mikyla was caught completely off guard, preoccupied with trying to gather the garments that were draped over the saddle and rein her stallion a safe distance away from Cale to realize the roan was bent on stirring trouble.

Sundance's powerful hooves slammed against the gelding's shoulders. The strawberry roan's shrill whinny mingled with Mikyla's startled shriek as water splattered everywhere. Cale had witnessed the nip and the retaliatory kick, but he couldn't paddle to safety before Mikyla was launched through the air. Her fists were clenched around her chemise and gown and her legs were entangled in each other. She resembled an oversize pelican making a fumbling descent to the water—and Cale was in direct line with her point of entry.

Cale swallowed two quarts of water when Mikyla landed on his head, forcing him beneath the surface. Thrashing and gasping for breath, Cale fought to untangle his arms and legs from Mikyla's. He came up cursing a blue streak.

"That horse is nothing but trouble," he sputtered furiously.

Mikyla, who had gulped a couple of pints of water herself, coughed and choked to catch her breath. "It wasn't Sundance's fault," she defended. "That long-eared, skinny-legged roan of yours caused the ruckus. Sundance was minding his own business until that gelding took a bite out of my horse's rump!"

"Minding his own business?" Cale hooted as he hooked an arm around Mikyla's midsection to drag her ashore. "That devil stallion intended to drown me! If you had any sense you would sell him to the highest bidder, take the money, and buy yourself a railroad ticket home."

"I don't have a home," Mikyla blurted out, allowing her tongue to outrace her brain. "My father gambled it away in a poker game, along with our farm in the Ozarks. He drank away what was left of my inheritance. Don't you understand? I had nothing to lose by coming here. There is nowhere else to go!"

Her remarks and the bitter tone in which she conveyed them dowsed the fire of Cale's temper. He stared down at the lovely nymph who was clutching her wet garments to her breasts. Her long, waist-length hair clung to her damp skin.

She looked so damned enticing and yet so vulnerable Cale felt his heart melt.

Mutely, Cale strode over to fasten himself into his breeches. When he turned around, Miki had wiggled into her chemise. His silver-gray eyes darkened under the full impact of her barely clad flesh. He was vividly aware of the turmoil of emotion that puckered her elegant features.

"Is that why you race Sundance? To gain enough money to put food on the table? Is that why you are so obsessed with making the Run alone, staking a claim with *your* name on it?" he pried.

Mikyla gazed soulfully at him, blinking back the mist of tears. Absently, she struggled into her clinging gown. "Without the money I would be penniless," she quietly confessed. "It isn't my father who takes care of me, but rather the other way around. I have done, and I will continue to do, what I must to survive. That includes entering horse races against men, even when they prefer not to have me there . . .

Cale had never met Emet Lassiter but he despised the man, sight unseen. No wonder Mikyla was so ferociously determined, so incredibly daring. She *had* to be to survive. Cale could not help but admire her, but neither could he prevent disliking a man who would shove such enormous burdens of responsibility onto his daughter's shoulders. Muttering to himself, Cale snatched up his shirt and boots and then stalked around the bank, gathering his horses.

In silence, they rode toward the small store located on Caddo Jake's crossing, the shallow point of the channel where wagons and horses could safely cross the South Canadian River. While Mikyla ambled around the dry goods store selecting a few supplies, Reuben Stubbs took Cale aside.

The old man smiled wryly as he glanced back at the shapely lass Cale had brought with him. "Your new lady?" he questioned.

Cale didn't know exactly how to answer the inquiry. He couldn't really label Ky as his lady. And yet they had been as close as two people could get. Indeed, Cale doubted he would ever forget the splendor he had experienced at Blue Lake.

"You ought to latch on to this one," Reuben snickered as he lit his corncob pipe. He blew a smoke ring into the air and scrutinized Cale through the hazy cloud. His twinkling eyes darted sideways to inspect Mikyla once again. "If I were twenty years younger I'd damn sure be giving you a run for your money."

"Since when did your age ever slow you down, Reuben?" Cale mocked lightly. It was wiser for Cale to tease the bushy-haired old man than to admit to an interest in this contrary, complex female.

Ushering Reuben outside, Cale paid him for keeping a watchful eye on the herd that grazed north of the store. As they led the new mounts to the barn, Reuben heaved a disappointed sigh.

"I'm afraid I wasn't much good at caring for your stock," he confessed. "I found two cows struck down by lightning when I checked on them after the storm." He gestured an arm toward the two orphan calves that were penned in the barn. "I've been giving them goat's milk for a week."

Cale nodded grimly. It wasn't the first time he had lost stock during a storm. "They're yours, Reuben," he said quietly. "If you hadn't taken them in they would have starved to death."

"But I don't expect to . . ." Reuben protested, only to be interrupted by Cale's firm command.

"Take them. I usually meet myself coming and going, and I don't have time to nurse orphan calves."

After a brief conversation, Cale and Reuben reentered the store to find Mikyla waiting to pay for her supplies. As they ambled toward their horses, Cale clasped Mikyla's hand and folded money into her fist.

"This is payment for the wager we made at Fort Reno and the rest is a gift," Cale told her soberly. "Take it and leave before the Run. You are facing impossible odds and I don't want to see you get hurt."

Mikyla's chin tilted, her blue eyes burning with determination. "I told you I have nowhere to go, and I have a

136

dream. I am going to have a home of my own in Oklahoma country."

His fingers bit into the tender flesh of her arm, giving her a sound shake. "Dammit, woman, you'll never see that childish fantasy come true. If you can't go back to the Ozarks, then come to Texas with me . . ."

Angry pride caused her to stiffen. Mikyla shook free of his grasp and leveled him a glare that was meant to maim. "And do what?" she smirked sarcastically. "Live out of *your* tent, play your strumpet while you wander around, swapping mules and horses for enough cash to purchase your next meal?"

Her sassy tone cut a mile-wide gash in Cale's temper, one that he had difficulty controlling in Mikyla's presence. He might have explained that he was wealthy beyond her wildest dreams, that his family owned and leased enough land to form their own state. But his male pride was a fragile thing. If he told her the truth about himself and she *did* come with him, he would never be certain if she cared more for the man or his money.

Damn her, was that all she could think about, land and fortune? Didn't it matter that they had shared a rare and special brand of passion? Hell, he didn't consider her his private whore. What did she think he was anyway? Some irresponsible rake who used women to . . .

Well, of course she did, he suddenly realized. That was the very impression he had projected in his attempt to keep Mikyla at a safe distance, not that it had worked worth a tittle. His method of self-preservation had been his defense *and* his defeat. He was involved all right—up to his ears!

Confound it, he didn't want to care about Mikyla, but he didn't want to see her dream shatter like crystal, either. It would be easier on her to walk away from her fantasy now than to see it destroyed by powers that defied her own fierce spirit. This was a man's world, and Mikyla had intruded upon it. Couldn't she see that? This insane Land Run would poison even those with the best dispositions. It would turn humans into greedy animals. Even Mikyla was so obsessed with staking her claim that she would fight to the death to have her precious land!

A piercing pain stabbed at Mikyla's heart when Cale didn't bother to defend himself against her harsh accusations. So that *was* what he had in mind, she thought acrimoniously. He saw her as a convenience. He wanted a resident harlot who could cook his meals, share his bed, and follow him while he traipsed into parts unknown. She had dared to give herself to a man who considered her an object for his lusty pleasure, not a woman with feelings and dreams, not his equal but his *slave*.

Suddenly, Mikyla felt diseased, like a tramp who had shamelessly surrendered to a lurid whim and would never be able to live down her one-sided affair. She had thought—at least she had *hoped*—those precious moments of intimacy had meant something special to Cale. Oh, how wrong she had been to delude herself. Cale was a rake in every sense of the word. She had offered herself to Cale because she was helplessly drawn to him, and he had merely accepted the invitation to ease his sexual appetite for women—*any* woman. Mikyla could have been any of a dozen other females for all Cale cared.

A mortified gasp gushed from her lips. Mikyla pivoted on her heels and stamped toward Sundance. "Good-bye, Cale Brolin. With any luck at all I will never see you again."

Before Cale could move or utter a word of protest, Mikyla was thundering over the ridge with her tangled hair trailing wildly about her. She rode as if the devil himself were on her heels and she never looked back, not even once.

Cursing furiously, Cale snatched her floppy-brimmed bonnet from his saddle bag and stomped on it. Yes, *stomped* it into the ground, dammit! He wanted to crush the sweet memory of their lovemaking, to smash the vision of wide-eyed innocence and stubborn determination.

Muttering several unrepeatable epithets, Cale stabbed a booted foot into the stirrup and then changed his mind about mounting the gelding. Why should he go chasing off after that bullheaded minx? It would do no good to reason with her. Once she made up her mind to something, nothing could change it. He might as well argue with a stone wall. It would be just as receptive to logic.

Let her crowd in beside the endless rabble of settlers who would be pushing and shoving their way to the boundary line to make that damned Land Run. Let her be trampled by some greedy homesteader who put human regard second to staking a lousy one-hundred-sixty-acre homesite.

Scowling, Cale wheeled around to march back to Reuben's store. He could use a drink . . . or three. Blast that woman, she was stubborn to the core!

A knowing smile pursed Reuben's lips as Cale buzzed through the door madder than a hornet. The old man had been eavesdropping, and he had seen Mikyla thunder off in all directions at once. Before Cale even had to ask, Reuben shoved a drink in his hand. Cale downed it in one swallow and refilled the glass, inhaling the second one just as quickly.

"Women!" Cale snorted disdainfully. "A man can't live *without* them and he sure as hell can't live *with* them!"

Reuben poured himself a whiskey and nodded agreeably. "Indeed, but a man gets lonely sometimes, especially when he gets old," he sighed. His narrowed gaze slid down Cale's inflated chest, one that was still heaving in frustration. "You're stuck on that pretty blonde, aren't you?"

"Not hardly," Cale scowled in contradiction. Still growling like a grizzly bear, he guzzled another drink. "If I wanted to settle down, that obstinate pigheaded female would have to be the last woman left on earth for me even to consider putting up with her!"

Reuben's weather-beaten features crinkled in a sly smile. If Cale honestly believed that, he was a fool. Cale Brolin would never ask a woman to accompany him to Texas if he didn't truly want her with him. Reuben had known Cale for five years and he had been keeping watch over Brolin's vast herd. Cale came and went with the wind, but Reuben had never seen this giant of a man get himself so worked up over a woman.

"Since when did you become such an accomplished liar?" Reuben wanted to know. "You're carrying a torch for that feisty little lady and we both know it. In fact, *she's* probably the only one who doesn't know, and you ought to tell her."

"Since when did you start dishing out advice to the lovelorn?" Cale muttered caustically, and then poured down another drink.

"Since you started inviting ladies to go home to Texas with you," Reuben shot back, undaunted.

Cale's stormy gray eyes riveted over Reuben's ruddy face. "You were eavesdropping!" he accused harshly.

Reuben smiled unrepentantly. "What else is there to do around here? It gets damned boring tending the store and staking a safe crossing on the river for travelers." His breath came out in a rush. "And every time I set the stakes, a big rain floods through here, changing the channel, and I have to start all over again."

"That is no excuse for listening in on private conversations," Cale grumbled grouchily.

Reuben's shoulder lifted like a duck shedding water. "I still think you're a fool for letting that pretty little thing slip through your fingers," he said.

The audacity of the man!

Cale came up out of his chair as if he had been sitting on live coals. "If I want your advice, I'll ask you, old man!" he roared.

The storekeeper guffawed at the irony of Cale's remark. "You don't take advice any better than that gorgeous female you brought here with you. I don't know why you're so put out with her when you reacted just as indignantly as she did. She didn't want your advice and you refuse to accept mine. What's the difference?"

Cale opened his mouth to fling a sarcastic rejoinder, but he was too irritated to speak. He knew he would be uttering a random string of curses that would make him sound as if he were just learning how to swear.

A wide grin stretched across Reuben's wrinkled face. "Yes siree, love has a pitiful effect on a man's brain. It makes him behave like a raving lunatic," he declared. Raising his glass in toast, he flashed Cale a taunting smile. "Here's to the light and love of your life, Brolin. For sure, that pretty Miki Lassiter set a fire under you."

With a wordless scowl, Cale slammed the empty glass on

140

the table and stalked outside. Reuben was supposed to be a friend. Some friend, Cale snorted resentfully as he swung into the saddle. Reuben didn't have the foggiest notion what Mikyla was like, how infuriatingly stubborn and contrary. If he did, he wouldn't have insisted that Cale tie himself to that witch's apron strings.

Love? Cale snarled ferociously. He was *definitely* not in love with that flighty female. Hell, he wasn't even sure he liked her! And he was not going to get involved with her . . .

Cale switched his curses back to that blue-eyed hellion who was tying his emotions in knots, even when he swore he didn't want her or need her. But, just the same, Cale found himself directing his mount toward the precious dream site Mikyla had described to him the first day they met. Cale was familiar with the lay of the Unassigned Lands that would soon be open to the Run. He felt the insane urge to view the sight that had obsessed Mikyla, to puzzle out why she was so entranced in her foolish dream.

After presenting his government license to the army patrol that scouted the area for Sooners, Cale thundered over the rolling plains and rode into the plush valley of the South Canadian River. He knew the moment he pulled the strawberry roan to a halt that he had located Mikyla's treasured site. She had mentioned the stately clump of cottonwoods that formed an arched pathway to the sandy shore, the gradual descent of the prairie that flowed south until it was swallowed by the ever-changing channel of this restless river.

Yes, it was spectacular country, Cale begrudgingly admitted. But was it worth her life? Apparently Mikyla thought so, since she was dead set on risking her prized stallion against ten thousand other land-hungry settlers who would form a human boundary line along what was soon to become Oklahoma country.

Still grumbling over the insanity of a Land Run and the mountains of obstacles Mikyla faced, Cale pointed his steed toward his camp. Damn, he needed another drink to wash away the lingering taste of kisses sweeter than cherry wine, the timid yet curious touch of a woman whose passion exceeded the limits of imagination. Reuben's whiskey hadn't eased the tormenting memories. Three or four drinks never would, Cale told himself bitterly. It was going to require an entire bottle to forget that impossible female. And if he knew what was good for him he would mind his own business after he drank that woman out of his thoughts. Mikyla had her onw life to live and he couldn't live it for her. The last time he interceded in someone else's affairs it had . . .

The dismal thought caused Cale's bronzed features to turn to granite. Dammit, he didn't want to think about that tragic incident, either. He just wanted to sprawl on his cot and drink until he couldn't see or feel or think! And that is exactly what he did . . . for the first time in years!

Chapter 10

Depression settled over Mikyla like a suffocating fog. Listlessly, she paced around the tent, packing her belongings in preparation for the move to their position for the Run. She should have been dancing on air, anticipating the great race that would place her dream closer to reality. But she was wallowing in moody frustration. She had returned to camp, still fuming from foolishly giving in to her passion for Cale and the heated argument that had come after. It was downright humiliating to realize she had given her innocence to a man whose heart was carved from marble. She had explained her father's failings and her craving to build her own home, her own life. But obviously Cale was unmoved by her motives for wanting to make the Run. Arrogant dolt that he was, Cale dared to invite her to become his harlot and sacrifice what meant more to her than that rudderless cowboy could ever understand.

Mikyla's constant pacing finally roused Emet from his sleep. Groaning, he pried open a bloodshot eye and attempted to focus on his daughter. Inhaling a breath to clear the haze that clogged his brain, Emet pushed himself into an upright position.

"It's time we had a talk," Emet declared hoarsely. Reaching out a shaky hand, he grabbed the dipper from the bucket of water and lubricated his vocal chords. "I want you to give up this foolish dream of yours, Miki. Together we are going to stake a townsite and establish a store. You should be there working beside me, not out on some confounded prairie, building fences and starting a ranch."

Her temper, already sorely put upon, exploded. Mikyla glared at her stubble-faced father who could barely hold his head in a position that didn't hurt. "I would prefer to blister my hands from a hard day's work than to mind the store while you drink and carouse in the first saloon that is erected in Oklahoma country," she muttered resentfully.

Emet glowered at his disrespectful daughter. "You are still my responsibility, young lady," he reminded her gruffly. "If you don't do as I demand, you may find yourself without a tent over your head or food in your stomach!"

Mikyla sniffed at his empty threat. "I think you are forgetting who has been supplying the funds to put this roof over our heads, flimsy though it is, and meals on our table. It certainly wasn't you," she snapped insolently. "You have drunk and gambled away every cent you have made peddling your goods, not to mention the ill-gotten gains you stole from honest citizens who bought your worthless maps!"

"How dare you use that hateful tone with me!" Emet sputtered in outrage. "If you don't remember your place, I might just take what is mine and leave you with whatever is left."

Emet stumbled to his feet to snatch up his belongings. As he reared up to full stature a fierce headache plowed through his skull and pounded on his brain. Damn, he felt awful and Mikyla wasn't helping his disposition with her fiery words. "And I don't want to hear you say you are not going to help me get my claim! You will do exactly what I tell you because you are my own flesh and blood, though today I can barely stand to admit it!"

He could barely stand, period, she thought acrimoniously. Mikyla yanked the coffeepot and tin cup from her father's grasp. "I paid for these things with my money after you sold the other utensils to pay your gambling debts," she reminded him hotly. "And you cannot disinherit *me* because *I* am disowning *you!*"

Emet did something he had never done in his life. He backhanded Mikyla across the cheek, sending her sprawling

144

on the floor of the tent, upending the small nightstand. A scowl erupted from his lips when he stared into her wide, teary eyes—eyes that reminded him of his departed wife. Michelle would have been heartbroken if she could have heard her husband and their daughter screeching at each other. Suddenly, Emet wasn't scowling at Mikyla. He was scowling at himself.

"Miki, I'm . . ." Hating himself for what he had become and cursing his abuse, Emet stepped forward to assist Mikyla to her feet.

Mikyla shrank back, certain her father intended to strike her again. "Get away from me," she shrieked hysterically. "Don't ever come near me again! You aren't my father. You are a miserable shell of a man who sees the world from over the rim of a liquor bottle and between the edges of your cussed cards! I want nothing more to do with you!"

Emet wheeled around, snarling at himself and his defiant daughter. It was all because of that damned stallion, he told himself bitterly. That horse had Mikyla living on dreams of ranches and prize stock. But that stallion was going to race to a townsite, Emet vowed to himself. He didn't have the funds to purchase a certificate from the townsite companies that were scheming to post stakes for citizens who were interested in building communities. He had to depend on Mikyla to make the Run for him. Emet was in no condition to battle the other settlers. He would have to rely on pure luck if he ever hoped to claim a site.

Grumbling under his breath, Emet stalked out of the tent. He needed a drink to clear his senses and start his heart pumping again. Maybe then he could decide how to handle his strong-willed daughter and convince her to do his bidding.

While Emet was weaving his way toward the gambler's den, Mikyla was scraping herself off the floor and crying buckets of tears. *My God,* she thought disparagingly. *My life is in shambles.* She had just disowned her own father and he had struck her! Father? Mikyla muffled a sob. Emet wasn't behaving like a father, more like a selfish, grisly despot!

Well, she didn't regret saying what she said to her father.

145

Perhaps it would bring him to his senses, make him realize she was not going to cater to him each time he fell into his cups and had to be toted to the tent. Emet no longer cared what she wanted or needed. He was too wrapped up in his dreary existence to pay her any mind.

What more was expected of her? How much longer was she supposed to indulge her father's failings? Mikyla let out her breath in a shuddering rush. It was time she took care of herself. Emet certainly hadn't looked out for her the past two years. And she was not about to venture to the gambler's den to drag him home once again. No doubt the Land Run would be over and done before Emet roused from his drunken stupor to realize he had sacrificed any chance of locating a town lot. Not that it would have mattered, Mikyla mused cynically as she pressed a cold cloth to her stinging cheek. Emet would have gambled away his lot and his merchandise before the month was out.

But *she* had not spent two years trekking through the rough country of the Ozarks and wandering across the flat western plains of Kansas like a vagabond for nothing! When the cannons from Fort Reno exploded, she would thunder off to stake her claim. And it would be *her* claim, not Emet's to gamble away or trade to pay his gambling debts.

Mikyla stormed around the tent, sorting her belongings from those of her father's, packing possessions that would have to be left behind until after she had staked her claim. Because of Cale Brolin and her own father, Mikyla was destined to become a manhater overnight, she thought. Both of them scolded her for living on a dream, a hope for a brighter future. But she was going to fulfill her dreams. *Because of* Cale and Emet and *in spite of* them! she vowed stormily.

Cale silently assessed the two immaculately dressed gentlemen who rolled toward his camp in a fringed surrey. One of them had a mop of hair that resembled corn shocks jutting out in all directions. The second man had a face like an exotic bird and he walked like a strutting peacock when he stepped from his carriage to greet Cale.

Joseph Richards, who specialized in developing townsites for the benefit of the railroad and his nameless associates, extended his manicured hand. A greeting smile bordered his pinched lips as he faced the tall, muscularly built man who was regarding him curiously.

"Mr. Brolin, I would like a word with you, one that could increase your good fortune." After introducing himself to Cale, who looked as if he had been trampled or severely hung over, or both, Joseph unfolded his scheme with grand diplomacy. "My associates have requested that I locate a man to make the Run for us, one who will act in the best interest of the railroad line and the directors of our Kansas-based townsite company. We have surveyed several potential areas that would benefit settlers who desire town lots near the approaching railroad. In six months there will be miles of tracks stretching between Kansas and Texas. These good citizens will require supplies and equipment to improve their new homes. My associates and I have come to aid settlers in locating cities and depots that will service this new territory."

Joseph inhaled a quick breath and flashed Cale a complimentary smile. "We feel you are just the man to put progress in motion. We need a competent rider with a swift horse to claim the acres on which we have decided to locate a town, one that will sit beside what will become the railroad right of way."

A suspicious frown knitted Cale's brow. "And just how did you decide I was the man to serve as the means to this end?" he wanted to know.

Joseph fidgeted beneath Cale's penetrating gaze, purposely avoiding visual contact with those steel-gray eyes. "My associates and I were on hand for the race at Fort Reno last week," he explained. "Your reputation speaks for itself. And you do own one of the fastest horses in the territory."

If Joseph thought compliments would win Cale over, he thought wrong. "How is this noble service you are providing for settlers going to benefit me?" His tone was frankly suspicious and vaguely sarcastic.

147

Joseph retrieved his wallet and allowed Cale to tabulate the bills that bulged from his leather purse. "A tidy salary for a worthy cause," he tempted with a smile.

Cale brushed his fingers over his stubbled chin, pretending to ponder the offer. Leaning negligently against the corral of timber and wire, Cale crossed his arms over his broad chest. "I assume you have already contacted settlers who are interested in townsites and that you have offered them choice lots in this soon-to-be city of yours."

Mikyla would have recognized that low rumble in Cale's voice as denoting irritation. Joseph, however, did not realize he had stoked the flames of Cale's temper.

Joseph nodded affirmatively. "We have . . . er . . . distributed certificates for townsites to almost three thousand anxious settlers. They would all be grateful for your assistance."

Thick dark brows formed a cynical line over those silver-studded eyes that could look right through a man and pluck out his secretive thoughts. "And how much does it cost a settler to purchase one of these plots of what is supposed to be *free* land?" His voice was rustling like the warning of a disturbed rattlesnake.

Joseph inwardly winced at Cale's emphasis on the word *free*. It was obvious Joseph wasn't dealing with the local ignoramus. Cale Brolin's competency with horses and his ability to defend himself with his hands and a pistol were well known in Indian Territory. But it was apparent this rough-edged horse trader and stockman was keenly intelligent as well. Cale had already deduced there was money to be made in these land transactions. There was nothing to be gained by lying to this man.

"We are selling lot certificates for a nominal fee of a few dollars," he began, only to be cut off by Cale's deep skirl of cynical laughter.

"And the prime sites go to those who can afford the exorbitant prices," he smirked in prediction. "Who would have thought *free* land could be so expensive!"

A patronizing smile elevated one side of Joseph's puckered mouth. "My superiors and my business associates

148

have the best interest of the homesteaders at heart," he proclaimed self-righteously. "Our preplanning will save considerable distress to some poor soul who will inevitably be forced to sell his land for the railroad right of way. Towns will spring up on choice locations near the railroad tracks. We have foreseen the problem and we plan to make the most of opportunity."

Cale could have hit the squatty little man with his black, beady eyes and a nose like an eagle's beak. This was a prime example of the opportunistic scheming Cale had tried to warn Mikyla about.

What would transpire in this Run for free land? It would become a scramble for property that would lead to arguments and gun fights. Nothing was free. Cale had tried to tell Mikyla that, but she was too obstinate to heed his warning. Some of the settlers would pay for these cherished sites in newly formed towns and men like Joseph Richards, the wily, conniving ones, would be grinning and counting their ill-gotten gains. Damn these swindlers! Cale would like to pound both men flat and mail them back to Kansas.

"And just where have you and your other associates, all of whom, I presume, will remain nameless, surveyed a townsite for the betterment of mankind?" Cale managed to ask without growling the question in Joseph's birdlike face.

Pivoting southeast, Joseph gestured a stubby finger toward the probable site. "Our surveys have determined that a prime location for a thriving community would lie on the two quarter sections of land, just north of the South Canadian River. There is an ample water supply and accessible ground for the railroad to build its bridge across the river. The trees along the nearby creek and along the river will provide shade and sufficient wood."

The wide brim of Cale's Stetson concealed the flash of stunned annoyance in his eyes. Joseph had just described the location of Mikyla's dream site. Even if that daring minx managed to stake her claim ahead of the townsite company—which was obviously in cahoots with the approaching railroad and God only knew who else—the railroad would condemn her land for a right of way. Mikyla could fight to keep her land but she couldn't possibly win against the powerful railroad and the wealthy backers of the townsite company. Cale was willing to bet his right arm that the town location had been laid out in the railroad drafting office the moment surveyors returned with their reports. That information was then transferred to investors, after a good deal of cash was passed under the table, of course.

A woman alone wouldn't have so much as a prayer when it was highly likely that railroad officials were also on the board of directors of this townsite company. Mikyla would be approached in a civil manner. If she refused to sell, she would be threatened. And if she didn't budge . . .

A slow burn simmered through Cale's rigid body as he pushed away from the corral to loom over Joseph Richards. "What you are proposing is fraud," he growled contemptuously. "In essence, you will be bribing me to stake a claim and then, in the name of humanity, I am supposed to graciously sacrifice the land for your community, one which you and your nameless friends will have sold to greedy settlers who don't wish to take their chances with the ten thousand citizens who are going to trample all over each other to obtain *free* land!"

Cale's voice had risen until he was shouting in Joseph's peaked face. The little man took two retreating steps before he dared to defend himself. He had only opened his mouth when Cale stomped forward to breathe down his neck.

"And don't give me that sugar-coated sales pitch about how your townsite company is benefiting the common settler," he sneered viciously. "If it weren't for the money you have collected, you would still be sitting in your tufted chair in Kansas!" Inhaling a deep breath, Cale shot an arm toward the cowering man who had wisely chosen to remain in the surrey. "Now get the hell out of here, Richards. I want nothing to do with your deceitful scheme!"

Joseph scampered toward the carriage and the safety of his friend before he flung Cale a condescending glower. "It's your loss of profit, Brolin," he snorted haughtily, now that he was seated a safe distance away from this snarling giant of a man. "If you won't ride for us in tomorrow's Land Run, someone else will. You won't stop progress by rejecting our generous offer."

"Your kind of *progress* has price tags all over it!" Cale bellowed as he stalked toward the surrey.

Joseph's eyes were as round as saucers when Cale stormed toward him, breathing the fire of dragons. Quick as his rotund little body would move, Joseph clambered to retrieve the reins and popped them on the horse's rump. The steed thundered off with his harness jingling, leaving Cale to silently consign both men to the eternal fires of hell.

Damnation, Cale swore as he watched the carriage disappear in the distance. He knew something like this was going to happen. Men like Joseph Richards swarmed in like flies when there was a possibility of making money. The Land Run was their opportunity, and they would make Mikyla's life a veritable hell if she managed to stake the same property the townsite company had selected.

Confound it, Mikyla was on a collision course with disaster. Grumbling, Cale stomped back to his tent to gather fresh clothes and then aimed himself toward the creek. He was going to soak in the stream until his temper cooled and then he was going to . . .

Cale didn't know exactly what he was going to do. But one thing was for certain. Mikyla couldn't make the Run. If she did, she would lose, even if she won!

Chapter 11

The glow of lanterns cast flickering light on Emet Lassiter's cards. It was all he could do to focus on his cards and determine the strength of his hand. Emet had ventured to the gambler's den to forget what he had become, to forget what he had done to his only child. But the more liquor he consumed, the more blame he placed on Mikyla for turning against her own flesh and blood.

"Defied her own father," Emet mumbled as he squinted at his cards.

If only Michelle were here to give his life purpose, to take Miki in hand. If only Miki had been more like her mother—patient, gentle, understanding. But Miki was no help, no help at all. She wanted a home and land, all of which meant hours of hard labor, none of which Emet wished on himself. What good was a home without Michelle? She had died and his fighting spirit had perished with her.

Grumbling, Emet wiped the liquor from his chin with his shirtsleeve. Mikyla was going to do his bidding this time, he told himself confidently. He needed her to tend his mercantile store, and, by God, that was what she was going to do!

"Are you gonna bet, old man?" an impatient gambler snorted. "I . . ." His voice evaporated when Morgan Hagerty clamped a hand on his shoulder.

"Why don't you give your backside a rest, friend," Morgan suggested. "It's obvious you haven't the patience to allow Mr. Lassiter the opportunity to carefully consider his hand."

The gambler jerked around to see Morgan's right hand poised over the Colt that lay in his holster. Deciding it best to back away, the gambler relinquished his wooden barrel to Morgan. A wry smile pursed Morgan's lips as he gathered the cards to deal a fresh hand. His reputation with a gun had proceeded him to the improvised saloon that sat on the creek bank. There were few men who disputed his suggestions. And, for the most part, Morgan played the gentleman, unless someone was foolish enough to cross him.

Tonight Morgan was prepared to do whatever he must, employing any available means to get what he wanted. There was a great deal at stake, more than the usual challenge of relieving one of the other gamblers of his money. Joseph Richards had sought him out to ride for the townsite company. Morgan accepted, provided he was allowed a share of the profit. To ensure that he staked the land, Morgan wanted to be sitting astride the fastest horse in the territory—Sundance.

And there was the matter of the sassy Miss Lassiter, he mused with a roguish smile. Once he had Sundance in his possession he would find a way to ease Mikyla's disappointment. Morgan hadn't quite puzzled out what he intended to say, but he would worry about that after he persuaded Emet to stake the stallion in a poker game.

"Does seven-card stud suit you?" Morgan questioned pleasantly.

Emet shrugged a droopy shoulder and reached for his empty glass, which Morgan made certain remained level full. Damn that Miki, Emet scowled half aloud. He was going to find a way to bring his contrary daughter under thumb. She had *forced* him to strike her, he consoled himself. She should never have proclaimed she was going to disown her own father. No matter what, they were blood kin and she was going to stand by him.

"Deal me in, too, Morgan."

The deep, rich voice came from the shadows, but Morgan would have recognized it anywhere. It was part of a recurring dream. Morgan felt hatred flood through his body like molten lava when Cale Brolin swaggered over to seat himself at the table of crates and planks. Instinctively, Morgan eased his fingers toward his pistol, but he reminded himself that this was not the time or place to satisfy his vendetta against Brolin.

A deadly smile thinned Cale's lips as he sank down beside Emet, who was too busy mumbling to himself to realize he was about to become bait for a wily shark. For a moment Cale and Morgan stared at each other, noting the changes that had taken place in the past three years. Morgan's handsome features had matured with age, but they were still more refined than Cale's had ever been. His blond hair was, as always, styled and clipped to complement his expensive clothes and dignified manners.

In Morgan's estimation, Cale had changed very little. He was still as hard and unyielding as he had always been. Time had deepened the lines that bracketed Cale's mouth and jutted from the corners of those unnerving gray eyes. The lines of experience held a cynical slant. Cale's full mouth could still narrow in that infuriating way that implied he wasn't budging an inch.

The last man Cale had wanted or expected to see tonight was Morgan Hagerty. But it seemed the fickle hand of fate had flung them together once again. After Cale had run Joseph Richards out of camp, he had bathed and shaved and plotted his plan of action. His first order of business was to locate Mikyla's father. After asking directions to the Lassiter tent, Cale had weaved his way through the prairie schooners and campfires, only to run headlong into Greta Ericcson. She had informed him that Mikyla and Emet had parted company on the most unfriendly of terms and that Emet had aimed himself toward the gambler's den to drown his troubles.

Muttering an imaginative string of curses Cale threaded his way through the maze of trees and underbrush. He had arrived at the makeshift saloon to seek out Emet Lassiter and give the man a good piece of his mind. The sight of Morgan Hagerty hovering over Emet like a vulture spoiled

Cale's already sour disposition. Morgan hated Cale with a passion, and he had since the first of their many confrontations in Texas. Although Morgan could portray the distinguished gentleman with his impeccable manners and charismatic charm, he was a dangerous man when he was provoked to anger. No one was aware that Morgan had an evil streak until they defied him, Cale mused as his probing gaze picked the gambler apart. When things were going his way, Morgan was suave and debonair. And when he wanted something badly enough, he began to scheme and maneuver. Morgan was deliberate and methodic and Cale detested the idea of having this potentially dangerous man near Mikyla or her father.

"It must have been an ill wind that blew you in from Texas," Morgan said after a long, brittle moment. His simmering green eyes swung to Emet. "Have you had the pleasure of meeting the meddlesome Cale Brolin?"

Ignoring Morgan's sarcastic jibe, Cale extended his hand, waiting for Emet's bloodshot eyes to guide his arm toward Cale. God, the man was so far into his cups that his hand was as limp as a wilted weed. Cale scowled in disgust, knowing he wouldn't have been able to reason with Emet if they had been permitted a private conversation. Emet was too intoxicated to think, and he was about to become easy prey for whatever scheme was hatching in Morgan's head.

Cale's disapproving gaze flooded over Emet's improperly buttoned shirt, rumpled hair, and stubbled chin. One look at this miserable man assured Cale that Emet couldn't control his high-spirited daughter. The man couldn't even take care of himself! Damn him. Emet wasn't good enough to be Mikyla's father. Because of Emet's pitiful condition, Mikyla was forced to assume the lion's share of responsibility for both of them. Cale was stung by the overpowering urge to jerk Emet off his wooden keg and shake some sense into him. He was further infuriated, remembering Greta's remark about Mikyla being forced to retrieve her father from this den of gamblers and thieves. She could have been molested by any one of these vermin, for Christ's sake!

"What are the stakes, Hagerty?" Emet slurred out as he

fumbled to retrieve the two cards that lay facedown on the table.

Morgan's face was a well-disciplined mask that revealed nothing of his thoughts. "The stakes are the highest ones around," he declared as he took a quick glance at his cards.

"I'm nearly out of money," Emet said sluggishly. He stared, blurry-eyed, at his "hole" cards, trying to determine if he were staring at a jack of diamonds or hearts.

Morgan's shoulder lifted nonchalantly. "Why not stake that fancy stallion of yours to cover your bets," he suggested. "If you win, I'll match Sundance's worth. If I win, the stallion is mine."

Mutinous fury glistened in Cale's eyes. So that was what this was all about. Morgan was after the stallion that was coveted by every settler awaiting the Run. Had Morgan found a buyer for the steed, or did he covet Sundance for himself? Or maybe Morgan had his sights set on the fiesty blond hellion. Knowing Morgan (and Cale knew him all too well), it was safe to say that the wily gambler was after both the lady and her stallion. Morgan pursued beautiful women with the same avid lust that he hungered for wealth. And if Morgan had the slightest idea that Cale and Mikyla were . . .

Cale shuddered at the thought. Morgan wouldn't bat an eye at using Mikyla as a method of revenge if he thought she meant something to Cale . . .

"Are you in, Brolin?" Morgan inquired with a seemingly disinterested glance. "In case you haven't heard, Lassiter's stallion is worth at least seven hundred dollars. I'm sure you would enjoy winning this particular steed, knowing how fond you are of horses."

The remark sounded pleasant enough, but Cale detected the scathing edge on Morgan's voice. It was a test of Morgan's self-control to pretend to be civil to Cale. In truth, Morgan would have preferred to drop Cale in his tracks than look at him.

"It isn't exactly my horse," Emet confessed over his thick tongue. "My daughter raised and trained him . . ."

One blond brow climbed to a mocking angle. "Do you mean to imply that you have no authority over your

157

daughter's business?" An intimidating chuckle tripped from Morgan's lips as he eased back to reassess the two cards that lay facedown on the table. "If I were you, I wouldn't admit that my daughter made the ultimate decisions about business *or* my prize horse. It leaves me to wonder who wears the breeches in your household, you or your daughter."

Emet sat up out of his slouch and squared his shoulders as best he could. By damned, Morgan was right. If Emet wanted to bet that blessed horse, he most certainly could. After all, he was the one who bought that scrawny colt for Mikyla. As a matter of fact, Emet wouldn't have found himself in conflict with his daughter if not for that confounded stallion. Without Sundance, Mikyla would have no choice but to help Emet locate a townsite.

Emet had approached one of the men who was selling town lots prior to the Run and he had requested a choice lot. But since Emet couldn't afford a certificate he had no alternative but to make the Run and stake whatever site hadn't been snatched up.

While Emet's foggy mind was turning over the thoughts, Cale was gnashing his teeth, determined to play along with Morgan and keep a watchful eye on this cardsharp. "How do I know this stallion is worth that kind of money? I haven't laid eyes on him," Cale lied convincingly.

"Sundance is worth every penny," Morgan declared as he scooped up his cards and then folded them into the palm of his hand—a maneuver Cale was quick to decipher as trouble. "The horse can run like the wind and he's won every race he's entered the past year."

"And Sundance will back my bets," Emet blurted out with a gloating smile. Just let Miki steam and stew over the future of that troublesome stallion. It would serve her right if Emet lost. Indeed, he didn't care if he did!

Cale inwardly cringed at the cards Morgan dealt him. They were what any poker player would distastefully refer to as "trash." Knowing Morgan, he had begun cheating from the first shuffle.

A crowd began to gather as the game progressed. Cale willed himself to concentrate on Morgan, but it was damned

158

difficult with Emet mumbling to himself, cursing his daughter and pining for a woman Cale assumed to be Mikyla's mother. And all the while Cale kept seeing Mikyla's bewitching face in his mind's eye, knowing it would crush her to lose Sundance the night before the Land Run. Morgan wanted the stallion, for what particular purpose Cale couldn't say. But Cale knew he wasn't about to hand Sundance over to Mor—

"Are you seeing the bet or raising it?" Morgan inquired, jolting Cale from his pensive deliberations.

Although the question sounded bland to the spectators, Cale noted the impatient irritation flickering in Morgan's eyes. Cale smiled to himself. Half the secret of defeating Morgan at his own game was to needle him until his composure cracked.

"I'm thinking," Cale murmured as he lifted the corners of the two "hole" cards he had the pleasure of dealing himself for this final hand. The king of hearts and the ten of hearts were peering up at Cale. The four of diamonds and the king of clubs were lying faceup on the table. His eyes shifted to the two cards—the queen of clubs and ace of clubs—that lay on Morgan's side of the table. Possible flush, Cale speculated before swinging his attention to the pair of threes that sat in front of Emet. "I'll raise the bet an extra hundred," Cale finally announced, and then watched both men match the stakes.

Cale dealt three more cards, faceup. He had added a three of hearts to his hand. Morgan was boasting a joker and Emet was grumbling at his recent arrival—the jack of spades.

"The pair of aces and possible flush has the bet," Cale said nonchalantly.

Morgan had to force himself not to grin as he raised the bet another hundred dollars. Cale was a fool, he laughed under his breath. Even though Cale was dealing, Morgan was sitting on a winning hand. His anticipation mounted when Cale dealt him the nine of clubs and gave himself the king of diamonds. The odds were against Cale and in favor of Morgan running a flush. Although Emet was still betting heavily, staking the stallion on the last hand, he didn't have a prayer. And neither does Cale, Morgan mused confidently.

After Cale dealt the final cards facedown, Morgan eased back in his seat. He had gained the four of clubs—the card that completed his flush. Cale had only a pair of kings showing. When the last bets were placed, Morgan let the four of clubs glide over his fingers for Cale to examine.

"Flush," he chuckled triumphantly.

Cale's face registered neither surprise nor chagrin. Leisurely, he unveiled his "hole" cards. "Full house, kings over fours," he declared.

Emet tossed in his cards. "Well, it looks like Brolin has himself a new stallion . . . and you're welcome to him." He slumped back in his chair to down the remainder of his drink. "But you'll have to fetch him yourself, I'm not sure I can find my way back to my own tent, much less round up Sundance."

Raw fury seared Morgan's body. He couldn't believe Cale had beaten him. He was certain his flush would hold. But Cale had somehow managed to collect a fistful of kings and fours. For a moment he sat there, stunned, infuriated, hating Cale more than he already did . . . if that were possible.

Leisurely, Cale unfolded himself from the table. God, Emet Lassiter was a pitiful sight. No wonder Mikyla was so bitter and resentful. She had every right to be, Cale decided.

After gathering his winnings from Morgan, Cale aimed himself toward the Boomer camp. He was in no mood to bicker with Morgan at the moment. All he wanted to do was fetch the stallion and return to his tent. But Cale was not to be granted his wish. As he weaved his way through the brush, he heard the crackling of twigs behind him. Cale didn't need eyes in the back of his head to determine who was following him. But what did surprise him was that Morgan hadn't yielded to the temptation of shooting him in the back.

"You cheated, you son of a bitch," Morgan sneered viciously.

Cautiously, Cale turned, his right hand hovering over his pistol. The faintest hint of a smile touched his lips and then evaporated as he stared into Morgan's handsome features, which were now twisted in a satanic snarl. "I only cheated

160

more effectively than you did," Cale corrected. "You dealt me so much trash, I almost couldn't overcome it. But it was your misfortune that I was allowed to deal the last hand. I knew you couldn't resist the temptation of betting all seven hundred dollars on that joker. Why the hell do you think I let you have a wild card?"

The taunt snapped Morgan's temper, which he had been forced to control for over an hour. "You always turn up to disrupt my well-laid plans," he growled mutinously. "First you destroyed my happiness with Jessica and now you have meddled in my affairs again. But you aren't going to interrupt my plans this time. I mean to have that stallion and his lovely lady." His chest was heaving with barely restrained fury. "I don't give a damn if I have to go around you or over you to get what I want."

Cale raked Morgan with disdainful mockery. "You always did blame everyone else when you were refused your whims, didn't you?" Cale scoffed in question. "You always thought you had been cheated, always looking for the easy way out. Even Jessica was your way out, nothing more, nothing less."

"I loved Jessica and you killed her," Morgan hissed poisonously. "You self-righteous bastard, you killed her!"

Cale inwardly winced at Morgan's hateful tone and his condemning words. Even Morgan couldn't know that vicious remark cut through him like a double-edged sword. But this was not the time for a display of emotion, not when Morgan was boiling with murderous fury. If Cale didn't keep his wits about him, Morgan would have his wish of seeing his enemy as deep in hell as a falcon could fly in a week.

"Love?" Cale's laugh was hollow and humorless. "You don't know the meaning of the word, Morgan. Jessica was your meal ticket. You planned to use her for the wealth she could provide to support your gambling habits when your luck ran amuck or when someone else cheated better than you did at cards."

Morgan trembled with outrage. God, how he hated Cale, had always hated him and always would. He despised Cale's capabilities, his air of authority. "Someday, Cale, you're going to find a woman who truly means something to you. And I'm going to take her away from you, the way you stole Jessica from me." His eyes blazed in the dim light. "You couldn't stand the thought that Jessica loved me, could you? You were determined to come between us, and I will never forgive you for what you did to her!"

Hatred poisoned Morgan's thoughts, provoking him to assert his rage and satisfy a meager portion of his vengeance. With an animalistic growl, Morgan threw himself at Cale. Oh, how Morgan itched to wrap his fingers around Cale's throat and choke the life from him. Cale reacted with a well-aimed blow to Morgan's belly, which doubled his assailant over and left him gasping for breath. But Morgan thirsted for blood. Unfolding himself, he lunged at Cale again, swinging wildly.

Cale agilely ducked away from the oncoming fist and coiled to strike before Morgan could regain his balance. Flesh cracked against flesh like the clap of thunder. Morgan was propelled backward and landed with a thud. His left hand involuntarily moved to his face to wipe away the blood that trickled from his nose and lips while his right hand crept toward his holster.

Before Morgan could draw his pistol he heard the deadly click of Cale's Colt .45. Damn, how he wished he had shot Cale in the back when he had the chance. Now he found himself staring down the silver barrel of Cale's pistol. For fifteen years Morgan had longed to be more competent than Cale at *anything,* whether it be women, weapons, words, or wealth. But even Morgan's best was second to Cale Brolin.

"The stallion is mine," Cale ground out between clenched teeth. "I only hope the horse is as valuable as you seem to think he is. I should hate to kill you over a worthless nag."

"You only wanted that horse because you didn't want me to have him. That is what motivates you, isn't it, Cale? I wanted Jessica, and you didn't want me to have her, either," Morgan sneered contemptuously. "Does it give you a feeling of superiority to take what you know I want? Can you live with yourself, knowing Jessica would still be alive if you had left well enough alone, if you hadn't been so intent on depriving me of what I wanted?"

Cale tolerated Morgan's verbal abuse. Maybe it was his own deeply embedded feelings of guilt that prevented him from voicing his defense. Maybe it was the fact that Cale realized Morgan had just cause to despise him. Three years ago, Cale had attempted to intervene in Morgan's life, to save Jessica from inevitable misery, even when she had shown her preference. And from that day forward Cale had carried a burden on his conscience that equaled the weight of the world.

Morgan's mocking laughter shattered the tense silence. "Just you wait, Cale. One day the tables will be turned and I will decide what you can have and what you cannot have. And when that day comes, you're going to understand what I felt the night Jessica died. And then, by damned, you are going to be consumed by the same maddening hatred that boils in my blood each time you cross my path and interfere in my life! If you think I'll ever let you forget the agony, the grief you forced on me, you are sorely mistaken!"

Without a word, Cale shoved his Colt into his holster and spun on his boot heels. Well, maybe Morgan's hatred was justified, Cale mused disconcertedly. Maybe he should assume the full blame for Jessica's death. But he was damned well going to save another woman from her untimely demise, from inevitable heartache. Mikyla might despise him for what he intended to do, but it was for her own good. She wasn't going to make the Land Run to her dream site on that devil stallion. Without Sundance, Mikyla would not be forced to confront the powerful railroad or the fraudulent townsite company. It was far better for her to be disappointed now rather than later. It would break her heart to claim her precious land and stand helplessly by while it was snatched out from under her.

Cale knew he was inviting Mikyla's wrath and her hatred. But, dammit, he had to save her from herself and from those who lusted after that precious piece of land. Chewing on that determined thought, Cale aimed himself toward the string of horses guarded by the various settlers who had united to

163

protect their prized steeds before the Land Run.

After Cale explained that he had won Sundance in a poker game, he was graced with a condemning glower.

"Miss Lassiter isn't going to like it when she hears her father lost her horse," the man grumbled. "If you had a heart you wouldn't collect on this debt."

Cale grabbed the lead rope and strode off into the darkness with Sundance reluctantly following in his wake. "I have a heart, friend, and sometimes a man has to do a woman a favor, even when she won't recognize it as one. Actually, Miss Lassiter should thank me for relieving her of this troublesome horse."

"Well, she won't," the guard guaranteed with a derisive snort.

"I know," Cale murmured half aloud. "But I'm afraid that can't be helped."

The guard slumped back against a nearby tree. Lord, he wouldn't want to be the one to explain this to Mikyla Lassiter. She wasn't going to like losing her horse on the eve of the Run. No, sir, she wasn't going to like it a damned bit!

Morgan Hagerty's summons drew Mikyla from her pensive deliberations. She had completed her packing in preparation to moving to the boundary line the following morning. She still had several chores to tend to and she wasn't enthused about Morgan's interruption, especially when her mind was cluttered with dozens of frustrating thoughts. Her argument with her father had upset her, and her shameless surrender to Cale made it even more difficult to live with herself. Mikyla had thrown herself into her tasks, deliberately trying to preoccupy herself. But Cale's strong, commanding image had moved in to take up permanent residence in her brain, causing conflicting emotions to churn within her.

"Miss Lassiter, I have to talk to you," Morgan insisted when Mikyla didn't immediately respond to his call.

Heaving an exasperated sigh, Mikyla walked over to raise the tent flap. Her mouth dropped open when she spied

Morgan's tattered clothes and the discolorations on the side of his face. "What happened to you?" she gasped in alarm.

Morgan managed to contain his fury. Mikyla had never seen him lose control of his temper, and he preferred that this attractive minx didn't even know he had one. "I'm afraid I'm the bearer of bad news," he told her, avoiding her question.

"My father did this?" Mikyla was leaping to conclusions.

"No, not exactly," Morgan clarified. "But indirectly, I suppose you might say Emet was responsible. He bet Sundance in a poker game."

The color drained from her exquisite features and no words formed on her lips. She stood paralyzed, gaping at Morgan's battered garments and bloody lip. Oh, God, had Emet taken her only prized possession and gambled him away, just as he had her home and her inheritance?

"When I realized what Emet planned to do, I immediately sat in on the poker game, hoping to win your stallion for you before someone else took advantage of your father."

Icy dread settled over Mikyla. She sat down before she fell down.

Ducking beneath the tent flap, Morgan followed Mikyla inside to complete his twisted rendition of what had transpired. "I wasn't as lucky at cards as I had hoped. Another man won the stallion. I tried to convince him to sell Sundance to me, no matter what the price. When I became insistent, he became abusive. We fought and . . ." Morgan touched his fingertips to his tender jaw and swollen lip. "Well, you can see for yourself that lady luck wasn't fighting on my side."

Mikyla stared straight ahead, seeing the inside of her tent through a furious red haze. Damn her father! He knew how much Sundance meant to her! He had purposely lost the horse because he had become angry with her. Now what was she to do? Buy a horse at the last moment? And if she did, what, pray tell, was she going to use for money to purchase building materials and supplies after she staked her claim—*if* there were any left after the Sooners and settlers with swift horses marked their property?

"Who won my stallion?" Mikyla hissed bitterly. Tears

scalded her eyes but Mikyla fought them back, forcing herself to listen to Morgan's answer.

"A man named Cale Brolin," he informed her, his voice thick with hatred. "A man without a conscience."

Mikyla vaulted to her feet, her body rigid with outrage. Cale had purposely drawn her father into that card game. He was doing this for some perverted kind of revenge against her! She had blurted out that her father had gambled away his own fortune. Emet had purposely wagered her stallion to spite her. And Cale, with malice and forethought, had set Emet up.

Damn them both to hell and back! Emet was repaying her for her hateful remarks, and Cale didn't want her to make the Run so he had swindled her out of her horse. God, how she hated his deceit! Well, he wasn't going to get away with this, she seethed. Mikyla would refuse to admit defeat. Her future was at stake and she wasn't about to lie down and let Cale Brolin walk all over her.

When Mikyla stormed toward the exit, Morgan was one step behind her. "What do you intend to do? Believe me, it's a waste of time to confront Brolin. I don't even know where he is or what he did with Sundance. For all I know, Brolin may have already sold the stallion."

Morgan's hands glided up and down Mikyla's tense forearms. "I'm afraid Sundance is gone, Mikyla. But I will take care of you if you let me. We could be very good together, and I will see to it that you have a claim, if that's what you want."

Mikyla didn't answer him. She was too busy planning to shoot, poison, and stab Cale Brolin. As she sailed through the maze of tents and campfires, Morgan studied her shapely backside. His version of the story would endear Mikyla to him. And when she returned from her fruitless search, needing consolation, Morgan would be here for her.

An annoyed frown replaced Morgan's sly smile. Dammit, he had business to attend to before the night was out. Now that he had lost Sundance he was going to have to find himself a swift steed for the Run. Yes, he wanted that feisty little bundle of femininity in his bed, but he would have to

166

wait until he was ensured that *he* wouldn't be riding a plodding nag in tomorrow's Run.

Finally, a Machiavellian smile tugged at the side of his mouth, the side Cale hadn't punched. "One day, Mikyla, you and I will be lovers. I will make sure of that."

Humming that positive tune, Morgan strutted off to make other arrangements. Mikyla was well worth the wait, he assured himself. No, she wasn't as wealthy as Jessica had been, but she could amuse him for a time. The thought of Jessica soured Morgan's mood. If not for Cale Brolin, Jessica would still be alive. Morgan would never forgive Cale for what he had done. And Cale's hell on earth was knowing that someday, somehow, he would endure the same agonizing grief, the same tormenting frustration, and the same poisoning hatred. Morgan would dedicate his efforts to ensuring that Cale Brolin was constantly hounded. That meddlesome bastard deserved no better than spending the rest of his life glancing over his shoulder, wondering how and when Morgan would strike.

"And I *will* have my revenge," Morgan promised himself stormily.

Chapter 12

The sound of Mikyla's piercing whistle brought Cale straight out of bed. In two long strides he reached the exit to his tent. He could hear Sundance pawing and snorting, but that stallion wasn't going anywhere. Cale had hobbled Sundance and staked him inside the corral in case Mikyla thought to whistle to him without confronting Cale first.

After several minutes, Cale heard the thunder of hoof beats approaching his camp. He was expecting that fiery minx, but as of yet he hadn't decided what he was going to say when Mikyla let loose with both barrels. And she would do exactly that, Cale predicted. Ky was going to be mad as hell.

Propped carelessly against the corral, Cale surveyed the silhouette who sped toward him. Wild tendrils of silver-gold hair glistened in the moonlight. Even at a distance, as Mikyla galloped toward him on one of her father's mules, Cale could detect the livid fury that exuded from her. She was riding bareback on the mule. Her chin jutted out in a pout and her spine was as stiff as a flagpole. And when she bounded to the ground Cale could decipher her outrage in every exquisite feature on her face. If looks could kill, Cale would have endured a hundred kinds of hell and died a thousand torturous deaths.

"Damn you, Cale," Mikyla spat, as if his name left a bitter taste in her mouth. "First you took my innocence to add to your collection of conquests and now you have stolen my horse! I shall hate you until my dying day!"

My, but she was in a fit of temper. Her eyes were burning hot blue flames and her breasts were heaving with every agitated breath she inhaled. The top two buttons of her trim-fitting shirt had come undone, exposing the inner swell of her bosom. Her elegant cheeks flushed bright pink to match the tempting color of her lips. The dim glow of the campfire framed her curvaceous figure, bringing to mind the vision Cale had witnessed the previous day at Blue Lake.

Discarding his arousing musings, Cale focused on her furious frown and deflected her glare with a reckless smile. "Don't you want to add that you will hate me through all eternity?" His calm tone implied that her tirade hadn't even fazed him.

"That too!" she hissed like a disturbed cat.

Mikyla wanted to slap him silly, but she had tried that before and Cale had hit her back. That insufferable ogre. He made her so furious she wanted to kick him into splinters. "I want Sundance back . . . NOW!!" she yelled at him as if he were stone deaf.

Cale shrugged lackadaisically. "Fine, Ky."

His bland acceptance of her demand took the wind out of her sails. For a moment she could only gape at him in astonishment. "That's it? All I had to do was ask?"

He gave his dark head an affirmative nod. When Mikyla wheeled around to retrieve Sundance from the corral, Cale grabbed her arm.

"I said you could have him back," Cale acknowledged. "But we have yet to dicker over the price I'll accept."

Her head swiveled on her shoulders to glare poison arrows at him. "How much do you want?" she questioned begrudgingly.

"How much have you got?" A devilish smile settled on his craggy features when her blue eyes flared, speaking unvoiced volumes.

"Six hundred and fifty dollars," she gritted through clenched teeth.

"That's a pity," he sighed in mock sympathy. "I was thinking perhaps eight hundred . . ."

170

"Eight hun—" Mikyla swallowed her tongue.

His smile spread from ear to ear when Mikyla practically fell through the ground. "How much is Sundance worth to *you,* vixen?" he taunted mercilessly. "If you cannot come up with the cash, perhaps we could settle on something to compensate for your shortage of funds."

Her eyes narrowed cynically. "Such as . . ." she prompted on a bitter note.

His all-encompassing gaze made a deliberate sweep of her luscious figure, missing not even one alluring detail. *"You,* Ky," he told her simply. "All night, as many times as I want to make love to you . . ."

Cale wanted this feisty sprite in his arms. He felt the unfamiliar need to protect her from trouble, to shield her from the disappointment that would inevitably come. And it was for damned sure that Cale wanted this firebrand nowhere near Morgan Hagerty!

Her outraged gasp caught in the evening breeze. "You miserable son of—"

Lean fingertips touched her lips to shush her. "I've already been called that once tonight. Try to be more inventive and less vulgar. Profanity doesn't become you," Cale chided in taunt.

Earlier, Mikyla had itched to kick Cale to pieces. Now she was leaning toward hanging him by his ankles in a musty dungeon full of snakes and rats. "You are beneath contempt, Cale Brolin," she sneered into his craggy features.

His fingers increased their pressure on her forearm, drawing her resisting body against his. "In my bed, Ky, without a fight . . . the way we were the first time you gave yourself to me . . ."

Her body betrayed her by trembling when it made familiar contact with his rock-hard flesh. The masculine scent of him swirled around her senses, making her all too aware of him. How could she hate Cale so thoroughly and still respond to the feel of his sinewy body brushing seductively against hers?

"I was a fool then," she ground out, commanding her voice to remain steady. "I'd be a bigger fool now if I submit to you."

"Not even for Sundance's sake?" One dark brow lifted as his head moved diligently toward hers. His smoky gray eyes focused longingly on her lips.

"Even Sundance would understand." Mikyla gulped over the lump that had suddenly collected in her throat. "I won't subject myself to that humiliation . . ."

His warm, moist mouth feathered over hers, skillfully demolishing the barriers she had tried so hard to construct. He was tantalizing and arousing her with the sweet threat of a kiss that transformed her legs to limp noodles.

"Why not, Ky? Because you know what happens when we make love?" he murmured huskily. "Because you know you enjoy my touch and you don't want to admit it, even to yourself?"

"I hate you," Mikyla snapped as she struggled for release.

"You already told me. You needn't repeat yourself . . ."

His mouth captured hers, depriving her of precious breath. His arms encircled her, tormenting her with pleasure. Mikyla blinked back the tears of frustration when she felt herself melt beneath his practiced touch. He was forcing her to face her vulnerability, her ill-founded attraction for this loathsome scoundrel.

Was this another cross she had to bear? Was she to be forever reminded she had shamelessly surrendered to desires of the flesh, the compelling lure she felt for a man who used her to appease his lusts? Cale knew she was magnetically drawn to him. He was playing upon her weakness to break her spirit, to prove his male dominance. Damn him, he had a heart encased in granite and he knew nothing of compassion. He saw her as a challenge and nothing more. To Cale, she was like a wild mustang to be tamed, broken, and led around on a halter.

When his arms slipped beneath her knees, lifting her from the ground, Mikyla could not locate her tongue to protest. She was making this sacrifice for the return of her stallion, she told herself. But deep down inside, Mikyla knew it was more than that. She despised Cale for taking Sundance when he knew how much the steed meant to her, how much she depended on Sundance's swift flight during the Land Run.

172

Yet, when Cale touched her, when he held her hostage in those liquid silver depths of his eyes, Mikyla found herself wanting him with the same irrational hunger she had experienced the previous day.

His kiss unlocked the sweet memories. Mikyla could feel his masterful hands gliding over her innocent body. She could feel those same heart-stopping sensations that followed in the wake of his gentle caresses. She remembered, with vivid clarity, the way his long, muscled body could mold itself to her pliant flesh, spreading wild, erotic pleasure that defied description.

Cale could see the contradicting emotions pursuing each other across her flawless features as he set her to her feet beside his cot. She wanted to hate him—body, mind, and soul. But she, like he, was in the grip of something more potent and forceful than logic. They could curse each other. They could hurl biting insults. But when they touched, pride and resentment fell away, exposing the simmering passions they evoked in each other.

Although Cale had remained steady and unerring during his ordeal of matching talents with Morgan Hagerty, he could not control the tremble in his hands. His fingertips quivered as they drifted over the buttons of Mikyla's shirt. It was as if he were meticulously unearthing a priceless treasure, one so fragile and delicate that it might disintegrate if he did not employ dedicated care.

As the garment fell away, Cale's hungry gaze sketched her alabaster skin, watching the rapid rise of her breasts above her racing heart. She was so perfect, so exquisite, that he marveled at the striking contrast between his tanned, calloused hands and the soft, pale texture of her flesh. His fiery silver eyes darkened with unfulfilled desire as they lifted to lock with those vivid blue pools. Cale monitored the disturbing effect of his caresses, watching all the sensations that flitted across her face.

Seeing her like this, watching her respond to his exploring touch provoked a wild stirring of passion deep inside him. It was a gnawing, burning hunger that created a monstrous craving that rivaled nothing he had ever experienced. Cale had presumed their splendorous tryst had been the pinnacle of desire. He had assumed that, once he had taken this lovely nymph, he would never again be overwhelmed by such a soul-shattering need.

Cale realized how wrong he had been. Their first encounter had been a mere stepping stone. The sensations he had experienced the previous day were now compounded by more complicated feelings. Cale was throbbing with forbidden hunger. He found himself swamped and buffeted by something deeper than simple, lusty passion, something more potent than physical desire. It was as if a part of him were missing, as if Mikyla had taken possession of some portion of his heart. He was stung by an obsession to make himself whole and alive again. He needed this wild, high-spirited minx to complete the circle that linked him as one body and soul.

Marveling at the direction of his thoughts, Cale fanned his hands over Mikyla's ribs and allowed his thumbs to drift over the thrusting buds of her breasts. She was the contrasting piece of the puzzle that he required to be content and satisfied. She was soft velvet and he was raw muscle. Her graceful beauty complemented his masculine strength. And together they formed the unique combination of life that blended brute force with feminine gentleness.

His worshipping caresses caused Mikyla to arch involuntarily toward him. Her lips parted to emit a ragged moan of pleasure. Cale's entire body shuddered with longing. He yearned to teach this exquisite nymph all the miraculous joys of lovemaking. Arousing her aroused him. He wanted . . . no, he *needed* to see the effects of his touch, to know that her hatred for him was a superficial thing. He wanted to know if she was feeling the same wondrous sensations he was experiencing.

Cale slid his fingertips beneath the band of her breeches to ease the garment from her hips. Another gasp tumbled from Mikyla's lips when she felt his adventurous hands mapping the landscape of her body. She closed her eyes to the rapturous torture Cale was employing to crumble the last barriers of her defenses.

"Look at me, Ky," Cale commanded, his voice no more than a ragged whisper. "I want you to watch me make love to you. I want you to see that I am not taking, but rather giving and sharing pleasure."

As if hypnotized, Mikyla's long, curly lashes fluttered up. And while his practiced hands made their slow, delicious descent, she saw and felt the magical flight of his fingertips over her skin. When her clothes lay in a pool around her ankles, Cale's adoring caresses flowed to and fro, investigating each sensitive point as if he were committing each curve and swell of her body to memory.

There was no taunting sparkle in those silver-studded eyes. Gone was the teasing smile that could inflame her temper. This complex, sometimes frustrating man was cherishing her as if she were his most precious possession.

For such a large, powerful man Cale was being unbelievably tender and patient with her. But then that was part of the paradox, Mikyla reminded herself as she peered into his ruggedly handsome face. And God forgive her for admitting it to herself, but she *did* care for him, more than enough to yield to the ecstasy of his lovemaking.

She knew the moment could not last forever and she knew her submission would come back to haunt her. But when she was in his arms it all seemed so right. It was as if she belonged here with him. She knew she was every kind of fool for permitting herself to be deceived into believing his affection would linger after their loving. But it was impossible to be sensible when his caresses and kisses were doing such incredible things to her body.

When Cale bent to press his sensuous lips to the throbbing tip of her breast, Mikyla clutched at his shoulders. The world was sliding out from under her. She was compelled to cling to his solid strength while the universe teetered wildly about her. But holding on to him didn't help. The world was revolving faster and faster, like a carousel spinning out of control. His butterfly kisses were drifting everywhere, setting wildfires to burn back upon each other until the leaping flames were a blazing holocaust of unfulfilled passion.

"Cale, please . . ." Her voice was a breathless whisper. Mikyla wasn't even certain what she wanted from him—to ease the gigantic craving or intensify it.

"Do I *please* you, little minx?" he rasped.

She felt his question ripple across her skin. And then, as if he had sprouted an extra dozen pair of hands, Cale began to weave a web of silken rapture, like a spider meticulously creating a snare from which there was no escape. It was a maze that led her deeper into a world of mystical sensations, a dimension of time and space that could not be seen, only experienced.

The purposeful path of his hands and fingertips, the lazy draft of breath that flowed in the wake of his kisses was maddening bliss. Mikyla arched closer, aching, burning up inside. She was his slave, his puppet, responding to the silent commands of his exquisite kisses and caresses.

And when she swore she would die in the sublime pleasure of it all, Cale laid her on his cot and stood back to devour her with molten silver eyes, those penetrating beams of liquid fire burning brands on her tingling flesh, holding her suspended.

Slowly, he worked the buttons of his tan shirt. With a shrug, the garment drifted down to join Mikyla's discarded clothes. Mikyla lay there, entranced. Her gaze traversed the rippling muscles of his forearms and chest, lingered on the thick matting of hair that shadowed his belly. She waited, her body aroused, her mind numb with the sensuous rapture of watching him push his trim-fitting breeches from his hips. He was raw masculine strength—rock-hard muscle and sun-bronzed flesh. He was magnificent, every well-sculptured inch of him, she mused as her eyes made a titillating journey over his naked flesh.

When Cale bent one knee upon the bed and towered over her, Mikyla reached up to comb her fingers through the crisp raven hair that framed his face. She drew his head to hers, her lips hungry for his kiss. Her hands began to explore with the same arousing techniques he had employed on her. Each time his massive body shuddered in response she became bolder in her explorations. She learned the rugged terrain of his body, discovered what pleased and aroused him. She was shameless with her touch, reveling in her ability to make this lion of a man respond to her adventurous kisses and caresses.

Cale allowed her intimate privileges, but it cost him dearly. Passion raged, coming dangerously close to bursting like a dam besieged by flood waters. Primal need had assumed command of his mind and body and he instinctively responded to her imaginative techniques. A guttural groan erupted from his lips when she enfolded him, stroking him, leading him ever closer. He wanted her, ached to satisfy the insane craving of being so close and yet so far away. He would have surrendered life itself to appease the wild torment her touch evoked.

"Do I please you?" Mikyla whispered back to him. Her hands glided upward to cup his face, bringing his lips within a hairbreadth of hers.

Ah, her lips, he remembered with a ragged sigh. They would melt like gentle rain upon his mouth. They were sweeter than wine and twice as intoxicating. He wanted her lips beneath his, craved to drown in the honeyed taste of her. But Mikyla denied him nourishment. She held him at bay, refusing to allow him to take her until his tangled lashes swept up to meet her penetrating gaze.

"Look at me, Cale," she demanded in a hushed whisper. "I am not just a woman, not just *any* woman. When we make love there will be no other memories from the past, no other face but mine . . ."

Mikyla knew it was pride that put such thoughts to tongue. But she didn't want to be a mere memory of passion, one among many. She longed for this to be a magical moment, an entity unto itself. She had never felt this way about a man and she refused to permit their lovemaking to become sordid and cheap.

Cale lifted passion-drugged eyes, allowing her to witness the fierce currents of emotion he should have concealed. Mikyla had turned his words upon him, demanding of him what he had earlier demanded of her. She was seeing the sweet agony as it swept through the craggy features of his face. She was watching him revel in the sublime sensations of possessing her.

And as he became a living part of her, every ardent emotion that had converged upon him exploded. His shuddering body surged into hers. He watched her arch to meet his demanding thrusts, observed the bubbling passion that was mirrored in the misty blue depths of her eyes.

They studied each other with a sense of wonder while they made wild, sweet love in the golden lanternlight. They reveled in the maddening sensations that avalanched upon them. With a gruff groan, Cale clutched her to him in sweet, satisfying release. He was living and dying, engulfed in the heady sensations that tumbled, helter-skelter about him. Aftershocks rippled through him like tidal waves. Cale surrendered to the intense pleasure that touched every nerve and muscle in his spent body.

The afterglow of their lovemaking could be bottled as a sedative, Cale reflected wearily. The tension that had claimed him for two hectic days drained from his body, depleting every ounce of strength. Mikyla's wild passion had exhausted him, mentally, physically, and emotionally. Cale felt utterly helpless, oddly tired, and yet incredibly satiated.

While the golden light glowed on his dark skin, Mikyla lay beside him, surveying his handsome profile, watching him drift into peaceful slumber. Impulsively, her hand glided over the rhythmic rise and fall of his chest, marveling at the tender emotion that tugged at the strings of her heart.

Why did this man, this giant of a man whose philosophies directly contradicted hers, arouse her to the limits of sanity? He delighted in mocking her and all that she represented until he made her positively furious. And then he would touch her with extraordinary tenderness and she forgot why she was so aggravated with him.

And through it all, Cale was transforming her into a hypocrite. One minute she was spouting her contempt for him. The next moment her emotions had reversed themselves and she was shamelessly begging for his kisses and caresses.

The memory of their wild, uninhibited lovemaking,

triggered another round of sensations. Her eyes darkened with renewed desire as her inquiring hands ventured down the rugged planes and muscled swells of Cale's body. Boldly, she caressed him, learning the feel of his flesh. Her kisses were light and inquisitive, tasting his masculine skin, feeling the rock-hard expanse of his chest and abdomen beneath her moist lips.

Cale came slowly awake to the most incredible sensations he had yet to experience. It was as if he were bobbing somewhere just beyond reality's shore. Gentle waves lapped against his skin like an incoming tide. Mikyla's caresses rolled over him, touching him everywhere and then quietly receding. Again they came, following in the wake of wispy kisses that ever so gradually built into the sweet crescendo of passion.

It wasn't the fierce savagery of desire that engulfed him, but rather the tender blossom of passion. The sensations came, toppling over him like a cresting wave, spilling through him like an eternal spring. And then, one delicious feeling gave way to another. Each surge of pleasure warmed him by degrees, altering his breathing, igniting subtle fires that nipped at his nerves and muscles, bringing them back to life.

Her hands and lips investigated and aroused, prowling everywhere, until Cale's entire body was besieged by a thousand tingling sensations. He had been consumed by a need that had virtually sneaked up on him. A groan of torment rumbled in his chest as Mikyla crouched above him. The dim light sparkled in the tangled mane of hair that cascaded around him. The lantern's glow captured the enchantingly lovely features of her face hovering just inches above him.

Cale could feel her silky skin upon his. She came softly to him, like the slow deliberate progression of day into night, easing the craving she had aroused in him. As she set the incredibly gentle cadence of lovemaking, his hands folded around her face, drawing her ever closer. She was teaching Cale things *he* had never known about passion, the tantalizing aura of innocent ingenuity. He had become *her* possession. She had taken him to her in her own unique way.

She no longer required hands and fingertips to caress him. Her body now caressed his as they moved together. Cale could feel the taut peaks of her breasts brushing ever so lightly against his laboring chest. He could feel her satiny flesh moving in perfect harmony with his. And when her lips melted upon his, Cale swore he had somehow been removed to a higher sphere. Passion enveloped him like a cocoon, and he was suffocating in splendorous paradise.

"Ky . . . ?" Her name burst from beneath her kiss in a helpless moan of rapture.

Suddenly, passion burst upon him and Cale was falling like a shooting star that had consumed itself in the heat of a thousand suns. A trail of ineffable sensations followed him as he was swallowed up in the darkness. It was as if he had floated in an incredibly exciting dream. But even in sleep, a hauntingly elegant face formed above him, leading him deeper into the bottomless sea of pleasure. The wild, free-spirited nymph who had inflamed him with desire was there, calling softly to him, accompanying him into the limitless depths of ecstasy, again and again . . .

A contented smile bordered Mikyla's lips as she quietly eased away. But just as suddenly as her smile appeared, it vanished. Sweet mercy! *She* had seduced Cale! Wasn't it enough that she had surrendered to passion? Did she have to compound her humiliation by rousing Cale from sleep to make love to *him?*

The thought pierced her soul like the stab of a newly sharpened knife. No matter how she sought to rationalize, she knew she couldn't blame Cale for this second encounter. She had made him want her after she had allowed him to exploit her. Cale had placed a price on her affection, her vulnerability. He had lured her father into a poker game that had left Sundance as the coveted stakes. Even when Morgan tried to prevent him from following through with his conniving scheme, Cale reacted without scruples. No doubt Cale saw Mikyla as a challenge and had set about to conquer her, using Sundance as a weapon against her. And now he had claimed the ultimate victory, Mikyla mused with a choked sob. She had sold herself for his lusty pleasure and she had condoned his actions by seducing him when he had not demanded it. Damn her foolishness! She had just become another notch on his bedpost.

With her pride smarting, Mikyla slipped from the cot to gather her clothes. Quietly, she snuffed the lantern and tiptoed outside. How could she ever face Cale again after the shameless way she had behaved? She couldn't even protest that she had given in to his bargain for the sake of her stallion, for *she* had initiated lovemaking while Cale slept. *She* had made him love her when he would have been satisfied to sleep beside her!

Mortification washed over Mikyla as she darted toward the corral to rescue Sundance from the restraining ropes Cale had placed on him. Why had she agreed to his wily bargain when the stallion was hers to begin with, not her father's? Mikyla almost hated Cale all over again for manipulating her. But she despised herself far more for permitting him to maneuver her. If he truly cared for her, perhaps she could have lived with her shame. But Cale was only interested in passion, nothing more. He only wanted to drive home the degrading point that she could never be his match, only his possession. She was like one of his blasted horses and mules—all objects with a price that were easily dismissed and quickly replaced.

Fearing she might awaken Cale and be forced to endure his humiliating taunts, Mikyla walked Sundance for more than a quarter of a mile before she swung onto his back. And then she wept like an abandoned child. It had taken a while, but Mikyla finally realized why she was hurting so deeply. It was because she truly cared for that horrible, deceitful monster. She was a pitiful judge of character and she wanted to see things in Cale that weren't really there. She wanted to believe their moments of passion were special to him, that he had lured her to him because of his own undeniable attraction. But it was her stubborn defiance that intrigued him, compelled him to demolish her protective armor and make her one of his many conquests.

Some men sought to seduce women just as confirmation

of their irresistible charm. Mikyla was only a challenge to be confronted. Cale Brolin had employed all methods at his disposal to seek victory in all his amorous conquests and Mikyla was no exception. That mortifying realization provoked her to dig her heels into the stallion's flanks and Sundance quickly responded, flying like the wind, drying her scalding tears.

Mikyla clung to Sundance's powerful neck, absorbing his strength, reviving her failing spirits. Tomorrow she would make the Run to her dream site. She would throw herself into building her own private world, a castle that would defend her from her haunting memories of the one man who was bold enough to touch her wild heart and gentle enough to crumble the walls that protected her from her own foolish desires.

Cale was now a closed chapter. Tomorrow would be the beginning of her new life. She had learned a valuable lesson from Cale's cruel tactics. Never again would she permit a man to prey upon her emotions the way Cale had. Now she knew what made men like Cale Brolin tick. He was like most of the ruthless, scheming creatures of the male species, and she would respond accordingly. No man would ever take advantage of her again. She had lost her innocence, but maybe it had been time for that. Maybe, in his own wicked way, Cale had done her a favor.

Mikyla no longer viewed the world through rose-colored glasses. She could see cold, harsh reality, the kind Cale warned her to expect when the Land Run began. She was going to have to fight for herself and her rights. Her dream of land and a prospering ranch was all she had left, and she found herself clinging fiercely to it. No man would ever use her heart as a doormat ever again. And Mikyla promised herself she would be prepared for anything.

But even her self-inspiring sermon would not be enough to sustain her in the following weeks. If she had known then what she learned later, she might not have condemned Cale. When he proclaimed the Land Run would lure wolves and other dangerous predators he wasn't exaggerating. But Mikyla was from Missouri, the "show me" state, and she wouldn't believe Cale until she experienced his prophecies for herself. She was laboring under the ill-conceived notion that if she were determined and perseverant she could see her dreams come true. But little did she know what lay ahead of her, of the battles she faced.

At the moment Mikyla couldn't see past the Land Run or her need to protect her heart from a man who had ridden into her life and turned it every which way but right-side-up. She had the uneasy feeling she had lost more than just her innocence to Cale Brolin, but she was too stubborn and determined to follow her heart. That was what had gotten her into trouble in the first place, Mikyla reminded herself as she thundered across the prairie, depending on Sundance to guard his steps. If she had been sensible she would have found a way around Cale Brolin instead of confronting him head-on. It was like attempting to plow through a brick wall. All Mikyla had received for her efforts was a bruised heart and a six-foot-four-inch headache that she feared would never go away, not when his memory kept unfolding itself from the shadows of her mind and blanketing her thoughts.

"Get out of my mind!" Mikyla muttered as she sailed across the countryside. But the vision of laughing silver eyes and a rakish smile rose like a specter in the night, granting Mikyla not a moment's peace.

She was stuck with Cale Brolin, perhaps not in body, but most definitely in spirit, Mikyla realized dismally. She could not outrun a man who had become a part of her emotions. But she would make certain no other man ever turned her inside out the way Cale Brolin had. Mikyla felt reasonably certain she could defend her heart against the rest of the male species, but Cale Brolin was an entirely different matter! It was going to take some doing to rout that man from her thoughts and extract him from her bleeding heart. His taproot ran deep, every bit as deep as the towering cottonwood trees that dotted the countryside.

Part II

There are two tragedies in life.
One is not to get your heart's desire.
The other is to get it.
     —George Bernard Shaw

Chapter 13

A furious roar exploded from Cale's lips when his heavily lidded eyes swept up to find Mikyla gone. That was not what he had intended! She was supposed to be by his side all through the night. He had planned to detain her, even if he had to nail her feet to the ground. Cale wanted Mikyla with him until *after* the cannons exploded, signaling the start of this insane race for land. Once Mikyla realized that she could not stake her dream site and finished cursing him to hell and back, Cale planned to persuade her—force her, if he must—to accompany him to Texas.

Muttering a string of colorful expletives, Cale vaulted out of bed and stumbled in the darkness to gather a fresh set of clothes. Cale wasn't so optimistic to believe Mikyla had wandered from bed for a predawn stroll. And sure enough, when he stormed outside, Sundance was gone. Damn her! She was supposed to have fallen into an exhausted sleep after they made mad, passionate love. But not that minx. For her, passion seemed to serve as a stimulant, not a sedative. Lord, he knew he should have tied her to the cot. Now he would be forced to dash frantically through a crowd of thousands to locate that determined firebrand. He had to dissuade Mikyla from this idiocy. The townsite company and railroad line would never allow her to enjoy her obsessive dream. Mikyla was running for a plot of ground that could never be hers!

Still cursing a blue streak, Cale tossed the saddle on the

strawberry roan. And, with fiend-ridden haste, Cale sailed off to find one comely blonde amidst ten thousand settlers who were about to swarm the borders of the Unassigned Land that lay in the very heart of the Indian Nation. In Cale's estimation, he didn't have a snowball's chance in hell of locating her before the cannons exploded and a tidal wave of humanity flooded in from the north, south, east, and west to claim coveted land. But that didn't prevent Cale from trying.

A shiver of anticipation skitted down Mikyla's spine. April 22, 1889, would be one of those days that divided history, and she was going to be a part of it. With a hopeful sigh, she stared up at the cloudless sky that was smiling down on the anxious settlers. Trees were in full leaf and the rolling hills were graced with the varying shades and colors of wildflowers. The sun shone with tropical radiance and a strong south breeze undulated through the thick carpet of grass.

All around her was the bustle of activity and the murmurs of excitement. Wagon wheels were being greased and given last-minute repair before the Run began. Riders had checked their saddles and bridles to ensure that all was in proper working order. By evening, cities would be established. Homesteaders would be sitting on their claims, occupying what had been vast prairie only hours before.

Every soldier who could straddle a horse had been sent to the Oklahoma line to monitor the movements of eager settlers and prevent them from charging into the area before noon. The shout of cavalry officers giving instructions, the barking of dogs, the whinny of horses mingled with the voices of homesteaders who were making a mass exodus to their position on the boundary lines.

Mikyla felt herself being swept along with the living wall of humanity that inched toward the Unassigned Lands. Those who were making the Run were wedging through the masses, literally toeing the line the cavalry had staked. As far as the eye could see, there was a string of horses, prairie schooners, carriages, mules—whatever means of transportation was to be had.

In each settler's hand was a long stick that resembled a fishing rod or lance. Each peeled willow limb was pointed at one end. The hopeful owner's name had been painted on the claim stick, which would mark possession of free land.

Those who had come as spectators or as the cheering families who encouraged their loved ones fell back to observe the first Land Run in the nation's history.

Those settlers who had intended to approach from the southern boundaries, marked by the South Canadian River, found the channel to be frothy red after the recent rains that had swept soil and uprooted trees downstream. Settlers crossing the river for the Run were forced to employ ropes to brave the raging swells of the channel, taking precious minutes away from their flight to free land.

Mikyla, however, had chosen to line up south and west of her dream site. It was difficult to hold her position with wagons and other horses bookending her stallion and ramming him broadside. At ten minutes until noon, blue-uniformed soldiers trotted up and down the line, shouting for the homesteaders to take their mark behind the stakes or risk being excluded from the Run.

Her gaze drifted down the human boundary line, wondering if her father had roused from his drunken stupor to climb upon one of his mules. Emet had been intent on staking a townsite lot that was not far from the approaching railroad. But Mikyla seriously doubted that Emet could stay on the back of his mule long enough to reach *any* claim.

Bitterness rose up inside her, thinking of her heated argument with her father and his spiteful scheme to lose Sundance in the poker game. Why was she even fretting over what had become of her father? It was obvious he had little consideration for her feelings. If he had, he would never have gambled Sundance away and she wouldn't have found herself in Cale's . . .

Mikyla squelched the vision of taunting gray eyes. This was the first day of her new life and she was not going to spoil this history-making moment by dwelling on a man who had been sent up from hell to torment her. She was participating

189

in the Land Run, whether or not Cale Brolin thought it was insanity. In fact, Mikyla didn't care what Cale thought about anything. Their stormy affair was over and she was on her way to a new beginning, to a long-awaited dream!

The grumbling of voices behind Mikyla drew her from her pensive musings. She swiveled in the saddle to see someone shoving bodies and horses out of the way. Mikyla's mouth dropped off its hinges when she recognized the man who was fighting his way through the human wall to approach her. Cale Brolin, looking as unpleasant as a coiled rattlesnake, elbowed his way through the maze of wagons and horses.

What the devil did he want? Mikyla asked herself sourly. He knew the cannon would sound off in nine minutes. This was no time for conversation. Dammit, she didn't want to see Cale again . . . ever. Why wouldn't he leave her alone?

"That is *my* stallion you are riding and I want him back," Cale scowled into her bewildered face.

"Your stallion?" she parroted in astonishment. "Are you mad? You know perfectly well what I was forced to pay to retrieve Sundance. And damn you for making me submit to such a bargain, Cale Brolin," she added in a quiet hiss.

Cale's eyes were brewing like storm clouds, ominous and threatening. "What we agreed to was an extra compensation, in *addition* to the six-hundred and fifty dollars in cash you promised to pay me," he snapped brusquely.

Cale was fit to be tied. For eight agonizing hours, he had battled his way through a sea of greedy settlers like a fish fighting its way upstream against the current. He had returned to Mikyla's camp, but she was nowhere to be found. After a frantic search, Cale had finally located Emet Lassiter. And by that time, Cale was so furious he had employed no tact or compassion with that miserable excuse for a man.

Emet had backslid as far as he could slide and Cale was itching to read him the riot act. Jerking Emet out from under the card table where he had been sleeping off his drunk, Cale had shaken the man until his teeth rattled. Firing questions like a barrage of bullets, Cale was aggravated to learn that Emet had seen nothing of his daughter since their argument the previous afternoon. The man didn't have a clue where to find his missing daughter and he behaved as if he could have cared less.

Cale had been so annoyed that he completely lost his temper with Emet. After several minutes of breathing the fire of dragons, Cale had finally gotten through the haze that clouded Emet's brain. When Emet was finally able to understand the ultimatum Cale delivered, he dragged himself into an upright position, but by the time Cale finished his bellowing tirade, Emet was cowering, afraid he was about to be beaten to a pulp. And if Cale hadn't been so anxious to find Mikyla he might have taken the time to do just that. Instead, Cale issued several venomous threats and stalked off to continue his frantic search.

And now, with only eight minutes to spare, Cale had located this headstrong vixen and it was going to require a full-fledged argument to remove her from the front line. "Since you neglected to pay in *full,* the deal is off," Cale growled at her. "Sundance is mine and I have no intention of selling him back to you."

This was the most important instant in Mikyla's life, a monumental moment of history and Cale Brolin was trying to spoil it. "You miserable . . ." Mikyla snarled mutinously as she fished into her saddlebag to retrieve every last cent she had in the world. "Take the money and be gone, you conniving scoundrel. Oh, how I hate you!"

"Tsk, tsk," Cale clucked with a goading smile. "There are ten thousand pair of ears listening." When Mikyla shoved the purse of cash at him, Cale shoved it back at her. "I told you the deal is off. All I want is my horse and don't you dare make a scene in front of the biggest audience in history."

Mikyla shoved the money into his midsection, along with her doubled fist, causing Cale to expel his breath in a pained grunt. "The deal is *not* off," she snapped at him. "Take your cussed money. Take it and leave me alone!"

Her voice had risen steadily and it was all she could do not to scream the words at him. Several pair of eyes swung toward her, but Mikyla didn't care. She wanted this infuriating man out of her way and out of her life forever.

191

Cale took her hand in a bone-crushing grasp and promptly removed it from his belly. "You aren't listening. I said there is no bargain, Ky. You should have paid the remainder of the price last night . . ."

"I did," she hissed through a grimace. Cale was dangerously close to breaking all twenty-seven bones in her hand at least once. "I paid more dearly than the normal person who purchased a horse for the Run."

"That's because you aren't a normal individual," Cale smirked.

Mikyla glared bullets through his dark shirt. "Nevertheless, you were amply paid," she gritted out through clenched teeth. "Indeed, I'm surprised you didn't extract, along with everything else, several pounds of my flesh!"

His steel-gray eyes narrowed on her, fierce and unrelenting. "You are not making this Run and especially not on *my* horse . . ." Cale broke off into several muttered curses when the rider beside him slammed against the roan, who then collided with Sundance. The mishap uncoiled like a serpent and for the next few minutes, everyone within a mile wrestled to regain control of their fidgety horses.

Two minutes and counting . . .

Cale was becoming desperate! If Mikyla didn't retreat they would be trampled by thousands of hooves and wagon wheels. "Dammit, I want you to come to Texas with me before you get yourself killed!" Cale demanded gruffly.

"No, I am making the Run and no one is going to stop me, especially not you, not after what you did," Mikyla sneered venomously.

"What *I* did?" Cale hooted like a disturbed owl. "What about what *you* did while I was trying to sleep? That wasn't the response of a reluctant, begrudging woman!"

Mikyla's face was suddenly stained with furious red splotches. She should have known Cale would taunt her about that. Indeed, he could probably survive months without nourishment, so long as he could feast on her humiliation and frustration.

One minute and counting . . .

"I hate you, Cale Brolin," Mikyla spewed poisonously. "If

192

I never see you again I will be the happiest woman on earth!"

When she twisted her head around to glower at the fertile prairie that sprawled before her, Cale clasped her hand, clenched around the saddle horn in a stranglehold. His silver-gray eyes were fixed on the determined frown. God, she was gorgeous, even when she was simmering like an overheated teapot. Cale allowed his admiring gaze to run from the hat that was pulled down over her blond hair, across the cotton shirt that complemented her high-thrusting breasts, to the form-fitting jeans that hugged her hips and thighs.

Thirty seconds and counting . . .

"Ky, don't do this. Believe me, you're going to regret it." When she refused to look at him or even acknowledge his presence, Cale expelled an exasperated scowl. "Come to Texas with me. I love you."

"You do not!" Mikyla came unglued.

She hated him even more for thinking she was foolish enough to fall for that empty phrase. Cale Brolin didn't know what love was—and neither did she for that matter. But he was still clinging to the offensive theory that every woman was an idiot and all a man had to do was tell her he loved her and she would succumb to any of his commands.

"I do too love you!" Cale spat the words at her.

It was the most ridiculous confession of affection Mikyla had ever heard. If Cale cared for her he had the strangest way of showing it. At best, Cale had mistaken *possession* for *love,* but she had difficulty believing Cale felt *any* sort of affection for her. She felt certain Cale was stung by his need to dominate her, to order her about as if she were a witless idiot.

He certainly wasn't behaving as if he cared for her. His actions spoke louder than words. What he should have said was that he had singled her out to make her life miserable and he was willing to say or do anything to spoil her dream of land and a home. She may have been a fool where Cale was concerned, but she certainly wasn't stupid! Cale Brolin did *not* love her. he didn't even like her and she detested her illogical attraction to him. He was deceitful and calloused and cynical and . . .

And then suddenly, resounding from over the hill, came the echoes of the exploding cannons from the distant Fort Reno. Before the bugler, who stood at the line, had lifted the horn to his lips, before the other officer could discharge his pistol, a wall of anxious settlers surged forward. All hell had broken loose and a human stampede thundered across the prairie to locate choice sites.

A cloud of dust mushroomed into the clear blue sky and a roar of cheering and yelling erupted as horses, carriages, and wagons trampled the prairie grass. Wagon poles splintered. Horses bolted and ran in all directions at once. Axles snapped under pressure. Those who were prematurely dumped on the ground fought to prevent being run down, each of them loudly exclaiming they had staked the first claim where they had fallen.

It was pure pandemonium, like a human cyclone demolishing everything in its path. Cavalry officers, wide-eyed and horrified, sought to fling themselves from the path of oncoming disaster. They rushed to save themselves and to aid the misfortunate settlers who had been injured by stumbling horses and careening wagons.

In the first few minutes of the Run, the swiftest horses formed the leading tidal wave that crested on the boundless meadows. Behind them was a second wave of wobbling wagons and prairie schooners that were engulfed in a cloud of congesting dust. Within several more minutes, riders began to fan out, searching for a suitable claim, determined to defend their land from other greedy settlers.

Cale found himself in the midst of something so overpowering that he was forced to race his strawberry roan or risk being gobbled alive. The cannons and exploding pistols had put Sundance to flight, and Mikyla had shot off with the first wave of greedy humanity, leaving Cale in midsentence. He swore if he were trampled, he would rouse long enough to insist that Miki Lassiter's name be listed on his death certificate, under cause of . . . She most certainly would be responsible, Cale thought bitterly. He wouldn't be here if it weren't for that high-spirited minx. Dammit, he was risking his life in a human stampede that he had condemned from the beginning!

Swearing in Spanish, Cheyenne, and English, Cale gouged his gelding to pursue the swift stallion with the flaxen mane and tail. Cale could barely see the shapely bundle whose long blond hair had fallen from the hasty bun she had pinned atop her head. Her wide-brimmed hat had flown off in the wind long ago. Through the suffocating dust of thousands of pounding hooves and rolling wheels, Cale finally realized Mikyla was leading the pack.

Cale's temper was at a rolling boil. He had employed every possible method to dissuade her, to prevent her from this insanity. And she had the audacity to scoff at him when he became desperate enough to say he loved her. Damn that stubborn hellcat. He had confessed to love her (whether he meant it or not) and the *least* she could do was hear him out. And then, if nothing else, she should have murmured a quiet, gracious thank-you . . . or something! But not that ill-tempered, ungrateful, ill-mannered spitfire, Cale silently fumed as he urged the roan into his fastest gait. No, Mikyla had ridiculed him in front of thousands of people. When he finally caught up with that infuriating woman he was going to strangle her!

Muttering to herself, Mikyla noted the existence of prepounded stakes all across the countryside. Sooners, she grumbled bitterly. Some of the settlers had managed to remain inside the boundaries without being spotted by cavalry patrols. No doubt they had slithered out from under their rocks before noon to set their stakes and then sat back to watch the less fortunate homesteaders scramble for claims. If anyone had sneaked in before the designated time and staked *her* dream site, she would . . .

Mikyla wrestled with the vicious thoughts that sizzled through her mind. If she gave way to violence, Cale would have one more reason to mock her obsession for land. Well, maybe she wouldn't kill anyone for cheating or attempting to stake the same claim she craved, but she wasn't going to *like* them for crossing her. Damned Sooners. They should have been forced to take their chances with the thousands of Boomers who stampeded into Oklahoma country! It wasn't fair. This Land Run was supposed to have provided equal rights for all those who gathered on the line to await the explosion of the cannons.

Her musings evaporated when she neared the rise of ground just north of her site. Mikyla held her breath and prayed nonstop as her eyes darted frantically about, searching for someone else's stake, hoping none would be there. Urging Sundance to push himself to the limit, Mikyla thundered toward the designated corner to set the stake which would register her legal claim. She heard the sound of approaching hooves closing in on her, but she didn't dare let herself become distracted, not now, not when she was so close to grasping her dream—her only chance at happiness!

Relief washed over her face when she realized the corner of her one-hundred-sixty-acre claim stood empty. Clutching the stake in her hand, a marker she had designed with thin strips of cloth to serve as a waving banner that could be seen at a distance, Mikyla yanked back on the reins. Sundance reared, his hooves thrashing the air, his eyes wild with excitement. Mikyla didn't wait for him to come down on all fours. She slid from his back and ran, stumbling toward the boundary stakes the government officials had placed on each claim.

To her disbelief, another stake struck the ground beside hers, just as she stabbed the marker into the grass. Cursing, Mikyla tugged the renegade strands of silver-blond hair from her eyes and bolted to her feet to confront the rapscallion who had set his claim stake the exact moment she had. Blind fury shot through her when she saw Cale Brolin looming over her. His broad chest heaved to such extremes that he very nearly popped the buttons off his dusty shirt. It had taken every ounce of energy and agility to dismount while his horse was at full gallop and arrive in time to place his improvised stake—a broken tree limb—into the ground.

A triumphant smile pursed Cale's lips as he towered over Mikyla. There he stood with his feet firmly planted on *her* land, *her* claim, mind you! Cale had done this just to spite her. Cale Brolin was the devil incarnate and his mission in life was to frustrate, humiliate, and annoy her until she went stark-raving, wild-eyed mad!

"What did you do? Rouse this morning and ask yourself how you could thoroughly and completely ruin my life?" she railed at him.

Cale didn't take the time to dignify her snide question with a suitably nasty response. He simply blurted out his declaration. "This land is mine. I staked it the exact moment you did and you were riding *my* stallion when you placed your claim. That makes this property *doubly* mine!

Mikyla might have taken time to appeal to his sense of decency and fair play, but she doubted he had any. She had had more than enough of this ornery, insufferable varmint. In a burst of fury, she lit into him with both fists, hammering on his chest as if she were driving nails and kicked his shins to bruised splinters.

"You'll have to kill me before I sacrifice my claim to you!" she spumed in outrage.

Cale blocked the flying fists and feet like a swordsman parrying the deadly jabs of his opponent's rapier. "Ky, get hold of yourself!" Cale barked sharply. "You're behaving like a maniac!"

"I'm not getting hold of myself until I get hold of *you*," Mikyla snarled at him, losing the last remnants of her temper. "You contest and counter everything I do. There will be no more of it! Get off my land and out of my life!" Her voice was growing higher and wilder by the second and she was so furious that she was seeing Cale and the entire world through a crimson red haze.

While Cale and Mikyla were sparring with words and fists, Morgan Hagerty galloped up to see the ruckus. It infuriated him that one of the two claims he was to seize and hold for the townsite company had already been staked. Although he was none too pleased about the complications, he found small consolation in the fact that Mikyla was lunging at Cale with claws bared. Morgan spitefully hoped she would tear Cale to bloody shreds. It was obvious they had both staked the same claim, one neither of them could keep. And it pleased Morgan even more to know that Cale would eventually be run off this land, whether he managed to snatch it away from Mikyla or not.

"Who placed the first stake?" Morgan demanded to know.

"I did." Cale and Mikyla called a cease-fire to answer in unison.

When Mikyla opened her mouth to protest that Cale was not the legal owner, he clamped his hand over the lower portion of her face and maneuvered behind her to dodge another swinging fist. "It's my claim, Morgan," he growled, annoyed to see his archrival while he was in the middle of fisticuffs with Mikyla. "And if she will give up and leave peacefully I won't file charges against her for stealing my horse."

Muffled curses exploded from beneath Cale's hand, which was squashing Mikyla's nose against her cheek and preventing her from saying all the rotten, degrading things that needed to be said about Cale Brolin.

Morgan gazed sympathetically at the wriggling bundle in Cale's arms. He might have climbed down from his mount to come to her rescue but he had yet to claim the adjoining property for the townsite company. "Find another claim, Miss Lassiter." His glittering green eyes drilled into Cale's carefully controlled stare. "You will find your satisfaction in watching Brolin lose this site and wind up with nothing. That might well be reward in itself."

With that, Morgan nudged his steed to seek out the other plot of ground the railroad and townsite company had designated for their community. Wicked laughter bubbled from his lips. He was going to enjoy watching Cale buckle beneath the pressure of the railroad and anxious settlers who had paid good money to establish a town on the banks of the South Canadian River. Before long, Cale would be without a claim and Mikyla Lassiter would detest the sight of him more than she already did. Morgan would personally see to it that Cale was paid the minimum price for his acreage. It would serve that bastard right for getting in Morgan's way twice in the span of two days.

While Morgan was driving his stake into the ground to

claim part of the land wanted by the townsite company, Mikyla and Cale were squaring off to go at each other again.

"Why are you antagonizing me?" Mikyla screeched into his amused face. "You don't want a homestead. You told me as much. What have I done to deserve your constant harassment?"

His gray eyes danced with devilment as they wandered over her shapely figure. Her hair was in wild, unruly tangles. Her face was smudged with dirt and perspiration and her clothing was twisted sideways after their scuffle. But even when this adorable spitfire was at her worst, no other woman could hold a candle to her natural beauty, her fierce determination.

"I'll make a deal with you," he stated, purposely ignoring her rapid-fire questions.

Mikyla's flaming glower was meant to burn Cale to a charred crisp. "I've tried to bargain with you before, and now I find myself facing charges of horse theft, though I cannot imagine how anyone can be accused of stealing one's own horse!" she yelled into his face.

From beneath the brim of his Stetson, Cale's veiled gaze reassessed her rigid stance. He knew he had dragged her as close to a ranting temper tantrum as she had probably ever come. "We will register the claim in both of our names at the land office."

"I am to share this claim with you? What a marvelous experience that will be," she sniffed sarcastically. "The next best thing to hell, that is."

Cale ignored her mutinous glower and her snide remark. "If you can manage to control that blazing temper of yours for *two consecutive weeks,* I will surrender the claim to you," he bartered. "No money will exchange hands and Sundance will again be yours."

Mikyla regarded him with a calculating stare. She was not about to agree to that proposition until she held some sort of advantage. Betting against her legendary temper was not exactly what one could call wagering on a sure thing. Her mind raced, attempting to determine how she could even the odds and hit this annoyingly arrogant weasel below

199

the belt . . .

When she stumbled over that thought a mischievous smile replaced her contemplative frown. Oh, how she was going to delight in watching Cale Brolin lose this bet. He had one weakness and she was going to prey heavily on it.

"And *I* will agree to relinquish my claim on this homestead if, for *two consecutive weeks,* you can curb your lusts . . ."

Cale laughed out loud. "All I have to do is keep my hands off you for fourteen days? You think I can't?" He let loose with an incredulous chuckle. "Honey, you should have conjured up a difficult challenge. This one is a piece of cake!"

"You have to curb your lust for *all* women," Mikyla stipulated with a wicked smile. "You cannot touch another woman, even if she throws herself at you, even if she wrestles you to the ground and demands that you . . ." Her chin tilted and her eyes darted away to prevent making visual contact with this loathsome scoundrel. "I think you know what I'm driving at . . ."

A deep skirl of amusement echoed in his chest. "I know what you're thinking, minx. But regardless of your low opinion of me, I can observe extended periods of celibacy without reducing myself to a pile of frustrated ashes," he boasted proudly.

"We'll just see about that," Mikyla sniffed caustically. "With your voracious appetite for women you will be suffering withdrawal symptoms by dusk."

Mikyla wheeled around and whistled for Sundance, but Cale intercepted the stallion's reins before Mikyla could grasp them. A taunting smile bordered his lips as he held the leather straps out of her reach.

"Sundance still remains in my possession until the end of two weeks. If you wish to use him you will have to ask permission," he said with a devilish grin.

Angry red stained Mikyla's features, but she caught herself the split second before she erupted like a volcano. "Very well, you can see to the feeding and caring of my stallion," she relented. "But if you abuse or neglect him . . ."

"You'll what? Lose your temper?" Cale snickered mischievously.

Although Cale was annoying her to no end, Mikyla drew herself up and pivoted on her heel, cursing the ornery rascal with every departing step. Cale monitored the gentle sway of her hips as she wandered to the river to drink, leaving him to defend their claim. When she disappeared into the clump of cottonwood trees, Cale sank down on the ground to chew thoughtfully on a blade of grass. All he had to do was badger that hot-tempered termagant until she exploded. *That shouldn't be too difficult,* he mused confidently. Mikyla was constantly flying off the handle and it required only the slightest provocation to set her off.

Once Cale forced Mikyla off the property, he would sell out to the railroad. There was no sense fighting the inevitable. Mikyla's dream site was only that—an unattainable fantasy. But it was for damned certain Cale wasn't going to inform her of the railroad's and the townsite company's intentions. That proud hellion would fight them both, tooth and nail, to save this piece of ground. And when the whole unfortunate affair was over Cale would . . .

Cale's thought processes bogged down when Mikyla sashayed over the rolling hill. Struggling to catch a breath, Cale swallowed over the lump that had lodged in his throat. So she intended to tempt and taunt him into defeat, did she? Cale's spirits plummeted as his eyes roved over her luscious body. Winning this wager might not be as simple as he had predicted. From the look of things, Miki planned to tempt him until the lusty beast within him took control of his mind and body.

Mikyla had indeed begun her sensuous assault on Cale's senses. With malice and forethought, she had tied her shirt just beneath her full breasts, refusing to fasten even one button. The gaping garment exposed the inner swells of her bosom to anyone who dared to look. The shirt, tied just so, also displayed her midriff and the trim indentation of her waist. Naturally, she had slopped enough water upon herself to leave the thin fabric clinging like a second skin. She had also tucked the hem of her tight-fitting jeans into her boots in order to accent her curvaceous hips and slim calves. Cale hated to hazard a guess as to what else was in store for him these next two weeks. Judging by this first effective assault, it was going to be a long, agonizing fortnight!

This was only the first phase, Mikyla mused when she caught Cale's blatant stare from the distance. That raven-haired devil wasn't going to believe to what extent she was willing to go to dispose of his aggravating presence. By the time she finished with this lusty creature he would be sneaking off to find a female to appease his animal needs. And Mikyla would be there to catch him red-handed. Then, Cale Brolin would have no choice but to walk out of her life once and for all. He would have lost the bet, hands down, because Mikyla vowed to maintain her good disposition for two consecutive weeks.

Nothing Cale Brolin did was going to upset her. She wouldn't wear her feelings on her sleeve. She wouldn't allow him to creep beneath her skin. No matter how much he provoked her, Mikyla was going to smile and count to ten, and even *ten times ten* if the situation demanded. Cale had met his match, and within fourteen days he would realize that he had been bested by a woman. Let him chew on that pride-crushing thought and see how he liked it!

And so began this great test of wills. Never had two people been more intent on deteriorating the other's firm resolve. Each action, each word was a meticulously calculated maneuver. Cale was never at a loss for pricking jibes and Mikyla sauntered about with as few clothes as possible without being dragged off to jail for indecent exposure.

Even though they were determined to dislike each other, they did not realize how quickly they would join forces at the first sign of trouble. Without giving the matter second thought, Cale and Mikyla would come to each other's defense when they were threatened. And Mikyla did not stop to realize that she had come to depend on this infuriating man who kept meddling in her life. All she knew was that Cale *was* interfering and she didn't have the foggiest notion why he was so hellbent on snatching her dream away from her when it was all she had to sustain her.

202

Chapter 14

The sun set in fiery splendor, flinging the last remnants of sunlight over the prairie. Mikyla dumped her belongings on the ground and prepared to erect her tent. For two days she and Cale had clung to their claim, protecting it from anyone who thought to seize it. The morning of the third day Cale had ridden to Reno City, a community that had literally sprung up in one afternoon. While he was recording their claim in the land office, Mikyla guarded their property. When Cale returned, Mikyla had gone to retrieve her supplies that had been guarded by the cavalry. It had been a long, exhausting day and Mikyla was anxious to erect her canvas home and collect wood for a campfire.

Mikyla had surveyed the landscape and had decided to pitch her tent on the bank of the river. Cale immediately objected to her foolishness, thankful he was not the one who was forced to control *his* temper.

"You can't set up housekeeping so close to the river," he snorted when Mikyla unfolded her tent. "The South Canadian is notorious for changing its channel. When the rains come, and they most certainly will, you might find yourself neck deep in quicksand and torrential waters. I've seen this river cut as much as fifteen to twenty acres from the north bank and create the same size sand barge on the south bank."

Mikyla didn't appreciate being told where to pitch her tent, but she countered Cale's domineering tone with a sugar-coated smile. "I do appreciate your free advice," she purred in sticky sweetness. "But considering what it's worth, I think I shall do as I please."

"Don't you usually?" Cale sniffed just as sarcastically.

"Now that we understand each other, why don't you crawl back under your rock before some other snake slithers up to steal your underground den?" she suggested before wheeling around to spread out the canvas and secure the supporting poles. "I have work to do and I cannot spare the time to spar with you. In fact, I find your conversation tedious and boring."

Cale glowered mutinously at her lovely backside, which was clad in jeans that were so tight they had to be squeezing her in two while they sent his blood pressure soaring. For the past few days, this spiteful nymph had flaunted her body at him with agonizing efficiency. She would breeze by him, leaving the scent of her perfume to clog his senses. She knelt directly in front of him, visually assaulting his eyes until they came dangerously close to popping out of their sockets. But all his attempts to rile her seemed sadly inadequate. Each time he hurled a biting remark, Mikyla refused to rise to the taunt. In fact, she was so civil and pleasant most of the time that it made Cale nauseous.

And then there were those occasions, like this one, when she cut him to shreds with her double-edged tongue—smiling all the while. Her remark had him grumbling under his breath. It had been a full, rich day. After waiting in line with at least two hundred other citizens who had come to stake claims and being pushed and shoved around like livestock, Cale had finally registered their deed for the land. As he strode across the street to buy himself a drink in one of the many saloons that had already been established in Reno City, Cale had stumbled on none other than Emet Lassiter.

The last time Cale confronted the worthless vermin he had issued threats. Cale was obliged to enforce them when he scraped Emet off the street. Yes, he had been rough on Emet, but the man deserved it, Cale decided. And Lord, what he had done to that pitiful-looking man! By the time Cale finished with him, Emet was alternately cursing him or whimpering like a whipped puppy. After making several arrangements, Cale had . . .

"Would you please move your tree stump of a leg?" Mikyla requested. "You are standing in the way of progress."

Cale not only moved, he left. He was not about to set up his camp on a flood plain like this stubborn minx who could not tolerate justified criticism.

It was after Cale had stomped off to erect his tent that Mikyla spied the movement in the underbrush. Fear riveted through her when four scraggly-dressed men waded from the river, armed with Winchester rifles and a various assortment of pistols.

Quick as a striking snake, Mikyla lunged for her rifle and dived for cover in the tall grass. Her frantic yelp only encouraged the intruders who swarmed in from all directions like an invading army. Her warning shot didn't faze the claim jumpers and she was forced to twist from side to side, firing at one approaching outlaw, permitting the others to rush in on her.

Despite her valiant efforts, Mikyla found herself surrounded. She didn't know which direction to point her rifle when there were four answering weapons aimed at her chest.

"Well, look what we have here?" Argus Freedman snickered. Resting his rifle on his hip, Argus scratched his bristled chin. "What do you think we ought to do with this pretty little thing, boys?"

"I've got several ideas," Samuel Thompson enthused, ogling Mikyla's seductive curves.

"This is my land and I am not giving it up," Mikyla spat at them. "I have already registered my claim in the land office and nothing you can say or do will force me to hand over the deed."

"My, ain't she the sassy one," Argus mocked. His expression became a hard glare when Mikyla shifted the barrel of her rifle to his sunken chest. "Four to one ain't too good of odds. Put the gun down before one of the boys has to do some bloodletting."

"*Two* to one odds," Cale's deadly voice suddenly corrected from behind them. "Now there are two rifles trained on you. That means maybe, just maybe, two of you might manage to walk away in one piece. But, being a betting man, I wouldn't want to put money on it . . ."

Argus nearly jumped out of his skin. "Who the hell is that?" he hissed furiously.

A victorious smile blossomed on Mikyla's features as the claim jumpers fell back, glancing around to determine the exact source of that gruff voice. "That is my partner," she informed them. "And if you have any regard for your hides, you better turn tail and run. But I won't guarantee that 'Dead-eye' Brolin won't be tempted to blow you to kingdom come just the same. He is as ill-tempered as a rhinoceros."

The implication that the unseen avenger who stalked them was deadly accurate with a rifle discouraged the claim jumpers, especially since it seemed it was their blood that was about to be shed. If "Dead-eye" Brolin was as daring as this feisty female, they would have a full-fledged battle on their hands. Deciding it best to prey on someone less capable of defending themselves, the desperados backed away and disappeared into the dense underbrush from whence they came.

"It certainly took you long enough to get here," Mikyla grumbled when Cale rose from the sea of waving grass.

"You're lucky I bothered to come at all," he snorted. "We made no pact about defending each other to the death. I could have saved myself a helluva lot of trouble if I had left you to your eager friends."

"Why *did* you come?" she asked him seriously, staring at his handsome physique as he strode toward her.

Cale broke stride. His arms dropped, dangling the loaded rifles beside his hips. "Damned if I know," he snorted, after giving the matter careful consideration.

Mikyla laid her weapon aside and walked purposely toward him. Opportunity was too ripe to ignore. Although Cale was not to touch her or any other female for two weeks, there was no stipulation that she couldn't touch *him*. That thought caused Mikyla to grin impishly as she closed the distance between them.

When Cale noted the ornery sparkle in her wide azure eyes, he frowned warily. "What are you up to, Ky? Whatever it is, I swear it's no good."

She paused directly in front of him. Reaching up on tiptoe, she curled her arms over his rigid shoulders to toy with the curly raven hair that hugged the nape of his neck. Wantonly, her body pressed into his, her breasts brushing suggestively against his rock-hard chest.

"I'm thanking you for saving my life," she explained in a soft, husky whisper. Her lips fitted themselves to his as she arched forward and upward, forcing Cale to brace himself or risk being knocked off balance by her enticing momentum.

Cale took it like a man—a man who was burning up on the inside and who could not return her overt display of affection without losing the bet. Suddenly, he wished he were a turtle so he could crawl into his shell to defend himself from her seductive charm. The feel of her luscious body left a searing imprint on his skin. The taste of her kiss was a thirst-quenching drink. Her feminine scent, flavored with the whole outdoors, was enough to drive a sane man mad. But Cale willed himself not to respond to the heart-stopping tenderness of her kiss or the potent impact of her touch.

Although he had endured the worst of her seductive affront, Mikyla was far from finished with him. Since he had accepted her kiss without responding, Mikyla rose to the challenge by bringing this giant of a man to his knees. Her fingertips nimbly worked the buttons of his shirt to reveal the hair-roughened expanse of his chest. Hands and lips that had been apprenticed by the master himself began to weave across his flesh, monitoring the accelerated thud of his heart.

Mikyla continued to arouse him, bit by agonizing bit. If there had been a wall nearby, Mikyla would have driven Cale up it. She had become a skillful seductress who knew how to excite a man, how to make him melt like snow on a roaring campfire.

"I have always been curious about the male species," she murmured against his tense flesh. "But until now I have never been able to appease my inquisitiveness without fearing repercussions."

Her hands slid inside his shirt to investigate the corded muscles that lined his spine. Cale swore an invisible pianist was playing an erotic tune on his vertebrae. It was a mark of heroism that he stood his ground without dropping his handful of rifles and clutching her luscious body against his.

"It is fascinating, is it not, that woman was created from a man's rib?" Mikyla mused philosophically. "She was not produced from his head to rise above him." Her wandering caresses scaled his shoulder to rearrange the ruffled hair that lay across his perspiring brow. "She was created from his side to be equal to him." Her hands migrated down the strained columns of Cale's neck to feather over his abdomen, feeling him flinch in attempt to control his disintegrating willpower. "Woman was made from a man's side to be protected by him . . . and near his heart to be cherished by him . . ."

Never did Cale imagine that being thoroughly thanked for rescuing a damsel in distress could be such bittersweet torment. Gnashing his teeth, Cale endured her tantalizing seduction and glared down at the appetizing bundle of femininity who forced him to tolerate a torture worse than death.

"If you are quite finished with your philosophical babbling, I should like to get to work," he muttered, his voice not as steady as he had hoped. "I have a stock pen to build before I sleep."

Cale was feeling the effects of her seductive ploy. Mikyla knew that as surely as she knew her own name. But Cale had shown incredible willpower . . . or perhaps she no longer appealed to him as much as she once had. The speculation cut deeper than it should have. It hurt to realize Cale saw her as a conquered challenge, one that could no longer tempt him past distraction. She wanted him to lose this crazed wager they had made in the heat of an argument. It would prove that he did feel something for her . . . although why it mattered so much Mikyla couldn't say for certain. But she needed to know Cale cared for her, even a smidgen.

Even during those times when Cale made her so furious she couldn't see straight, Mikyla could not contain the stirring deep inside her that resulted from having Cale within ten feet of her. Maybe she was attracted to him for all the wrong reasons and he didn't deserve one iota of her affection, but there was no getting around it. The man was impossible to resist, with his virile physique, his deep resonant voice, his devil-may-care smile.

Cale had deceived her and used her as his gambit. He had manipulated her and taken unfair advantage in every situation. And yet, she was like a senseless moth lured into a flame, knowing she would be cremated. But, confound it, Mikyla had grown accustomed to that ruggedly handsome face of his, accustomed to his tantalizing kisses and caresses that set her aflame. Cale had become an addictive habit. But within two weeks, one or the other of them would have to go. And then where would she be? She would have her precious land, the foundation of her dream, she encouraged herself. It would be enough. It would ease the heartbreak of finding herself the wounded pawn of this one-sided affair.

Mikyla was jostled back to reality when Cale, grumbling under his breath, pried her arms from his neck. The look that had captured Mikyla's elegant features tore at Cale's heart. God, he ached to gather her close, to end this pretense that she didn't arouse him, that her effect on him had diminished. But, dammit, Cale had to win this bet. Mikyla would accept her defeat from him—she wouldn't like it, but she would *accept* it. But she would fight to the bitter end to defy the railroad and the townsite company. Cale was not going to put Mikyla through that cruel ordeal. Let her think he had sold her out. She loved to hate him anyway, he reminded himself. She could cope with her contempt for him, but watching the powerful railroad company steal her precious land out from under her would be the crowning blow. It would be easier on her if she lost this bet, Cale reassured himself as he did an about-face.

"I hope Sundance is accustomed to work," Cale said out of the blue, drawing Mikyla's befuddled frown. "He is going to drag a stack of posts to the spot where I intend to erect my corral."

Mikyla stiffened. "Sundance is not a work mule," she

209

protested, careful not to lose her temper as Cale had anticipated. "He is a race horse."

An intimidating smile dangled on the corner of his mouth as he flung her a parting glance. "Not today he isn't," Cale drawled.

"Now that you have confiscated my stallion, what am I supposed to do if I need Sundance to steady posts while I build *my* fences?" Mikyla inquired after counting to ten twice. "I can hardly erect my pens without some kind of assistance."

Cale half turned, his smile broadening to display perfect white teeth. "That's your problem, little Miss Stubborn and Independent," he taunted.

As Cale strutted away, Mikyla hurled imaginary boulders at him. That low-down, good for nothing . . . Oh! If she wouldn't risk losing the bet she would pound him round and use *him* as fence post!

Thrusting herself into her chores, Mikyla wrestled with her tent and finally managed to leave the canvas structure standing upright. Well, almost. It tilted slightly west, but it was the best she could do without Sundance to steady one side of the tent while she secured the other.

With that accomplished, Mikyla aimed herself toward the pile of posts Cale had purchased for her in Reno City. Although the townsite was still no more than a congregation of tents and prairie schooners, lumber had been hauled into the area by the railroad that was rapidly building its way south. Mikyla had heard talk that the recently formed city might be forced to pull up stakes and migrate west to make use of the railroad that was rumored to miss the town because its citizens would not put up the money to lure the rails into their community.

Damned railroad, Mikyla muttered as she staggered forward with her fence posts. It seemed the directors of the railroad were out to make money at every opportunity. Mikyla knew of the townsite corporations that were alleged to have formed alliances with the railroads, but obviously the three powerful land companies that settled Reno City thought they could pressure the railroad. Apparently, they thought wrong. Trouble was brewing in Reno City. Several of the townspeople wanted to move to the new site where the railroad would cross the North Canadian River. Those citizens who had bought choice lots were threatening their neighbors to stay put.

Mikyla hoped the railroad and scrambling townsite companies would veer around her quarter section of land. She pitied the owners of the property that lay in the direct path of the railroad. It did not seem fair that the owners would be shuffled aside for a town that had set up housekeeping in the wrong location. Mikyla wouldn't have wanted to find herself in the middle of a bustling city. This land was going to be a prospering ranch, and that was the beginning and end of it!

While Mikyla labored over her corral, which stood empty until Sundance was returned to her, Cale ambled over the rise to prop himself against a tree. He had to give this little termagant credit, Cale mused with a reluctant smile. Mikyla was an industrious individual. The sun had set long ago but she employed a campfire and lanterns to continue working into the night.

"Would you mind holding this post while I nail the fence rail in place," Mikyla requested, balancing on one leg.

"Yes I would," Cale told her frankly. "Since you were so all-fired determined to claim this homestead for yourself, you can construct the improvements all by yourself. Besides, you already informed me that women were men's equal, and I already warned you the first heavy rain would wash out your corral. I am not about to expend my energy helping you erect a pen that is too close to the river."

Mikyla was sorely tempted to use the fence rail that was clenched in her hands as a club with which to beat Cale over the head. Damn him. He thrived on antagonizing her.

Resolving to perform the task that required four hands, Mikyla braced one leg against the corner post to hold it in place. Lifting the rail, she attempted to drive the spike. Suddenly, Cale was there to relieve her. But his hurried assistance knocked her off balance. Mikyla landed in a heap with the fence rail atop her. The hammer came down on her

211

shin. Muffling a curse, Miki untangled herself and climbed back to her feet, certain Cale had purposely rammed into her, determined to irritate her. This constant test of self-control was wearing her nerves thin and she wondered how she could endure eleven more days with Cale constantly preying on her temper.

"I'll make a deal with you, Ky," Cale offered.

"Lord, not another one," Mikyla groaned in dismay. "The last two were *two too* many!"

"We'll pool our supplies and work together on our building projects . . . that is, if you are agreeable to the suggestion. We will also combine our food. And if you will graciously consent to wash my clothes and prepare the meals, I will help you construct your livestock pens, even though they won't be standing after the first rain."

Despite his taunt, Mikyla realized she had to consider his proposition. There were simply times when two hands were not enough and she did not possess the strength required to construct sturdy corrals, fences, and sheds. And she certainly didn't have enough cash left to hire the tasks done. It had drained most of her funds when she purchased the tools and material to begin her land improvements.

When she glanced up to voice her compliance to Cale's suggestion her breath caught in the back of her throat. His shirt had gaped open and his bronzed skin glistened with perspiration. He was regarding her with a strange, undecipherable expression. It seemed a combination of frustration, concern, and desire. But it was always difficult to tell with Cale. He could guard his emotions so effectively when it met his whim. He could be masking killing fury or boredom, and it wasn't always easy to determine which one unless she caught the rumbling purr in his voice. The rumble was there, but it wasn't as gruff and ominous as it had been when he was truly angry with her.

Mikyla sighed disappointedly. She would never know what Cale was thinking or what he was really feeling. His facade was well controlled and he was not a man who expressed his private thoughts and emotions. He guarded his inner feelings like a protective watch dog. Except when he was mad as hell, Mikyla clarified. In that instance no one was safe within half a mile of him!

Hesitantly Mikyla inched toward him, permitting her own conflicting emotions to show in her wide blue eyes. Again, she reached up on tiptoe to bless him with a kiss, knowing Cale would assume she was taunting him. But somehow, tonight was different. She was feeling a need to display her affection for him, feelings she hadn't wanted to take root, feelings that had deepened, just the same.

"Thank you, Cale. It seems my lot in life is to possess a man's determination and dreams. But I will always be tormented because I don't have a man's physical strength to see my dreams through." Impulsively, she gave him a hug, one that could not be and would not be returned, even when it was killing Cale not to throw his arms around her and crush her to him. Her face nuzzled against the crook of his neck, her breath tickling his skin. "I sorely resented your intruding in my dream, but, to be honest, I am ever so thankful you are here now."

Clamping an iron grip on himself, Cale tolerated the sweet tormenting assault on his senses. Lord, he was left wanting things he couldn't have. It seemed an eternity since that mystical night he had lain beside Mikyla, watching her respond to his lovemaking, feeling her return his touch, caress for caress. She was the devil's own temptation and Cale was forced to defy his primal needs. But it was damned difficult when his body was making titillating contact with her supple curves and swells. And oh, how he ached to lose himself in a kiss that was sweeter than cherry wine.

Finally, Cale mustered the will to set her from him. "After we complete your corral in the morning, I need to tend to my own business. While I'm gone, you can prepare our meal. Agreed?"

Mikyla was aching for his skillful touch, longing for the feel of his sinewy arms. She didn't know who was being tortured the most, but from all indications it was she. Cale appeared to be functioning quite nicely while she was trembling from the aftereffects of molding herself to his warm, powerful body.

Not trusting her voice, Miki nodded affirmatively. When logic cut through the haze of desire that fogged her brain, Mikyla frowned suspiciously. "Will there be other women in the vicinity while you are *tending to business?*" she demanded to know.

Cale scooped up the fence rail, smiling secretively to himself. "No, but I wonder if you will *trust* me enough to take my word for it."

Her tapered fingers folded over his muscled arm, feeling the mass of potential strength beneath her hand. "Tell me the *truth* and I will trust you, Cale."

He fell, pell-mell, into the depths of those sparkling blue eyes like a swimmer diving from the towering rock above a river channel. Cale sorely needed a substitute for passion, a crutch to lean upon while this gorgeous minx was off limits. What he needed was to get rip-roaring drunk and forget this feisty female who was turning him wrong side out. But after seeing Emet Lassiter, Cale wasn't all that sure if he wanted to employ whiskey to forget what he didn't want to remember.

"I'm going to Blue Lake to retrieve another string of horses," he told her in a strained voice. "As you well know, there are no women at Caddo Jake's trading post. And I hardly think Reuben would appreciate my hugging the stuffing out of *him.*"

The mention of the secluded lake where they had first made love caused Mikyla to wince uncontrollably. The forbidden memories came flooding back, making her even more aware of the private, intimate moments they had shared, the sensations she had experienced, the incredible tenderness, the ardent passion . . .

Expelling a frustrated sigh, Cale shook off Mikyla's lingering hand. He was suffering the same longings that plagued Mikyla. And he remembered, with painful clarity, how perfect, how unique that day had been . . . until it had been spoiled by their argument. And Cale had sworn he wasn't getting involved, he reflected pensively. Now, wasn't that the shining example of "famous last words"?

"Yes, well . . . I suppose we should get back to work," he mumbled, deliberately focusing his attention on the corner post instead of the ripe swells of her breasts that were exposed by the daring décolleté of her shirt.

Mikyla was too preoccupied with her inner turmoil to question whose horses Cale would be retrieving the following day. If she had bothered to inquire she might have realized Cale had an inexhaustible herd of livestock grazing on the land he had leased from the Cheyenne and Arapaho. She had assumed, and quite erroneously, that Cale's funds came from the horses he had sold for exorbitant prices to settlers.

For more than an hour, Cale and Mikyla worked in companionable silence. Mikyla was oddly content to have Cale laboring beside her, helping her construct her dream, offering suggestions and instruction without intimidating her, even when opportunity presented itself.

When they parted company, Mikyla watched Cale disappear into the darkness and then she fished into her saddlebag. Chewing on the dried beef that served as her supper, Mikyla pondered the events of the past few days. And each of her musings was centered around Cale. She kept seeing him change moods, feeling his passion as he . . .

Mikyla squeezed her eyes shut and blocked out the arousing thought. She had to concentrate on her dream, not on a man who would soon ride out of her life. She was a fool if she became so attached to Cale Brolin that his leaving would spoil her dream. Cale had no desire to stay and build a ranch, to put down roots. When he lost this ridiculous bet he would be long gone and there would be a string of women to replace her. If she was smart, she would never allow herself to forget that.

Grappling with that thought, Mikyla crawled into her tent and collapsed on her cot. She was exhausted. There would be no reason to fret if Cale might steal into her dreams this night to frustrate her. She was much too tired for that . . . or so she thought. It was dispiriting to learn that the night had silver-gray eyes and protective arms that wrapped themselves around her like a warm security blanket. Even in sleep Cale was there to haunt her, to rekindle the memories of passion and pleasure that defied rhyme or reason.

Chapter 15

The sun played hide-and-seek behind the clouds that paraded across the Oklahoma sky while Mikyla and Cale worked together to construct a small shed that would hold her supplies. They had roofed the structure earlier that morning and had begun the north wall. Mikyla hoped they would complete at least two walls by evening. She was impatient to construct all the necessary out buildings. And, even with Cale's help they could not erect the structures quickly enough to satisfy her.

"I saw your father in Reno City yesterday," Cale said before hammering a board into place.

For a moment Mikyla didn't respond. She well remembered Morgan Hagerty telling her that Cale had taken advantage of Emet while he was overindulging in liquor. Mikyla was hounded by bitterness toward both Cale and her father.

"What was he doing?" she questioned quietly. "I didn't notice his wagon in town when I was running errands last week."

Cale could tell he had broached a sensitive subject, but he couldn't understand why Mikyla had flung him a reproachful glare. "I know you think I deceived you," he felt compelled to say. "But Emet was about to lose Sundance to Morgan Hagerty and I didn't . . ."

His comment was interrupted by her incredulous laugh. "To hear Morgan tell it, which I most certainly did, *he* was attempting to save Sundance from *you*. And when Morgan offered to buy Sundance from you he said you beat him up!"

Cale's head swiveled around to survey Mikyla's disparaging glower. "And you think that's the way it happened," he speculated, his voice carrying an undertone of bitterness. "You would take the word of a professional gambler over mine?"

"Why shouldn't I believe him? Morgan has been a perfect gentleman in my presence," Mikyla defended tersely.

"I'll just bet he has," Cale growled sourly.

His snide remark caused Mikyla to bristle with indignation. "Morgan is easier to hold at bay than you are," she declared, forcing herself to control her temper. "When I rejected his advances, he respected my wishes while you tromped all over them!"

Cale wheeled around to glare down into her face. "Stay away from him, Ky. Morgan Hagerty is dangerous, whether you believe it or not."

"More dangerous than you are?" Mikyla's delicate brow elevated to an inquisitive angle. "From experience, I can safely say it's the other way around."

The topic of conversation spoiled Cale's mood. "I only intended to tell you that your father set up shop at the north end of Reno City."

The topic of conversation put a strain on what had been a pleasant morning. Cale busied himself with completing the north wall of the shed and then stashed the tools inside it. Without another word, Cale strided over the hill toward his own camp. Disconcerted, Mikyla watched Cale ride off, leaving her to defend the claim and prepare a meal. Cale had only been gone an hour when Morgan Hagerty, dressed immaculately as always, appeared from the east boundary of her property.

Touching his black felt hat in greeting, Morgan dismounted. "I thought perhaps you had settled your disagreement with Brolin and had located elsewhere," Morgan commented as he reached out to wipe a smudge of dirt from Mikyla's cheek. "I've been concerned about you, Mikyla.

The thought of leaving you to fend for yourself against Brolin unnerves me."

Cautiously, she backed away, uncertain who to believe—Morgan or Cale. "Mr. Brolin and I have a working arrangement. Within the next nine days, one or the other of us will become sole owners of this property. Until then, we are each making the improvements required for legal ownership, dictated by the Homestead Act."

"I would like to buy your quarter section," Morgan announced abruptly. "You will be paid top price."

Mikyla's eyes took on a determined glow. "I have no intention of selling to anyone. Mr. Brolin will soon realize I have come to Oklahoma country and that is where I plan to stay, for better or worse. When he becomes restless and decides to move on, I will still be here. But no amount of money will purchase this quarter section of land!"

Morgan surveyed the stubborn tilt of her chin, an expression he had noted on several other occasions. "I don't want to see you hurt, Mikyla. But I think it wise to inform you that a townsite company has interest in this site. It is also rumored that the railroad will cross the river just below your newly constructed corral."

The news set fuse to her temper. "I am not moving. The railroad can find another location to cross the river."

A tight smile thinned his lips. It seemed Mikyla was going to put up a fuss. She might need to be taught a lesson before this matter was settled. "If you make waves, you may also be forced to suffer the consequences. I have been contracted by one of the townsite companies and I have consented to sacrifice my quarter section, which joins yours on the east. You will see, as I have, that one man cannot fight hundreds of anxious settlers who wish to build a town, not to mention the powerful executives of the railroad who have predetermined where they will lay their rails. The railroad is rapidly building south and no one is going to stop them from taking the most practical route."

As Morgan strode away, Mikyla silently fumed. Dammit, she wasn't sacrificing her dream site for any amount of money! This was her property, *free* property claimed in the Run.

Still steaming over her conversation with Morgan, Mikyla flounced about camp to gather wood for a fire. She had to win her wager against Cale and force him off her land. If he won the property, he would sell out in a minute. But Mikyla wasn't going to be moved as if she were a sack of dirty laundry! This was her claim. She had staked it, abiding the regulations set by the government. Anyone who thought to remove her from the premises would have to carry her away, kicking and screaming, and at gun point!

The spring of 1889 was plagued with rain. Every time Mikyla turned around the sky was threatening to open up and dump several more inches of rain upon her. Just when the prairie was about to dry out, another drenching rain came pouring down. An annoyed frown puckered Mikyla's brow when threatening black clouds gobbled up the sun, engulfing her in gloomy shadows. A distant rumble of thunder shattered the peaceful serenade of crickets and bull frogs and set Mikyla to grumbling. Hurriedly, she water-proofed her campfire and glanced west, wondering what had detained Cale. He had been gone since morning, and she was itching to know if he had spent the day with some eager female.

As darkness settled over the prairie the black shadows stretched toward the towering cottonwoods and bowed willows that lined the river. Another clap of thunder broke the silence, causing Mikyla to glance skyward. Confound it, where was Cale? She had spent the entire afternoon plotting their evening encounter. If he didn't return to camp all of her planning would be for naught.

Mikyla had garbed herself in the most provocative gown she owned, hoping to force Cale to break his vow of keeping his hands off her. She knew she had to gain sole ownership of the property . . . and quickly. If Cale learned the townsite company was interested in the land, he would try to persuade her to sell. This land meant nothing to him. It was only his way of harassing her. But this site meant everything to

Mikyla and she was determined to keep it.

When she finally caught sight of Cale's striking profile against the gathering storm clouds banked in the northwest, her heart leaped in pleasure. If only they weren't constantly at cross-purposes, if only Cale felt some affection for her . . . Mikyla squelched the wistful notion. She promptly reminded herself of her purpose and proceeded accordingly.

Cale tripped over his own feet when a vision of pure loveliness floated toward him. Mikyla was dressed in a sheer muslin gown that matched the dazzling color of her eyes. The provocative dress exposed her bare shoulders and swooped low on her bosom. The flickering campfire sprayed through the gossamer fabric, displaying her enchanting figure with such devastating effectiveness that Cale reduced himself to a cloud of steam.

He had already spent the day listening to Reuben heckle him about the feisty vixen who had him building corrals and sheds instead of roaming the plains, as was Cale's usual custom. And now this, Cale thought glumly. Tonight looked to be another maddening assault of his senses.

Dammit, it couldn't have come at a worse time. He had escaped Reuben's teasing, only to find himself lingering on the shores of Blue Lake. There, through the waning shafts of sunlight, he had been visited by sweet, arousing memories. He could see Mikyla drifting upon the sparkling water like a graceful swan. He could see her luscious body in the clear depths. He could hear her irrepressible laughter and feel the warm, fierce passion that had consumed them . . .

Her small hand slipped into Cale's, jolting him back to reality. "Come, love, I have prepared a feast for a returning king," she whispered before leading him back to the fire.

Cale wasn't certain if it were distant thunder or the explosion of his heart that rumbled in his ears. God, this night would surely be the unique combination of heaven and hell. He was to be granted a view of this bewitching nymph, but he was not allowed to touch. She would seduce him with her beauty and her feminine wiles and he would be forced to battle the beast within him once again.

Determined not to fall prey to her charm, Cale immediately set about to counter her alluring spell. After consuming one bite of the freshly roasted rabbit she had hunted and prepared, Cale began cursing and choking simultaneously.

"My Lord, woman," he sputtered. "What did you put on this meat?"

Mikyla sat upon her wooden stump, staring frog-eyed. "Nothing, especially not poison if that's what you're thinking."

"I wouldn't put it past you." Cale sucked in a ragged breath and then burst into another coughing spasm. "Killing me would be the perfect solution to your problems," he managed to choke out.

Unsympathetically, Mikyla whacked him between the shoulder blades, spitefully wishing she had a hatchet in her hands. "I may want you off my homestead, but I had *not* planned to see you buried beneath it." It hadn't occurred to Mikyla that Cale was feigning his act. She hadn't tasted the meat and she honestly thought he was on the verge of choking to death.

Although Cale was famished and Mikyla had prepared the meat superbly, he cast it away, plate and all. "You obviously can't cook. You certainly can't build fences, and you can't even pitch a tent that stands perpendicular to the ground. I'm doing all the work and *your* input couldn't fill a thimble!" he growled at her.

Instinctively, Mikyla doubled her fist and cocked her arm, wondering wickedly how this big ape would look with both eyes on the same side of his face.

The transformation of Cale's expression halted her arm in midair. He was preparing himself for a sound smack in the jaw. Indeed, he was inviting it! He wanted her to pound him into the ground with the vigor of a carpenter driving nails and she had come dangerously close to delivering a blow that would officially end this wager!

"Come on, Ky," Cale taunted with a goading chuckle. "Hit me. You know you want to. You know you have wanted it since the moment I staked this claim alongside you." When she stood frozen like a pillar of stone, Cale raked her with scornful mockery, antagonizing her, testing the very limits of her self-control. "You're a lousy cook. I seriously doubt you can boil water without botching it up. The reason you're so trim is because you can't choke down your own meals. Indeed, they aren't fit for human consumption. I would rather sink my teeth into roasted bark. It would be more appetizing than the skunk meat you tried to feed me."

Cale's cutting jibes would have tried the patience of a saint, and Mikyla was a far cry from sainthood. She was the first to admit she had a devil of a temper, but she was slowly learning the meaning of self-control.

Defying Cale's infuriating smile, she unclenched her fist and allowed her arm to drop to her side. Slowly, she closed the distance between them and her arms looped over his shoulders, her hands linking behind his neck. Tilting her head just so, the glorious mane of silver-gold hair trailed down to her waist like a cascading waterfall. When she inched closer, her generous display of bosom was pressed upward, leaving Cale drooling in desire.

She might as well have laid a hot branding iron upon his flesh. It could not have seared him more thoroughly. From his towering height, Cale could look down into the most enchanting face ever to cross his line of vision. Eyes as brilliant blue as the coming dawn drilled into him. Hair that was the lustrous combination of sunlight and moonbeams framed her oval face. Her peaches-and-cream complexion was aglow with the luminous firelight. Long lashes, incredibly thick and curly, feathered from the rim of those entrancing brilliant azure eyes.

Sweet tormenting agony, the kind that stemmed from wanting and having not, ricocheted through Cale's body. His assessing gaze skimmed her delicate features, wandered down the ivory column of her throat, and settled on the full mounds of flesh that were pressed against his heaving chest. Through the thin fabric that separated them, Cale could feel her abdomen against his loins, her thighs imprinted on his muscular legs, legs that suddenly felt as sturdy and supportive as melted butter.

"You're right, Cale," she agreed in a piquant voice that reduced him to a puddle of liquid desire. "I can't cook." Her

223

skillful hand mapped the craggy lines of his face, turning his commanding features into mush. "I'm incompetent with a hammer and nails." She moved, strategically placing herself full-length against him, leaving not one inch of them separated. "Indeed, there is very little I can do and do correctly. And because of my shortcomings I envy you."

Her fingertips speared into his crisp hair, directing his head toward hers, bringing his full mouth within inches of her sensuous lips. "You are the personification of what I would like to be, but never can be—a tower of strength, a force to be reckoned with, undeniable vitality . . ."

When her lips took his into captivity, Cale didn't feel much like a reckoning force. He rather thought he resembled a burnt marshmallow—crisp and crusty on the outside and soft and gooey on the inside. Cale didn't dare move. He couldn't breathe while he was being subjected to this tenderly devastating affront. If he responded to her tantalizing kiss, all would be lost—his male pride, their wager . . . Hell, just about everything would go up in smoke, Cale reminded himself shakily.

How easy it would have been to disregard his purpose, to satisfy his selfish craving for a woman. But not just any woman, Cale amended as he held himself rigid while Mikyla continued to work her sweet hypnotic magic on his emotions. There was only one female who remained just beyond his grasp. She was a woman with the heart of a lion and the exquisite gentleness of an angel.

Only one woman haunted his dreams and tormented his waking hours. Cale wanted Mikyla in ways he had never wanted another woman. And yet he didn't want her at all. She made him feel vulnerable, out of control. She was the quintessence of graceful beauty and undaunted spirit. She was every man's dream, but, more specifically, Cale Brolin's nightmare. He had pitted himself against a female who defied the laws of nature. Although she had modestly denied it, Mikyla was any man's equal. What she lacked in strength she compensated in sheer will and perseverance.

When Mikyla realized she had lost this battle of wills, she withdrew, fighting like the devil to mask her disappointment. It was no longer the challenge that motivated her. The feel of Cale's steel-hard flesh meshed into hers provoked forbidden memories of intimacy. Although Cale appeared unruffled, Mikyla was a mass of unfulfilled desire. She ached to lose herself in the splendor of his passion, to allow her senses to take flight and soar beyond the horizon.

The flash of lightning and delayed rumble of thunder tugged Mikyla from her pensive contemplation. "I suppose I had better retire to my tent," she murmured softly. "I have been told it isn't wise to defy the thunder and lightning."

Cale remained immobile, as if he had been planted there. His devouring gaze followed Mikyla as she ambled across camp to take refuge in her tent. Cale wondered if Mikyla had planned this next bit of torment. Somehow he doubted it. After she had failed to see him buckle beneath her charms, she had suddenly become withdrawn and preoccupied. Had she known how dangerously close Cale had come to casting their wager to the wind she would have enjoyed some small consolation. But he wasn't about to confess that having her so close and yet so far away had very nearly melted the glue that held him together?

Moaning in misery, Cale stared unblinkingly at the dark silhouette cast by the lantern in Mikyla's tent. Unaware of her audience of one, Mikyla pulled her gown from her shoulders and pushed it from her waist. Cale swallowed his Adam's apple while he gawked at the perfectly formed feminine silhouette. She stood unclad inside her tent, oblivious to the fact that Cale was being granted a view that made his body shudder in frustration. There, sketched in the light and the shadows, protected by canvas walls, was a sculpture of unrivaled beauty—the ultimate dream.

Cale watched, totally entranced, until Mikyla pulled on her nightgown and stretched out on her cot. When the lanternlight finally evaporated into darkness, Cale felt himself collapse. On weak knees, he wobbled back to his camp to wait out the approaching storm. But the storm within was far more frightening than the one that whipped around his tent.

Rain came in torrents, drumming at the canvas like

impatient fingers. The wind howled like a banshee and lightning ripped jagged holes in the bleak sky. Cale swore he had lain there for hours, fighting to regain control of himself and constantly losing ground.

Damn his promises! He could have been cuddled in Mikyla's silky arms, riding out the thunder, lost in passion's stormfire. But no, he had to go and suggest this ludicrous wager. Hell, what difference did it make who won? Mikyla was going to be bitterly disappointed, no matter how he chose to handle the situation. She would lose her dream site. That was as plain as the nose on his face. Cale had only stayed in Oklahoma country to lessen the blow and protect her from harm.

Perhaps he should just tell her the truth, admit defeat, and cure this fever of wanting that was burning him alive. After the loving, when logic returned, Mikyla would instigate their final argument and he would walk away. That would be the end of this maddening preoccupation with Mikyla Lassiter. It would be over and done, and her dream site would become a thriving city, served by the coming railroad.

Deciding that he was only prolonging agony, Cale swung his long legs over the edge of the cot and walked outside. Although buckets of rain were still pouring from the sky, the worst of the storm had followed the river and lightning flickered only in the distance. Swiftly, Cale marched across the soggy meadow. Inhaling a courageous breath, Cale drew himself up at the entrance of Mikyla's tent.

"Ky, I want to talk to you. It can't wait," he declared in a no-nonsense tone.

Mikyla didn't answer.

"Dammit!" Cale swore savagely as he fought his way through the canvas flap. "Mikyla, did you hear me? We have to talk . . . now."

Another curse exploded from his lips when he discovered Mikyla wasn't in her bed. Had those claim jumpers returned to have their revenge? Had she cried out for his assistance, only to have her pleas drowned by the clatter of rolling thunder and driving rain?

A terrified shriek reached Cale's ears and his heart turned

back somersaults in his chest. The startled cry had come from the river, now swollen from the heavy rains. Cale took off like a shot, stumbling over the driftwood that had washed across the flood plain.

Mikyla's second bloodcurdling cry caused Cale to veer east toward what had been the corral site. But there were no corrals or stock pens. The angry river had changed its course, carving a new channel through what had previously been ranch improvements that were shaded by stately cottonwood trees. Now the trees stood in the middle of foaming water and quicksand!

Swiftly, his keen eyes scanned the river that danced with raindrops And there, clutching the trunk of a tree, was Mikyla. She was sobbing hysterically and her hands bled from her attempt to clutch the bark while the raging current sought to drag her into its whirling depths. Cale wheeled, running blindly back to Mikyla's camp, frantically searching for a rope.

The channel was running too high to swim a horse through it without the risk of being washed downstream. His only hope was to lasso Mikyla and drag her ashore. But even if he succeeded in roping her among the tangle of uprooted trees and shifting sands, he couldn't guarantee she wouldn't drown while he pulled her to solid ground.

Cale's hands finally landed a rope that was piled among Mikyla's belongings. He glanced north to release a piercing whistle. Although Sundance was penned with the herd of horses, Cale didn't doubt the stallion would answer the summons. If Sundance thought his mistress was calling to him he would make short work of finding a way over or through the corral. And Cale didn't care if Sundance kicked the pen to smithereens and the other horses thundered off in all directions. He would gladly spend a day rounding up horses if it would ensure Mikyla's safety.

The thud of hooves on the soft, sandy flood plain brought relief to Cale's tense features. Although Sundance didn't appear particularly thrilled to see Cale, he didn't bolt and run. Speaking softly, as Mikyla would have done, Cale laid the rope over Sundance's head and urged him toward the roaring river. It wasn't until Mikyla's hysterical scream shook the darkness that Sundance stopped dragging his feet and followed Cale without being forcefully tugged.

Cale's breath stuck in his throat when he realized what had evoked Mikyla's frightened shriek. The tree to which she clung had given way to the fierce, overpowering current. No doubt, Mikyla had to fight her way back to the surface when the tree crashed into the river. The cottonwood had swirled sideways, lodging against two other upended logs. The wooden dam blocked the channel, causing a rolling wave of water to topple over Mikyla.

Although he had hurled a lasso a thousand times and was confident that he could perform the feat in his sleep, Cale suddenly questioned his abilities. The one time he needed to be perfectly accurate, he felt like a quivering mass of jelly. Gritting his teeth, he circled the loop over his head. His eyes were fixed on Mikyla's partially visible body bobbing in frothy water and draped in gloomy shadows.

His first attempt at rescue tangled in the protruding branches. Swearing under his breath, Cale snapped the rope to release it from the snagging limbs. After he finally managed to retrieve the lariat, he tried again. This time, almost miraculously the loop landed around the protruding limb and over Mikyla's shoulders.

Cale barked a sharp order for Mikyla to loose one hand and push the rope to her waist, but she was too petrified to obey. Holding on for dear life was an instinctive reflex and Mikyla was frozen in place. Scowling, Cale pulled off his boots and grabbed hold of the lifeline between Sundance and his half-drowned mistress. Cale was thankful he had taught the sturdy stallion to respond to a few commands while they were dragging posts to build stock pens. Now Sundance had to perform the same task. The only difference was that this was a matter of life and death for both Cale and Mikyla.

With his hands clenched around the taut rope, Cale fought the cold, raging current to reach Mikyla. Widening the loop, Cale wedged himself in beside her and then shouted a command to the waiting steed. Mikyla, half-dazed with fear, screeched at the top of her lungs when she felt her fingers being pried away from the tree bark. It seemed unnatural to unclench her hands, now bloody from clinging to the bark. She heard Cale's harsh, impatient voice, remembered the protective feel of his arms around her, but her brain was too waterlogged to respond.

Cursing the fact that Mikyla was as much help as a wet dish rag, Cale shoved her face into his shoulder. When he had pried her loose from her death grip on the tree, Cale shouted for Sundance to drag them across the swollen river. The ominous current towed them under and Cale swore the muscles in his arms would snap from the intense pressure. The breath he had inhaled seemed insufficient to sustain him while he was being churned and spun in the sandy depths.

Submerged limbs reached out to ensnare him like the oppressive arms of death. Cale felt Mikyla go limp in his arms and he cursed vehemently to himself when his lungs threatened to burst. Thrashing wildly, Cale tried to determine which way was up, but in the frothy water and swirling darkness even that was next to impossible.

The split second before Cale thought he had breathed his last breath, he felt the water ebb. Risking all, Cale gasped for air, thankful he wasn't inhaling another gallon of water. He could feel the slow, methodic pull of the rope, but he couldn't see Sundance on the shore. The pelleting sand stung his eyes, virtually blinding him.

Suddenly there was solid ground beneath his feet. Cale was never so happy in all his life! Calling to Sundance to freeze in his tracks, Cale wrestled out of the loop and scooped Mikyla's lifeless body into his aching arms. A mass of muddy blond hair trailed over Cale's elbow as he struggled to fling Mikyla over Sundance's back.

After smacking Miki on the back several times, she sputtered and choked. But then, drawn back into the looming arms of darkness, Mikyla collapsed against the stallion's ribs. Praying frantically, Cale urged the steed up the incline to his tent. There was no way in hell that he was setting foot in Mikyla's canvas cabin. It was too near the raging river to be considered safe.

229

"Blast it, if you would have listened to me in the first place this wouldn't have happened," Cale scowled at his unconscious companion. "You do not go traipsing out in the middle of a storm to determine if your corrals have been swept away!"

Feeling consolation after he had scolded her for her idiocy, even if she hadn't heard a word of it, Cale dragged her lifeless body from the steed. After staggering into the tent, Cale placed her on his cot. With the lantern illuminating the tent, Cale inspected his unconscious patient. Her body was a mass of scrapes and bruises. She reminded him of Sleeping Beauty, lying there so still, so utterly motionless.

With no concern for her garment, Cale clenched his fists on the bodice of her gown and ripped it away. Hurriedly, he wrapped her in quilts and then lifted her head to pour brandy down her throat. Cale knew he risked choking her, but he was desperate and he had no medication at his disposal. His heart fluttered with a glimmer of hope when Mikyla instinctively gulped twice before collapsing into a deep sleep.

Cale sank back on his haunches to stare into her peaked face. Her lips were still a frightening shade of blue and her features were as white as linen. But he could detect the slight rise and fall of her chest beneath the quilts.

Too restless to sit and wait, Cale stalked back outside to survey the damages to his livestock pen. As he suspected, Sundance had burst through the top rail to answer the summons. Horses were scattered in every direction. Only the mules had bypassed the opportunity of leaping over the broken rail and trotting off to graze.

Deciding to wait until morning to retrieve his herd, Cale wheeled south. He was determined to move Mikyla's tent to higher ground—and immediately adjacent to his own, whether she approved or not. Cursing and growling, Cale hauled Mikyla's belongings outside and then folded her tent. Using the stallion as a pack horse, Cale toted the gear and supplies back to his camp. Within a half hour, he had erected the canvas structure. And this time it *was* perpendicular to the ground instead of leaning like the Tower of Pisa. Nervous energy kept him pacing about, reconstructing

Mikyla's crude home exactly as she had arranged it.

And then the bottom fell out from under him. Cale was suddenly assaulted by incredible fatigue. He had been running on raw nerves for more than three hours. But now there was nothing left and Cale felt the need to lie with Mikyla, to protect her, to ensure that she was still among the living. And yet he didn't want to approach her to find that she had . . .

Cale squeezed back the dreary thought. Ky was full of will and determination. She would live, he encouraged himself. But even while Cale repeated consoling platitudes, he wondered if he were being realistic. The thought caused his confidence to backslide. The moment he eased down beside Mikyla he felt the fierce compulsion to clutch her to him, to share his vitality, his warmth.

But she felt so cold and lifeless, Cale mused dispiritedly. As if he were coddling a frail, defenseless infant, Cale drew her tenderly against his bare flesh. Odd, he couldn't remember experiencing these emotions before when he held Mikyla in his arms. Then he had been engulfed by passions, the savage need to possess her, yet, it wasn't only desire that churned within him now. It was gentle compassion, a quiet stirring of affectioin and concern. He wanted to hold her to him and go on holding her until she came back to life, until he witnessed the familiar sparkle of living fire in her eyes.

Although Cale knew Mikyla would protest if she were conscious, he pressed his lips to her unresponsive mouth. All right, so he had cheated on their wager. But she was never going to know he had kissed her and held her while they slept. Sundance couldn't tattle on him, and Cale wasn't about to tell her.

At long last, after the tormenting agony of enduring her sensuous assaults, Cale could express his emotions. He was lulled to sleep by the steady patter of rain against the canvas tent, by the contentment of lying full-length against this luscious angel. The dull thud of her heart against his bare chest was meager encouragement, but it was enough to take Cale into a world of dreams—some terrifying, others arousing.

And all through the night, Cale clung to Mikyla, offering her comfort and easing his long-denied needs of touching the one woman who had somehow managed to burrow into his heart. The hold she held over him frightened Cale. But he couldn't pull away, not when she needed him, not when she was lying so close to death's door.

If this was all there was, Cale promised himself that Ky would leave this cruel world with his memory entangled with her fleeing spirit. But if Cale was allowed to have his prayer answered, Mikyla was going nowhere without him. The thought of life without this hot-tempered, impossibly stubborn sprite was a grim prospect. Cale could not even begin to comprehend how the world would look without sunshine beaming down upon it. For certain, it would wallow in gloomy shadows without the sparkle of Mikyla's dazzling blue eyes and the heart-warming radiance of her smile.

Chapter 16

The incessant tap of raindrops on the top of the tent brought Mikyla from the depths of drowsiness. Her body felt as if it had an anchor attached to it. When she tried to move, her muscles screamed in complaint. A muddled frown puckered her brow as she glanced about her. This looked like her tent, but somehow Mikyla had the feeling she was lying in Cale's tent. Why? Had she surrendered to her compelling need for him? Had she managaed to . . . ?

Suddenly the nightmare rolled over her like the angry river that had very nearly swallowed her alive. Mikyla whimpered at the terrifying sensations that riveted through her. Although her body rebelled, she dragged herself out of bed and away from the horrible scene that cascaded over her like a suffocating flood.

Wrapped only in a quilt, Mikyla forced her feet to move toward the exit of the tent. Before she could step outside, Cale loomed over her like a dark cloud.

"What the hell are you doing out of bed?" he growled in question.

Mikyla was too weak and dazed to counter in her usual saucy manner. Her tangled lashes swept up to study Cale's disapproving scowl. He was soaked from head to toe, and his raven hair was plastered against his head. His clothes clung to his muscular physique as if they had been glued to his skin.

But it didn't matter that Cale resembled a wet mop. Miki was never so happy to see anyone in all her life. The thought

233

of spending the day within the canvas walls reliving her nightmare had little appeal.

When her waxen features blossomed into a smile Cale melted into sentimental mush. Her contagious greeting mellowed his stern expression. For a moment they stood a foot apart, both of them aching and yet hesitant to fly into each other's arms. Mikyla didn't want Cale to know how much she was beginning to care about him and Cale refused to lose a wager that boasted higher stakes than Mikyla realized.

"Feeling better?" he asked awkwardly.

"I think I'd have to be dead three days to feel better,"Mikyla choked out hoarsely.

Cale shifted from one foot to the other. Her comment wasn't amusing. After watching her lie there so motionless for several agonizing days, Cale wondered if she would survive.

Wedging past Mikyla, he stepped into the tent to peel off his dripping shirt. "I've been rebuilding your corrals on higher ground. This is a thorough, soaking rain—no lightning," he commented offhandedly.

Mikyla nodded, aware of Cale's fearful respect for electrical storms. If the sky had been flashing with streaks of silver, Cale would have been in the tent instead of working outside. Wearily, she shuffled toward the cot and sank onto it before she collapsed. And then she realized she had seen her own tent standing not twenty feet away from Cale's. She had noticed that the canvas structure had been relocated, but when Cale appeared to fill up her world and her thoughts, tents were the last thing on her mind.

"Why did you move my tent?" she questioned tiredly. "I don't think it wise for us to be living so close together. People might get the wrong impression."

Cale spun around to fling her an annoyed glare. "I transplanted your tent because your campsite was on the flood plain to begin with. I tried to tell you, but being stubborn from head to toe and all parts in between, you refused to listen. If I hadn't pulled up the stakes to your tent it would be downstream with your corrals."

Cale graciously allowed time for Mikyla to interject a snide rejoinder, but she just sat there with her hands folded primly in her lap, her eyes downcast. "No sarcastic remark? You must truly be exhausted," he sniffed in taunt.

Still, Miki did not snatch up the gauntlet. She needed time to clear the fog that clouded her brain and regain her energy.

After shrugging on a dry shirt, Cale regarded her for a long, pensive moment. "I hardly see what difference it makes about what people might think," he said flippantly. "After all, we have been as close as two people can get . . . or did the flood conveniently wash away that memory, Ky?"

His candor put a rose-tinted blush on her otherwise colorless cheeks. Wounded pride gave words to tongue, even when Mikyla didn't feel much like engaging in a battle of wits. "I can hardly forget what happened between us in a reckless moment. But I have no wish to broadcast my mistakes *or* habitually repeat them."

Cale winced as if he had been stabbed from behind. It seemed he and this feisty minx were back to swords and daggers again. "Would you prefer that I post a sign on our property, informing passersby that we are living side by side because necessity and flood waters dictate and that we are not sleeping together as they might suspect?"

He didn't think her ashen face could explode with so much color so quickly or that her sluggish movements could send her bounding off the cot with so much vigor. But his taunt was like lighting a fire beneath her. Mikyla opened her mouth to hurl a barrage of hateful remarks, but she caught herself in the nick of time, much to Cale's chagrin, for he had hoped to make her lose her temper and end this tormenting wager.

"I hardly think that will be necessary," she cooed in sticky sweetness. "I suppose I merely overreacted because I'm not feeling up to snuff." Heaving a tired sigh, Mikyla wilted back to the cot, clutching her quilt to her bosom. A wry smile pursed her lips as she stretched out in bed. Turn about was fair play, she decided. If Cale thought to annoy her, even when she had just roused from the dead, then she would waste not a minute reverting to her ploy of arousing him past temptation. "Would you be so kind as to offer a massage. My muscles feel as if they have been tied in Gordian knots."

Cale sank down beside her before he realized his foolishness. Like a butterfly worming its way from its cocoon, Mikyla wiggled out of the quilt, exposing her back and shapely hips to Cale's reluctant and yet devouring gaze. Another test of self-control, he mused dismally. Cale found himself questioning his confidence, wondering if he possessed one iota of self-restraint. The fact that he had worried himself sick about Mikyla while she lay in bed only compounded his need for her. Her last bit of mischief could cost him dearly.

Mustering his willpower, Cale fanned his hands over her exquisite flesh, kneading the knotted muscles until they relaxed beneath his gentle ministrations. While Miki was "ooing" and "ahing" in relief, Cale was inwardly groaning in torment. So much for the platonic concern and compassion he had experienced while Mikyla was recovering from drinking half the South Canadian River. Damn, he was back to wanting her the way a man hungers and lusts after a beautiful, desirable woman.

When Mikyla eased onto her back to peer up at him with those beguiling blue eyes, Cale couldn't determine what she expected next. His gaze left hers to flow over her swanlike neck and the satiny mounds of her breasts. If he hadn't been so distracted, he might have noticed the longing in her features. It was no taunt, no spiteful need to end the wager and win back her land. It was raw desire, the kind that was aroused by the feel of his masterful hands gliding over her skin.

Oh, Miki knew she was breaking her solemn vow to avoid Cale, not to become involved with him for her heart's sake. Yes, she had religiously lectured herself on the subject. But it just didn't seem to matter anymore. In fact, she really didn't care what anyone thought about her camping out on the same property with Cale. What mattered most to her was what this mountain of a man felt for her. If only he could stare at her with something more than desire. If only he could see her as his equal, his partner, his friend . . .

When her hands migrated along his forearms, Cale was off the bed in a single bound, as if he had been sitting on a bumble bee. "Crawl back under your quilt, Ky," he ordered gruffly. "I'm not much good at playing a lady's maid. I made my attempt to inflame your legendary temper and you tried your hand at freeing the lusting beast within me. That should be enough for one day."

Mikyla swore Cale could hear her heart breaking in two as he stomped outside to construct the corrals. But if he did, he didn't bother to mention it. Mikyla knew she was losing every battle in her private war with Cale Brolin. He had learned to read her moods. He knew what she needed, better than she herself knew. With each passing day she had come to rely and depend on him. When she lured him close it wasn't because of their wager. It was because she wanted him, ached for him. She had begun to live for his laughter, his teasing smiles, his skillful touch.

For the next four days, Cale took a wide berth around Mikyla. She silently yearned to end this farce of controlling their worst faults—*her* notorious temper and *his* rakish reputation with women. To dampen both of their moods, it rained again, bogging the Oklahoma prairie in mud.

When they ventured to town to restock supplies, they found that half of Reno City had pulled up stakes and moved to higher ground. A new community known as Elreno had located near the railroad right-of-way. The city had split in half and bitter feelings ran rampant.

Mikyla was informed by those who were irate about the separation of the initial townsite that Emet Lassiter had moved his place of business to the new community. Although she was curious to know if her father was still drinking and gambling his life away, she refused to travel to Elreno to confront him. She was still resentful of his attempt to gamble her stallion out from under her.

As they ambled down the muddy streets, Cale announced that he intended to visit one of the score of saloons that lined the main road of Reno City. Mikyla eyed him with mistrust. The town was swarming with painted ladies who were all too eager to accommodate a lonely man. Each time Cale had ridden from camp without her, she had wondered if he were secretly easing his needs for a woman. And now that they were in town together, she intended to keep a close surveillance on his activities. If Cale was about to lose their bet, she had every intention of catching him redhanded. And if Cale thought she would refuse to follow him inside the saloon, he had sorely misjudged her! Though Mikyla wasn't certain if it was jealousy that made her so determined, she couldn't help but wonder if Cale had been visiting one of these calico queens on the sly.

A stunned expression settled in Cale's rugged features when Mikyla marched onto the boardwalk beside him, giving indication that she was about to enter the saloon. His hand clamped around her elbow, pulling her back before she could burst through the door. "What the devil do you think you're doing?" he croaked. "Decent women don't frequent saloons!"

"Neither should respectable men." Her stare was frankly condemning. "Which is it you can't live without?" she wanted to know. "The drink or the bar fly who serves it?"

"Do you really care?" he snorted in question. "I rather thought you wanted me to lose this blasted bet."

Her chin tilted to a proud angle. Cale was as blind as a bat if he couldn't see that it was jealousy that inspired her far more than their bet. Dammit, couldn't a man tell when a woman was falling in love with him? Wasn't it printed on her face, brewing in her eyes like an Indian smoke signal?

"Cale Brolin, you are a fool!" Mikyla burst out suddenly.

Cale did a double take. What had brought on that unexpected defamation of his character? "If I'm a fool, what, pray tell, does that make you, Miss High and Mighty?" he growled down into her bewitching features.

"Another one," Mikyla admitted honestly. "And if you so much as touch someone of the female persuasion, I'll chop off your hand at the wrist. Not only will you lose the bet, but I will despise you until the end of eternity."

As Mikyla sailed into the saloon, wearing her traditional garments of tight breeches and a form-fitting shirt, Cale broke into a wry smile. Was she really jealous? Was that her subtle way of telling him she cared about him?

Cale's disposition was a sweet as honey . . . until he swaggered inside to find none other than Morgan Hagerty bowing over Mikyla's hand. Damn, with twenty-three saloons to pick from, Cale had the misfortune of selecting the one with Morgan in it. Of all the rotten luck!

Morgan was all smiles until Cale's shadow fell over him. A scowl swallowed his handsome features. "I'm disappointed to see you are still keeping company with Brolin, no matter what the circumstances," he sniffed distastefully, shifting his attention from Mikyla to Cale.

There was an odd tension in the air when these two men came within ten feet of each other. Mikyla glanced from one hard, glaring face to the other. She supposed their animosity stemmed from the poker game that had ended in fisticuffs—a conflict that, even to this day, Mikyla didn't know who had instigated. Both men had assured her that the other was at fault. But little did she know that the fierce competition and bitterness between them had been brewing long before they set foot in Oklahoma country.

"There isn't, by some remote possibility, something going on between you and Miss Lassiter, is there?" Morgan questioned Cale, his green eyes glittering menacingly.

Cold dread formed icicles on Cale's spine. He could see the cogs of Morgan's brain cranking. Morgan was grasping for a weapon of revenge, anything he might employ to satisfy his personal vendetta. The bitterness he felt for Cale had blossomed into a poisonous hatred. And for that reason, Cale was forced to dispel any suspicions Morgan might have had.

In order to protect Mikyla, who might find herself used as a gambit in Morgan's game of vindication, Cale was forced to deny any attachment for this saucy beauty. "Come now, Morgan," Cale chuckled sarcastically. "You should know better than that. All I want is the claim all for myself. I hardly consider Miss Lassiter my kind of woman. What is between us is strictly business."

If all they had been doing was business, one of them was most certainly a fool, Mikyla mused. And she knew exactly which one of them it was—her. Mikyla's heart fell down around her knees. Cale might as well have come right out and said he didn't give a tinker's damn about her.

Cale's eyes narrowed meaningfully on his nemesis. "You, of all people, ought to know why I want that particular quarter section of land."

Mikyla felt as if Cale had drawn a knife from his boot and twisted it in her back. He couldn't have hurt her worse. The moment before they entered the saloon she had hinted at her affection for him. Obviously, Cale didn't care a smidgen about her feelings. He had just announced to the crowd that she was a necessary convenience who stood in the way of what he wanted

Damn him! He knew about the proposed townsite and railroad site, just as she did! How had he found out? Cale had been away from camp the day Morgan rode in to inform her. She had purposely kept the news from Cale. Mikyla had adamantly rejected Morgan's suggestion of selling out at a high price—but that was exactly what Cale intended to do, *if* and *when* he gained possession of the property.

Double damn him! Every time she turned around she found Cale playing her for a witless idiot. She was willing to bet Cale knew all along that the land was coveted by a townsite company. That was why he had been so intent on staking the claim before she did. Lord, would she ever learn? Couldn't she recognize a lost cause when she was staring him in the face? All Cale saw was profit in their wager and she was willing to bet her right arm that it was *Cale* who tried to win Sundance from her father, just as Morgan insisted. No doubt Cale had intended to ride her stallion to claim the site. Then he had planned to sell the property to the townsite company, take the profit, and buy himself another herd of mules and horses.

While Mikyla was standing between both men, fighting to prevent erupting in a fit of temper and becoming even more determined to win this wager, Joseph Richards arrived upon the scene. Hell and damnation, Cale muttered to himself. Why did disaster always fly in formation like a skein of geese, one tail-ending the other? First Cale had been confronted by the one man who hated him with a passion. Then he was forced to announce to all the world, and to Morgan in particular, that Ky meant absolutely nothing to him. And then, like spoiled frosting atop a sour-milk cake, Joseph Richards had appeared. If Mikyla hadn't already deduced that Cale knew about the townsite's plans, she would now. Joseph would open his big mouth and offer them a generous settlement for the property that lay on the north bank of the river. Mikyla's darkest suspicions about Cale's integrity would be confirmed and he couldn't defend himself because Morgan was looming like a waiting vulture.

Cale would have praised himself for being so clairvoyant if he wasn't so busy cursing fate. And sure enough, Joseph fluffed his feathers, lifted his beaklike nose, and squawked out his offer for the deed to Mikyla's dream site. And to make matters worse, he began by mentioning that he and Cale had been in contact *before* the Run. Dammit, the man could have rattled on all day without blurting that out!

"My company is prepared to offer you thirty dollars an acre for your claim," he announced to Mikyla, cautiously avoiding the glare of the man who had run him out of camp.

What was the use? Cale mused sullenly. *Why prolong the inevitable?* "We'll take it," he affirmed, only to be contradicted by Mikyla's "We most certainly will not!" And something about "Over my dead body!"

Damn, Cale wished she hadn't said that. The last thing he needed was to have Mikyla plant ideas in these two men's heads, especially Morgan's! He already wanted Cale dead. There was no reason to have Morgan speculating on the possibility of a double funeral.

When Mikyla puffed up like an overinflated balloon, preparing to tell Joseph Richards and Morgan Hagerty what she thought of their proposition and where they could stash it, Cale clamped his hand over her mouth. "If you lose your temper, you lose everything," he reminded her

241

sharply. "And then the land will be mine to do with as I please."

That depressing thought was like throwing ice water on a fire. Mikyla cooled down immediately—at least on the outside. On the inside she was burning on a hot blue flame. Damn men everywhere! They made a woman's life a veritable hell. Mikyla was used to being knocked around, but she detested being walked all over. And that was exactly what all three of these men were trying to do to her.

Worming from Cale's grasp, Mikyla stamped out of the saloon and stormed toward Sundance. Even when she marched through a mud puddle, slopping water all over her, she didn't break stride. She was seeing the world through a furious red haze. Mikyla was struggling like the devil to get herself in hand before Cale came along to make some goading remark. She would lose what was left of her temper, which already had been stretched until it was on the verge of snapping.

Deciding it best not to allow the molten lava of her temper to cool, Cale hurried to catch up with Mikyla as she thundered away from Reno City. If the rigid set of her back was any indication of the degree of difficulty involved in restraining herself, Cale had predicted she would go through the sky, given the slightest provocation. And that was exactly what Cale did—provoked her now that Morgan was out from underfoot. He hadn't wanted her to make a scene in the saloon, but now he was eager to end their wager before Joseph Richards and Morgan Hagerty stooped to drastic measures of procuring the land they wanted.

"I'm selling the land," Cale announced as he eased up beside Mikyla. "If I don't comply with the request now, the railroad will condemn the property and force me to settle for bottom price. I can make a tidy profit and I'm not going to allow opportunity to slip through my hands."

To Cale's utter amazement, Mikyla did not eject herself off the saddle and skyrocket into orbit. She simply sat on her stallion, looking like a grenade that was about to explode. Mikyla refused to give Cale the satisfaction of winning. She did not say a word until she had silently counted to one hundred.

"You have yet to win this wager," she managed to say without spitting the words in Cale's face. "When the bet is settled, the *winner* will determine whether to stay and fight or to sell out."

Cale couldn't help but admire her willpower. He knew she was mad as hell after the agitating procession of events that had occurred at the saloon. If he hadn't been trying to control his own temper he would have vaulted from the saddle and kicked a hole all the way to China to relieve his frustration. The day had been a total disaster.

"You knew all along, didn't you, Cale?" Mikyla questioned, her lovely face alive with a riptide of emotion—anger, disappointment, and indignation. "That's why you wanted to stake my claim, because you knew about the townsite company. You knew how much the land meant to me and yet you wanted it so you could turn a profit."

"I knew but . . . " Cale began diplomatically, only to be interrupted by Mikyla's disgusted sniff.

"I don't want to discuss it further," she ground out as she dug her heels into Sundance's flanks and took flight across the prairie.

Cale slumped in the saddle, watching the shapely bundle soar on her winged stallion. What purpose would it serve to explain, he asked himself sourly. Mikyla had always believed the worst about him. Why should he waste his time crawling to her with explanations and apologies? She didn't want to hear them. Indeed, she had her heart set on hating him and she was doing it quite well.

Damn, he had two days to win his bet. And what was he going to do if he didn't win? Cale hadn't puzzled that out yet. He was too preoccupied countering Mikyla's seductive assaults and plotting to make her lose her temper. That was a full-time job, Cales mused as he urged his strawberry roan into a swifter gait.

Chapter 17

When Cale returned to camp, a curious frown knitted his brow. Sundance was standing outside Cale's tent, which was billowing as if a cyclone were rumbling through it. Hastily dismounting, Cale whipped open the flap to see Mikyla rummaging through his supplies like a eager puppy digging a hole to unearth a previously buried bone. His garments and cooking utensils were flying in all directions.

"What the devil are you doing?" he wanted to know.

Mikyla finally located Cale's stock of liquor. Grasping a bottle, she rose to full stature and spun to face him. "I'm borrowing your brandy," she declared before presenting him with a cold shoulder, complete with icicles.

One dark brow lifted in surprised amusement. "Do you intend to return the bottle to me empty or full?"

Mikyla uncorked the whiskey. "Empty." Without ado, she helped herself to a gulp.

"You don't drink," Cale reminded her a moment too late. Mikyla was already coughing and sputtering to catch her breath. Unsympathetically, Cale slapped her on the back to reactivate her stalled heart.

"I've just started," she wheezed.

Her eyes watered in reaction to the fire that blazed down her throat to inflame her stomach. Recomposing herself, Mikyla marched stoically toward her own tent, only to find Cale following in her shadow. Purposely ignoring her irritating companion, she guzzled another drink. The second taste of liquor was not as repulsive as the first, she supposed. By that time her throat was numb. Mikyla then chugged her third swallow. A peculiar tingle riveted through her body, taking the edge off her nerves. She detested drinking, but she decided there were times when whiskey served its purpose. This was one of those times.

Cale sank down on the edge of the cot and frowned disapprovingly when Mikyla inhaled another swallow of brandy. "If you don't slow your pace, you might find yourself lying *under* that chair rather than sitting in it," he prophesied.

Her shoulder lifted and drooped in a careless shrug. "If the liquor erases every memory of you and your treachery, I don't care if this chair is sitting on *me,"* she slurred out and then frowned at the odd sound of her own voice.

Cale's eyes rolled in disbelief. This firebrand was going to get herself looped before she knew what hit her. She had begun drinking the way she approached all else—with not the slightest restraint. Cale supposed the proper term for her behavior was *whole hog*—which was rather appropriate, he thought, considering she was the most pigheaded female he had ever encountered.

"I really don't know why you dislike me so. I'm only trying to help you," he said in self-defense.

"Dislike you?" Mikyla repeated with a distasteful sniff. "That is putting it mildly." Her eyes fell to the bottle she had clutched in her hand and she promptly tipped it to her lips. A strange numbness seized the tip of her nose. Staring cross-eyed, Mikyla inspected the unfamiliar object with her fingertips. It was her nose all right, but it suddenly didn't feel as if it belonged in the middle of her face. "With a *friend* who is trying to sell my claim out from under me, I hardly think I need enemies, though I seem to have acquired my fair share along the way."

Muttering at her ridiculous antics and now her insult, Cale leaned out to snatch the bottle away from her. After he had poured down a gulp of brandy, he thrust the bottle back into Mikyla's waiting hand. Damn, he couldn't beat her. He might as well join her, he decided.

"You're going to hate yourself in the morning when you wake up to a helluva hangover," he predicted, waiting for Mikyla to offer him a second drink.

"It's far better than remembering how much I despise you this afternoon," she countered, flinging him a condemning glare and the brandy bottle.

"I don't know why I'm even bothering with you," Cale scowled before downing the brandy.

A silly smile was draped on the corner of Miki's mouth. Brazenly she assessed the rugged, muscular man. "That makes us even. I don't know why you *bother* me. But I can't seem to look past your magnificent body," she declared abruptly.

Her pointed stare caused Cale to do a double take. Mikyla was leering at him with feminine appreciation. That was the last thing he anticipated from a woman who had, only moments before, exclaimed that she detested the very sight of him.

A rakish grin curved his lips as he returned her bold stare. "You realize, of course, that I could take advantage of your compliment and of *you* when you are in no condition to resist," he taunted.

Unsteadily, Mikyla pushed out of her chair and weaved past Cale on her way outside. "If you dare to touch me, you would lose the bet," she reminded him before she gulped another drink.

"I doubt you can recall what might happen, drunk as you're going to be," he smirked as he watched Mikyla wobble over to unsaddle Sundance.

"I'm sure I would thoroughly enjoy our tête-à-tête and you would tell me how I reveled in the pleasure of your touch. Indeed, I imagine you would hold it over me for the rest of my life," she threw over her shoulder, along with a provocative smile.

Cale shook his raven head in astonishment. The brandy certainly had warped Mikyla's defensive veneer. She was rattling off seductive remarks that Cale was amazed to learn she was even *thinking*. He was even more surprised she had put the comments to tongue in his presence. Her compliments were usually so few and far between that Cale hoarded them as if they were gold nuggets.

After downing another hasty drink, Mikyla set the bottle aside to tend her stallion, but her reflexes were shaky. When she attempted to steady the saddle in her arms, her legs folded like an accordion and she found herself sitting down when she hadn't intended to. A bewildered squawk erupted from her lips when she hit the ground with the saddle straddling her belly.

Cale's uproarious laughter might have ignited her temper if the liquor hadn't numbed her so thoroughly. Instead of becoming outraged to find herself the brunt of Cale's amusement, Mikyla burst into giggles. When she struggled to unburden herself, Cale came to her assistance. He jerked her to her feet, sending the world spinning furiously about her. Mikyla clutched at the only stable force in her revolving universe.

"If you knew how foolish you looked you would be humiliated," he chuckled into her droopy smile.

"Mmm . . . if you knew how good you felt, you would wonder how I can summon the willpower to resist you . . ." she slurred impishly. "Indeed, I am wondering that myself and I am finding that I have not an ounce of restraint."

Her body moved suggestively against his, her hands weaving across the buttons of his shirt to bare his hair-matted chest. A groan of unholy torment flew from Cale's lips. Mikyla was doing incredible things to his flesh with her adventurous caresses. She looked so damned desirable, so utterly defenseless. Her lips were parted in invitation. Her eyes were glazed with vulnerability and her luscious body was speaking to his in a language all its own.

His thoughts were derailed by Mikyla's silly shenanigan. Cale was overly tempted to lower his head, to taste those brandy-flavored kisses, to ease the maddening ache she aroused in him. He could feel her curvaceous body melding to his and he was all too aware of the differences between a man and a woman. Cale wanted her like a drowning man longs for a life preserver.

Mikyla's owlish stare was focused on Cale's chiseled features. Like an acolyte worshipping a saint, she reached up to trace the bronzed skin that covered his face, mapping the smile lines that sprayed from the corners of his eyes and mouth. He was so virile and commanding, so utterly masculine, she mused appreciatively.

If she hadn't been so numb with liquor perhaps she could have puzzled out which emotion was more potent—her love or her hatred. But Mikyla was far past contemplating anything. Her inhibitions had floated away with brandy and she could only respond to the warm, tantalizing sensations that flooded over her.

"Did I ever mention that I find you terribly irresistible?" Miki slurred over her thick tongue.

Cale's eyebrows jackknifed. "I thought you said I was terrible, period."

"Did I?" A comical frown of pensive deliberation captured her features. "I don't remember."

"Why doesn't that surprise me," Cale tittered as he slipped his arm around the intoxicated sprite and herded her toward the tent.

"I do find you attractive," she admitted, the brandy working like a truth serum. "Do you suppose you could ever really love me?"

Cale very nearly stumbled over her abrupt question. "Mikyla Lassiter, you are drunk," he grumbled in evasive response.

Her reckless laughter tickled Cale's senses, "I am, aren't I?"

"Most definitely, and you are behaving shamelessly," he scolded as he nudged her toward her cot.

"I thought you liked brazen women," she purred as she pivoted to drape her arms over his shoulders.

Removing her wandering hands before he lost what was left of his self-control, Cale redirected Mikyla toward her cot. "Lie down and go to sleep, minx," he commanded sternly.

Like an obedient child preparing for bed, Mikyla began disrobing right before Cale's hawkish eyes. What he *didn't* need at the moment was a titillating display of Ky's bare flesh. He was all too aware of this shapely nymph as it was. But neither could he force himself from the tent. And so he just stood there devouring Mikyla with his eyes, battling his frustrated desires, wishing he had a blindfold.

As the garments fell away, Mikyla shook her hair free, allowing the silky strands to ripple about her in splendorous disarray. When she stretched out on the cot, Cale steadied himself against the support pole, fearing his knees would buckle and he would wind up crawling to this gorgeous witch, begging for whatever scraps of affection she might offer.

"Cale?" Mikyla's voice was a drowsy whisper. "Aren't you going to tuck me in?"

"Absolutely not!" Cale snapped. If he allowed himself that close there was no telling what might happen next.

Lazy blue eyes drifted toward him like unfolding tentacles that pulled him against his will. "Please . . . I would do the same for you if you asked . . . "

Cale cursed every step he took when he was magnetically drawn to this tempting enchantress. Willing his eyes to remain glued to her face, Cale clutched the sheet that concealed the shapely form that had been, and would forever be, etched on his mind.

"Do you find me attractive?" Mikyla questioned out of the blue.

"Very much so," Cale croaked like a sick bullfrog. Lord, her devastating effect on him not only disturbed the vital parts of his anatomy, but had also constricted his vocal chords.

Her expression was so pathetically sincere and innocent that Cale had to bite his lip to prevent bursting into snickers. "Then why haven't you touched me, despite our wager?" she dared to ask. "Is it because you don't find me as appealing as the other women you have known?"

Cale braced his arms on either side of her bare shoulders to peer into her exquisite face. "Believe me, vixen, I deserve a medal of valor for resisting the constant temptation you present," he told her honestly.

250

Her lips trembled and her wide blue eyes clouded with remorse. "But the money you'll recieve if you sell my claim holds more appeal than I," she murmured deflatedly.

His hand lifted to trace the inviting curve of her mouth, but Cale caught himself before he committed the error and lost the wager. Although Cale summoned enough willpower to hold himself at bay, Mikyla had not one iota of self-restraint left. Her hands glided up his forearms to map the sinewy expanse of his shoulders and chest. She marveled at the man and the riptide of emotions he evoked from her. Irresistibly drawn to him, Miki levered herself up to brush her lips over his unresponsive mouth, wishing he would return her hungry kiss and enfold her in his magical embrace.

Cale suddenly found himself in the grips of something so tenderly overwhelming that his entire body quaked. Lord, why had he proposed this ridiculous wager? It was going to drive him to an early grave!

And then, like a dainty flower, Mikyla wilted back to her pillow. Her lashes fluttered against her cheeks and she surrendered to the drugging effects of brandy. For a full minute Cale struggled to inhale a normal breath. Mikyla had him aching in places he didn't realize existed. Sweet mercy, how much longer could he endure this torture? Cale asked himself miserably. Mikyla tempted him so often that he found himself on the verge of waving a white flag and satisfying the monstrous cravings that tormented his days and haunted his nights.

Reluctantly, Cale dragged himself to his feet and strode outside to complete the task of unbridling Sundance. His eyes fell to the whiskey bottle and he was tempted to polish off the contents in hopes of easing his unfulfilled passions. But he didn't dare. If he lost command of *his* senses, he might find himself joining Ky in bed.

Grumbling, Cale swatted Sundance on the rump, urging him into his pen. When Cale had tended the strawberry roan, he aimed himself toward the river for a cold bath. Damn, he had followed this prescription to ease his primal needs so often the past few days that he wondered if he would shrivel up like a raisin before they determined the winner of this tormenting bet.

Well, it was better than losing and forcing Miki to face Morgan and Joseph alone, he consoled himself. He could surely suffer through several cold baths if it would save that feisty spitfire from confronting those two scoundrels. Mulling over that thought, Cale peeled off his clothes and waded into the river, standing in midstream until his teeth chattered.

Mikyla awakened to the sound of the percussion section of a band echoing in her head and pounding in her eardrums. Groaning, she eased into an upright position. Her stomach pitched and rolled, causing her to emit another agonized moan. She swore she was staring at the inside of her puffy eyelids until she had dressed and staggered outside to see the sliver of the crescent moon draped on the horizon. Had she slept the afternoon away or was this the way the world looked when one was suffering a skull-splitting hangover?

Determined to relieve her queasy stomach Mikyla weaved toward the coffeepot that hung over the fire. This was the first and last time she would attempt to drown her troubles in a bottle of liquor, she resolved. She had never felt so miserable in all her life! How could her father punish his body like this on a regular basis? He must have acquired a lead-lined stomach, she speculated.

"How's your head?" Cale inquired as he watched Mikyla overextend herself to grasp the coffeepot.

Mikyla had no idea Cale was clinging to the shadows. His voice startled her and the coffeepot leaped from her shaky hands to sizzle in the coals. While she was fumbling with her sluggish reflexes, Cale retrieved a hot pad, snatched up the pot, and set it on the ground.

"Would you like me to spike your coffee with some brandy?" he teased cheerfully, waving the whiskey bottle beneath her nose.

When the smell of brandy infiltrated her senses, Mikyla felt herself becoming sick all over again. Cale was deliberately taunting her in her misery and she wished he would go away and let her die in peace.

Cale chuckled when Mikyla turned green around the gills. He watched in wicked amusement as she collapsed to her knees to pour a cup of coffee. "Allow me," he insisted, stealing the cup from her trembling fingers.

"Don't try to be nice," Mikyla muttered crossly. "You should stick with something you are familiar with."

"Several hours ago you were plying me with compliments," Cale informed her as he offered her a steaming cup of coffee.

A muddled frown puckered her brow, causing her to wince uncomfortably. Lord, even her face ached from her bout with brandy. Had she blurted out some reckless confession in her drunken stupor, she wondered bleakly.

Since Mikyla appeared befuddled by his comment Cale decided to badger her until she lost her temper. Casually, he stretched out on the carpet of grass to enjoy his own cup of coffee. "I had no idea you were so crazy about me," he remarked and then awaited her reaction. As he anticipated, Mikyla choked on her coffee. A low rumble of laughter shattered the silence. "Ah, the things you said . . . the things you did. You truly amazed me, minx."

Mikyla was feeling sicker by the second. Without daring to glance in Cale's direction, she contemplated the contents of her cup. She wasn't going to allow her curiosity to get the best of her. She didn't want to know what she had said and done.

"I've known some wild, uninhibited women in my time, but your antics . . ."

"I don't want to hear it!" Mikyla growled and then grimaced when a splitting pain slashed across her skull.

Cale frowned in feigned concern when he noted the lack of color on Mikyla's features. "You don't look at all well, my dear." Suddenly Cale was on his feet, pulling Miki up beside him so quickly that it made her head spin like a top. "What you need is a soaking in the river," he diagnosed. "We'll have you functioning properly in no time."

"Why don't *you* go soak your head and leave me be,"

Mikyla grumbled crabbily.

But Cale was persistent. Despite Mikyla's protest, he hustled her to the river and led her into the channel. Before she even knew what he was doing, Cale grabbed the nape of her shirt and shoved her face in the water. He held her under much longer than Miki deemed necessary. She wondered if his true purpose was to suffocate her, rather than sober her up. The instant before she swore she would drown, Cale snatched her out of the water to grace her with an ornery smile.

"You see? You are feeling better already, aren't you?" he snickered mischievously.

Mikyla had her heart set on cursing him, but Cale pushed her down before the words could fly from her tongue. The longer he held her submerged the more furious she became. And when he finally granted her the smallest breath of air, she found herself mercilessly dunked for the third time. Damn the man. When the devil dished out orneriness Cale Brolin had sneaked through the line twice!

Just as Cale suspected, the christening did more to inflame her temper than cool it. Mikyla floundered to regain her feet. Sputtering, she tugged the soggy strands of hair from her face, squinting to see through the stream of water that poured from her scalp. She itched to claw that devilish grin off Cale's face, but she was forced to swallow her fury, along with a few gallons of water. Mustering what was left to her dignity, Mikyla stomped ashore, her back as rigid as a cottonwood tree.

"Now, don't you feel a hundred times better?" Cale teased relentlessly.

Mikyla whirled, shoving the damp mop of blond hair from her eyes so Cale could receive the full effect of her mutinous glare. "Not really, if you want to know. Before you dunked me I felt like killing myself because I was miserable. Now I feel like killing *you*. All that is preventing your untimely demise is this confounded wager, and I do not intend to lose."

"At least my cure for your hangover was effective," Cale enthused, preying on her barely restrained temper until it came within an inch of snapping in two. "You look as if you will live. Several minutes ago, I wasn't sure of your prognosis."

"Rest assured, *Dr.* Brolin, that I will never find myself in that condition again," Mikyla snapped as she twisted her clinging clothes back in place. "I'm never going near another whiskey bottle as long as I live." She leveled him another glare that was meant to maim and mutilate. "And I am never going to speak to you again as long as I live either. If I said anything nice about you while I was drinking I retract every compliment. It was the liquor talking. You, Cale Brolin, are a low-down, good-for-nothing rat."

Cale's shoulders slumped as he waded ashore. He had been so certain this last bit of mischief would sever the reins of Mikyla's legendary temper. He had hit her while she was down and still she hadn't yielded to the temptation of clobbering him.

Angry though she was, the woman had suddenly acquired the patience of Job. Cale, on the other hand, was wrestling with his unfulfilled desires and losing miserably. The sight of Mikyla in her clinging clothes did impossible things to Cale's anatomy. Some females resembled dish rags when they were wet. But not Mikyla. Her natural beauty always shined through, whether she was at her best or worst.

The depressing thought provoked Cale to reverse direction for another cold bath. And it was a half hour before he could torment himself by facing that lovely creature who refused to speak to him or even acknowledge his presence. Mikyla simply sat on a stump, staring into the fire and sipping coffee while Cale gnashed his teeth and wished for things he knew he couldn't have.

Mikyla stood outside her tent, staring sullenly to the east. The sky was enshrouded in a deep shade of blue and a bright, blood-red sun sent shafts of brilliant light spraying across the meadow. A mist of dewdrops rose from the gently swaying grass and sparkled like a halo of diamonds above the prairie. On the perimeters of the panoramic mirage that

255

encompassed the countryside at sunrise was a border of stately cottonwoods. Their foliage was kissed with sunshine and glittering with a mist of dewdrops, adding even more beauty to already breathtaking scenery.

Although Miki was in awe of splendor, her heart lay in her chest like ten pounds of lead. She and Cale hadn't spoken a word to each other since her battle with brandy. She pretended the infuriating cowboy didn't exist, and Cale ignored her to prevent being overwhelmed by lust. Without announcing his destination, Cale had rounded up a string of horses and left camp, not to return that night.

Mikyla knew for certain that Cale no longer desired her. He had made that clear at the saloon. All Cale wanted from her was the land and the profit it would bring.

But, no matter what, Mikyla wasn't giving up. This was *her* land, the dream she had lived and breathed since the President had proclaimed a section of Indian Territory would open for settlement. This property held only monetary value for Cale. He had built stock pens for no other reason than to contain his herd. And now that he and Miki were at odds, Cale was traveling the area, selling his stock and doing God only knew what else.

Heaving a melancholy sigh, Mikyla turned her back on the glorious sunrise and set about to construct another shed that would protect Sundance from inclement weather. It was almost noon when Mikyla was interrupted by the sound of approaching horses. The sight of Cale sitting so tall and proud in the saddle evoked a mixture of pleasure and pain. Why did she still feel this irrational yearning for a man who constantly betrayed her? Before Mikyla could contemplate the answer to that mind-boggling question, the clatter of yet another herd of horses heralded the arrival of a cavalry patrol.

"I wondered what had become of you, Brolin," Major Brock Terrel greeted before nodding courteously to the shapely blonde who was constructing a stock shed.

Cale returned Brock's smile and swung to the ground. "What brings you out here? No squabble between feuding settlers, I hope."

Noting the confusion in Brock's expression when he glanced at Mikyla the second time, Cale made the introductions. "Miss Lassiter and I had the misfortune of simultaneously claiming the same site. We are resolving our differences without pistols at twenty paces."

A wry smile pursed Brock's lips. Now he remembered where he had seen the attractive blonde and her magnificent stallion. And knowing Cale's craving for women, married or single, Brock surmised that Cale was reaping the full benefits of this arrangement. If Emily could see Cale with his latest lover, perhaps it would dissolve her fascination with him. Brock had managed to contain his jealousy when he saw his wife in Cale's lap, but irritation still gnawed at him.

"Actually, I came to invite you to the social affair at Fort Reno," he informed Cale. "Now that everyone is settled into their homestead we are formally celebrating the opening of Oklahoma country. There will be feasting, dancing, racing . . ."

Mikyla perked up at the opportunity of doing something besides moping around camp, wallowing in pity. "I would be delighted to accept your invitation," she enthused.

Cale growled under his breath. There were only one and a half days left to their wager. The last thing Cale wanted was to risk seeing Emily Terrel. Their most recent encounter had come dangerously close to being exposed. If Emily threw herself at him, Brock might see them. And if Brock didn't catch them, Mikyla certainly would, Cale predicted. He was doomed to lose the bet if Emily began pouring out her heart and complaining that she was a woman of frustrated passion, a woman neglected by her busy husband.

"Thank you, but no," Cale demurred. "Mikyla and I would like to attend, but we have chores . . ."

"I can spare the time," Mikyla contradicted. "And I would be happy to join in the festivities."

Cale glared holes in Mikyla's acceptance smile. But it was not until after Major Terrel and his patrol trotted away that Cale turned to breathe fire down Mikyla's neck.

"Since when did you become such a socialite?" he queried caustically.

257

Her sugar-coated smile was dripping sarcasm. "Since when did you care what I did, so long as I did it out from underfoot?"

"Well, I care!" Cale exploded, his booming voice coming at her from all directions. "You are not going to that celebration without me."

A confused frown knitted her brow. "I thought you said you weren't going."

"I'm not and neither are you," he had the audacity to tell her.

Miki's chin tilted to a defiant angle that Cale had come to recognize at a glance. "You are not dictating to me. I will go where I please, when I please."

When Mikyla pirouetted around and breezed toward her tent, Cale expelled his breath in a wordless growl. Damn it all! He wasn't turning Ky loose on a fort full of lusty soldiers, but he risked disaster if he accompanied her and Emily Terrel managed to corner him. Lord, he might as well lie down in the corral and let his horses trample over him. It would certainly be less painful than attending a feast at which Cale's *cooked goose* would be served as the main course.

Feeling as if he were walking under a black cloud, Cale stomped to his tent to retrieve a fresh set of clothes. As he burst out of the canvas abode to seek out the river, Mikyla exited with the same intentions.

"I trust you won't spy on me while I bathe," she said flippantly, matching him step for step, refusing to glance in his direction.

"That wasn't part of the bargain," Cale grumbled. "I can still look, so long as I don't dare touch."

Oh, how she wished he would! Mikyla's love-hate affair with Cale was driving her mad. She hated him for constantly maneuvering her. And yet she was hopelessly drawn to him. Just once more before they went their separate ways, she wanted to forget the world and everything in it. She wanted to create a cherished memory to sustain her until the end of her days.

When she glanced hesitantly at Cale, her whimsical thoughts shattered like crystal. His face looked as if it had been carved from quartz. There was no love or tenderness in his expression. He was angry and sulking and she didn't have the slightest notion what had put him in such a snit. What could be the harm in attending the festivities at Fort Reno, watching the soldiers march in procession, stuffing her face with succulent food, dancing the night away, racing on Sundance's back . . .

It was as if Cale had read her thoughts. "And don't delude yourself into thinking you are going to place any more bets on that devil stallion," he muttered grouchily. "This is one race Major Terrel is going to win."

Mikyla gaped at him. "Why should you care about Major Terrel?" Cale wasn't making any sense.

"He is the officer who decides whether to purchase my stock and he already thinks his wife and I . . ." Cale slammed his mouth shut before his runaway tongue voiced all his private thoughts. "Because it is important to Brock," he finished cryptically.

A suspicious frown clouded her brow. My, wasn't Cale the conniving scoundrel. He didn't want to jeopardize his business dealings by allowing the major to be defeated by the woman who was sharing Cale's property. She could understand Cale's motives, even if she didn't approve of them. But what baffled her most was the remark Cale started to make about Brock's wife. What did she have to do with anything? A speculative answer formed in her mind as Mikyla demanded to know if she had leaped to the correct conclusion.

"Have you slept with Brock's wife?" she inquired, pointblank.

Cale stared straight ahead as he picked his way through the underbrush that clogged the riverbank. "That isn't any of your business." His face twisted in a black scowl.

"You must have slept with her or you wouldn't be so up in the air," she predicted aloud.

Cale whirled around. His riveting gaze pinned Mikyla to a nearby tree. "It was a long time ago, before Emily and Brock were married. It was just after Jessica . . ." Cale swore vehemently to himself. He would have to bob his tongue if it didn't stop outdistancing his brain.

"Who is Jessica?"

Mikyla hated her inquisitive nature. She really didn't want a listing of all the women who had shared Cale's passion. No doubt the numbers of his female conquests were so extensive they would need to be catalogued in alphabetical order. The thought sent Mikyla's spirits plunging like an anchor. She was a fool to think she was woman enough to appease a man with Cale's voracious appetite for females.

To Cale, women were like horses, Mikyla reminded herself. When Cale found a good mare he purchased her and then sold her for a profit. When he liked the looks of a woman, he took possession of her until he found another female to replace her. But even after all she and Cale had endured together, Mikyla still meant nothing special to him.

She *had* to forget her foolish fascination with this raven-haired devil. She had to concentrate on her dream of land and a prospering ranch. It was all she had! Surely the railroad and the townsite company would locate elsewhere. She would make it understood that the property meant everything to her. Once they realized she wouldn't sell, they would seek out another area and leave her be.

Dejectedly, Mikyla presented her back to Cale's probing stare. She was hurt by his refusal to explain about Jessica Whoever-she-was. As Mikyla disappeared into the brush, Cale kicked angrily at a tree, very nearly breaking his toes. Why didn't he simply set Mikyla down and explain everything to her, from beginning to end? Then she wouldn't be staring at him like a wounded fawn, speculating on what she *thought* he was thinking and why he was doing the things he was doing.

Brooding, Cale limped toward the river. He knew exactly why he couldn't and wouldn't explain himself. It had nothing to do with redeeming his reptuation after he had fallen from Ky's good graces time and time again. It had nothing to do with him or Jessica or Morgan . . . or even Emily.

Dammit, it had *everything* to do with what was between him and Mikyla, not their compelling attraction for each other, not the unfulfilled desire that was eating him alive. It was that blessed dream of hers that stood between them. It was her confounded obsession, the inner driving force that kept her constantly at odds with him.

Cale pulled up short and glared at the river as if it were solely responsible for his woes. Was he making any sense at all? Well, of course he was! He was making perfect sense, he reassured himself. And until that vivacious spitfire sorted it all out in *her* mind, she and Cale would continue to be crosswise of each other. The problem was Mikyla didn't care enough to understand what motivated Cale. She was too preoccupied with her dream to see there was more to life than a quarter section of land and a string of colts Sundance had fathered.

On that frustrating thought, Cale tore off his clothes and waded into the water, which reminded him of his warnings to Miki about wandering into quicksand. If she didn't have enough sense to respect his knowledge of this treacherous river which was so swollen with rain that it was running as wide as the Mississippi, she could come to her own rescue! Cale was in no mood to portray the good Samaritan. At the moment he was annoyed enough to let that troublesome bundle of femininity sink.

All Cale wanted to do was stand there and sulk, knowing beyond a shadow of a doubt that the celebration at Fort Reno would be the beginning of the end for him and Mikyla.

Destiny and fate were about to join hands. Cale had the depressing feeling he would not emerge from the social affair with the same amount of dignity he possessed going in. Tomorrow, when the calamity was over, he would have to devise a new plan of action. Because, sure as hell, the one he was presently following would be outdated.

261

And sure enough, Cale was right. He was astute enough to predict disaster. His misfortune was being unable to determine how to avoid it, short of staking Mikyla to a tree and refusing to permit her to enjoy the long-awaited diversion of a festive celebration . . . or impending doom, depending on one's point of view . . .

Chapter 18

Mikyla surveyed her appearance in her small hand mirror, but it was difficult to obtain the full effect when she could view only one portion at a time. Finally, she gave up and focused her attention on her coiffure. She had taken particular care to pin her hair in fashionable curls. In the past, she had concerned herself with what was practical instead of stylish. But maybe tonight she wanted Cale to see the full-fledged woman who lurked beneath the boyish breeches and shirts. Maybe? Mikyla laughed at herself. There was no doubt about it. She was every kind of fool and she knew it. But for this one night she was going to attempt to charm a man—one man in particular: Cale Brolin.

When she and Cale had made their trek to Reno City, Mikyla had spent the last of her funds on a frivolous gown. It had been an impulsive buy with Cale in mind. But after the fiasco at the saloon she doubted Cale would ever see her in it. The celebration of the opening of Oklahoma country was the excuse Mikyla needed. She only hoped Cale would notice her.

Ah, such childish whims, Mikyla chided herself as she smoothed the gown into place. Cale was too wrapped up in his scheme to make money at the homesteaders' expense and too fickle to notice Mikyla Lassiter was still alive and well and living under his nose. But perhaps some nice young man (as Greta was in the habit of saying) would take note of her and ask her to dance. It was going to require a handsome diversion if she were to forget her one-sided fascination with that dark-haired rogue who had more concern for his livestock than his women.

Chomping on that depressing thought, Mikyla stepped outside to find Cale propped leisurely against the corral. Mikyla's knees threatened to buckle beneath her when her gaze sketched Cale's expensive black waistcoat and tailor-made breeches. The white cotton shirt accented his deep tan, and each of his garments called attention to his muscular physique. If it were acceptable to describe a man as gorgeous, that was the word for Cale Brolin. He resembled a dashing rake and a debonair gentleman, all rolled into one arrestingly attractive package.

Mikyla's wide, appreciative gaze ran the full length of him, not once but thrice. There was not one flaw in his appearance. Indeed, Cale Brolin was perfect . . . until he limped forward on an improvised cane.

"What happened?" she chirped bewilderedly.

Cale glanced at his booted foot and shrugged. "I kicked a tree," he declared. When Mikyla continued to study him, Cale elaborated. "I was throwing a temper tantrum to relieve my frustration. It's a pity I was not the one who wagered I could restrain myself from fits. It served to prove that a person's temper can be self-destructive."

Although Cale's foot wasn't paining him half as much as he pretended, he hoped his excuse not to dance would discourage Emily from sniffing him out and melting all over him. Damn, when a man ached for a woman's affection, there usually wasn't one within twenty miles. And when he preferred to be left alone there was inevitably one female who would get him into trouble. There was a strong possibility that Emily was that kind of woman.

Cale's pensive deliberation evaporated when he allowed his gaze to wander over Mikyla's stunning royal blue gown. The tissue silk dress was adorned with white lace-border gauze that bared her shoulders and swooped low over her bodice and back. The full bell skirt tapered to the tiny indentation of her waist, drawing enticing attention to her curvaceous figure. The gown, hanging on a manikin might have appeared appealing. But with this enchanting goddess in it, the garment was extraordinary. Mikyla looked dainty and exquisite, as if she had access to all the luxuries rather than only the bare necessities offered by their meager camp. Her silver-gold hair was a mass of lustrous curls. Wispy ringlets outlined her flawless features, drawing attention to her enormous blue eyes that were fringed with long, thick lashes.

Cale felt the quick rise of desire stirring in his loins. Damn the festivities. He would much prefer to have this lovely angel all to himself.

"This is the first time you have looked the part of a lady," Cale teased with a smile. "Remind me to make a note of it in my diary."

"I didn't know you kept one," Mikyla said saucily, pleased Cale seemed impressed with her appearance, despite his taunt.

Cale tapped the side of his head and broke into another wry smile. "My memoirs are all committed to memory," he murmured, his voice husky with unfulfilled passion. "And it will be forever etched in my mind that you are breathtaking in royal blue . . ."

He had noticed her, truly noticed her! Mikyla could not suppress the pleased grin that cut dimples in her cheeks. Cale felt his knees buckle beneath him when she blessed him with her radiant smile. It was the first time Cale could recall being the recipient of such a sunny expression. Usually, he invited her mutinous glowers.

"And may I say you look absolutely gorg—" She strangled the remainder of the word and her face flushed profusely.

Cale gestured toward their horses, silently indicating it was time to leave. "I appreciate the compliment, but I think it more proper to describe a man as handsome or attractive," he corrected, flinging her a wry grin.

Thrusting out her chin, Mikyla aimed herself toward Sundance. "Despite your faults, I find you far more than handsome. Since arrogant is already among your extensive shortcomings I cannot add to your failings by declaring that tonight you border on beautiful."

Amusement bubbled from Cale's chest as he watched Mikyla float gracefully toward her stallion. If anyone else had labeled him beautiful, Cale would have punched them in the mouth. But considering the source of the compliment, and knowing how Mikyla detested him at the moment, he wasn't about to become indignant over her choice of words.

The journey to Fort Reno was more pleasurable than Cale anticipated. Mikyla was looking forward to the festivities and she bubbled in conversation, apparently forgetting she disliked her companion. Cale was intrigued by this new facet of her complex personality. Mikyla was light and carefree and he yearned to reverse direction and bypass the celebration. Sharing this enchanting nymph with the male population of the fort depressed him. Mikyla would be swirling around the dance area in scores of other arms. And where would Cale be? Propped in a chair, pretending to be crippled.

Mikyla misinterpreted Cale's sullen silence as disinterest. He had complimented her appearance but it didn't take long for his thoughts to stray from her. Oh, why was she so determined to win his affection, or even a smidgen of it? Cale was Cale. He wasn't going to change *for* her, *because of* her, or *in spite of* her. She might as well hitch herself to a drifting cloud. Cale was just a restless tumbleweed who could never share her dreams of putting down roots and building a home brimming with love. He wasn't the kind of man who could be content to share a life with only one woman when the world was heaping with conquests. He preferred variety to steadfast devotion and she was too possessive to tolerate a man with his assortment of tastes.

When the music of an orchestra wafted its way across the rolling hills, Mikyla set her troubled musings aside. She was going to enjoy herself for this one night. Even if Cale purposely ignored her, she was going to find distraction, she promised herself faithfully

Cale limped along, leaning heavily on his makeshift cane, favoring his right foot. He was dreading this so-called celebration as thoroughly as a man who was on his way to his own execution. Just as he suspected, Mikyla was accosted by

266

a cavalry of men who ached to whirl her around the open arena with the pretense of dancing.

Distracted by the exquisite blonde who moved with sylphlike grace in the torch light, Cale sank down by a table, only to find Emily Terrel materializing from thin air.

"I hoped you would come," she murmured, sidling closer to lay a possessive hand on Cale's thigh.

Cale flinched as if he had been snakebit. "Em, I don't think this is the time or the place," he chided, giving her the evil eye.

Emily refused to take Cale seriously. He had never been the kind of man to ignore a woman's advances. "I told you I was a lonely, neglected woman." Her adventurous hand mapped the muscular column of his upper leg. "Come dance with me, Cale. I want to feel your arms around me, to remember what it was like between us . . ."

"I can't dance," Cale told her, edging as far away as the bench would permit. "I injured my foot." Cale waved his cane under her nose to confirm his proclamation.

A disappointed frown puckered Emily's features. "Cale, please, I need you. I need to feel needed . . ."

Cale rolled his eyes heavenward, requesting divine patience. If he angered Emily she might seek revenge by making accusations to Brock. And if Cale touched her, for any reason, Brock might see them. Cale was between a rock and a hard spot. No matter which way he turned he could feel the scrape.

Before Cale could delicately express his sentiments, Morgan Hagerty and Joseph Richards approached. Cale was most thankful for the interruption, even if he were forced to confront these particular scoundrels. Graciously excusing herself, Emily left the table and Cale breathed a sigh of relief.

The tension between Morgan and Cale increased when Morgan glared murderously at him. It was Joseph who finally broke the brittle silence with his annoying voice.

"Now see here, Brolin. You and that feisty young woman are making this business transaction very tedious," Joseph declared brusquely. "You are intelligent enough to know

267

you can't fight us. Sooner or later, you will have to succumb to our demands. Only a fool would hold out until the land is taken from him at a minimal price."

Cale thought Joseph would look more appropriate sitting on a perch. He truly resembled a parrot with his loud, colorful vest and red jacket. And he sounded like one, too, when he spoke in that nasal squawk of his.

"I would gladly hand the property over to you," he assured Joseph. "But my partner does not agree. I need a few more days to resolve my dealings with Miss Lassiter. Once we come to terms the deed will be yours for thirty dollars an acre."

"Then perhaps Mikyla is the one we should pressure, since you seem so agreeable," Morgan smirked, flinging Cale a devilish glance.

Cale's nerves were already as taut as harp strings. The insinuation and the wicked expression on Morgan's face set fire to Cale's temper. Impulsively, he reached across the table to clamp his fingers in Morgan's freshly starched shirt.

"You leave Mikyla alone," he hissed venomously. "When I have sole ownership of the claim, it will be yours. Until then, keep your distance from her. I'll handle her in my own way . . ."

"What is going on here?"

Mikyla had seen the two men approach Cale. She had also seen the comely redhead who had been practically sitting in Cale's lap. Although pride refused to permit her to interrupt when Cale was with one of his admirers, she had no qualms about barging in on this particular conversation. She had arrived in time to hear Cale declare that he would handle her. The remark hurt worse than being slapped in the face. Cale had just confirmed her darkest suspicions. He was conniving to steal her property out from under her and all three men had decided to go behind her back. But no one was going to snatch her dream site away from her!

Without taking his stormy gray eyes off Morgan, Cale growled at Mikyla. "Go Skip to My Lou with your long string of soldiers."

Her chin jutted out in indignation. How dare he talk to her

268

in that gruff tone of voice! "I will not be sent away like a misbehaving child," she informed him curtly. "The land is mine and I will never sell it."

Her firm declaration caused Cale to wince uncomfortably. The last thing Joseph and Morgan needed was to see just how strong-willed and determined Mikyla really was. "Dammit, shut up and get the hell out of here!" he snarled.

Cale had insulted her only a moment before. But she couldn't have hurt her more if he had doubled his fist and planted it firmly in her jaw. He was shoving her aside as if she had no rights, as if she were some simple-minded twit who couldn't determine north from south unless some man pointed her in the right direction. By damned, she had every right to voice her opinions. Just because she was a woman didn't imply Cale could tell *her* when to jump and exactly how high! The decision about the land was partially hers to make and she wasn't selling.

After flashing Cale a glare that was meant to slice him in quarters, Mikyla focused on the two greedy swindlers who wanted to shatter her dream for their own personal gains. "Cale can only speak for himself," she gritted out, fighting to contain her volatile temper. But it was damned near impossible. She itched to snatch up the Colt that hung on Cale's hip and blow all three men to smithereens.

"I have no intention of selling my quarter section, not to you or anyone else. There is nothing you can do to make me sell! Nothing!" Her voice was low, but there was no mistaking the determination in it. "I will take my protest to the courts, and the two of you will be exposed for fraud. And that is exactly what you are committing. This land was *free* land. It was not to be sold off in expensive town lots. It was to be staked by individual settlers on the day of the Run. Not you or the railroad is going to browbeat me into accepting *any* offer."

With that, Mikyla flung her nose in the air and turned a cold shoulder. As she flounced away, Cale muttered every curse word in his vocabulary. Damnation, now she had really done it! It was obvious that Joseph and Morgan saw Mikyla as a definite threat to their scheme. If she continued to protest, the settlers who anxiously awaited the purchase of the property would grow restless and locate elsewhere. Joseph and Morgan stood to lose a fortune if they couldn't establish a community near the railroad's soon-to-be right-of-way.

Totally exasperated, Cale pushed away from the table to limp after Mikyla, but Morgan's harsh voice froze him in his tracks. "You better talk some sense into that stubborn chit. She will soon regret her interference in our plans." A menacing smile curled Morgan's lips detracting from his handsome appearance. "There are ways to ensure her cooperation . . . and yours . . . if the two of you refuse to come to terms . . ."

Cale's glittering eyes drilled into Morgan's sinister smile. "It works both ways, Hagerty. If you harm Mikyla, you may not be around to reap the profits of your skulduggery. If you think I have interfered in your life before, you might find that I have only begun to meddle."

Leaving that threat hanging in the air, Cale hobbled off to locate Mikyla. She was surrounded with eager beaux who were vying for her attention and the opportunity of holding her luscious body against theirs. The moment Mikyla spied Cale, she latched on to the nearest soldier and led him toward the other dancers, quickly losing herself in the crowd that was lining up to dance the Virginia Reel. She was too furious to confront Cale and she couldn't risk exploding in a temper tantrum. She would be forced to concede the bet.

Scowling to himself, Cale wheeled around, deciding to locate a neutral corner and park himself in it. No such luck. Emily Terrel had been monitoring Cale's activities while her husband was in the stables, tending his palomino. Brock had won the horse race and he was so involved with his victory that he had momentarily forgotten he even had a wife.

Before Cale could elude her, Emily fluttered toward him, clinging like ivy. Cale was forced to endure her forwardness. "Em, it's time you and I had a talk," Cale said with a frustrated sigh.

Emily's face lit up like a lighthouse beacon. But the conversation she had in mind did not require words. "We can have privacy over here . . ." One trim finger indicated the shadows cast by the officers' quarters that sat beside the military drill field.

When they were safely concealed in the shadows, Emily flung her arms around Cale's neck, showering him with affectionate kisses. If the eager female had been Mikyla, Cale might have accepted his good fortune. But Emily posed a threat she couldn't possibly begin to imagine.

It was difficult to wedge a word in edgewise while Emily was climbing all over him. Cale tried his hand at diplomacy, but it didn't work worth a tittle. Emily was wrapping herself around him like an octopus.

While Cale was trying to fend off Emily's amorous advances without insulting her, Mikyla was picking her way through the crowd. She had seen Emily approach Cale and lead him away. Mikyla resolved not to go near Cale for fear of completely losing her temper. But jealousy got the best of her. If her suspicions were correct, the eager redhead was Brock's wife, the one who had been intimate with Cale after Jessica Whoever-she-was had done whatever she had done. Mikyla knew she was leapfrogging from one speculation to another, but she was hurt and angry and frustrated . . . and jealous, dammit!

She had dressed specifically for Cale. She had wanted tonight to be a fresh new start for them. But Cale was going behind her back to sell her land and now he was carousing with Major Terrel's wife. And if Cale laid one hand on that curvaceous redhead, Mikyla was prepared to fly into a rage. After all, she would have won the wager and she would no longer have reason to contain herself.

Mikyla focused her attention on the wooden structure around which the chummy couple had disappeared. Suddenly, Morgan and Joseph appeared on Mikyla's left flank. Approaching on her right flank was Brock Terrel, who was anxious to boast his winning to Cale and Emily and everyone else who would listen.

"Have you seen Cale?" Brock questioned Mikyla, still sporting a triumphant smile.

Mikyla grumbled under her breath and lied. Why she was

protecting that insufferable Cale Brolin was anybody's guess. He certainly didn't deserve one iota of consideration. "No, not in the last quarter of an hour," she flung over her shoulder.

"Mikyla, we want to talk to you," Morgan insisted, hastening his pace to catch up with her swift, impatient strides.

"Not now," Mikyla muttered in annoyance.

"Yes, now," Joseph Richards snapped at the back of her head. "You are making a grave mistake, young lady."

"Go away and leave me alone," she hissed, lifting her skirts to break into a run.

To her dismay, all three men loped along at her heels. As she skidded around the building hoping to elude her pursuers, she came face-to-face with the sight of Cale backed against the whitewashed building, his lips fastened on Emily's. The redhead had clamped herself around Cale so closely they resembled Siamese twins joined at the mouth. From where Mikyla stood it seemed Cale was thoroughly enjoying his tête-à-tête. But Cale was still relying on diplomacy—a tactic he quickly realized was a waste of time. He had opened his mouth to inform Emily that he was not going to come between her and Brock, but before he could utter two words, Emily had engaged her lips in something far more stimulating than conversation.

Before Cale could alert Emily to the sound of visitors, Mikyla appeared, followed by Brock, Morgan, and Joseph. Cale prayed for the earth to open and swallow him alive. But the answer to his prayer was *no*. He was forced to confront Mikyla's outraged glower, Brock's furious gasp, Morgan and Joseph's wicked smiles.

Mikyla was the first to find her tongue and she exploded like a keg of dynamite. "Our wager is over, Cale Brolin." She spat his name as if it were poison. "The property is mine alone, to do with as I see fit." Unable to face Cale without bursting into humiliated tears, Mikyla wheeled around to confront Joseph and Morgan. "You can take your offer elsewhere, gentlemen. I won't sell. Do you hear me?" Her tone bordered on hysterical. She struggled to see through the flood of tears that splashed in her eyes. "The land is mine and it shall remain mine, even if I have to carry my battle all the way to the high courts!"

In a burst of mortified fury, Mikyla crashed through the wall of men and ran blindly ahead. All she could see was Cale holding Emily full-length against him, plying her with those heart-melting kisses of which *she* had been deprived for two agonizing weeks. Damn him! The Lord should call down his wrath on one of his most obvious sinners. Cale deserved to pay penance.

Why had she fallen in love with a man without a soul, without a conscience, without a heart? Oh, how she hated Cale. She had endured her last round of humiliation because of that man. She didn't want to see Cale again . . . ever!

"Ky, come back here!" Cale bellowed furiously. But Mikyla never broke stride or glanced back. She just ran as fast as her legs would carry her.

As Cale charged after her, Brock's hand snaked out to detain him. "Wait just a damned minute. You have some explaining to do," he snarled.

Cale's temper snapped like a dried twig. Brock was glaring murderously at him. Emily was wailing and sobbing hysterically and Morgan was gloating over Cale's misfortune.

"Before you condemn me, Brock, perhaps you had better take a good long look at yourself," Cale muttered, shaking his arm free. "If you would spend more time with Em, she wouldn't turn her attention on the first man who crosses her path."

Brock puffed up like a bullfrog. "It is *my* fault that you were taking outrageous privileges with my wife?" he croaked. "You miserable coward! Aren't you man enough to assume the blame for what you did?" When Emily flew into his arms like a homing pigeon returning to roost, crying and blubbering senselessly, Brock gathered her close. "Don't you think I know you took advantage of Em before we were married?" His tone suddenly resembled a panther's growl. "I'm not a fool, Brolin. I tried to overlook your lusty advances on my wife since we were involved in business

273

dealings. But our arrangements are off. Go peddle your horses somewhere else!"

As Cale stomped off, Morgan's taunting voice nipped at his heels. "It seems you also misjudged Miss Lassiter's affection for you," he chuckled devilishly. "She flew off like a woman scorned. I wonder if she would be upset or delighted if you were to meet with disaster . . . Or do you even care what she thinks or what becomes of her?" He waited, carefully scrutinizing Cale's reaction to the remarks.

Morgan left the implication dangling in the air, allowing Cale to draw his own conclusions. Cale wasn't certain if Morgan was suggesting that *he* was to become the tool to be used against Mikyla or if it was to be the other way around. Knowing Morgan's scheming mind, Cale prepared himself for trouble, an armload of it. But it would be a contest to determine who would dispose of him first. Morgan had hated him for years. Joseph wanted to see him crushed for his own personal satisfaction. Brock wanted him skinned alive, and Ky . . .

Cale swore vehemently. Mikyla would hold this over him for the rest of his natural life, he predicted grimly. If she hadn't hated him in the past, she surely would now—enough to refuse to speak to him. Well, she might not wish to talk to him, but she would, just the same. But damned, Cale had a few things to get off his chest and Mikyla was going to hear him out!

Gnashing that thought between his teeth, Cale stalked toward his horse, forgetting his limp. After all, the ploy hadn't saved him from disaster. It only served to slow the pace of impending doom. Lord, what else could possibly go wrong? Cale asked himself dismally. He had made so many enemies the past few weeks that if he wound up dead, he wouldn't know who to accuse. So much for good intentions, Cale breathed miserably. He had only tried to spare Mikyla inevitable heartbreak. But if damnable oaths had any effect on a man's afterlife, Cale imagined that Mikyla's curses would earn him an agonizing, torturous death and consign him to the fiery pits of hell.

Chapter 19

Mikyla flew across the moonlit meadow as if a prairie fire were blazing behind her. The tears she had managed to contain earlier streamed down her cheeks. She felt empty and raw inside. She had been betrayed by the only man who had the power to hurt her. God, how she loathed the image that rose to torment her over and over again.

Cale was a despicable bastard, she reminded herself for the umpteenth time. He didn't care enough about her to keep his hands off another woman—a married woman, the wife of his business associate! He had attempted to bargain with Morgan and Joseph as if her feelings counted for nothing. He didn't respect her. He didn't care an ounce. Damn that horrible man!

The sound of hooves pounding the ground behind her provoked Mikyla to glance over her shoulder. The last man she ever wanted to see was thundering across the rolling hills, pushing his gelding to the very limits. Muttering several more unprintable epithets, Mikyla spurred Sundance into his fastest gait.

Cale bided his time as he followed the billowing bundle of blue silk. He knew Mikyla would eventually slow her breakneck speed. She wouldn't risk winding her precious stallion. True to his prediction, Mikyla was forced to bring the laboring stallion to a walk. When she did, Cale kept the strawberry roan at a bone-jarring trot. The steed was far more accustomed to long journeys and he slowly gobbled up the distance that separated them.

"Ky . . ." Cale called just loud enough to be heard over the methodic clop of hooves.

"Don't ever call me that again. Don't speak to me at all," Mikyla bit off, her voice crackling with emotion.

Cale nudged the roan. When he was directly beside the stallion, Cale leaned out to grasp the reins, bringing Sundance to an abrupt halt. "I love you." His soft words broke the strained silence and they were followed by the sharp crack of Mikyla's palm colliding with Cale's cheek.

How could he say such a thing in the wake of what he had done? He had barked at her as if she were a witless ignoramus. He had schemed to sell her land out from under her. He had dallied with one of his former lovers. And after all that, he had the audacity to ply her with empty phrases of love. That was the second time he had voiced that preposterous declaration. He hadn't meant it then and he most certainly didn't mean it now. How stupid did he think she was? Did he think he could profess undying devotion when she knew for a fact that he was lying through his teeth? Did he think those three little words made everything right, no matter how wrong things were?

Well, she was not a sentimental fool who would grasp at the possibility of love. She knew Cale for what he was and nothing was going to change her low opinion of him. Thanks to Cale, she was now a devout man-hater. Thanks to Cale, she now had a dried-up soul and a heart that was as shriveled as a prune. No one would ever hurt her again because she would never let anyone that close. She was her own island, an entity unto herself, and Cale Brolin could sizzle in hell for all she cared!

Ignoring the stinging sensation that throbbed in his cheek, Cale stared Mikyla squarely in the eye. Tears were gushing down her face like torrents of rain. Her silver-blond hair was a mass of wild tangles and her knuckles were white from clutching the saddle horn.

Tearing off an arm would have been less painful than enduring her flood of tears, her scathing glowers. But Cale couldn't see that he had much choice, not until he reasoned with this high-strung minx.

"You are fighting a hopeless battle, Ky," he told her solemnly. "Morgan holds an interest in the townsite company. He staked the adjacent property and had intended to stake your dream site as well. Now you have defied Joseph and Morgan. They can't risk taking the matter to court when they face fraud. And after you went spiriting off like the betrayed lover, you put ideas in Morgan's head."

Cale expelled the breath he had been holding. "Morgan is no fool. He knows there is something between us. Unless I miss my guess, he will continue to pressure you off your property. Joseph and Morgan won't bat an eye at using either of us to influence the other." Cale's features were grave with concern. "I'm referring to threats of violence, perhaps even death. Now that you have allowed Morgan to think you are in love with me . . ."

"I am not!" she piped, her voice shrill with protest.

Cale shrugged for the sake of argument. He was not about to be detoured into a fiery debate when there were critical issues to discuss.

"What matters is what Morgan *thinks,*" he emphasized. "If he believes you will buckle if my life is in danger, or that you will concede the land if Sundance is crippled . . ." Cale could tell his remarks had penetrated her armor of anger and humiliation.

Allowing her the opportunity to digest his speculations, Cale tugged on Sundance's reins, leading the stallion and his sulking mistress toward camp. "It may not be just your life that is in danger," he elaborated. "Morgan will seek out your weaknesses and prey upon them until you bend to his will. He has grown tired of attempting to charm you into submission. And before long you will meet the real Morgan Hagerty, the one who lurks beneath that sophisticated veneer of polished manners and persuasive smiles."

From where Mikyla was sitting, Morgan didn't seem half as threatening as Cale Brolin. Cale was the one who had preyed on her vulnerability, who had betrayed her, spited her at every turn.

"That is all nonsense," Mikyla burst out as she rerouted

the river of tears with the back of her hand. "You have twisted everything to redeem yourself." Her bitter laughter shattered the silence. "You concoct such convincing lies that even Saint Peter would fall prey and place you next in line to receive a halo. But I have been burned so often that I can see through your scheming lies. I saw you talking to Morgan and Joseph. I heard you tell them that you would see that I conformed to their wishes. And I most certainly witnessed your attempt to seduce Emily Terrel."

Her voice was becoming higher and wilder by the second. "Don't try to confuse me with any more lies. Just leave me be." As they approached their camp, Mikyla gestured a trembling finger toward his tent. "I want you and your belongings off my property in one hour. If you're not gone, I will scatter your horses and set a torch to your tent. As of this moment, you are trespassing on my property and you are guaranteed only sixty minutes of amnesty!"

Damn, was there any conceivable way to reason with this woman, Cale asked himself as he stared into her tear-rimmed eyes. She had her heart set on thinking the worst of him. Indeed, she delighted in hating him. It was her inspiration, he mused sourly.

When Mikyla swung from the saddle, Cale followed suit. As she stormed toward her tent, Cale outthrust an arm to halt her.

"I want you to pack up and come with me," he demanded more gruffly than he intended. "Forget this fantasy before it gets you killed. If you want a ranch I'll build you one. If you want a herd of Sundance's colts, I'll supply the best brood mares in the country."

Blast it. She didn't want to hear empty promises. He only wanted her off the land and he was willing to say anything to have his way. She didn't want him to erect a ranch for her. She didn't want his brood mares, purchased with money he had swindled from settlers who had been desperate for a swift horse to make the Run. She wanted his *love* and his pledge to help her protect her dream.

Her affection couldn't be bought and neither could her acceptance of his demands. Both would have to be freely given and there were too many lingering doubts about Cale's integrity to sway her. She could never profess to love this confusing, complex man until she knew beyond all shadows of a doubt that he honestly cared for her. And she knew he *didn't*.

A man in love did not betray the woman he cherished time and time again. He had told Morgan and Joseph that all they were conducting was business. He had exemplified his flagrant disregard for her feelings by groping in the shadows with Emily Terrel. Come to think of it, the two times Cale had mentioned love he had been hellbent on making Mikyla do his bidding. He hadn't wanted her to make the Run. So what did he do? Cale insisted that he loved her and commanded that she accompany him to Texas. Now he wanted her to take the profit for the land—(and undoubtedly split it with him!)—and relocate on a site *he* selected. Cale used a confession of love as a means to an end. But Mikyla wasn't *bending* to his will and she wasn't *breaking* either!

She glared furiously at the tanned fingers that were clamped on her forearm. "Remove your hand or I will retrieve my pistol and blow it away," she hissed vindictively. "I am going nowhere with you. I came to Oklahoma country chasing a dream and I have found it. I've lived like a gypsy for years and I will have no more of it."

She was just gathering steam and she was determined to expend every ounce of it before she said her last good-bye to Cale Brolin. Mikyla drew in a deep breath and plunged on. "You offer nothing lasting or permanent. A promise of a home elsewhere?" she laughed bitterly. "The stars are your ceiling, Cale. You couldn't put down roots if you were placed in a hole and watered regularly. In two weeks you would grow restless and all your empty vows would be forgotten. You don't love me. You don't know what love is. You wouldn't recognize it if it marched up and sat down on top of you!"

Cale was so infuriated with this mule of a woman that he wanted to shake the stuffing out of her. Swearing a blue streak, Cale watched her sweep into her tent. Hell, he ought to ride off into the darkness and allow Morgan to eat her alive. Giving way to that spiteful thought, Cale stalked off to fold his tent and gather his gear.

Let her do battle with the townsite company and the railroad, he silently fumed. Even if she tried to drag those swindlers through the court of appeals it would take forever to reach a decision. There were so many disputes stacked up already that it would be years before Miki could present her case. By then, Morgan would have disposed of her. When she realized she couldn't win she would come crawling to Cale, begging him to help her. Then he would scoff into her beseeching blue eyes and ridicule her for permitting her stubborn pride to defeat her.

How dare she declare he didn't know the meaning of love. She was the one whose heart was inflated with dreams that blinded her to reality and left her deaf to sensibility.

While Cale stormed around camp, clanking and cursing, Mikyla sat on the edge of her bed. Her ears were tuned to the sound of Cale preparing to walk out of her life. She was anxious to see him go. Now she could sulk without guarding her emotions. If she felt like crying buckets of tears she could. If she felt like throwing things, no one would be here to taunt her for her tantrum.

Lost in dreary thoughts, Mikyla didn't glance up until Cale's brawny form filled the entrance of her tent. But when she did, her heart wilted like a delicate rose besieged by hot summer winds. Cale's wide chest was heaving from exertion and frustration. His silver eyes were stormy with anger. As his shadow fell over her, Mikyla shrank away, terrified that he would touch her and she would melt like a sentimental fool.

He's leaving and you will never see him again, her broken heart screamed. *Good riddance to him,* logic scoffed in contradiction.

Roughly, Cale jerked Mikyla to her feet. His hands were like vise grips on her elbows, cutting off the circulation. "Don't you ever tell me I don't know what love is," he scowled into her blanched face. "Not when you don't have the foggiest notion what love *isn't.* Love *isn't* giving half your heart and withholding the other portion for a silly damned dream of Thoroughbreds and sprawling ranches. Love *isn't* thinking the worst of a man, refusing to trust him, defying your belief in him." Cale's craggy features were clouded with frustration and he yielded to the temptation of trying to shake some sense into this staunchly independent, incredibly stubborn female. "Go ahead, think the worst of me, put your faith in Morgan. We'll see where it gets you."

Suddenly Cale released her. The back of her knees collided with the edge of the cot and she sprawled on her bed, petticoats billowing everywhere. Cale loomed over her, ominous and threatening. Clutching the lace bodice of her gown, he rendered the garment to rags, eliciting Mikyla's startled shriek. Before she could gather her wits and fight back, Cale's fingers tangled in her hair, twisting the long strands around his hand like a rope. She was forced to move her face toward his or risk having her hair yanked out by the roots.

"You want to believe I'm a rough-edged savage who uses women to curb my animal lusts?" he breathed into her colorless cheeks, setting them aflame. "Perhaps I should live up to your expectations. It would be a pity if you had no justifiable basis upon which to form your low opinions of me. If you want to despise me, perhaps it's time I truly gave you cause."

His mouth came down hard on hers, bruising her lips, stripping the breath that would have voiced a loud protest against rough abuse. He was showing her how he would behave if he wished to prove his male dominance, to display his total lack of respect. In less than a heartbeat Mikyla's recently purchased gown was lying in a heap. His hands were flooding over her quaking flesh, wanting to hurt, to leave lingering marks of abuse. But even while Cale was motivated by frustrated fury, he couldn't bring himself to injure and maim. He was provoking Mikyla to hate him more, but Cale could not have hated *himself* less.

His anger transformed into gentle passion, the healing kind that erased his bruising touch and replaced it with pleasure. The need that had lain dormant for two tormenting weeks began to burn within him. Cale no longer wanted to humiliate Mikyla. He longed to make her respond to him, to persuade her to defy her own stubbornness. There had been times, when the storm of desire had engulfed them, that Mikyla had come to him in eager abandon. That was what Cale found himself wanting now. Just once before he walked out of her life, he wanted to relive those splendorous moments, to forget the fury that now raged between them.

Her quiet whimpering stabbed at his heart and Cale whispered his apology against her kiss-swollen lips. What Mikyla truly needed, whether she would admit it or not, was to be loved, thoroughly and completely. She needed to understand that there was more to life than delusions, than famed ranches and legendary horses. And once before he left, Cale was determined to set a torch that would inflame her dreams—not the ones focused on prairie grass and winged stallions—but the ones that touched the heart and smoothed the wrinkles from the soul.

Gently, Cale took her lips under his. He kissed away her salty tears, assuring her that he had no wish to hurt her. His worshipping hands smoothed away the pain his roughness had wrought. In the wake of his anger came the tenderest of passion, and the sweet sensations healed the wounds of humiliation. His skillful caresses swam over a sea of bare flesh, creating a river of rapture that channeled into every fiber of her being. His kisses were like warm sunshine after a devastating summer storm. Soft, full lips whispered across her skin, provoking her flesh to quiver like the gentle stirring of leaves in a breeze.

Cale quickly unbuttoned his shirt and brought her hands to his hair-matted chest. "Touch me, Ky. I am no monster, although I can behave like one when I am aroused to fury. But I am only a man who wants you for what you are, for what we share when we shed the defensive armor of pride. This is what is between us—this insatiable, ever-constant craving to possess and be possessed. When we make love we need nothing else . . ."

As his flowing caresses sketched the shapely contours of her body, Mikyla's hands also began to investigate and explore. She didn't want to remember the wild, ecstatic moments, not when she knew they would become her ruin. But when she set her hands upon his rock-hard skin, her heart took control of her thoughts. She adored touching this powerful mass of masculinity. She reveled in the feel of his rough flesh melting beneath her inquiring caresses.

For several moments they lay together, stroking and touching, scrutinizing each other. Her deep blue eyes followed the flight of her hands as they drifted down the slope of his shoulder. She watched as her inquiring fingertips splayed across his massive chest. She saw the shimmer of awakened passion in his eyes.

Caressing him aroused her, left her craving more than this quiet intimacy. She ached to fulfill the unsatiated passion that had long been denied. She yearned to create a memory that would sustain her when loneliness threatened to destroy her.

After Cale walked away, she would never again experience the stormfire of sensations that set her heart ablaze. Never again would she hear the soft enchanting melody that strummed on her soul. This night would have to last her a lifetime. It was all she had, all she could ever have.

When Cale crouched above her, Mikyla's moist lashes swept up to survey those craggy, bronzed features that could become rigid with anger or mellow with desire. His eyes were like sparkling moonbeams as they slid down her body in total possession. His sensuous mouth parted in invitation. The corded muscles of his arms bulged as he held himself at bay, waiting for her to come to him.

The faintest hint of a smile bordered Mikyla's lips as she looped her arms around his broad shoulders. "I know I'm going to hate myself for this," she murmured up to him.

A slow grin rippled across his lips and sparkled in his eyes. "I can endure your hatred, as long as I know you still want me." One heavy brow arched as he bent to drop a light kiss to her lips. His masculine body brushed provocatively against hers and then withdrew, teasing and arousing her. "Do you want me, Ky? No matter how many obstacles stand like mountains between us?" he questioned hoarsely. "Do you need me to fulfill the empty dimension of your life? How deep does this hatred run? And how long will it sustain you when I'm gone?"

His sensuous assault was sweet, tormenting agony. He was so close and yet maddeningly far away. He knew how to make a woman ache to her very core, leaving her craving to become his total possession. A surrendering sigh tumbled from beneath his feather-light kiss, and her body helplessly arched toward his, throbbing with pulsating desire.

"Damn your pride," Cale breathed huskily. "Tell me what you feel, even if you consider me to be Satan himself. Do you want another man . . . *any* man . . . or *me*, Ky?"

He was doing incredible things to her self-control. Her entire body was aflame with a longing that only Cale Brolin could generate and fulfill. "I want you," she whispered against his warm lips. "And damn you for making me admit that no one else arouses me the way you do."

"Ky, I need you . . ." Cale rasped as he settled over her. "Take me to paradise . . ."

She was absorbing his strength, draining his thoughts. Cale had held himself away from her, testing his restraint, waiting to hear her begrudging words. Even if there could be nothing else between them, he needed to know she was driven by the same potent attraction that defied rhyme and reason.

Groaning in bittersweet torment, Cale buried his ruffled raven head against the tangled mass of silver-gold strands and inhaled the poignant scent of her. His body moved upon command, matching her ardor, giving of himself, sharing the splendor that couldn't be translated into words.

They were like a living, breathing puzzle that would make no sense until they were one. His soul took flight, soaring toward the boundless horizon. His heart hammered against his ribs like a wild bird fighting captivity. He sought unattainable depths of intimacy, driven by a need that consumed his mind and body.

Cale could feel himself losing control. He could feel Mikyla's nails digging into the whipcord muscles of his back. And when she gripped him so fiercely, Cale responded. He held her to him as if they were about to plummet from a towering precipice. Ecstasy drenched them like a waterfall of fire. Sensation after sensation tumbled over them until they were a part of the living flame. Rapture burned away time, leaving them suspended in space for that one endless moment only lovers can experience. Cale and Mikyla reveled in the ineffable pleasure of their union, in the wondrous sensations that their lovemaking evoked.

It was long breathless minutes later that the fiery pleasure ebbed and Cale regained a small degree of sanity. He knew he had to leave, but it was pure hell to force himself from the silky circle of her arms. Quietly he eased away and sat up on the edge of the bed. When he glanced down, his breath stuck in his windpipe, very nearly strangling him. Lord, she looked enchanting as she lay there with those wild tendrils of sun and moonbeams spraying about her exquisite face. Her lips were red and swollen from his kisses. Her cheeks were tinted with the afterglow of passion. Her shapely body was soft and pliant and warm with intimacy.

Unable to restrain himself, Cale cupped her face in his large, calloused hands. Holding her unblinking gaze, he lowered his head to treat himself to one last kiss. With the taste of her lingering on his lips, Cale scooped up his breeches and fastened himself into them. Silently, he gathered his boots and shirt. When he reached the exit, he paused to formulate his thoughts. Turning, he waved several bills he had retrieved from his pocket and then set them on the table beside the door.

"I didn't mean to rip your gown to shreds," he murmured apologetically. "You looked lovely in it. I hope the one you purchase to replace it will be just as exquisite as the lady who wears it . . ."

As Cale disappeared into the darkness, Mikyla bounded to her feet, snatching up her mutilated gown. It was a simple matter to shrug on the garment since Cale had split it down the middle. At the moment she didn't care about the dress or the anger he had displayed earlier. Cale was walking out of her life and she couldn't let him go!

"Cale, don't leave me. Stay here and help me build a home we both can share," she choked out as she ran toward him.

He swung into the saddle and then glanced down to see Mikyla dashing toward him. Her silver-gold mane was trailing behind her. Her gown gaped to reveal the alluring swells of her breasts and the shapely form of her legs. Lord, it would have been so easy to climb down off his horse and envelop her in his arms. But they would resolve nothing if he stayed with her.

A rueful smile grazed his lips as he leaned out to brush away the tears that bled down her cheeks. "It won't work, Ky," he murmured softly. "You will have to come to me when you are no longer blinded by your dreams. Come to me when you want *me* instead of your prospering ranch and prize Thoroughbreds."

His hand curled beneath her chin, forcing her to meet his somber gaze. "If you come, I will know it's me you want and that you will expect no more than to stay by my side, even if I decide to live out of a tent and wander the plains like a vagabond." His silver eyes drilled into hers as he softly uttered his last request. "Come to me, Ky, only when you desire no more than *me* . . . when *I* become the only dream you'll ever need . . ."

Mikyla jerked away, her back stiff in annoyance. Damn, but he was arrogant. He wanted her to forget what *she* wanted, what *she* needed.

Cale expected her to follow him to the edge of the earth. And yes, she loved him. But she refused to fetch and heel, to assimilate her life with his. Cale wanted her to do all the giving while he did all the taking. Well, she was too proud to grovel at his feet. Damn him! He didn't need a woman, he needed a lap dog!

Even if she did humiliate herself by consenting to follow him, what kind of life could she expect with Cale? The same kind she had endured with her father, she assured herself bitterly. She had enough of drifting from town to town, scratching and clawing to provide meals and clothes. Cale was asking too much of her. He wanted her to sacrifice everything she had dreamed of having. He demanded far too much when he was offering nothing in return. And if Cale really loved her he would have whispered his confession in

286

moments of passion, not when he wanted to sway her from her anger and maneuver her to do his bidding. If he cared for her he would have said so while they lay in each other's arms, not while they were in the middle of one of their arguments!

"And what shall we build *our* dreams on, Cale?" she questioned, her voice quivering with resentment. "Will our home be constructed of invisible stones, our corrals of imaginary wire and timber? And what shall bind us together when we have another of our explosive arguments?" Her hollow laughter split the darkness. "We will always be at odds. Sometimes I think all we truly have in common is our differences."

Cale chuckled deep in his throat as he took up the lead rope to his long string of horses and mules. "Sometimes, my lovely little nymph, invisible walls and silken bonds are more durable than wood and stone." When a muddled frown knitted Mikyla's brow, Cale chortled again. "You still see everything in terms of boundaries—something with stone walls and written agreements, don't you, Ky?" He didn't allow her to respond. He simply confirmed her darkest suspicions. "I'm not offering a marriage contract that says we are to hold the vows sacred. A piece of paper may prove legality, but it can't promise fidelity or affection." A heavy sigh escaped his lips as he stared into her oval face. "One day you may begin to understand what I have been trying to tell you. But I doubt that will happen until you stop *thinking* and begin to trust your instincts."

His fingertips touched the brim of his Stetson and a smile grazed his sensuous lips. "Good luck, Ky. You're going to need it if you plan to cling to this dream of yours."

Mikyla stood like a marble statue until Cale and his procession of livestock became one of the swaying shadows. Seeking consolation, Mikyla strode over to stroke Sundance's soft muzzle. But even the stallion's eager response failed to lift her drooping spirits.

"Invisible walls, indeed," Mikyla muttered in exasperation. The day she left Sundance and pulled up stakes to follow that rootless rake would be the same day the sands of the Sahara Desert sprouted tropical vegetation!

Why should Cale Brolin become the most important thing in her life when he had lied to her, cheated on her, and betrayed her? Why, even his crippled leg had been a ploy. And he didn't think she had noticed! Well, she had. The man was utterly mad and she would have to be crazy as he if she adopted his philosophy and went off in search of the sun.

Mikyla climbed into bed and cursed the lingering scent of the man who had made her want him despite her firm convictions, despite her wounded pride. No matter which way she turned the memories were there to haunt her. For what seemed hours Mikyla tossed and turned on her cot, imagining what her world would be like without Cale in it. He had been with her so long it seemed incomprehensible to think she wouldn't be greeted each morning by his lopsided smiles.

"You are made of sturdy stuff, Miki Lassiter," she encouraged herself. "You can lead a perfectly normal life without Cale Brolin."

But somehow her self-inspiring lectures lacked enthusiasm, especially when the following day dawned bleak and dreary. Mikyla caught herself wondering if Cale had spitefully lassoed the sun and tied it behind his procession of horses. She wouldn't have put it past that ornery rascal. He was determined to leave her miserable. And what galled her to no end was that he had efficiently accomplished his purpose. Facing each new day without Cale was a dozen kinds of hell.

Part III

He who has a thousand friends has not a friend to spare, and he who has one enemy will meet him everywhere.
—Ralph Waldo Emerson

Chapter 20

Reuben Stubbs puffed pensively on his corncob pipe, monitoring the progress of Cale Brolin and his procession of livestock. Even at a distance Reuben could detect Cale's irritation. He sat in the saddle like a bronzed statue. A sour frown carved distinct lines in his craggy features as his hand clenched on the reins in a stranglehold.

"Kicked you out, did she?" Reuben speculated as Cale swung to the ground.

"I don't want to discuss it," Cale said crossly. "Fetch me a bottle of your best whiskey."

Reuben's bushy brows puckered bemusedly. "The last time you were here you said you had sworn off liquor."

"That was *last* time," Cale grumbled as he pulled the bit from the roan's mouth.

When Cale strolled into the rear portion of the trading post that served as Reuben's modestly furnished home, a bottle and glass awaited him. Dropping down into a chair, Cale inhaled his drink in one swallow.

"Are you sure you don't want to talk about it?" Reuben prodded, sipping his whiskey at a more reasonable pace.

"I'm sure," Cale muttered as he slopped more liquor into his glass. A bitter smile rippled across his lips. Carelessly, he raised his glass in toast. "To whiskey—may it always be a substitute for a hardhearted, pigheaded woman."

Reuben broke into a wry smile. "You know you're going to have to wind up marrying that feisty female," he declared.

Cale's frosty glower left icicles dripping from Reuben's mocking grin. "I thought I said I didn't want to talk about her," he snapped gruffly.

A lackadaisical shrug lifted Reuben's thick shoulder. "You did," he affirmed. "But that doesn't mean *I* can't talk about her."

Gnashing his teeth, Cale grabbed a piece of paper and jotted down a list of errands. "I have a few things I'd like for you to do for me while I'm in Texas."

"How long will you be gone?" Reuben questioned, straining his eyes to read Cale's scribbling upside down.

"Until I get damned good and ready to come back," he grumbled, concentrating on his list of tasks to be performed.

"That soon?" Reuben teased, loving every minute of it. "I knew you couldn't stand to be away from that woman too long."

Cale slammed down the pen, slopping ink on the round table. "You don't need to *practice* being obnoxious," he scowled. "You already have years of experience." Huffily Cale shoved the list under Reuben's nose. "Take care of this while I'm gone."

As Cale's long swift strides took him outside, Reuben scurried to keep abreast. "When you come back, are you still going to be as unfriendly as a grizzly bear?"

Growling, Cale replaced the bridle and stepped into the stirrup. He was determined to escape Reuben's badgering, but the stout old man grabbed the reins before Cale could make his break for freedom.

"Why don't you just tell her you love her and get it over with?" Reuben suggested.

"I already did," Cale scowled disgustedly.

His bushy brows elevated in surprise. "What did she say to that?"

"She called me a liar . . . among other things," he snorted.

"Well, are you?" Reuben had the nerve to ask.

Cale's response came in the form of a bruising glower. Nudging the roan, Cale forced Reuben to remove himself from the gelding's path or be run down.

As the steed trotted away, Reuben broke into an amused

smile. He was willing to bet this was the first time Cale had been rejected by a woman. Cale's male pride was smarting, Reuben surmised. It wasn't easy for a man to be jilted when women had always chased after him like kittens on the trail of fresh milk.

Easing the steed across the staked crossing of the river, Cale expelled a harsh breath. If he knew what was good for him, he would remain at the ranch until spring. By then, he would have recovered from his stormy affair with that blond-haired hellion. By then, Morgan and Joseph would have taken control and Mikyla would have left the area in search of another rainbow.

By damned, that was exactly what he ought to do! If he never saw that woman again he would be a fortunate man. But try as he might, Cale couldn't forget the magical night they had shared before he had collected his belongings and ridden away. The forbidden memories gnawed at him with a hunger that nothing could appease. Blast it, that woman was in his blood! She had taken possession of his mind. She was *stormfire*—a turbulent, raging flame that blew the stars around and left no stone *unburned*.

"Confounded female," Cale muttered to himself. He and Ky could have enjoyed each other. They could have lived and loved the years away. But no, Mikyla was hellbent on that dream of hers. She wouldn't follow him unless he signed a marriage contract. That woman wanted everything cut-and-dried, and in black and white, staked and claimed!

Marriage, hell! Cale wasn't about to scribble his signature on a worthless piece of paper just to pacify that minx. And stubborn pride refused to allow Cale to confess that he could afford to make all her materialistic fantasies come true, that he could lay fortune at her feet. But he wanted that proud, willful vixen on *his* terms—without contracts, without a financial statement of his worth. By damned, he wasn't going to compromise. Obviously, he wasn't man enough to sway Mikyla from her obsessive dream. If he really meant something to that feisty free spirit of a woman she would have accepted him however she could have gotten him! But he didn't and she wouldn't.

Cale released a wordless scowl as he pointed himself toward Texas. It would take a strong-willed, courageous man to control that fiery female. And even an invincible man would meet with mountains of difficulty when it came to that blond-haired hellion. The simple fact was, there were some horses that weren't meant to be broken and some women who couldn't be tamed. Mikyla Lassiter was one of those rare women who was determined to live her life on her terms.

So why was he wasting another thought on that spitfire? There were passels of women who were eager for his kisses, who would take what he had to offer for as long as he was inclined to give it. Cale could have had any woman he wanted at the snap of his fingers. Except one, his male pride reminded him resentfully.

Cale pulled the strawberry roan to a skidding halt and stared toward distant Texas. Then he twisted in the saddle to glance back at Oklahoma country. And there he sat for several minutes, battling a mental tug-of-war. Cale knew he should put as many miles between himself and Ky as possible. And yet the strings on his heart had stretched just about as far as they would go.

Cale breathed a frustrated sigh. Should he follow his common sense or his heart? Both were debating the issue of Mikyla, spouting the pros and cons of involving himself with a woman who could brew trouble faster than she could boil water. Was he really going to wait until the spring thaw to check on her, to determine if she had ridden off into the sunset, defeated, disillusioned, disenchanted? Was he really going to abandon her to a man like Morgan Hagerty, knowing how dangerous Morgan was when he was hellbent on having his way?

Reuben's mouth dropped open wide enough for a dove to nest when Cale Brolin came splashing through the river. In stunned silence he watched Cale swing to the ground and sling his saddlebag over his shoulder.

"Would you mind sharing your home with a man who can't seem to shake the dust of Oklahoma off his boots?"

Cale questioned sheepishly.

Reuben stepped back from the doorway to allow Cale to pass. "I'd be pleased to have the company," he enthused. "It gets damned dull around here, staking the river crossing, only to have it wash away after one of those toad-strangling downpours . . ."

While Reuben rattled on, Cale dropped his gear at the foot of the extra bed. Although Mikyla had told him good riddance, Cale couldn't bring himself to turn his back on her. She needed him, of course. She was just too stubborn and independent to realize it. But Cale was going to be there to pick up the pieces of her dream when it shattered around her. It was the least he could do for the one woman who refused to bend to his will. He was obliged to pay his due to the one female who had resisted him, whether he employed brute strength or gentleness with her.

Yes, it was fitting and proper that the only woman who remained just out of his reach should receive the consolation prize of leaning on him when her world came tumbling down. And it would eventually, Cale prophesied grimly. Morgan Hagerty would ensure that it did. Mikyla had yet to see the ruthless, destructive side of Morgan. Unless Cale missed his guess, Mikyla would meet the real Morgan Hagerty very soon. The man had to be getting desperate and he would deplete his patience if Mikyla continued to defy him. Knowing Mikyla, she would fight Morgan with her last dying breath. And that was what brought Cale back—to keep a watchful eye on her.

Wearily, Mikyla plopped down on the ground to face another meal alone. Her back ached, her hands were blistered, and she had dropped two fence posts on her toes before lunch. But she was proud of her accomplishment. She had completed the digging of post holes and had strung wire along the northern boundary of her property. Using the stack of wire and posts Cale had left behind as the spoils of their private war, Mikyla had erected a half mile of fence. Her labors had helped to distract her from her most recent confrontation with Morgan and Joseph. She had ushered them off her land with a Winchester rifle, listening to Joseph squawk threats and watching Morgan eye her with a sinister smile. That man was up to something. Cale's warnings had finally gotten through to Mikyla. She had noticed the subtle changes in Morgan's attitude toward her. Each time he and his fine-feathered friend, Joseph Richards, appeared, Morgan was less pleasant than the time before.

Mikyla was annoyed by the constant harassment but what disturbed her most was that she missed the infuriating Cale Brolin. Every day for two weeks she had gazed west, hoping he would appear. But Cale had vanished and Mikyla had heard nothing from him.

Cale was the master complicator. There had been a time when the possibility of staking her home was enough to sustain her. Although her dream site still inspired her, she was less enthusiastic now that Cale had walked out of her life. She was going through the paces of living without actually enjoying herself. It had occurred to her that she even missed their trenchant arguments, the challenge of matching wits with that domineering man. Now her conversation was limited to Sundance and he . . .

The rumble of a wagon brought Mikyla's head up. She glanced north to see Greta Ericcson and her three children approaching camp.

"Well, dere you are, at last!" Greta greeted cheerfully.

Mikyla had almost forgotten the sound of Greta's heavily accented voice. So much had happened since they had seen each other that it seemed a lifetime ago they were sitting side by side in the Boomer camp.

"I hope you and Dag found a fertile homestead for your farm," Mikyla murmured as she returned Greta's zealous hug.

"Yah, thanks to that swift horse Mr. Brolin sold us," Greta enthused with a beaming smile. "And since Mr. Brolin let us have de mare for only fifty dollars, we had enough funds left to purchase lumber and supplies for our home."

Fifty dollars? Mikyla was thunderstruck. She had assumed that Cale had scalped the homesteaders with his outrageous prices of livestock. Obviously, though, he had been more than generous, since good horses were selling for ten times that amount.

"I have organized our first social," Greta declared proudly. "Ve are having a *pound party* so all de young ladies and gentlemen can become better acquainted." Her eyes twinkled impishly. "I have met some very nice young men who are most anxious to be introduced to you."

So Greta was back to her matchmaking, Mikyla realized, but Mikyla wasn't feeling sociable. She could not stop thinking about Cale and she doubted any of Greta's "nice young men" would compare to the ruggedly handsome Cale Brolin.

"I have so much to do," Mikyla demurred. "I really don't think I should attend. Perhaps . . ."

"Nonsense," Greta sniffed, refusing to take no for an answer. "Dere is plenty of time for building and stringing vire. You vill come to the pound party tonight. Everything is already arranged."

When Mikyla looked as if she were about to register another flimsy excuse, Greta held up a hand to forestall her. "You vill arrive at seven o'clock at our home. And if you are the slightest bit late, I vill send several young gentlemen to escort you!"

After rattling off the directions to the Ericcson homestead, Greta pulled onto the wagon seat and sped away. Mikyla's shoulders slumped. The last thing she wanted was to meet eligible bachelors who could not hold a candle to Cale. But Greta was a determined woman. Mikyla doubted she would be permitted to miss the social function to which every eligible bachelor was to bring a pound of candy, crackers, apples, or other tempting morsels to share with the young ladies. After sitting and visiting for fifteen minutes with a particular woman, the hostess would announce that each man was to shift to a new conversation partner. It was like playing a version of musical chairs, and Mikyla could think of dozens of other games she would prefer to play besides this social spin-off of a childish pastime.

Resigning herself to the fact that she would be a guest at

the Ericcson homestead, Mikyla gathered her tools and went back to work. Ah, well, she consoled herself. She could eat herself out of her gloomy preoccupation with Cale Brolin. After she gobbled up all the goodies the eligible bachelors brought along as temptation she would be too nauseous to dwell on Cale.

Garbed in a plain homespun gown and a floppy-brimmed bonnet, Mikyla approached the Ericcsons' farm, chagrined to see the numerous men outnumbered the women three to one. When Greta spied Mikyla's dowdy dress and oversize bonnet she frowned in disapproval.

"I expected you to drag your feet, Miki, but I did not think you vould purposely set out to discourage your suitors," she sniffed as her eyes swept over Mikyla's uncomplimentary attire.

Mikyla shrugged, undaunted. "I said I would come, but I did not promise to enjoy myself."

Greta's gaze soared heavenward. "How vill ve ever get you married to a nice young man if you do not show the slightest interest?"

A teasing smile pursed Mikyla's lips as she followed her hostess to the throng of young people who were awaiting the last arrival before they could begin their social affair. "I do appreciate your interest, Greta. But I am not ready to marry and I won't be until I have fulfilled my dream."

Greta was not giving Mikyla up as a lost cause. Indeed, she made certain that Mikyla was allowed to spend time with the most attractive and personable bachelors she had selected from the area. These men were handpicked and all of them would make suitable matches for this lovely but independent young woman.

As far as Greta was concerned, Mikyla needed a man in her life to replace her father. Emet had been a terrible burden on his daughter and Mikyla deserved a little happiness. It was apparent to Greta that the shapely blonde had been strapped with more responsibility than she was due. Once

298

she was married she could begin a new life and enjoy a bright future. But the first thing Greta had to do was get Mikyla married to one of these industrious young men who could not see this diamond in the rough for what she was when she was garbed in that outlandish dress that would have better suited her grandmother!

While Greta was stewing about the success of her plans, Mikyla was gorging herself with a variety of sweets and nodding politely while her most recent beau was boasting of his accomplishments on his claim. Mikyla listened disinterestedly, purposely adding little to the conversation.

When Greta indicated it was time to change partners, Mikyla choked down her crackers and chased them with a sip of lemonade. As her next suitor eased into the chair beside her, Mikyla raised her gaze, which was obstructed by the oversize brim of her bonnet. Her eyes made contact with a pair of twinkling silver pools that rippled with amusement. Mikyla strangled on her drink. An odd constriction tightened her chest. A strange ache overwhelmed her. It was like seeing a treasure that one had lost and knowing it would never again be hers. Seeing Cale Brolin was the most peculiar combination of mental, physical, and emotional pain Mikyla had ever experienced.

Cale leaned over to whack her on the back before she turned another shade of blue. "The way you have been wolfing down every treat that has been placed under your nose, one would think you're a glutton," he mocked her.

"What are you doing here?" Mikyla squeaked, her voice one octave higher than normal.

"Socializing," Cale informed her as he picked up a bonbon and stuffed it in her mouth. "Or should I say amusing myself by watching you become a human garbage can." His tanned fingers curled beneath her chin, tilting her face so he could look into her eyes instead of into that ridiculous calico bonnet that was plastered on her silver-blond hair. The head gear looked even more atrocious than the one Cale had stomped into the ground the day Mikyla thundered off from Reuben's trading post. "How can you eat this menagerie of

299

sweets without making yourself sick?"

"I can't," Mikyla confessed after she swallowed the bonbon.

"Then why are you doing it?" Cale wanted to know.

His touch sent tingles leapfrogging across her skin. Willfully, Mikyla concentrated on her reply rather than the arousing caress of his hand. "Because this is a *pound party,*" she reminded him tartly.

Cale burst into chuckles. "I think you have misinterpreted its purpose. The idea is not to see how many *pounds* you can put on by eating everything in sight! You'll be as full as a tick and you will have to be toted home in the bed of a wagon."

"I hardly see what concern it is of yours if I return to my homestead on my feet or on my back," Mikyla sniffed before snatching up another piece of chocolate-covered candy.

Cale stifled a snicker when Mikyla gobbled the sweets and then licked her fingers clean, employing not a tittle of good manners. He might have been offended by her outlandish attire and behavior if he hadn't known this ornery minx was deliberately projecting an image of social impropriety. Cale had been scrutinizing this lively bundle all evening. She could have had every man at the party drooling over her, but her apparel and her bad manners were as effective as Reuben's pasty concoction of insect repellent.

For the remaining minutes allotted them, Mikyla continued to stuff herself while Cale swallowed his amusement. And when Greta signaled the guests to change partners, Cale folded back the brim of her bonnet to peer into Mikyla's bewitching face.

"If you need someone to cart you home, just let me know." His voice was like rich velvet, holding secret promises that could buckle Mikyla's knees and turn her muscles to jelly.

Mikyla couldn't say for certain what Cale was doing at this social event or why he hadn't packed up and ridden off to Texas. But she did know a proposition when she heard one. She also knew that if she followed her foolish heart she would permit Cale to escort her home and they would inevitably wind up in . . .

The thought caused a riptide of emotions to churn within

her. Yes, she ached for his masterful touch, the feel of his sensuous lips drifting lightly across hers. But their lovemaking would resolve nothing. Cale would ask her to follow him hither and yon and she would refuse. They would lash out at each other and part company on a sour note.

"I . . ." Mikyla hiccupped loudly. Hurriedly, she covered her mouth and glanced around, noting the amused stares she was receiving from the other guests. Lord, her stomach felt like a boiling caldron.

Why in the world was she sitting here, gobbling down these nauseating sweets when she would have preferred to be in her tent? All she had accomplished was making herself sick and facing the bleak realization that no other man in the country could compare to Cale Brolin.

When Cale turned and walked away, Mikyla pushed out of her chair and scurried into the darkness, leaving her approaching suitor to gape after her. Mikyla was going home where she belonged. If she had known Cale was to be present she wouldn't have come at all. She didn't need to see him while she was still so vulnerable. It had only been two weeks since he rode away from her camp. The memories were still too fresh, the wounds too raw.

As Mikyla veered around the side of the house to fetch Sundance, Cale materialized from the shadows. Her startled gasp erupted in another unladylike hiccup.

"Will you please go away," she grumbled as she attempted to pull into the saddle.

Before she could seat herself on Sundance's back, Cale drew her against him, his moist breath caressing her neck. "Stuffing yourself with sweets won't replace my kisses," he teased mercilessly.

The feel of Cale's rock-hard body molded to hers was bittersweet torment. Mikyla resented the soul-shattering sensations that consumed her when Cale held her so familiarly. "That was *not* what I was doing," she protested, wriggling for release.

"Wasn't it?" he murmured as he turned her in his arms. "You haven't forgotten, have you, Ky? We can set fires in each other's blood . . ."

"My blood is pumping normally and without even so much as a spark," she lied to protect her pride.

A rakish smile caught the corner of his mouth. "Then let's see some proof that I have no effect on you . . ."

His head came steadily toward hers, his silver eyes boring into her tormented features. His lips fluttered over hers in the softest breath of a kiss. His hands glided down her ribs to settle on her hips, drawing her trembling body into contact with his solid length. His fingertips mapped her shapely curves and swells. His thumbs brushed across the tips of her breasts and then drifted to and fro, arousing her. Trickling drops of sensations poured across her flesh and through her body like sprinkles that signaled the onslaught of a downpour. And then it came—the cloudburst of emotions, the pounding raindrops of pleasure.

Mikyla sighed as if she had been granted a thirst-quenching drink after a prolonged journey across a barren desert. And when her betraying body melted in his arms, mindless to all except her insatiable need for him, Cale tucked his arms beneath her knees and planted her in the saddle. With an owlish stare, Mikyla surveyed Cale's roguish grin. It annoyed her that Cale knew how strongly he affected her, had *always* affected her. He touched her, and her emotions and her protective defenses turned to mush.

"There is a shapely brunette awaiting my return," he told her matter-of-factly. "She isn't you, but she seems infinitely more interested in my conversation than my bonbons."

Mikyla reacquainted him with her look of irritation, as if he could have forgotten how her blue eyes flared, how her sensuous lips compressed, how her chin tilted to that proud, aloof angle. "I hope you and your brunette and your bonbons will be very happy together," she gritted out. "I have more important matters on my mind than idle conversation and reckless affairs. I have a ranch to defend and I cannot do it long distance."

As Mikyla galloped off, her floppy bonnet flapping in the wind, Cale broke into a wry smile. Mikyla hadn't forgotten even one sweet memory of their times together. Although they were still at cross purposes, the fires burned just as fiercely and uncontrollably as they ever had. But as always, Miki was too proud to admit it.

A curious frown knitted Cale's brow as he reversed direction to join the young lady who awaited his return. Why had Mikyla appeared at the Ericcsons' in that outrageous getup? Why wouldn't she allow herself the opportunity to attract a beau? Heaven knew, all she had to do was flash men a come-hither smile and they would hover around her like bees swarming nectar.

A quiet smile replaced his pensive frown as Cale sank down into his chair on the front lawn and focused his attention on the comely brunette. But his senses were still filled with the taste of chocolate-covered kisses and the fragrance of roses. And throughout the remainder of the evening, his thoughts kept drifting to that arousing kiss he and Mikyla had shared.

It wasn't over between them. It would never truly be over. Mikyla knew that, even though stubbornness and pride refused to allow her to accept it. And *that* was why she had arrived in her old-fashioned gown that hung on her shapely figure like an oversized bedspread.

Perhaps Mikyla didn't love *him,* but nor did she want any other man. At least that was encouraging, Cale consoled himself as he trotted cross-country to return to the trading post. And maybe one day that defiant beauty would resign herself to the fact that they could create their own dreams which they could share together.

Cale breathed a heavy sigh. The only trouble was, he might not live long enough to see the day Mikyla admitted she felt something special for him. As obstinate as she was, it would take her a century to realize she cared enough for Cale to open her heart and give love a chance to blossom and grow.

After attending the pound party, Mikyla had her heart set on returning to camp, sitting down, and feeling sorry for herself. She wanted to have a good cry while she lamented that Cale would never again be a part of her life. But she was deprived of enjoying a long evening of wallowing in self-pity. Morgan had seen to that!

A muttered growl escaped Mikyla's lips when she rode back into camp. During her absence, someone had trespassed on her property and ransacked her tent. Tools and lumber were strewn about as if a tornado had ripped across her land, scattering her belongings to kingdom come. Although her stomach ached and her thoughts centered around her encounter with Cale, Mikyla set about to reconstruct her camp and gather her supplies.

"Morgan." She vehemently spat the man's name. So he intended to harass her until she threw up her hands and admitted defeat, did he? Well, she was going to hold out until the settlers who intended to stake a new town on her property gave up and went elsewhere. She was not buckling beneath Morgan's aggravating tactics. This was *her* land and she wasn't moving! If only Cale were here to help her protect . . .

Mikyla immediately discarded that wistful thought. Cale didn't think the land was worth the battle. He wanted her to cast aside her aspirations and trail obediently after him. Blast it, he didn't need a woman. He needed a slave! And Mikyla needed a home, a place to which she could run when the world closed in on her, a haven that was hers to arrange and design as she saw fit.

"Forget him," Mikyla scolded herself as she placed the last of the lumber back into a neat stack. "You lived without that impossible man before you met him and you can survive without him now."

Heaving a weary sigh, Mikyla plopped down on the cot she had just uprighted and tugged off her bonnet. It was like removing her suit of protective armor. Within an instant the warm sensations came swirling back to haunt her. She could feel Cale's sinewy arms enfolding her, smell the musky scent of his cologne, taste those inviting kisses that left her craving a dozen more just like them.

Oh, why had she fallen in love with a tumbleweed? she asked herself bitterly. There were several men at the Ericcsons' party who shared her convictions of building a home in this new territory. But none of them interested her. They were all so predictable, so dull, so—God forbid her for saying so—gentlemanly!

Her heart was still tied to a man whose ideas were in direct contrast with hers. Why, Cale Brolin didn't even believe in marriage. If she flung aside her dreams and accompanied him as he rode aimlessly across the Great Plains, he would expect her to go as his paramour, not his wife. Cale wanted her to shrug off every inch of pride and integrity, to blindly trust him.

The words Greta had spoken that morning came flitting back as Mikyla stretched out on her cot and stared at the canvas ceiling. Well, maybe Cale wasn't quite the rapscallion she believed him to be. Perhaps he had been reasonable and just with the settlers who begged to buy his horses. But he had still manipulated her. He still didn't think the way she did. And because of that, they would always be at odds.

A tear formed in the corner of her eye and slid down the side of her face. If she and Cale could have met at another time, another place, perhaps their differences wouldn't have seemed so insurmountable. Sometimes loving a man wasn't enough. This was one of those times. She needed Cale's love in return, not empty phrases uttered to bend her to his will.

Why couldn't Cale compromise, even a smidgen? Stubborn man! He had called her muleheaded, pigheaded, and bullheaded more times than she cared to count, but he was just as mulish, opinionated, and determined as she was!

Mulling over that thought, Mikyla closed her eyes and begged for sleep without the complication of dreams—at least not the kind that had been haunting her, the kind that contained Cale's looming image and his soft, tormenting voice. He had been visiting her each night since he rode out of camp, taunting her, refusing to allow her to forget the magic they shared.

Will it ever be over? Mikyla wondered as she curled up in a tight ball to counter the queasiness in her stomach. She had attempted to work away Cale's lingering memory. And tonight she had sought to *eat* away his memory. There wasn't a cure for Cale Brolin, she realized glumly. He was like a terminal illness from which she could never truly recover. Once a woman had him, there was simply no getting over him. She was destined to spend the rest of her natural life fighting a fever that nothing could cure! She was trying to treat the symptoms of love, but there was no treating the *problem*. And Cale Brolin was definitely her problem!

Chapter 21

Mikyla mopped the perspiration from her brow and peered up at the blazing sun. For four days she had worked herself into exhaustion, constructing fences and dragging stones to camp that would form the foundation of her home. This endless labor had not proven to be an effective medication for what ailed her. Cale Brolin was still ever present in her thoughts, constantly frustrating her.

Even Greta's unexpected visit that morning had failed to satisfy the loneliness that gnawed at her. As Mikyla had anticipated, Greta had raked her over the coals for appearing at the party looking like a character out of a history book. Greta had proclaimed that Mikyla owed her a favor after that annoying stunt. This time Greta was organizing a box supper to raise funds for the building of a school. She had demanded that Mikyla make an appearance and that she dress to fit the occasion. Although Mikyla had intended to decline, Greta would not hear of it. She issued another threat of having Mikyla dragged to the social function if she did not come on her own accord, *and* with a box supper in hand.

With a flourish and a warning frown, Greta clambered into her wagon and rumbled off to extend the invitation to the rest of the countryside. Although Mikyla was afraid of what would happen if she left her property unattended at night, she decided to join in the festivities. After all, the box supper supported a worthy cause and she was lonelier than she had been in weeks. Perhaps it was the anticipation of seeing Cale that convinced her to go, she mused as she stretched the wire for the new east fence. She knew she was a fool to throw herself in the way of temptation. She knew the sight of Cale would stir forbidden memories and leave her aching for what she couldn't have. But how did one totally neglect a part of one's self? Cale had taken half her soul when he left and she yearned to make herself whole again, even for those few brief minutes that would be a mixture of both heaven and hell.

Well, this time she wasn't going to go strolling to a party looking like an outdated old woman. She would take pains to look her best, even if she were plagued with a sunburned nose and calluses on her hands. It was time she journeyed to the newly established community of Elreno that had literally picked up and moved away from the mosquito-infested site of Reno City.

At the pound party Mikyla had learned that the dispute of relocating near the rapidly approaching railroad had practically turned Reno City into a ghost town. Since Elreno was destined to become a thriving metropolis served by the railroad, Mikyla decided to have a look at the community.

After Mikyla finished her lonely meal, she aimed herself north to make some purchases, including a dress to replace the one Cale . . . Her mind froze when the image of laughing silver eyes and an ornery smile returned to haunt her for the tenth time that day.

"Leave me be, Cale Brolin!" Mikyla commanded sternly. Cale was out of her life and he wouldn't be back. There would be no more splendorous nights in his arms. He probably wouldn't even attend the box supper, she told herself sensibly. He had probably gone to Texas to do whatever he did in the Lone Star state with whatever female caught his roving eye. If Mikyla allowed herself to dwell on the memories they had made together she would only make herself more miserable than she already was . . . if that were possible.

After delivering another of her self-motivating lectures, Miki resolved never to spare Cale another thought. But he was a difficult habit to break and she felt as if she had been wrestling with his memory forever.

Mikyla had ridden all of three miles before she noticed two riders galloping toward her. Dragging her Winchester rifle from the saddle sling, Mikyla continued north, armed and ready. She knew who the two men were—the same sidewinders who heckled her three times a week and ransacked her camp while she was away. Well, they were not going to intimidate her, she vowed fiercely. It was time they paid penance for scattering her belongings and voicing continuous threats.

Joseph and Morgan slowed their pace when the sunlight reflected off the rifle barrel. They had never been well received by the stubborn Mikyla Lassiter, and apparently she still held them in contempt as they refused to accept the fact that a woman could manage a homestead all by herself.

"I told you two to stay away from me," Mikyla growled in warning. "I meant what I said. I am not selling out, even if you demolish my camp every night of the week!"

Joseph waved the paper he had clutched in his fist, as if he were holding a flag of truce. After closing the distance between them, he burst into a triumphant smile. "You no longer have a choice, Miss Lassiter. This is a court order to condemn your land for a railroad right of way . . ."

Mikyla felt as if she had been punched in the midsection. Damn those scoundrels. They wouldn't give up! Frustration sizzled through her veins and her jaw clenched in angry defiance. Bringing the rifle to her shoulder, she took aim on the legal document Joseph was waving over his head.

"Now wait just a min—"

Joseph's eyes popped out of his head when the rifle discharged, making confetti of his court order. But then, it wasn't all that legal in the first place. It was only a scare tactic to oust Mikyla off her land. With a frightened yelp Joseph wheeled his horse in the direction he had come and thundered off like a house afire.

Morgan sat rigidly in the saddle, his expression as hard as granite. "You're asking for trouble, Mikyla," he told her in a low, threatening growl. "You will live to regret that impulsive retaliation. Now you are all alone on your claim. Your *lover* isn't around to pro—"

When Mikyla grasped her rifle, Morgan bolted out of firing distance. The spray of buckshot on his horse's rump sent him riding off in all directions at once. He fought to keep his seat on what had suddenly become a bucking bronc.

"Damn you," Morgan roared furiously. "I'm going to enjoy watching you receive your just reward, bitch!"

Muttering several explicit curses, Morgan galloped away. That woman was worth her weight in trouble. There had been a time when Morgan had fantasized about seducing Mikyla, but now she had earned his *fury,* not his *affection.*

Time was running short and Morgan had grown tired of patronizing that feisty misfit. It was time to employ drastic measures. The settlers were irritable because they were forced to hang in limbo, waiting for the investors of the townsite company to resolve their differences with Mikyla. Many of them requested that their money be returned. To pacify them, Morgan had promised to obtain the land as quickly as possible. But the days had dragged into a month and the homesteaders wouldn't wait much longer before they degenerated into a mob and forcefully *demanded* the return of their money.

It was time to decide what was to be done with Mikyla Lassiter, Morgan mused as he caught up with Joseph. And he had several suggestions to offer the investors of the company!

After regaining her composure, Mikyla calmed Sundance, who had nearly jumped out of his hide when the weapon exploded so close to his ear. Odd, Mikyla had once thought Morgan to be a gentleman who was a mite out of his element in the gambler's den. But it seemed he was a wolf in sheep's clothing and not one bit better than the scalawag he associated with.

Had Morgan truly been the one who lied about the poker game in which Sundance had been named as stakes? Was Morgan the one who wanted possession of Sundance so he could ride for the townsite company? Had Morgan been playing up to her because he wanted something from her?

310

Her affection and trust? Her prize stallion? Or was it because of something else?

Turning those thoughts over in her mind, Mikyla reined her steed toward Elreno. As she neared the community, she found the trail between the old site and the new town littered with broken timbers and the wreckage of buildings. Migrant settlers had been attacked by Reno City citizens who were outraged about the relocation. Those homesteaders who had paid the premium for prime sites in Reno City had formed vigilante groups to prevent the exodus. But some of the homesteaders had slipped away at night to reconstruct their homes and businesses. Since the new townsite was closer to Fort Reno, soldiers frequented the growing city, leaving the dwindling community of Reno City to flounder and die.

Mikyla rode through the dirt streets, wondering if her father was still in town after relocating in this new community. Her gaze scanned the half-canvas houses with sod dugout annexes, the false-front stores, and the sparse smattering of frame buildings that had been hurriedly nailed together. As was true in Reno City before its collapse, Elreno was overrun by more than two dozen saloons, restaurants, or a combination of both—not to mention numerous dance halls and calico queens.

Her eyes widened in surprise when she spied the framed mercantile shop that boasted the name Lassiter's. Had Emet actually acquired sufficient funds to build his store?

Oh, how Mikyla hoped her father had taken a new lease on life and relinquished his vices. But she doubted Emet would ever reform. He no longer had a purpose and he carried the memory of Michelle around in his mind, allowing the past to torment him.

After purchasing a new gown and sampling the food at one of the more respectable restaurants, Mikyla finally worked up enough nerve to approach the mercantile shop. She and her father had flung a barrage of insults at each other during their last confrontation. Mikyla was indecisive about how to proceed. But she was going to be bitterly disappointed if Emet had lost his store and was lying under his wagon, sleeping off his latest bout with liquor.

311

Mustering her courage, Mikyla strode inside the shop that appeared to be doing a thriving business. She was greeted by an attractive middle-aged woman who blessed her with a friendly smile. Since Emet was nowhere to be seen, Mikyla assumed that Emet no longer owned the establishment. If he had, he would have been managing it.

Mikyla hesitated to inquire about her father, but finally curiosity got the better of her. "Could you tell me who owns this business," she questioned politely.

"Mr. Emet Lassiter is the proprietor," Belinda Grove informed Mikyla. She gestured toward the door that led to the small home attached to the store. "Would you like a word with Emet?"

Nodding mutely, Mikyla was ushered into the modest home to find her father fussing over the inventory of newly arrived merchandise. Mikyla nearly fell off her boot heels when her father spun to greet her. Lord-a-mercy, Emet didn't look like the same man she had dragged home from the gambler's den. He was scrubbed so clean that his cheeks shined like polished apples. His fashionable garments were starched and pressed and they hadn't been *slept* in! His shaggy mane of hair had been neatly clipped and there wasn't a whisker on his face. Talk about miracles! Mikyla thought delightedly.

"Miki?" Emet's mouth curved into an awkward smile. "I wondered if I would ever see you again after the awful things we said to each other . . ."

Sentimental emotion overcame Mikyla. She dashed to her father, hugging the stuffing out of him. "I'm so proud of you, Papa. My, you look wonderful!"

Emet chuckled as he returned her hug. "I won't for long if you crinkle my waistcoat and rain tears on my starched collar." He glanced affectionately at Belinda, who was viewing the scene with misty eyes. "I want you to meet the woman who is partially responsible for my rehabilitation. Belinda Grove, this is my daughter Mikyla."

Wide blue eyes swung to the woman who stood with her hands primly folded gracing Miki with a quiet smile. Mikyla was utterly speechless. This must surely have been an angel sent to answer Mikyla's prayers.

"Cale Brolin picked me up out of the street and hired Belinda to put me back on my feet." Emet's eyelid dropped into a teasing wink. "Belinda looks to be gentle and compassionate, but for a while there, I swore she had missed her calling. She could have made an excellent prison warden."

Cale Brolin? Why hadn't he told her he had taken it upon himself to turn Emet's life around? Why hadn't he defended himself when Mikyla accused him of selling his horses to settlers for outrageous prices? And what supported him, if not the exorbitant sum he received for all his livestock? Mikyla was thoroughly confused by the questions that buzzed through her mind. She thought she knew Cale, but it seemed she didn't understand that man at all!

"The second time I met Brolin, he delivered me a sermon on temperance that was physical as well as vocal," Emet admitted, rubbing the jaw that had been so sore he had been unable to eat comfortably for a week. "When he found me again in Reno City, down on my luck . . . facedown," he added sheepishly. ". . . I thought he meant to kill me. He had me locked in jail for a week and hired Belinda to cook my meals and clean my clothes. When he returned to release me, he entrusted me to this teetotaler." Emet's eyes lingered affectionately on Belinda who blushed beneath his warm regard. "Mr. Brolin swore that I would wish I were dead if he happened into town and found me reverting to my old ways."

"Do not forget to mention who purchased this lot in Elreno, and who paid for the lumber and inventory for the store," Belinda prompted. "Mr. Brolin has been a godsend to both of us. He has put new purpose in both our lives . . ."

Mikyla sat down before her legs collapsed beneath her. Cale had done all this? With what money? Was that why he had hoped to sell her dream site for a high price? Had he borrowed the money for Emet? Her mind reeled with befuddled questions. Why hadn't Cale mentioned any of this to her? Why had he allowed her to form her own conclusions about him? The man totally baffled her. She didn't know

313

what to make of him!

Emet's abrupt announcement that he wanted Mikyla to serve as Belinda's maid of honor at their wedding the following month knocked the props out from under her. It seemed everyone was getting on with their life and she was wallowing about, struggling to fulfill her dream—one she was dangerously close to losing.

"Belinda, will you excuse us for a moment?" Emet requested, his gaze still focused on his daughter.

With a nod of compliance, Belinda returned to the store, granting Miki and Emet privacy. Sighing heavily, Emet dropped into his chair. Casting Miki a quiet smile, he gestured for his daughter to take a seat across from him.

"Miki, I owe you an apology," he began solemnly. "The past few years have been difficult for me and I have made them miserable for you. Because of my selfishness, my grief, I forced you to grow up all by yourself. I'm afraid I haven't been much of a father to you lately."

"It's all right, Papa, I . . ."

Emet waved his hand for silence. "No, it isn't all right," he contradicted. "I tried to drown my troubles in liquor and gambling, to forget the life we once knew when your mother was alive." His downcast eyes lifted to hold Miki's unblinking stare. "I have been terribly unfair to you. It seemed you accepted the loss much better than I. And for a time we even exchanged roles. I became *your* responsibility, one you should not have been forced to accept." His breath came out in a rush. "I sorely regret the anguish I put you through and I promise it will never happen again."

Emet leaned forward to clasp his daughter's hands. His touch was warm, confident, and steady, just as Mikyla remembered from childhood. "Things are different now. You have your own dream and Belinda has given my life new purpose. I have no wish to disappoint either of you, nor myself."

Miki threw her arms around her father's neck, uncaring that she dampened Emet's freshly starched collar with her tears. The words she wanted to voice caught in her throat. She was choking on the tender emotion bubbling inside her.

314

"I owe my life and the return of my self-respect to Cale Brolin," Emet confessed brokenly. "I was a miserable wretch who had lost his will to live. But Brolin forced me back on my feet. He sought out Belinda, who had come to the territory with her sister's family. She had been mourning the loss of her husband, and Cale decided we would be good for each other. And we have been, Miki." His pale blue eyes misted with sentimentality. "I hope we have your blessing."

"I wish the best for both of you," she whispered, giving her father's hand an affectionate squeeze.

Emet grasped Miki's shoulders to stare into her tear-rimmed eyes. "If there is anything you want or need for your homestead, just ask and I will see that you have it," he insisted.

Mikyla forced the semblance of a smile. "Seeing you happy and content once again is all I need, Papa."

"That's the same thing Cale Brolin said when I offered to repay him for his investment in this store," Emet snorted as he rose to full stature. "Perhaps he won't accept the payment of my loan, but a father can most certainly aid his daughter if he is so inclined. I'm sure you could do with a few supplies and I will see that you have them, compliments of your father!"

With that declaration, Emet shepherded Miki through the store. He presented her with goods to sustain her for several weeks. Although Miki protested his generosity, Emet insisted on making gifts of the supplies.

After the delightful reconciliation with her father, Mikyla loaded the goods on the mule her father had given to her. As she rode toward her homestead her spirits were inflated for the first time in weeks. Her darkest suspicions about Cale had shattered in the light of what she had learned, first from Greta, and now Emet.

Cale had permitted her to think the worst of him while he sneaked around, assisting those who needed his help—Mikyla included. But why had he been so negative about her dream site? Had he known she would face difficulty? Had he tried to convince her to relocate only for her own safety? Had he actually been trying to spare her heartache by allowing himself to become her scapegoat?

Mikyla reined Sundance and the pack mule her father had bestowed upon her to a halt. Anger and frustration sizzled through her veins when she spied the tangled remains of the east fence that had taken days to construct. Damn that Morgan Hagerty! He wasn't forcing her off her property, no matter how many times he demolished her fences and her camp! This was all she had.

Even if she could let go and turn her back on her dream there was nowhere to run. Cale only wanted her on his terms . . . if even at all. And Mikyla could not bring herself to kneel like a subservient slave. Her pride would not allow her knees to bend into that humiliating position. Nothing would ever be right between her and Cale until he could accept her love without *using* it as a weapon against her. If they couldn't be equal partners in life they had no future.

Mikyla expelled a downhearted sigh. If she *were* forced off her land, she couldn't run to her father for assistance. He was about to begin his new life with Belinda. What was she to do if she lost this battle with Morgan Hagerty and that cussed townsite company?

The closer she rode to camp the more furious she became. Morgan had not only destroyed her fence, but he had taken an ax to the supporting beam of the shed. The roof drooped toward the east, as if it would collapse when besieged by the slightest onslaught of wind.

Damn those scoundrels! She would not bend to their will! They presumed that just because she was a woman she would crawl into her shell like a turtle when she faced adversity. Well, they had sorely misjudged her. Mikyla had toiled and sweated over this land. She had come dangerously close to drowning in the river that formed the southern boundary to her property. And she wasn't giving up! This land was a part of her. It was all she had left now that Cale had ridden out of her life.

Determined to prove her fortitude, Mikyla set about to restring the fence and repair the shed. And she cursed Morgan with every angry breath she inhaled. Cale had certainly been right about Morgan, she mused as she wiped

316

the perspiration from her face. The man was dangerous when he wasn't allowed to have his way.

Mikyla leaned tiredly against the fence post, her gaze scanning the distance. She was surrounded by other families who labored to carve homes on the prairie. Her father was prospering, and Greta was determined to see Mikyla properly married. Yet, with all that was right with the world, two things were very wrong. Her conflict with Morgan and Joseph frustrated her. And secondly, and more important, there was a hole the size of Oklahoma country in her heart.

Even when she threw herself into her chores her mind drifted to that muscular cowboy with the lopsided smile. Thoughts of Cale continually cluttered her brain and inflamed her dreams. He had allowed her to think he was an unscrupulous rascal while he went about helping those who were down on their luck.

For a time, she and Cale had become lovers and friends. He could read her moods and determine what she needed, even when she didn't know herself. He had given Emet back his self-respect and offered Belinda a purpose in life. He had seen to it that the Ericcsons and countless others had the opportunity to stake their free land and build a future.

The man had saintly qualities, but he possessed one major flaw that kept him and Mikyla from enjoying a compatible coexistence. Cale refused to compromise. Why, they didn't come more obstinate and perseverant than Cale Don't-give-an-inch Brolin. That iron-willed cowboy wanted her to make all the sacrifices in their rocky relationship, as if he were testing *her* worthiness to follow in his shadow! But until he shared her dream of land and a home they would never see eye to eye.

As if that matters now, Mikyla told herself dismally. All her pensive reflection changed nothing. Cale was gone. Why, he had probably drifted to Texas, or New Mexico Territory, or wherever the wind blew him. Mikyla suddenly found herself scoffing at all men in general and Cale in particular. He didn't really love her, she told herself. He only wanted to dominate her, to see her bow to his superior strength, to his strong will. Yes, she wanted him in ways she had never wanted or needed a man. And yes, she was miserable without his teasing smiles, his tender embraces, those mystical nights of love . . .

Squeezing her eyes shut, Mikyla forced back the sweet, tormenting memories. If she kept carrying a torch for him, she would burn herself up. Cale probably hadn't given her a second thought since the night of the pound party. There were women aplenty to replace her, women who asked no more than a smile and a moment of his time. But Mikyla had demanded more of Cale than those splendorous hours between dusk and dawn. She had wanted to share a life and a dream, make decisions together, discuss alternatives . . .

Come to think of it, *compromise* wasn't all that familiar to her, either, and she never had appreciated being told what to do. Well, it was all for the best, Mikyla consoled herself. She and Cale were too much alike to live in peace. She wanted her way and Cale wanted his. They were like two competitors on the opposite end of a rope, playing a tug-of-war with each other's emotions, fighting a constant power struggle.

Heaving another sigh, Mikyla plopped down in bed. She was too tired to wade through the depths of her emotions. It had been a long, eventful day. She was a fool to rehash her conflicts and her craving for Cale. He was probably in another woman's arms at this very moment, taking passion where he found it.

Did he ever allow her to cross his mind? she wondered as she stretched out in bed. Did he ever speculate on how she was faring with Morgan and Joseph? Would he have applauded her for shooting the affidavit out of Joseph's fingertips? Or would he have scolded her impulsive fit of temper?

Mikyla smiled in spite of himself. Cale would probably have read her the riot act after that crazy stunt. He would have shaken her silly and then he would have . . .

Warm, full lips captured hers. Strong, capable arms enfolded her, blotting out the world. The masculine scent that was so much a part of him, and now a part of her, encircled her senses, leading her into a sensuous dimension of . . .

"You'll drive yourself mad if you keep thinking about him," Mikyla chided herself. "Cale Brolin is probably a thousand miles away and you are probably a million miles out of his mind!"

Counting the brood mares that would one day grace her pastures instead of the traditional flock of sheep that were supposed to put one to sleep, Mikyla closed her eyes. But Cale was her constant companion, stealing softly from the corners of her mind, reviving the sweet memories, provoking inner turmoil.

Mikyla was still clinging fiercely to her dream. But try as she might, she couldn't forget the raven-haired devil who had left her wondering if her priorities were misplaced. Damn but that Cale Brolin was an exhausting man. Mikyla was wearing herself out trying not to think about him. And the harder she tried, the more difficult it became not to wonder if she hadn't made a grave mistake by refusing to follow after him. What good was a dream if there was no one with whom to share it? That was one question that haunted her all through the night. Even if she won her battle against the townsite company she had lost something that had become precious and dear to her. Without Cale, even a victory would be as depressing as defeat.

Mikyla felt a tear trickle from her eye as she flounced on her cot. Maybe she was every kind of fool. Maybe she wanted things she could never hope to acquire. But if she could turn back the hands of time to that night when Cale had walked out of her life, she might have set aside her obsessive dreams. Yet, what would she have accomplished? she reflected pensively. She could have remained at Cale's side, but until she knew he loved her, truly loved her, she still would have had nothing. She would have been an even bigger fool than she already was, Mikyla consoled herself.

Yes, she had done the right thing by rejecting his offer. It would just take some time to convince her heart of that! But how much longer could she endure this torment before she went stark raving mad? Now here was a question she had better seriously contemplate, she advised herself. If she didn't get herself in hand she would be a lunatic, dwelling on the memories of a man who had given her a chance to follow him, expecting her to accept whatever he offered. She had refused and now she had to live with her decision, difficult as it was!

Chapter 22

Garbed in her new cherry red gown, Mikyla collected the meal she had prepared for the social. The box wasn't heaping with delicacies because Mikyla didn't have the whole day to fuss over the Dutch oven, cooking a gourmet dinner. It had taken her most of the morning to complete her fence and she considered it far more important to labor over her claim than over the fire.

Mikyla was surprised to note the number of riders who approached the Ericcsons' homestead. Greta must have invited everyone in the western half of Oklahoma country. Although Mikyla had been reluctant to attend this affair, afraid and yet anxious to know if Cale would be among the guests, she felt her spirits lift when assaulted by the ripple of laughter and the squeal of children.

Perhaps this is just the therapy I need, Mikyla told herself. She still enjoyed the serenity of the prairie, but there were times, especially when Cale's image followed like her shadow, when she desperately needed a distraction.

Greta clasped her hands delightedly when she spied Mikyla. "Ah, dis gown is much better!" she exclaimed. "It complements you instead of detracts from your beauty like dat God-awful garb you wore to de pound party."

Mikyla found herself whisked off to meet the neighbors, some of whom she had seen at the pound party and others who were new acquaintances. Then, Greta steered her toward a cluster of men to put her on display. Embarrassed but amused by her well-meaning friend's tactics, Mikyla graced each eligible bachelor with a smile and a quiet how-do-you-do. Although she hid her emotions, Mikyla was disappointed that Cale was not among the guests. She suspected that he had pointed himself toward Texas, leaving Oklahoma and her memory far behind him.

The evening progressed without a hitch until Mikyla spied Morgan Hagerty propped leisurely against the corral. His goading smile caused Mikyla to stiffen like an arched-backed cat. It annoyed her to see how well Morgan wore that smug expression. She would have given anything if she could have slapped it off his handsome face.

"No Winchester rifle this evening, Mikyla?" Morgan taunted.

Her blue eyes blazed over his expensive garments, disliking him more by the minute. "Had I known there was to be a snake in our midst I would have made arrangements to exterminate it," she hurled at him, along with another disgusted glare.

The mocking smile slid off Morgan's lips. "You and I could still be on friendly terms if you weren't such a feisty little bitch," he growled at her.

Mikyla floundered momentarily for a suitably nasty rejoinder. When she had formulated one, she wrapped it around her tongue and flung it in his face. "I seriously doubt it, Morgan. I have no use for gamblers and even less respect for a man who connives to steal from his neighbors. You would sell anything, including your soul, for profit."

This chit's tongue is like a poison arrow, Morgan thought in annoyance. His hand bit into her wrist, causing her to grimace. "You would have been much better off if you would have remained in my good graces. I no longer feel guilt in seeing you run off your land." His green eyes scorched her and his low voice held a hint of ridicule. "Obviously you aren't worth any man's attention. Even your lover grew tired of your pestilence and sought out a female who knew how to please a man."

Mikyla responded without thinking. Although Morgan held her right hand in a vise grip, her left palm smacked against his clean-shaven cheek, immediately changing the color of his complexion to a shade that resembled raw liver.

"Exactly my point," Morgan hissed as he released her hand to inspect the welt on his cheek. "No doubt Emily Terrel poured out her affection instead of pouncing on a man with claws bared—like you have a habit of doing." One blond brow lifted to a mocking angle. "How does it feel to be abandoned, my dear? Did you beg and plead with that bastard to stay with you? Did you offer him your inexperienced body, only to be rejected?"

Mikyla decided she had to flee from Morgan before she made an unforgivable scene at Greta's social. He suddenly reminded her of a rabid dog, hissing and snapping, his face puckering in a vicious scowl. She could understand why Morgan disliked her, for she stood in the way of what he wanted. But the way he spat out Cale's name puzzled her. Cale would have sold the property at the drop of a hat. Was Morgan still fuming because Cale had made mincemeat of him during their fisticuffs? Why did he hate Cale so intensely?

Before Mikyla could speculate on Morgan's animosity toward Cale, Greta clamped onto her arm and herded her to the crowd that had gathered for the sale of the box suppers.

As the sun made its regal descent into the fiery spectrum of colors that graced the western horizon, the bidding began. Mikyla shifted uncomfortably from one foot to the other, embarrassed that the box suppers prepared by the other women were decorated with wild flowers and ribbons, while her meager offering appeared to lack the time and effort needed to impress a man.

Well, supper was the last thing on her mind, she rationalized. If a man wanted only a cook and laundress he could find himself a maid. And if a man was to judge her on the looks of a lousy box supper, he wasn't worth having, she contended. Perhaps she would become a spinster, she thought. The entire male population seemed to cause her nothing but trouble . . .

Her thoughts dispersed when Dag Ericcson grabbed her plain box supper and held it up for inspection. And then Mikyla herself was hoisted into the wagonbed like a slave

323

placed on the auction block. Mikyla endured the mortification with a faint smile until Morgan Hagerty entered the bidding.

What did that man intend to do, place poison on the food and force her to eat it? Or was he anxious to go another round, just for sport? He should know by now that nothing he could say or do would change her mind about selling her claim.

By the time the bid reached the outrageous price of ten dollars the other young men shrugged and turned away. While Morgan was grinning in spiteful satisfaction, another bid resounded from the back of the crowd. Mikyla squinted in the torchlight to determine who had offered twenty dollars for a meal that was hardly worth a quarter!

The sound of the man's voice sent a tingle riveting down her spine, but she supposed it was only her deteriorating mind that was playing tricks on her. Was it Cale? Surely she was mistaken. He should have been in Texas by now.

Morgan pivoted to determine if he had guessed the name of his competitor. A wordless snarl curled his lips when he saw Cale towering over the other guests. Damnation, he thought he had seen the last of Cale Brolin.

For a split second Mikyla's eyes locked with Cale's. It was as if they were suddenly alone, standing all too far apart. Her gaze left his to drink in the sight of his raven hair and broad shoulders. Her heart flip-flopped around her chest and bounded off her ribs. Lord, she didn't think she could forget how ruggedly attractive he was. But she had. His skin was a darker shade of brown than she had remembered, but his smile held its usual hint of teasing amusement. He looked absolutely "gorgeous!"

"Thirty dollars," Morgan growled resentfully.

A ripple of murmurs undulated through the crowd. Morgan's bid was unusually high, even if the profits were going to the establishment of a school.

"One hundred dollars," Cale offered without batting an eye.

Morgan elbowed his way through the crowd and paused beside Cale. "You're a fool, Brolin. You're getting yourself in over your head. Both you and that sassy bitch will live just long enough to regret antagonizing me."

"Leave her out of this, Morgan." Cale's voice had a deadly ring to it. "I've made it my ambition in life to see that you get exactly what you deserve, but Miki has no part in what is truly between us."

Morgan snorted contemptuously. "I haven't forgotten how you meddle in business that is none of your concern. You even went so far as to kill Jessica just so I couldn't have her. But if you don't convince that feisty witch to sell her land, I'm going to take drastic measures to remove her . . . permanently." Flashing Cale one last mutinous glance, Morgan made his hasty departure.

Cale had only a moment to dwell on Morgan's threat before the crowd parted like the Red Sea to deliver Mikyla and her shabby supper basket. She looked so humble standing there clutching her box supper that Cale burst into a chuckle. God, it was the first time he had smiled since he had watched this ornery minx devour pounds of candy at the last community social.

"It seems I overpriced this package," Cale snickered. "Not another sample of poison rabbit, I hope."

Mikyla might have risen to the taunt if she hadn't been so drunk on the sight of this powerfully built rogue. It was like staring at a cherished portrait that had been stashed from her sight for years on end. Each time she saw him it served to remind her how much she had missed the sound of his laughter, missed the teasing sparkle in those silver-gray eyes, missed his masterful caresses . . .

When Cale's strong hand enfolded hers to lead her away, Mikyla melted like butter left unattended on a hot stove. His confident touch triggered a barrage of sweet memories. Sensations pelleted over her as she blindly followed Cale's long, impatient strides.

"What are you doing here? I thought you would be in Texas," Mikyla chirped, her voice failing when she felt the need to appear cool and indifferent to protect her already wounded pride.

As quick as a pouncing mountain lion, Cale's sinewy arms

engulfed her, lifting her exquisite face to his. "I couldn't leave until I did this . . ."

His mouth captured hers in a devouring kiss. He was rough and impatient and insistent and Mikyla didn't care a whit. Her hunger for his embrace held no gentleness, either. She clutched him to her as if she meant to squeeze him in two, aching to be absorbed into his hard length.

The lunch basket fell to the wayside as Cale carried Mikyla into the sheltering clump of trees that crowded the creek. Mikyla made no protest. She knew she was behaving like a shameless trollop and was aware that she was reopening a closed chapter of her life. But she loved him, damn his foolish hide! Yes, she knew he would ride away again and she could not bring herself to follow him. But for now, just once more before they parted, she would offer herself to him, silently assuring him of what he could anticipate if he decided to stay and help her fight for her land.

When Cale set her to her feet, Mikyla worked the buttons on his shirt. After pushing the garment from his expansive shoulders, her hand sailed across the dark matting of hair that covered his lean belly. Cale sucked in his breath when her fingertips dived beneath the waistband. But he allowed her to tug at the garment until it gave way.

"Is this what you planned for whoever purchased your lunch basket?" he teased, his voice husky with mounting desire.

Mikyla's hands were never still a moment. They fluttered across his shoulders and chest, creating intricate designs on his muscled flesh. Her head tipped back to counter his rakish grin with her provocative smile. "You, better than anyone, can attest to my lack of culinary skills. What else do I have to offer a man who pays good money for a meal?" she teased.

When Cale made a grab for her, Mikyla retreated just out of his reach and tossed him a saucy smile. "If memory serves, you made rags of my last gown, lusty dragon. I prefer to keep this garment in one piece. It would be most embarrassing to ride home dressed like Lady Godiva."

Cale was treated to an enticing scene, even though he

wasn't certain he possessed the patience to enjoy it. Inch by tantalizing inch, Mikyla revealed the tempting package that was wrapped in red silk. She took his flaming silver eyes on the most arousing journey and Cale swore he would burn like a bonfire before she ceased her seductive game and returned to him.

"Come here, Ky," he growled hoarsely. "You are becoming too much the seductress. The very sight of you is temptation enough."

"But can I drive away the memory of the other women who have taken my place these last few weeks?" Mikyla would have punished herself for posing that question if she could have contorted her body to become both the donor and recipient of a swift kick.

Morgan's vicious taunts hurt more than Mikyla had allowed him to think. Cale was a passionate man, the kind who was never between women. It hurt to think she had lived on splendorous memories while Cale was making new ones with countless other women.

Like a looming giant, Cale closed the distance that separated them. His hand curled beneath her chin to lose himself in the radiant depths of eyes that were as brilliant blue as the morning sky. "Don't spoil the moment, Ky," he whispered softly. "I didn't come here to argue or debate. I'm here because I want you. For us there can be no past or future, only the present." His dark head was only a few tormenting inches away and his breath skipped across her trembling lips in tantalizing promise of what was to come. "What's that adage about east is east and west is west . . . ?"

She knew what he was implying. Cale was insinuating that they would never see eye to eye, that they could only live for the moment before it escaped them forever. "And never the twain shall meet . . ." Mikyla supplied in a throaty voice, thick with longing.

"Wanna bet?" he murmured upon her dewy soft mouth, leaving her to wonder if east were west and vice versa. But at the moment neither of them gave a tittle about twains or directions. They were like magnetic poles drawn together by a compelling attraction. "When I'm with you, I can believe most anything is possible . . ."

When Cale pulled her against his hard flesh, Mikyla's brain malfunctioned. Her entire body shuddered in response to his skillful, sensual intimacy. Sensations blended, one into another, as his exploring caresses rediscovered each sensitive point and set it aflame. Cale seemed to have perfect recall, as if it had been seconds rather than weeks since he had touched her. Mikyla reveled in the wild flight of her senses as she was swept into a sea of exquisite ecstasy.

Her head tilted back, allowing the tangled tendrils of silver-gold to flood over her shoulders granting Cale free access to the pulsating column of her throat. A trail of fire followed in the wake of his kisses, eliciting Mikyla's soft moan. Her long lashes fluttered down as his tongue flicked at the throbbing peaks of her breasts. Another wave of fire engulfed her. It was as if she were burning, inside and out. Rapture sizzled in the depths of her soul as his hands and lips spread white-hot flames across her quaking flesh.

Mikyla gasped to inhale a breath, but it was difficult to breathe, to think. She could only respond to his ardent caresses, the hot whisper of his kisses. The need Cale created with his practiced touch was so fierce Mikyla feared nothing could appease it. Restlessly, her hands fanned across his ribs and lean belly. But touching him wasn't enough. She wanted him. She ached for him. Instinctively, her body moved toward his, but Cale held himself away, tormenting her to the limits of sanity.

Cale urged her to the pallet of discarded clothes. He marveled at this nymph's flawless beauty, the enchanting way the moonlight and shadows caressed her shapely body. It had been forever since he had felt her silky flesh beneath his inquiring hands. He wanted to memorize each luscious curve and swell, to revel in the pleasure that touching her aroused. He longed to revive those hauntingly sweet memories and create new ones. And when he finally came to this lovely angel, his name would be on her lips, his caresses would be branded on her mind.

If it was Cale's intent to drive Mikyla mad with want, he had accomplished his purpose, for she didn't care if she sacrificed her last breath if it would bring an end to this wild, aching pleasure that demanded total fulfillment.

"Cale . . ." Her voice was ragged with breathless impatience. "Please . . . I need you . . ."

His eyes were upon her, burning like hot silver. He was visually making love to her long before he lifted her to him. Mikyla felt tears stinging her eyes as she was consumed by an ache beyond bearing. Boldly her hand folded around him, caressing him, urging him to love her in all the wondrous ways he had taught her, to hold her until the sweet, tormenting sensations ebbed.

As he stared into her lustrous blue eyes, deciphering her need for him, Cale became engulfed by emotions that transcended desire. Her body was his for a time, but he wondered if he would ever be able to capture her defiant heart. As his massive body covered hers he felt an odd shudder rock his soul. He wanted Mikyla the way he always had—wildly, irrationally. But possessing her satiny body wasn't enough. He wanted to touch her soul, to absorb that fierce, determined spirit that both intrigued and infuriated him.

Raw passion overshadowed the thoughts that spun tangled webs in Cale's mind. He felt himself consumed by emotions and turbulent sensations that demanded appeasement. Yet, even as he gave himself up to the stormfire, Cale knew he would never be content until he had earned this vixen's love. It was a whimsical dream that would never collide with reality. But it was Cale's secret obsession. Other females who had sauntered in and out of his life did not hold the same compelling challenge. But with Ky, lovemaking was different. It was the one special dimension of life in which they could join hands and hearts. It had always been . . .

That was the last fragment of thought to skip across Cale's brain before he was towed into the fiery current of mindless passion. His body reacted only to primal instinct, driving him into her, aching for desire's sweet release.

Mikyla cried out as the sensations which had diverged like beams of sunlight recoiled and then converged upon her with penetrating pleasure. She became the sun—a bubbly core of fire, rocked by devastating internal explosions. She felt Cale shudder against her, heard his guttural moan. It was as if she were entrapped in a universe that pursued and captured time. It was as if she were living and *reliving* each ineffable sensation, like an echo of erotic sensations coming at her from all directions at once.

A tender smile pursed Cale's lips as he held on to Mikyla's perspiring body. He knew he had taken her with him to passion's highest pinnacle. Perhaps he could never tame her, but he could arouse her slumbering passions and unveil the woman who girded herself in her armor of stubborn defiance.

When Cale felt her silent tears against his chest, he eased away to brush his lips across her damp cheeks. Gently he touched his index finger to her chin, lifting her cloudy gaze to his tender smile.

"I wonder if the other couples enjoyed the same satisfying feast," he whispered huskily. "Somehow I doubt the other young ladies could have packaged such an appetizing treat."

Even in the moonlight Cale could detect the rose-tinted blush that colored her cheeks. Turning her face into his shoulder, Mikyla nibbled at his aromatic flesh, refusing to speak for fear of shattering the sweet, companionable moment. They lay together, exchanging light kisses, touching, adoring the serenity they had created in the aftermath of love.

When Cale finally found the strength to move away, Mikyla felt a cold chill replace the protective warmth that had blanketed her the instant before. She watched in awe as Cale rose to collect his scattered clothes. She was reminded of a sleek, powerful panther prowling the darkness. Muscles bunched and rippled as he moved, alerting her to the strength that lay in repose. He was so perfect, so sensual, so masculine. She adored watching him. She was in awe of his virile physique.

Cale half turned and then froze in his tracks. He felt as if he had stumbled on a wood nymph reclining in her nest of leaves and grass. Lord, she looked so exquisite, he mused as

330

he fumbled with the buttons of his shirt. He would be content to spend half his life devouring this shapely beauty with his eyes and the other half . . .

A rakish smile tugged at the corner of his mouth, curving it upward. Cale wondered if Ky would chide him for being a lusting beast if she knew what he would do with his time and energy. Half the day would entail *thinking* about what he was going to do when he got his hands on this enchantress. The other fifty percent of the day would involve *doing* what he had contemplated. Before he yielded to the temptation of combining *thinking* and *doing* all over again, Cale clamped a tight grip on himself and walked away.

As Cale marched off in the direction he had come, Mikyla frowned bemusedly. Was he leaving her, just like that? No good-bye? No "We'll meet again someday?" No nothing?

"Don't go . . ." Her voice was raspy from the aftereffects of passion and undeniable disappointment.

Cale wheeled to torment his eyes with another tempting view of Mikyla's flawless body and radiant hair that streamed about her shapely curves. "I thought perhaps I should retrieve the box supper before someone happens along and begins to wonder exactly what we *did* have for dinner."

When his silver-gray eyes flooded over her flesh, Mikyla trembled in pleasure. Thank goodness he hadn't planned to leave her, she breathed in relief.

"Perhaps that would be wise," she murmured with a sheepish smile. "I should hate for you to pay such an exorbitant price for something you didn't enjoy—meager though it was."

A deep skirl of laughter rumbled in his wide chest. "Believe me, minx. I hardly feel shortchanged . . . even before I have the chance to examine the contents of that box supper."

When Cale swaggered through the clump of trees, Mikyla wormed back into her clothes and paced the shadows. Their stolen moments were as they had always been, she thought with a melancholy sigh. Cale could touch her and she misplaced the good sense she had been born with. She dared

331

not make demands on him for fear of spoiling a most enchanting evening. But there was so much she wanted to ask. Questions like why had he gone to the trouble of aiding her father? Why had he been so generous with the Ericcsons? Why were he and Morgan mortal enemies? Why couldn't he love her and remain with her?

Mikyla expelled a frustrated breath. She knew why Cale didn't love her. She was too willful and independent and headstrong. He wanted a woman who would pledge her life to him, mindless of her own wants and needs. Cale had been born under a wandering star and he reveled in the freedom to roam when restlessness overcame him. He didn't want to change any more than Mikyla wanted to cast aside her dreams . . .

When the seconds became minutes Mikyla glanced expectantly toward the trees into which Cale had disappeared. Where the devil was he? Why was he keeping her waiting? How long did it take to retrieve a lunch basket, for heaven's sake?

Mikyla endured several more minutes of curious impatience before she realized Cale hadn't intended to return at all. He had used the box supper as an excuse to abandon her before they found themselves entangled in another of their inevitable arguments. He had come and gone like a restless wind, leaving her to yearn for a man no woman could hold.

Her heart shrank in despair. Was this the way it would always be with Cale? Never knowing where he was or when he would return? Would he come again, just when her heart and soul began to heal? Would he reopen the tender wounds and leave them to bleed all over again, just as he had done now? Would she ever stop wanting him?

Cale had once demanded that she set aside her obsessive dream and chase after him. But confound it, she never knew where he was going or what to expect from him. A woman would have to be hopelessly, helplessly in love to follow a man without a destination. Yet that was what Cale expected of her, even when he knew she had an excess of stubborn pride, when he was aware that she was determined to fight for her land and her dream.

Yet this time Cale hadn't even asked her to accompany him. He had left her waiting and wondering. Perhaps he hadn't intended to invite her to go with him. Maybe he had come tonight to feed his male pride, to confirm his belief that Mikyla was still the world's biggest fool where he was concerned.

Hurt and frustrated, Mikyla picked her way through the maze of underbrush and trees. Her heart fell to her ankles when she passed the plain reed basket that held her supper. With trembling fingers Mikyla scooped it up. She didn't feel like eating, not when there was an aching vacuum where her stomach should have been.

Mustering her dignity, Mikyla milled through the crowd and then made her discreet exit. Following the moonlight, she traced her way across the prairie to her homestead. She chided herself for feeling betrayed, but she simply couldn't understand Cale. She would never figure that man out if she lived to be one hundred. He had seemed so warm and affectionate while they were together and when he had appeared to save her from another uncomfortable scene with Morgan, she had even wondered if she had wandered into someone else's fantasy. But, as if she meant nothing to him, Cale had made love to her to satisfy his lust, and then performed his disappearing act.

By the time Mikyla arrived in camp her spirits were scraping rock bottom. Sighing downheartedly, Mikyla unfastened the cinch and removed the saddle. As if Sundance were trying to change the color of her blue mood, he reached around to clamp his teeth on the blanket that lay on his back. When Mikyla spun back around, the quilt was dangling from the stallion's mouth.

A faint smile worked its way across her lips. "You're right. I should be thanking my lucky stars that I have such a talented, dependable steed, instead of dwelling on that impossible man."

Sundance snorted in agreement, dropped the blanket atop the saddle, and clomped over to his corral. Feeling a smidgen

333

better, Mikyla offered Sundance a fond pat and then ambled to her tent.

Little by little, Cale was eroding her resistance, Mikyla realized dismally. He had graced her with sunshine and then had flung her into the shadows of despair. He came. He went. And Mikyla, fool that she was, clung to the brief but magical moments, nibbling on the scraps of Cale's affection.

She kept reaching for that special feeling that had always existed between them. They had had it all and Miki had been too stubborn to admit it. She knew she couldn't live those wondrous times again, but she allowed her dreams to take her there—back to those glorious moments they had shared.

Mikyla flounced on her bed and pulled the sheet over her head. She lay there, staring at the inside of her bed linen, cursing the image that materialized to torment her. Would Cale forever haunt her? Would she ever get over loving that man? What had she done to deserve this constant punishment?

The thunder of hooves brought Mikyla straight out of bed. Morgan! He was back to his mischief. Mikyla snatched up her Winchester and pushed the barrel through the tent flap. But to her chagrin, it wasn't merely one masked man who stampeded toward her camp. Four riders set torches to her shed and lassoed the posts of the corrals, sending them tumbling down like the walls of Jericho.

With her heart hammering in fearful anticipation, Mikyla clutched her loaded rifle. She waited, expecting her tent to collapse around her. As the desperados thundered toward her, Mikyla took aim and fired, catching the lead rider in the arm. Instead of answering the challenge of Miki's weapon, the pack of men tossed a sack from one of the horses and then evaporated into the darkness.

Mikyla poked her head outside to see the shed go up in smoke. Her angry gaze flew to the corral where Sundance had been before he was startled by the thundering hooves and leaping flames. Apprehensively, Mikyla stared at the bulky sack that lay beside her tent. Had they left her a nest of snakes? Mikyla shuddered at the thought. Or was it perhaps a horde of rodents and pests that would overrun her camp?

Cautiously, Mikyla untied the oversize bag. A shocked gasp gushed from her lips when she realized a man's battered body had been stuffed inside the sack. Sickening dread gnawed at her as she pushed the man to his back.

"Cale!" His name exploded from her lips in a bloodcurdling scream.

Mikyla's trembling hands glided over the man's face, which was so bloody and swollen that it was barely recognizable. When she spied the note that had been tied around his neck, along with a rope, Mikyla pronounced every curse word she knew and then invented a few new ones.

Next time it could be you. And it will be if you don't abandon your claim . . .

Sobbing hysterically, Mikyla dragged Cale's unconscious body into the tent. Since she couldn't lift him onto the bed, she rolled his lifeless body onto a pallet, then, barefooted, she dashed to the river to retrieve water to cleanse his numerous wounds. As she stumbled through the brush, she retracted all her hateful, mistrusting thoughts of Cale. He had been caught in the cross fire of her war against Joseph Richards and Morgan Hagerty and they had used Cale as a threat to force her off her land. And if Morgan had his way, Mikyla would be next in line for a brutal beating. Damn him! Morgan would pay for this, she vowed through choking sobs.

When Mikyla returned to administer first aid she found bruises and scrapes all over Cale's body. His skin was raw, looking as if he had been dragged behind a horse. Rope burns marred his throat and wrists and his clothes were battered beyond repair.

If Cale survived this torture he would sure despise her for involving him in this grisly business, Mikyla predicted. Cale was an innocent bystander. He would have sold the land. But Mikyla, determined and stubborn to the core, had adamantly refused any and all offers. *She* should have been the one who was beaten within an inch of her life and dragged across the prairie, not Cale!

Once she had placed salve on the rope burns and bandaged Cale's wounds, she collapsed in frustrated exhaustion. But she was awakened several times in the night by piercing screams, only to find they were her own. Cale hadn't moved a muscle. He just lay on the floor, looking a great deal like a half-live Egyptian mummy.

Mikyla must have kissed him ten dozen times, whimsically wishing her embraces would bring him back to life. But kisses didn't breathe life back into him and frantic prayers didn't revive him.

She decided then and there that she would hunt Morgan down and have him hung if Cale died from his injuries. Morgan would not escape unscathed after this violent retaliation. No doubt he had hired henchmen to beat Cale within an inch of his life. This was Morgan's act of vengeance to counter what Cale had done to him during their fight. This was also Morgan's way of punishing Mikyla for refusing to sell the property.

What was it Cale had said about the Land Run degenerating into human greed and inviting vicious opportunists? He had foretold of the evils that might arise. And now, because of Mikyla's defiance, Cale had fallen victim to his prophesy. Lord, how could she live with herself when she knew she was responsible for Cale's misfortune? He would never forgive her and she wasn't sure she could blame him. She had brought him nothing but trouble.

Chapter 23

Cale dragged himself up from the black depths of a nightmare. He was certain he had died sometime during the night and no one had bothered to inform him that he had been removed to a higher or lower sphere. Definitely *lower,* Cale decided when he tried to move. He was tied down and his body burned all over. Obviously, he was frying over one of hell's blazing fires.

When Cale pried open one swollen eye the world was black as pitch. Yes, he must be dead, he concluded. No sound reached his ears. The air that weighted down his lungs was as thick as pudding. And then a deep, foreboding rumble of thunder resounded around him and a streak of silver flashed across his line of vision. Sweet mercy, he was to spend all eternity being tortured by lightning, thunder, and flames. He was paying penance for the sins he had committed, along with a few he hadn't.

An unbearable pain consumed him and Cale surrendered to unconsciousness, unaware that another dowsing rain was swelling the South Canadian River and turning the Oklahoma prairie into a swamp. Several hours later, a piercing light began to tap at his puffy eyelids. Weakly, Cale lifted one heavily lidded eye to see an angelic face haloed by radiant sunbeams. Lord, not this, too, Cale thought in anguish. Besides perpetual storms and fires, his private corner of hell was to be haunted by Mikyla's exquisite face. What totally unforgivable sin had he committed that had

337

brought him to this tortuous end? He hadn't behaved all that badly . . . had he?

"Cale, can you hear me?" Mikyla questioned softly.

"Am I dead?" Cale inquired in a voice that sounded nothing like his own.

Her expression was proof of her pity and concern. But a hint of a smile trickled across her lips when Cale plied her with his bewildered question. "No, and I am not about to let you die. I rode to Elreno to fetch a doctor to examine you. I think your left arm is broken."

A peal of pained laughter echoed in Cale's chest. "Are you sure I still have one? I can't feel it."

A light flush stained Mikyla's cheeks. Cale had been so badly bruised and scraped that she had bound him into one gigantic bandage. His left arm was disfigured and swollen, so naturally she had bound it securely to his chest. She had done the best she could with the salves and home remedies she had learned to concoct in the Ozarks. But after two days, Mikyla decided it was time to fetch a physician to set Cale's arm. Damn, if only he could have remained unconscious until the agonizing ordeal was over, she mused wistfully.

As the doctor approached the pallet to inspect his patient, Mikyla crouched down to press a careful kiss to Cale's swollen lips. "I'm so sorry, Cale," she choked out, unable to hide the turmoil of emotion that churned within her. "This is all my fault."

Cale attempted to frown in bemusement, but his face felt like a punching bag and the muscles were sluggish. "What happened? The last thing I remember was walking off to retrieve your lunch basket."

He hadn't abandoned her? Mikyla wanted to hug him for revealing that bit of information, but she didn't dare. Considering Cale's condition, she might squeeze the life out of him.

"You must have been set upon by someone's henchmen," Mikyla speculated. "After I returned home from the social, thinking you had left without saying good-bye, four men rode into camp to tear it upside down. They dumped you on the ground before they thundered off. There was a note

338

pinned on what was left of your shirt that indicated that I could expect to be next in line for such brutal treatment if I didn't sell the land."

Cale would have scowled, but since he couldn't perform the slightest gesture or contort his face into any expression without inflicting pain upon himself, he didn't move a muscle. "Morgan," he hissed, but very carefully.

Mikyla nodded in grim agreement. "That was my guess. And he will pay dearly for what he has done." Her voice was thick with bitterness and revenge.

"No," Cale feebly protested.

Mikyla's eyes bulged. "You can't mean you will permit him to go scot-free? That's ridiculous! The man very nearly killed you," she reminded him curtly.

"I owe him," Cale said cryptically.

"Indeed you do," she insisted caustically. "You *owe* him two black eyes, a broken arm, and the removal of both layers of his skin from various parts of his body."

"That isn't what I meant," Cale sighed wearily.

"I still think he should be charged with assault and . . ."

Before Mikyla could debate Cale's do-nothing policy, the doctor gave her several rapid-fire orders and sent her out of the tent to retrieve what he needed. He examined Cale's arm, finding Mikyla's diagnosis to be correct. The arm was definitely broken and it required a set and securely bound splints—both of which were going to be painful in Cale's battered condition.

After pouring a sedative down Cale's throat, the physician began his task. Between his ministrations and Mikyla's previous attentions, Cale did indeed resemble an Egyptian mummy. Part of his body was bound with wood and the remaining portions were wound in bandages to ward off infection.

When the doctor completed his splint masterpiece, he climbed to his feet to work the kinks from his back. Wearing a stern frown, he wagged his finger in Cale's disfigured face. "You stay put for a few days, Brolin," he demanded. "I see no reason why you can't move around occasionally, but don't overexert yourself."

Cale nodded in compliance. At the moment, he had no inclination to ever remove himself from his pallet. He seriously doubted he could, even if he wanted to. All six hundred and thirty-nine muscles in his body would have screamed in protest.

Mikyla accompanied the doctor outside and listened to her instructions for nursing Cale back to health. By the time she returned Cale was asleep. A tender smile pursed her lips as she surveyed the gigantic mummy. Cale looked so helpless lying there. Mikyla's heart went out to Cale. He wasn't accustomed to inactivity. No doubt he would be growling like an injured lion before he fully recuperated.

Another depressing thought skitted across Mikyla's mind. When the pain ebbed and Cale could think clearly he would be cursing her for his woes. Her stubbornness was responsible for his plight and Cale would make it a point to remind her of her failings.

Turning away, Mikyla ambled down to the river to be alone with her anguished thoughts. She stood on the cliff that overlooked the swollen waters of the South Canadian River, gazing at the flat plain that had once been the site of her corrals. Now the land stood under water. The river was rippling as it sped along its new channel, running away from her just like her dreams.

Mikyla knew she had to sacrifice her fantasy of a ranch and a home. She couldn't risk Cale's life again. Morgan had realized she cared for Cale and he was using her affection as a weapon against her. Perhaps if she hadn't been so transparent that night at Fort Reno, Morgan wouldn't have known she was suffering from a one-sided love affair. No doubt everyone who had seen her face at the box supper, when she spied Cale, had been aware of her feelings for that shiftless cowboy. Cale's face had been an impassive mask that revealed nothing of his emotions when their eyes locked. But Mikyla was certain her features had lit up like a lantern blazing on a long wick. Morgan knew of her affection for Cale and the scoundrel had preyed on her vulnerability, striking out to hurt the man she loved, forcing her to submit to Morgan's demands.

Her shoulders slumped dejectedly. Morgan had won. Mikyla could not live with the perpetual fear that her adversary would murder Cale if she didn't sell out. Losing Cale would be far worse than losing her precious dream site. One treasure had to be sacrificed to spare the other.

A mist of tears clouded Mikyla's eyes as she watched the river roll lazily toward the sea. Oh, how easy it would be now to ride off into the sunset with Cale. Now there was nothing to hold her. And now that she had come dangerously close to losing Cale, she realized how much he meant to her. But she couldn't follow after Cale when he recovered from his injuries. He didn't truly love her, not the way she needed to be loved. He wanted her physically, but his desire would fade once he overcame the challenge of having her accept his offer.

Cale was a dynamic individual who took control of situations. He would continue trying to dominate Mikyla. He would attempt to make her decisions for her. That was just his way. He had been trying to tell her what to do since the moment they met and he would never change.

Mikyla knew she couldn't survive an affair in which she would be forced into submission. Neither did she expect to dictate to Cale. It had to be an equal sharing of affection and responsibility. Love would have to overshadow both of their faults and Cale didn't love her enough to compromise.

Another heavy-hearted sigh passed her lips as she turned her back on the river and aimed herself toward the tent. While Cale was sleeping off his sedative, she would ride into Elreno and seek out Morgan Hagerty and Joseph Richards. Once she had been paid the meager price for her property, she would rent a room at the hotel. It would take a few days before Cale could be moved. But when he could, she would transfer him to her room. And then . . .

Mikyla didn't know what she would do after Cale rode out of her life again. All she knew was that she couldn't go with him, not if she wanted to salvage any of her dignity and independence. Emet had offered her a job at his store, but Mikyla couldn't intrude. Her father was happier than he had been in years. Belinda and Emet were preparing for their

341

wedding and Mikyla would only be underfoot. And yet, where else could she go when she lost her land?

Well, I'll cross that bridge when I encounter it, Mikyla told herself. But for now she had to prepare herself for her confrontation with Morgan and Joseph. It would be difficult to be civil to those miserable vermin, knowing what they had done.

Cursing in irritation, Mikyla tossed the saddle on Sundance's back. After she had checked on Cale to ensure he was resting as comfortably as possible and set food and drink within his reach, she galloped north. Mikyla dreaded this meeting, certain she would never be able to contain her temper. In her mind's eye, she would see Cale's bloody, bruised body and she would become furious all over again.

When Mikyla located Morgan and Joseph, she found it necessary to count to ten thrice before she dared to open her mouth. Sure enough, the bitterness and resentment came rushing back the moment she glared into Morgan's handsome features, which should have been as black and blue as Cale's.

"You have convinced me to sell my property," Mikyla muttered, her tone harsh with anger and frustration.

A triumphant smile captured Joseph's sharp, angular features. Morgan's poker face showed no expression at all. No doubt he was saving his goading grin until later, Mikyla predicted.

Grasping her arm, Joseph shepherded her down the street to the land office to transfer the deed. "It's a shame you waited so long to agree to a sale, Miss Lassiter," he mocked in his parrot-like voice. "We might have been more generous with you if you hadn't put up so much resistance."

Mikyla jerked away from his repulsive touch and flashed both men murderous glowers. "I may have been forced to sell out, but I don't have to like it. Dealing with conniving wretches like you has spoiled my opinion of the male species."

Flinging her nose in the air, Mikyla marched toward the

land office in stiff, precise steps. God, how she detested giving in to these two men! But she had no choice. Even if she took them to court they would rely on brutality, and she doubted she would live long enough to present her testimony to a judge.

When the deed had been transferred to the townsite company, Joseph waddled off to make arrangements. As Mikyla stepped outside the office she glanced back at the blond rogue who could change personalities faster than a chameleon could change colors. She had once thought Morgan to possess the manners of a gentleman, but now she realized that his appearance and proper airs concealed his deceitful character from his unsuspecting victims. When things were going Morgan's way he was all smiles and propriety. But when he was deprived of his desires he was vicious and ruthless.

"I admit I was fooled in the beginning," Mikyla confessed begrudgingly. "But now I realize you lied about the card game and the fight with Cale Brolin. You wanted my stallion, didn't you? You were the one who was taking advantage of my father."

Morgan shrugged nonchalantly. "The stallion was a valuable asset and I saw no reason why I shouldn't use him to accomplish my purpose. After I decided to become a member of the townsite company's board of directors I thought Sundance would ensure that I acquired the prime sites."

His veiled green eyes slid over Mikyla's curvaceous figure. It annoyed him that he still found himself attracted to a woman who had shamelessly offered herself to Cale Brolin. Damn her. Morgan could have given her all the things a beautiful woman wanted, but this feisty vixen preferred to spread herself beneath the one man Morgan despised with every part of his being.

It was fortunate for Mikyla that Cale saw her only as the object of his lust, Morgan mused. If Cale really felt something for her, Morgan would have been tempted to dispose of the minx, just to repay his long-standing debt to his mortal enemy. But Morgan wouldn't be satisfied with planning the demise of Brolin's whore. No, he wanted to take something from Brolin that meant more to him than life. Morgan was obsessed with leaving Brolin to suffer torment and grief, to make his life a veritable hell on earth.

As his thoughts circled back to the present, Morgan displayed the goading grin Mikyla had anticipated earlier. "I could have satisfied several of your feminine whims," he had the gall to say. "I might have even managed to persuade the other directors of the townsite company to let you keep part of your claim." When his hand lifted to touch her flawless cheek, Mikyla jerked away as if she had been stung. An unpleasant snarl swallowed Morgan's features. "But you were a fool and I can never forgive you for allowing yourself to become Brolin's plaything."

His words stung like a wasp. And it hurt worse to know Morgan was right. She could never win Cale's love, not in one week or one century. "And I suppose you are going to lie through your teeth and tell me you would have treated me with the utmost respect if I had buckled beneath your shallow charm?" she sniffed sarcastically.

Her taunting words and the caustic tone in which she conveyed them rankled Morgan's temper. "Bitch," he spat at her. "I can please a woman far better than Cale Brolin can."

It was Mikyla's turn to break into a ridiculing smile. "Although I am not woman enough to tame a man like Cale Brolin, he would always be my first choice if I were to pick between the two of you," she purred mockingly. "Cale is a man's man, as well as a woman's whimsical dream. He knows how to satisfy a woman. You would do well to take a few lessons from the master, Morgan."

Rage boiled through Morgan's veins. Dammit, he had spent half his life being compared to Cale Brolin. God, how he detested it. Nothing could make him furious faster than having Cale's name thrown in his face.

Instinctively, Morgan clamped his hands on Mikyla's arms, crushing them in his fierce grip. "Don't you ever compare my skills to that bastard's or you won't live long enough to humiliate yourself by sleeping with him again."

It was only after he had shoved Mikyla against the outer

wall of the office that he regained a degree of self-control. His rough treatment served to ignite Mikyla's temper. She itched to scratch his eyes out, but she doubted Morgan would allow her that close to him. Yet, if her silent curses had any effect, Morgan would die an excruciating death.

"I'm sure you're satisfied now that you can sell my property for enormous profit," she sneered at him. "No doubt you are enjoying double satisfaction after you hired your henchmen to beat Cale to bloody shreds." Her flashing blue eyes raked Morgan with scornful mockery. "Cale bested you all by himself, but you had to call in reinforcements to break him, didn't you?"

Morgan had thoroughly recomposed himself by the time Mikyla spat out her question. His emotions were masked behind a carefully disciplined stare. "I'm sure I don't have the faintest notion what you are talking about. But I cannot say I care what happened to Brolin. Even the news of his death would bear me more pleasure than grief."

The odious man, Mikyla silently fumed. He wouldn't even own up to his brutal treatment of Cale. What did she expect of an accomplished liar? He knew if he confessed to arranging Cale's merciless beating she would make a bee line to the newly appointed sheriff and have Morgan dragged to jail. Damn, if only she could have detected Morgan's face behind the bandanas the men wore that night. Then she would have concrete evidence that Morgan was responsible for the beating. But whether or not he was on hand for the dastardly deed, Morgan's handwriting was all over the violent act.

"Be warned, Morgan," Mikyla jeered contemptuously. "If you ever threaten Cale's life again, I'll shoot you myself."

A peal of laughter rang through the air. "You guard that worthless bastard like a she-dragon," he scoffed into her face. "Such misplaced loyalty for a man who will eventually leave you to wallow in your shame! What a fool you are, Mikyla."

Mikyla could endure no more of his grating insults. She cocked her arm to mash Morgan's smile into his face, but he was lightning-quick with his gun hand. The Colt was out of its holster and trained on her heaving breasts before she could strike. Mikyla's doubled fist remained in midair while she glanced around to note their boisterous argument had drawn a crowd.

It was daring, she did admit. But with a congregation of spectators surrounding her, Mikyla felt reasonably safe. Morgan would indeed be carted off to jail if he gunned down a *woman* for delivering no more than a well-deserved punch to his jaw. Morgan was vicious but he wasn't a fool. Operating on that theory, Mikyla satisfied her hunger for revenge. Her fist connected with Morgan's cheek and a bright red welt erupted over his deceitful features.

Smiling in smug satisfaction, Mikyla pivoted on her heels and sashayed across the street to retrieve Sundance. When she heard the deadly click of Morgan's Colt, she paused beside Dag Ericcson, who had ventured to town to purchase supplies.

"I don't mean to sound like a poor loser, but if I should die from a bullet in the back, shoot him for me," she requested. When Dag nodded in compliance, Mikyla straightened her shoulders and continued on her way.

Morgan was smoldering with murderous fury. Damn that bitch! She had struck him, daring him to retaliate while they were surrounded with eye-witnesses. Although he itched to squeeze the trigger, he couldn't, not without inviting his own lynching. But he wasn't finished with that spitfire, not by a long shot!

It was with a small degree of satisfaction that Mikyla headed back to camp. She had lost her dream site, true, but she had told Morgan what she thought of him and socked him in the face, just as she should have done each time she had confronted that wily weasel. If her sacrifice had saved Cale's life, it was worth it, she assured herself. Indeed, she might even find happiness if Cale would learn to love her the way . . .

Before she found herself wandering off on a whimsical tangent, Mikyla redirected her thoughts. She wasn't going to fool herself into hoping Cale would return her deep affection. She had to be realistic. She had lost her dream site

346

and before long Cale would be gone. She would have nothing and she might as well prepare herself for the emptiness that would inevitably overcome her. Soon the shock would wear off and she would be forced to cope with the desolation of seeing her dream shatter and watching the man she loved vanish into the sunset.

A tear formed in the corner of Mikyla's eye, and then another followed in its wake. She had fought hard to keep her land, but she should have dedicated her time and effort to the man who now lay in a bruised heap. It was too late for her and Cale to make a life together. Now Cale would never love her. He would always resent her stubbornness and her fierce independence. And *she* would never be satisfied unless she had a place to call her own.

Mikyla wanted to scream in frustration. Because of her obstinacy, she had lost everything she held dear. She couldn't blame Cale if he hated her for the rest of his life. She had given him little reason to care for her. It seemed everything she touched turned to disaster.

Grappling with that depressing thought, Mikyla rode across the rolling prairie, wishing she had selected another site, one that wouldn't have conflicted with the interests of the townsite company, wishing she had listened to Cale when he told her she was inviting trouble. But it was too late, she reminded herself again and again. She had made her mistakes and now she had to own up to them.

Chapter 24

By the time Mikyla returned from Elreno darkness had engulfed the small campsite. She had not even set a booted foot to the ground before she heard an almost inhuman growl behind her.

"Where the hell have you been?" Cale demanded gruffly.

"What the hell are *you* doing off your pallet?" she questioned just as sharply. "The doctor told you to . . ."

"I don't give a whit what the doctor said," Cale muttered in annoyance. "Now, where were you?"

She knew he was going to despise her when he roused enough to realize Mikyla was the indirect cause of his suffering. Sure enough, he was as friendly as a charging rhinoceros. Slowly, Mikyla drew herself up to peer into his stubble-faced scowl. Her defiance and stubborn pride sagged when confronted by this huge, sneering mummy.

"I rode to Elreno to sell my property to the townsite company," she murmured deflatedly. "Well? Aren't you going to say I told you so?" Bitter laughter burst from her trembling lips. "You have been waiting over three months to say it."

The anger and frustration drained from Cale's body like water pouring through a sieve. Mikyla looked so vulnerable standing there, fighting for hard-won composure, struggling to contain the tears. He knew how much it must have hurt her to make the inevitable sacrifice, and see her dreams collapse around her.

"I'm sorry, Ky," he said quietly. "I knew you would fight this battle to the bitter end. But this dream of yours wasn't meant to be. You were destined to lose before the Run began." Cale expelled a sigh. "Joseph Richards came to me, requesting that I race as the representative for the townsite company. He told me the exact location, and it was the site you had selected. Although I informed him in no uncertain terms that I wouldn't race for his fraudulent company, I knew he would pay someone else to do it for him."

"Morgan . . ." Mikyla bit off his name, her voice brimming with resentment.

Cale nodded somberly. "No doubt Morgan demanded a share of the interest in the company in return for staking the claim. I tried to convince you not to make the Run because I knew you would never be allowed to keep your property. There is too much power and wealth behind that company, not to mention the hundreds of settlers who paid those swindlers for lot certificates."

"And I was too stubborn and foolish to believe anyone could deprive me of my dream if I wanted it badly enough," Mikyla finished for him as she rerouted the tears that boiled down her cheeks.

Mechanically, Cale hobbled around to point himself toward the river. "I knew you thought I was being pessimistic and cruel, but I was only trying to spare you the heartache you are suffering now. I thought if we sold the land for a fair price you could find another homesite to suit you."

"Where are you going?" Mikyla blinked bewilderedly when Cale limped past the tent instead of ducking into it.

"To the river for a bath," he informed her without breaking his slow, uneven gait.

Mikyla darted after him. "You can't bathe yet. You'll warp the splint on your broken arm!" she protested. "And all the bandages will be ruined."

"I couldn't get up, either," Cale reminded her with a snort. "But I'm up, I'm staying up, and I'm going to take a bath. You can help or you can go to bed. But with or without you, *I'm* going to do as I damned well please."

An unnoticed smile pursed her lips as she followed in Cale's wake. He looked as if he had been trampled by a herd of wild horses, but it didn't stop him. It only slowed his pace, and Mikyla fell in love with him all over again. There was a rough sensuality about Cale that had always appealed to Mikyla. He was as rough as rawhide and tough as leather, doing as he pleased and not catering to a woman. Mikyla always lost interest in men who fawned over her, men who held little challenge. But Cale was a renegade and Mikyla was attracted to him, untamable though he was.

Wearing only the breeches Mikyla had cut off to facilitate caring for his many wounds, Cale waded into the river. A contented sigh escaped his lips as he peeled off the conglomeration of bandages Mikyla had meticulously wrapped around him. While Cale was splashing water on his chest, Mikyla shrugged off her clothes and waded in beside him.

Hearing her approach, Cale turned to voice a remark. The words evaporated on his lips when a vision of sheer loveliness floated gracefully toward him. Cale wasn't sure which hurt worse, his raw flesh or the ache in his loins.

The Indian summer moon was glowing like an orange ball in the eastern sky. Glittering stars, the forget-me-nots of heaven, encircled the glorious sphere. Through the canopy of tall trees, the twinkling beams poured down to caress Mikyla's silky skin. Even the chirps of the creatures of the night fell silent when this enchanting nymph entered their domain.

Her hair, a waterfall of silver streams intermingling with strands of gold, caught in the moon-dappled light. Cale reached out to lift the lustrous strands, to inhale their tantalizing scent. Suddenly his senses became aware of nothing but Mikyla. The pain seemed to ebb when he fell beneath her magical spell. And when her tapered fingers skimmed over his chest, Cale felt a shudder run all the way to his toes. Now this was the perfect prescription for pain, he decided. This sweet angel could cure any ailment.

Mikyla didn't know what possessed her, but she was stung by the fierce need to express her love for this incredible man.

351

But words were inadequate. Mikyla longed to convey her *feelings* for him, displaying all the wondrous emotions that consumed her when she looked upon this remarkable cowboy and remembered all they had endured together.

A muted moan tripped from Cale's tongue when her moist lips skimmed over his scrapes and bruises. She was unbelievably gentle. She knew the location of each wound and she had carefully kissed away the pain, creating an entirely new ache that came from deep within.

"Does it hurt much?" Mikyla murmured as her butterfly kisses fluttered from one male nipple to the other.

"Not anymore," Cale squeaked, wondering if it was indeed his voice that had uttered the words. As her kisses and caresses ventured lower, Cale struggled to untangle his tongue. "Don't do that . . ."

"Why not?" Her smile drifted across his whipcord muscles while her hands wandered at will, erasing the sting of raw flesh, replacing it with tingling pleasure.

"Doc said to take it easy," Cale gasped as Mikyla continued to excite and arouse him.

"He also told you to stay in bed," she whispered against his hair-roughened flesh. "You didn't. That makes you fair game, wouldn't you say?"

"Ky . . ." Cale drew her to her feet, pulling her delicious body against his hard, aching contours. "I'm not sure I can make love with one arm in a splint. I . . ."

"Have you ever tried?" she questioned huskily.

"Well, no but . . ."

Mikyla's face fairly beamed. "Good. I have always wanted to be around to share at least one *first time* with you . . ."

Her lips silenced his weak protest. When she finally came up for air, Cale inhaled a steadying breath. Damn, this woman was hard on a man's blood pressure, not to mention the devastating effect she had on his anatomy. She had become a skillful seductress and Cale hated himself for attempting to reject her. But he had the feeling she held herself responsible for what had happened to him. He didn't want Mikyla's pity. It would never be enough to satisfy him, not when he wanted to tame her defiant heart and capture her rebellious soul.

As her arms slid over his shoulders, her breasts pressed wantonly against his chest. Cale's resistance drooped another notch. Despite his attempt to frown in disapproval, a tiny sigh betrayed him. "You are a very persuasive woman," he rasped.

"It's because I took instruction from a most persuasive man," she informed him saucily. Her eyes focused on the sensuous curve of his lips, yearning to have him return her kiss, longing for him to hold her in his possessive embrace, even if he could only employ one arm.

The look on her face, the lure of those spell-casting blue eyes snapped Cale's willpower. "Hell, I can't resist you. I never could. I don't know why I should try now," he groaned as he clutched her to him.

"I'd rather you wouldn't waste the energy," she said with an impish smile.

Mikyla slipped from his arms to amble toward the sandbar that lay ankle-deep in the water. As she stretched out upon the shifting sand, Cale moved toward her, hypnotized by the enticing picture she presented in the moonlight. Silver ripples undulated about her as she sat back, resting her weight on her arms. Her head was tilted toward the sky, surveying the galaxy of stars that sprawled across the heavens. One leg was bent, the other stretched out in front of her. Although she was poised in the river like a mermaid basking in the moonlight, it was the expression on her face that turned Cale's legs to limp noodles. When she glanced at him, there was something in the way she smiled that left his heart dripping on his ribs.

"I want you, Cale, and I'm no longer ashamed to admit it. There was a time when I resented this attraction between us. But no more. For however long it will last, even if it can't be forever, I want you. I want to cherish the memories . . ."

Cale dropped onto a skinned knee, mindless to all except this goddess who formed the dimensions of his erotic dreams. He wondered momentarily if he were really lying on his pallet in the tent, imagining this titillating scene. But the instant he felt her sweet lips melt beneath his, he knew it was no fantastic dream. Mikyla was in his arms, creating new memories, evoking monstrous cravings that made him tremble in masculine anticipation.

There had been times when they had surrendered in wild, savage abandon. There had been those times when their lovemaking was embroidered with gentleness. But nothing compared to the way they touched and kissed while the silvery river trickled over them. They were drifting with the current, savoring each other, cherishing each soft, inquiring kiss and caress.

Mikyla felt as if she were melting and flowing away with the meandering river. The fact that Cale's arm was in a splint didn't seem to inhibit him at all. He drew her back against his chest, allowing his good hand to glide sensuously over her shoulder, along her arm, and across her thigh. While his fingertips languidly drifted and receded, his warm lips traced the swanlike column of her neck and cheek. He touched her with indescribable tenderness, worshipping her, arousing her in ways she had never experienced. His hand and lips migrated to the dusky peaks of her breasts and swirled across her abdomen, leaving her to burn, even while she was sitting in the river.

Mikyla twisted to face him. Although his features were discolored, he was still the most disarmingly attractive man she had ever seen. She longed to trace each scar, to feel his solid strength beneath her fingertips. She didn't want to rush this night, but to revel in it. Tonight might be her last night with Cale. The fact that he was up and moving, despite doctor's orders, indicated that he was growing restless. Soon he would feel the need to roam and he would leave her to drown in the magical memories of the way they were, the rapture they had shared. Cale was another of her dreams that would never touch reality, a longing she could never fully enjoy.

But this time, when they went their separate ways, Mikyla would have expressed her love for him. It would be in the way she touched him, the way she responded to his caress, the way she gave herself up to his skillful lovemaking.

She made no attempt to contain the quiet moan of

354

pleasure. Nor did she feel shame when she arched toward his seeking hand. His name was on her lips and love was in the whisper of each tender caress.

When Cale crouched above her, Mikyla lay back on the sand, studying him, commiting every treasured expression to memory. She watched his powerful muscles ripple down his chest and arm as he bent over her. She stared into those flaming silver eyes as he took possession of her body and soul. The intimacy of this moment would be forever branded on her mind. Mikyla could feel all the splendorous sensations that overcame him. She could see the wondrous emotions that engulfed him, and she made no attempt to disguise what she was feeling.

Sensations poured out in triplets. Each one tumbled onto the other until they mingled into one unique emotion—the essense of love, that ineffable combination that could never be duplicated or re-created without the perfect ingredients.

Cale felt passion filling him to overflowing as they moved together in rapturous harmony. And then, like wine toppling from the rim of a goblet, the sweet, soul-shattering sensations trickled through him and over him. They had somehow created their own unique brand of lovemaking. It was as special as Mikyla herself. He focused on her passion-drugged features as they made their spiraling descent from love's intimate journey. He couldn't trust himself to speak just then, too engulfed in the maelstrom of emotions to think rationally. In his present state, he would probably make some unreasonable demand on Ky and shatter this fantastic moment.

And so, he quietly eased down beside her, levering his upper body on his elbow, protecting his cumbersome splint from the gentle flow of the river. Mikyla cuddled up behind him, her chin resting lightly on his shoulder. Her hand absently followed the masculine terrain of his thigh and hip. They lay in the stream until the embers of passion cooled, each one afraid to speak and yet hounded by troublesome thoughts. Cale longed to know what Mikyla planned for her future and Mikyla ached to know how many hours she had left before Cale walked away, leaving her to collect the shattered remains of her heart.

Finally, Cale unfolded himself and pulled Mikyla up beside him. Keeping her small hand tucked in his, he led her ashore. Cale managed to walk all the way back to camp before he was overwhelmed by the need to make love to her all over again. He felt as if he were about to lose something precious and dear to him and yet he was helpless to prevent it.

Making demands on a woman as stubborn and willful as Mikyla accomplished nothing. Cale knew that for certain. After all, he had attempted to dictate to her dozens of times and with no success. Threatening her only made her all the more determined to defy him.

Her reaction to Joseph and Morgan's ultimatums was proof of her perseverence. And until Mikyla could accept him for what he was, they would never overcome the obstacles that stood between them. He could not bring himself to invite her to follow after him, knowing she wouldn't come because she truly wanted to, but only because she had very few alternatives left at her disposal. Her dream had crumbled around her. She felt alone and vulnerable. She held herself responsible for his troubles. Male pride refused to allow Cale to become Mikyla's *last resort,* and he was not about to accept her pity.

But no matter what tomorrow held, Cale was going to ensure the night lasted forever. He intended to take his Texas time with this seductive nymph. Yet, even before he could confess he hadn't returned to the tent to sleep, Mikyla was pressing eager kisses to his lips, doing incredibly delicious things with her hands. Cale found himself caught up in the gentle but potent force of passion. He tried not to think of what was to come when dawn intruded on them. He refused to think past the splendor of the night. The task wasn't difficult, not when Mikyla filled up his senses and accompanied him on another magical flight beyond the curtain of stars.

Chapter 25

Sunlight tapped against the canvas and Mikyla came slowly awake, feeling as if she had only slept an hour. A wry smile pursed her lips when she landed on that thought. Because of their fervent lovemaking, there *had* been little time for sleep. . . .

Realizing Cale was no longer beside her, Mikyla bolted straight up in bed. Had he left her again without so much as good-bye? Mikyla scrambled to her feet, grabbed a discarded shirt, and rushed outside.

Amusement glistened in her eyes when she saw Cale wrestling in a one-armed attempt to untangle the leather straps of the saddle. He was wearing his cut-off jeans and boots. He hadn't bothered to shave the stubble from his face, and his hair looked as if it had been styled during a cyclone. His appearance was so comical, Mikyla giggled at him.

Cale was in the process of saddling Sundance. Each time Cale flung the blanket over Sundance's back, the steed tugged it off and dropped it on the ground. Since Cale could use only one hand, he was forced to lay the saddle aside, retrieve the blanket, and begin the process all over again.

"Damned sorry nag," he growled, glaring mutinously at the contrary stallion. "I'm no more pleased about the possibility of riding you than you are. But since my gelding was stolen, you are the only four-legged beast of burden besides Miki's mule . . . which I am not about to ride!"

Sundance tossed his proud head and stomped his hoof

dangerously close to Cale's booted foot.

"Oh, you would love to see my entire body encased in wooden splints, wouldn't you?" Cale snorted derisively. He slapped the blanket into place and quickly whirled to retrieve the saddle before the ornery steed could shed the pad, as he had done twice already.

"Sundance, mind your manners," Mikyla scolded with an amused smile.

Both the steed and Cale swiveled their heads around to see Mikyla ambling toward them, wearing no more than a flimsy shirt that barely extended to her thighs. Ignoring Cale's all-consuming gaze, Mikyla lifted one perfectly arched brow in question.

"Were you planning to steal my horse and leave without telling me good-bye?"

"If I were, I'm not now," Cale growled as his good arm stole around her waist. He offered her a good-morning kiss that sizzled like the summer sun. "Actually, I intended for you to come with me."

Mikyla frowned in concern. "Are you well enough to travel?"

A rakish smile dangled from the corner of his mouth. "You seemed to think I was well enough for most anything last night," he reminded her, his eyebrows elevating provocatively.

A becoming blush worked its way from the base of her throat to the roots of her hair. Cale chuckled at her embarrassed response. But his smile evaporated when Mikyla turned to stare at some distant point. Her back was rigid with her usual degree of determination.

"You're planning to travel to Texas, aren't you?" she blurted out in a rush. "Don't ask me to follow after you again, Cale."

"I wasn't going to ask," he said after he had studied her for a long, meditative moment. "Where are you going, Ky? Cale turned to heave the saddle onto the stallion's back.

"It doesn't really matter *where* I'm going," she said defeatedly. "Only that I can never be where I truly want to be."

Reaching beneath the stallion's belly, Cale struggled to fasten the cinch without the use of his left hand. His expression was one of frustrated annoyance, and Mikyla wasn't sure if he was more irritated with her remark or his inability to fasten the girth all by himself. Pushing his hand aside, Mikyla assumed the task, wondering if Cale had misinterpreted her comment. No doubt he assumed he thought she was referring to her dream site and the fact that she could no longer call this property her own.

Cale glared at Mikyla's shapely backside while she bent to tighten the cinch under Sundance's belly. How could this gorgeous creature still evoke anger and desire in him, all in the same moment? Damn, she had always touched so many emotions in him that he felt as if he were sitting on both ends of an emotional seesaw, as well as in the middle!

"If you had listened to me in the first place, you wouldn't be without a home," he muttered sourly. Cale expelled an agitated breath as he jammed the bit into Sundance's mouth. All that interrupted the strained silence was the sound of Sundance rolling the bit with his tongue and snorting at Cale's unnecessary roughness.

Mikyla suddenly felt all alone and terribly depressed. If Cale had insisted that she accompany him to Texas, despite her refusal, she would have felt some consolation. But he had given up on her and she faced an emptiness that nothing could fill. Her land was gone and the man she loved had every intention of walking out of her life . . . again.

"Get dressed and pack your gear," Cale ordered impatiently. "No matter where we go, we have to get off this property." He gestured east, calling her attention to the approach of prairie schooners, wagons, and buggies. "Morgan is about to open the floodgates of humanity. This land will be crawling with townspeople in half an hour."

His bitter words reflected the resentment Mikyla suddenly felt when she glanced east. Damn that Morgan Hagerty. He had forced her off her land. All the long hours of labor, all the hopeful dreams . . . all of it was gone forever. Mikyla was bearing up as best she could, but she feared the time was rapidly approaching when the shock would wear off, leaving her to come to grips with the heartbreaking realization that she had truly lost.

In a stunned daze, Mikyla walked to the tent to dress and gather her belongings. When she had completed her packing, she helped Cale disassemble the tent. But before they could evacuate the campsite, a group of soldiers approached from the northwest.

Cale swore under his breath when he spied Brock Terrel leading the patrol. With a stiff nod, Brock greeted Cale. His eyes flooded over Cale's odd apparel and then settled on the splint that encased his arm.

"It appears you have run into some difficulty of late," he observed. Before continuing, he gestured for his patrol to proceed to the east fence to monitor the approach of settlers who were about to stake Mikyla's land as a townsite. "Joseph Richards and his associate from Kansas were found murdered last night."

The shocking announcement caught Cale and Mikyla off guard. They stood there gaping at Brock as if flowers were sprouting from his ears.

Brock's gaze swung to Mikyla, eyeing her speculatively. "It was reported that Miss Lassiter was very bitter about losing her land. Morgan Hagerty also informed me that she shot the affidavit out of Joseph's hand when he attempted to present it to her."

Cale's brows jackknifed as he glanced incredulously at Miki. "You did that?" he croaked aghast.

Mikyla gave a reluctant but affirmative nod. "I was angry and bitter and I. . . ."

"Did your anger over the situation also provoke you to kill Joseph and the other director of the townsite company?" Brock demanded to know.

"She was with me last night," Cale defended, glaring at Brock. "It seems you should be asking Morgan these questions. He is the one who stands to gain a great deal from the death of his associates."

"I already asked him," Brock snapped back. "Morgan seems to think the two of you might have been involved, and he has his own alibi." Suddenly, Brock's expression mellowed and he released the breath he had been holding. His eyes dipped to the toes of his polished boots and then refocused on Cale's battered features. "The truth is, I cannot imagine you taking such drastic measures. Nor do I believe you would allow Miss Lassiter to vent her frustrations over the situation in bloody violence. But it is my duty to investigate the deaths."

Brock's gaze scanned the rolling hills, watching the wobbling prairie schooners make their approach. "I also owe you an apology, Cale," he murmured quietly. "Emily admitted that you were not the one at fault during the celebration at the fort. She said you tried to reject her as delicately as possible because you and I were friends." His eyes swung back to Cale and a brief smile touched his lips. "Although Em felt she couldn't stay with me after she had betrayed my fidelity, I cannot, in good conscience, allow our friendship to end. You were right. I was partially at fault, and I will assume my share of the blame." His arm stretched across the distance that separated them to clasp Cale's hand. "Your business is welcome at Fort Reno and the unfortunate incident is forgotten. I regret my harsh words and my preoccupation that has finally driven Em away from me."

Mikyla had the feeling Brock and Cale needed time to speak in privacy. Sensing she was in the way, she strapped her belongings on the pack mule and wandered around her camp like a lost child. When Cale and Brock completed their private conversation, Brock rode off to join his troops and Cale strode up behind Mikyla.

It was difficult for Miki to restrain the tears that swam in her eyes as she glanced around her dream site for the last time. It was over, she told herself. There would be no more childish dreams of a home and a ranch. A town would soon be sitting on her claim and she would have nothing left but the bittersweet memories. It had been a brief, shining moment, a breath of hope for a bright future. But now it was gone like a shooting star bursting into light before being swallowed up in darkness.

Mikyla was too busy fighting to maintain her composure to notice the troubled expression on Cale's face. Absently he

361

led Mikyla toward Sundance. Something Brock had said disturbed Cale, but his attention was on Mikyla, knowing it was killing her to leave the land she had fought so hard to keep, losing it because of Morgan's ruthless tactics.

As the hordes of citizens swarmed the prairie to stake their homes and businesses beside what would soon become a path of spikes and steel rails, Mikyla and Cale rode north. After several minutes of unbearable silence, Cale finally expelled a sigh.

"I know you won't believe me when I say this is for the best," he began, only to be interrupted by Miki's choked sob.

"The best?" she sniffed bitterly. "What have I done so wrong to deserve being ousted from my dream site? Just because I am a woman alone, men seem to think they can walk all over me. Because I haven't the time and money to take my protest to court, Morgan pressured me with threats and violence."

Mikyla struggled to keep her voice from deteriorating, but it was difficult. She was aching inside and depression was closing in around her like a gloomy fog. The shock had worn off and she was feeling the full effects of losing her battle against the townsite company. "*Free* land, they said. A land of milk and honey that was ours for the taking, to build dreams and new hopes for the future." Slowly, Mikyla turned in the saddle to see the exodus of settlers rushing to set up housekeeping on *her* claim. She almost cried all over again. "I should have listened to you instead of gazing at the world through rose-colored glasses. Now I'm bitter and resentful. I dislike all those homesteaders and I don't even know them!" she wailed despite her attempt at self-control.

Cale grimaced when Mikyla reduced herself to tears. He could feel her body quaking against his, but holding her against him didn't seem to comfort her. Cale had never seen her fall completely apart and he wasn't much good at consolation. But he did try to comfort her. "I know you hate the world and everyone in it at the moment. I'm afraid the townsite companies are necessary evils. They have served their purpose in populating towns in practical locations. I don't condone their methods, but many people have relied

362

on their judgment."

Cale stared into her cloudy blue eyes, hoping she would accept what he was trying to tell her. "Think of all the settlers and their families who would have suffered if you hadn't sacrificed your claim. Those people paid good money to the townsite company. If you had miraculously managed to keep your land, Morgan and his friends would have skipped the country with their money. All those innocent, well-meaning people would have been out several hundred dollars and they would have to migrate elsewhere." Cale gestured his good arm toward the flock of excited settlers who were buzzing about unloading their supplies. "These are the people who would have been hurt, not Morgan. And now, because of their greed, Joseph and his friend are dead. It could have been *you*, Ky," he said meaningfully.

Mikyla knew Cale was trying to lift her spirits and she knew he had stated an important point. But it didn't prevent her from hurting. It angered her that a man like Morgan was flitting around, free as a bird. He had routed her from her land and then he had disposed of his partners. Would that man ever receive his just desserts? Perhaps not in this life, she mused. But one day Morgan Hagerty would be baking in one of hell's hottest ovens.

After Cale rode into Elreno to purchase another set of clothes, he reined Sundance east. Pausing on high ground, Cale gestured toward the stately, two-story house that was surrounded with sheds and corrals.

Mikyla peered at the ranch that had sprung up on the prairie. It reminded her of her dream, the vision of what she might have had. When Cale nudged Sundance toward the framed home, Mikyla tugged back on the reins.

"If you think seeing someone else's dream come true will somehow make me feel better, you are wasting your time," she muttered acrimoniously. "I had intended to spend the day feeling sorry for myself."

"Trust me for once in your life," Cale grumbled as he took the reins to steer the stallion.

Mikyla didn't want a closer look at someone else's dream. Why was Cale punishing her when he knew she was raw

363

inside? What did he think he was going to do, attempt to find her a job working for these people? Didn't he realize the anguish she would suffer if she were forced to be reminded daily of what she had lost?

"Cale, I don't know what you're planning or what you expect to accomplish, but I . . ."

"Hush, woman, I am doing this for your own good," Cale snapped.

Mikyla clamped her mouth shut, but she had already made up her mind to reject whatever suggestion was whipping through Cale's head. To her amazement, Cale pulled her from the saddle and led her toward the front door as if he owned the place.

"I have just been accused of murder and now you will have me hustled off to jail for breaking and entering," she muttered as she planted her feet at the door. Although she refused to stir a step, Cale uprooted her from the spot and shuffled her into the house. "Why have you brought me here? I don't want to see it. And who owns this pl—?"

Her voice trailed off as Cale strode into the sparsely furnished study. To her utter astonishment, he whipped open the desk drawer to retrieve a bulky envelope. Without ado, he closed the distance between them and laid the envelope in Mikyla's hand.

"*You* own this place," he informed her matter-of-factly. "Here is the deed and enough cash to furnish the house to suit your own tastes."

Mikyla's legs buckled beneath her. Her eyes bulged from their sockets and her mouth dropped open wide enough for a covey of quail to nest. "What?" she hooted incredulously.

Cale ushered her into the spacious parlor and planted her in a chair. "If you recall, I told you there were numerous opportunists who made the Run, only to claim property in hopes of selling it for profit. These two quarter sections of land were staked by just such men. They were looking for buyers, and I purchased their property. With Reuben's help, we contracted carpenters and assisted them in erecting the house and corrals. The house was built to my specifications and I ordered enough furniture to accommodate you until

364

you could purchase other pieces to your liking," Cale elaborated while Mikyla sought to digest his hasty explanation.

"But why? And how could you afford to buy the land and construct the home?" she chirped bemusedly. "Greta told me you weren't demanding exorbitant prices for your livestock. Where did you get the money for this ranch, as well as the cash to set up my father in business?" Wide blue eyes blinked up into his wry smile. "I didn't realize the territory had even established enough banks for you to rob! How could you afford to hire Belinda to care for my father and why . . ." The questions that had previously hounded her, plus a score of new ones, exploded from her lips in a stammering rush.

Cale put his index finger to her mouth to shush her. He squatted down on his haunches in front of her. A chuckle bubbled in his chest when Mikyla stared at him like a wide-eyed owl. "The moment I discovered Joseph Richards had his sights set on your property I knew you were destined to lose," he explained. "I set about to locate another site and ensure it was ready for you when you finally realized you couldn't keep your claim." His smile held a hint of remorse. "I can't give you back your view of the river, but this property boasts a spring-fed creek that will provide a lasting water source. I have left you enough money to have a well dug to supply the house. And with what you made off your property, you can purchase brood mares to start your herd."

His hands folded around her trembling fingers. Staring into her rounded eyes, he brought her fingertips to his lips. "Its all yours, Ky. The dream you thought you lost, your future, is all here for you to enjoy. I know I led you to believe I had nothing, but my family owns one of the largest ranches in Texas. We also lease the pastures near Blue Lake. Reuben works for me, overseeing the herd of livestock that grazes the reserve acreages of Cheyenne-Arapaho country. We also leased the very ground on which this ranch stands from the Creek tribe until it was offered in the Land Run." His finger curled beneath her sagging jaw before it dropped off its hinges. "I can well afford the land and the ranch. I want you to have it. Heaven knows you deserve it after all you have been through in attempting to carve a home in Oklahoma country."

Mikyla's heart was bounding around in her chest like a crazed jackrabbit and her eyes weren't functioning properly. She just sat there, blinking owlishly, opening and closing her mouth at irregular intervals. No words would form on her tongue, not when her jumbled thoughts were ricocheting off the corners of her brain.

"Don't you like it?" Cale questioned, wishing she would say something. Rarely had he seen this spitfire speechless.

After a long moment, Mikyla rewound her unraveled composure. "I like it just fine," she managed to say in a steady voice. "But I don't want it."

To Cale's astonishment, Mikyla replaced the envelope in his hand and headed out the front door. Dammit, now what was wrong, he asked himself in exasperation. He had given her the opportunity she wanted. He had offered her another dream to replace the one she had lost. For months now, Miki had lived and breathed this fantasy of a sprawling ranch and prize horses. Now he had handed opportunity to her on a silver platter, no strings attached, and she had turned it down flat! Confound it, if he lived a century he would never figure out this stubborn, willful, complicated female!

"What the hell do you mean you don't want it?" Cale growled as he stalked after Mikyla.

She presented her back, permitting him to breathe down her neck. "I think I made myself perfectly clear. I said I don't want your ranch and that is precisely what I meant."

Cale clamped his fingers into her arm and wheeled her around to face his unpleasant scowl. His stubbled face and ruffled raven hair gave him a foreboding appearance, but Mikyla didn't cower.

"I met myself coming and going, making arrangements, hiring workers, selecting a location that would give you the grandest view of the countryside. I invested my money to make you happy. Dammit, woman, the *least* you could do is say thank you!" he bellowed into her face.

Mikyla felt reasonably certain she had seen Cale's entire set of teeth when he thrust his face into hers and yelled down at her. "Consider yourself thanked," she insisted, elevating a stubborn chin. "I do appreciate the time and effort and the investment. But I cannot accept this generous gift."

"Why the hell not?" Cale snorted. He wanted to yank her up off the ground and shake her for rejecting his offer. But with one arm in a splint it would have been difficult, even when she was light as a feather.

Tears clouded her eyes and Mikyla sighed tremulously. "I really don't expect you to understand."

"I really don't expect me to, either, especially if you don't explain it to me!" he burst out angrily.

"It's only a dream, Cale," she began hesitantly, afraid he was going to explode before her very eyes. "Just like the dream I lost to the townsite company." Her dewy lashes swept down to caress her cheeks as she carefully chose her words. "I once thought the land and opportunity was all I needed to make me happy. But . . ." Damn, this was difficult, Mikyla thought to herself. Never before had she dared to bare her deepest feelings. Danger she could confront unafraid. Enemies she could meet head-on. But when it came to affairs of the heart, Mikyla realized she was the world's biggest coward. It took incredible nerve to force the words to tongue. "But each time you left me with my dream it became an empty fantasy."

Mikyla wrung her hands nervously. If Cale dared to laugh at her she would die of a broken heart. But she couldn't go on like this. The emotions had been piling up inside her until she feared she would pop. "If I could trade this ranch for your love, I would do it in a minute. But as much as I love you I won't tie myself to a man who doesn't need me the same way I need him."

Her long lashes fluttered up to peer into those entrancing silver eyes. "I can't be your slave when I yearn to be your equal. I can't be your lover if I cannot be your confidante and friend." There, she had said it. Now all she had to do was summon enough courage to hold herself erect while Cale let her down gently, the same way he had rejected Emily Terrel.

Cale stared at her lovely face, eyeing her with a smile that was both incredulous and a mite ornery. "I don't know why you put up such a fuss these past few months. I already told you I loved you. I wondered if you would ever get around to loving me back."

He was taking this all too well to suit Mikyla. Of all the things she expected him to say, that wasn't even on the list. And he had said it so nonchalantly that it annoyed Mikyla to no end. "You *said* you loved me, but you didn't mean it," she countered tartly. "You wanted something from me each time you said it. You thought I would wilt like a witless fool if a man declared he loved me!" Her voice rose until she was all but yelling into his face, which was now sporting a purely mischievous smile.

"What would you have had me do?" he chuckled in question. "Vow my undying love in the heat of passion? Knowing how mistrusting you are of me, you would have sworn I said the same thing to every other woman I've known." His silver eyes flooded over her rigid stance. "Where you are concerned, my lovely witch, it has always been *damned* if I do and *damned* if I don't."

Mikyla was so irritated she wanted to strangle this raven-haired devil. She had encroached upon this most serious subject and Cale was grinning and snickering as if she had just related an amusing anecdote. "I don't find this the least bit funny," she spewed indignantly. "Just once in your life, I wish you would show a smidgen of sensitivity!"

"You want sensitivity? You've got it, honey," he yelled back at her in the same booming tone.

Cale hoisted Mikyla over his shoulder and marched toward the house, thoroughly enjoying himself for the first time in weeks. If Mikyla didn't fear that she would inflict more pain on his scrapes and bruises she would have pounded her fists in his back. But it didn't prevent her from lashing him with her tongue.

"Put me down, you big ape. It's obvious you don't have the foggiest notion what sensitivity is." When Cale continued on his way without breaking stride, Mikyla stared at the house from her upside-down view. "Where are you taking me? I just told you I want nothing to do with this house."

Cale climbed the staircase and unceremoniously tossed her on the satin bedspread—the blue one he had purchased to match those hypnotic eyes. While Mikyla was sprawled on the bed, Cale sat down on her as if he were straddling a horse. And that made her all the madder.

"I told you I loved you and I meant it both times," Cale insisted. "But you didn't believe me because you didn't *want* to believe me. You were caught up in delusions of Thoroughbreds and ranches. I could have given you anything you wanted then, and I can now. Damnation, Ky, it's *you* who doesn't understand." His voice became softer when she ceased her struggling and hung on his every word. "I wanted you to want me for what I am, not for what I could give you. I wanted what we shared to be just as special for you as it was for me. I wanted those weeks we spent together to form the foundations of our own private dream, one that didn't include ranches and horses, but rather a dream that centered entirely around *us.*"

The back of his hand brushed across her flushed cheek, adoring the feel of her satiny skin. "We made it through the rough times, Ky. It's always been more than physical attraction, more than the challenge of matching wits and will. If we could survive living like roaming gypsies, doesn't it stand to reason that we can also make it through the good times?" His fingers slipped beneath her chin, meeting her searching gaze. "This ranch can be the beginning of the best of times . . . if you'll stay here with me in *our* home. If you're here, I won't feel the need to wander in search of an elusive dream. I've found it in you . . ."

Again Mikyla fell in love with the same man. She stared up at the towering mass of brawn and muscle and wooden splints and she burst into tears. But this time, they were tears of joy and relief. This time she truly had come home to strong, capable arms that would love and protect her. This time Cale wasn't leaving her holding the jagged pieces of her dream. He had formed the dimensions of a fantasy that she prayed would last her a lifetime.

"I do love you, Ky . . . I love you in ways I've never loved anyone or anything else in my life. I've said I love you a thousand times, perhaps not in so many words," Cale added softly. "But I cared about you to the point that I allowed you to believe the worst about me, just as long as I could be there to protect you." Cale eased down beside her to redirect the stream of tears, sending them trickling from the corner of her eyes instead of flooding over her cheeks. "I want you to marry me and give me children—the products of our love for each other. I want to transform this sparsely furnished house into a home that blossoms with love. I want it all. But first and foremost, I want you to love me in all the wondrous ways I cherish you, in all the ways I need you to make my life complete."

Mikyla traced a slim finger over the chiseled lines of his face and broke into an impish smile. "How many?"

Cale's features puckered in a muddled frown. "How many what?" Had he suddenly dozed off and missed part of the conversation?

"How many children do you want?" she whispered as she arched to mold her pliant flesh to the hard-muscled contours of his body, battered and bruised though they were.

"A half dozen should suffice, but I'm content to begin with one . . . if we haven't already . . ." His lips hovered over hers, holding intimate promises of what was to come.

"Do you know how very much I love you?" Mikyla murmured as her fingers trailed across the buttons of his chambray shirt, baring the bronzed skin beneath the fabric. "Better yet, let me *count* the ways . . ."

Cale lost count after the first dozen caresses that turned his mind to mush. He considered pinching himself to ensure this wasn't another whimsical dream. But Mikyla soon convinced him that what he was feeling was too vivid for even the most lifelike fantasy. She held nothing back when she touched him. The emotions were there. They whispered on her lips. They were embroidered in her caresses. And Cale matched her ardor, kiss for kiss, touch for touch, returning her precious gift of love.

It was a wild coming together, like a volcanic eruption of what had been carefully guarded emotion. The words they had so cautiously avoided resounded in their private world of ecstasy. What they shared was a rare instant in which past, present, and future blended into eternity. They were exploring the ultimate heights and depths of passion, voicing their love with words as well as the sweet physical expression of desire mingled with heartfelt affection. They were a living, breathing essence—like a bright, shining star that fed upon itself, growing more radiant with each glorious moment.

And when the loving was over, Cale knew it was only the beginning. Mikyla had become the flame within him, the light that lit up the night and lent purpose to his life.

"I want you to marry me as soon as possible," Cale murmured hoarsely.

"Is tonight too late?" Mikyla chortled as she nuzzled against his sturdy shoulder—the one without the splint.

A rackish grin dangled on the corner of his mouth as his eyelid dropped into a suggestive wink. "Not if I can find something to occupy my time until dark," he stipulated.

Her blue eyes flared with mischief. "We could rearrange the furniture . . . what there is of it . . ." she proposed, even as her hands began to weave across his steel-hard muscles, converting them to jelly.

"Nope," he drawled, looking displeased with the idea and obviously aroused by the wayward flight of her hands.

"We could rummage through my supplies and prepare lunch."

"Not hungry," Cale declared, his voice faltering when her caresses grew bolder.

"You are a difficult man to please, Cale Brolin," she teased provocatively.

"Yep," he agreed as he shifted to bring Mikyla's curvaceous body upon his. "I'm also a very demanding one. But what I want, you won't have to get up to fetch . . ."

Silver-gold strands fell about his face like a shimmering cape that blotted out all except her radiant smile. "What a coincidence," she giggled giddishly. "It just so happens that I don't have to climb out of bed to retrieve what I wish to give you . . ."

When Mikyla wove a tapestry of pleasure around him, a soft moan erupted from his lips. "I love you, Ky," he rasped before giving himself up to her honeyed kiss.

"And I love you more than any silly ole dream," she whispered back to him. "I have your love and that is more than enough."

As the sun beamed down on the frame house that overlooked the tree-rimmed creek, Mikyla and Cale loved away the hours. Sundance, who had been long forgotten, sought to find shade from the summer heat. If he could have unsaddled himself, he would have.

And by the time his master and mistress finally got around to venturing outside, Sundance was put out with the both of them. He had always been Mikyla's first concern. She never left him to chomp on his bit unless they were traveling. Now he had been abandoned and neglected as if he were just another horse!

The stallion did, however, forgive Mikyla later that evening when she treated him to a generous portion of oats and allowed him to graze to his heart's content.

Part IV

Love's of itself too sweet: the best of all
Is when Love's honey has a dash of gall.
                        . . . Anonymous

Chapter 26

The sound of cheering in the streets interrupted Morgan's pensive musings. Curious about the source of the excitement, he ambled out of the saloon to see the handful of guests who trailed after the bride and groom.

A wicked smile pursed Morgan's lips when he recognized the couple who had bounded into a buggy to speed off into the darkness. So Cale Brolin truly did have a strong attachment for that troublesome minx, Morgan thought with a derisive snort. All along, Cale had been trying to protect her, knowing his archrival would use the affection for Mikyla to settle the score.

No doubt Cale expected Morgan to be camped out on the new townsite, unaware that the marriage had taken place. Cale probably anticipated that Morgan would drift off to parts unknown now that he had made a profit on his most recent business venture. And Morgan had intended to do just that . . . until he discovered Cale's marriage to that blond-haired hellion.

A diabolical grin curled the corners of Morgan's lips upward. He had waited an eternity to avenge Jessica's death. Now that he had located Cale's most vulnerable spot, he would prey upon it. He would let Cale think he had abandoned Oklahoma country, enshrouding him in a false sense of security. And one day, when conditions were right, Cale would understand the hatred and agony Morgan had endured these last three years.

Grappling with vengeful thoughts, Morgan strode across the street to spread the word that he was leaving the area. But Morgan had no intention of abandoning Oklahoma until he had satisfied his personal vendetta. There were plans to make and a specific location to be prepared. Morgan could visualize the scene in his mind's eye. The thought provoked him to chuckle fiendishly.

What Cale would experience was going to be the maddening combination of haunting memories and a new, tormenting nightmare that would hound him for the rest of his days. And when Cale came looking for him, Morgan would dispose of that meddlesome bastard once and for all. At last he had formulated the perfect retribution to punish Cale Brolin for what he had done to ruin Morgan's life. Not only would he expose Cale to a torture worse than death, but it would also be Morgan's hand that felled the mighty giant.

Morgan couldn't believe his luck. Cale thought that feisty witch was the answer to his dreams. But Morgan would see to it that Mikyla became the human sacrifice for the woman *he* had lost. How ironic, Morgan snickered maliciously. He could re-create the incident as it had happened three years earlier. Satanic anticipation caused Morgan to burst into laughter as he trotted his horse south. Ah, this was ripe! In fact, it was the best scheme he had ever concocted. Cale was going to despise him as thoroughly and completely as Morgan despised the man who had interfered in his life all too often. But this would be the last time Morgan found himself in Cale Brolin's shadow. Morgan would be rid of Cale once and for all!

Cale's breath caught in his throat when Mikyla appeared in the doorway of the bedroom. His eyes hungrily devoured the sheer pink negligee. The lanternlight sprayed through the thin fabric, molding golden beams to her silky skin, accenting her luscious curves and swells. Lord, she was the most gorgeous creature he had ever seen! The mere sight of her set his heart to pounding as if it meant to beat him to death long before he satisfied the craving Mikyla inspired in him.

Mikyla's exquisite features blossomed into a smile when Cale stared at her with masculine appreciation. "I thought I would slip into something more comfortable..." she murmured lamely, wondering why she felt so awkward with her new husband. It wasn't as if this was to be the first time they had made love. But it was different somehow, even more special than all their splendorous nights together. Mikyla's dream had come true and she wanted everything to be right between them, now and forevermore.

A rakish smile tripped across Cale's lips as his possessive gaze sketched her perfect figure once again, not missing even the smallest detail. "The gown is enchanting," he complimented, his voice husky with unfulfilled desire. His dark head indicated the wooden rocker that sat in the distant corner. "But I think I would like the garment better if it were draped over the chair and you were here..." He patted the empty space beside him. "I spent the evening vowing to our friends that I would love and cherish my wife until the end of time." Although his naughty smile said it all, Cale felt inclined to elaborate. "I can't do any loving and cherishing with you all the way over there..."

"Beast," Mikyla teased him playfully. "I dressed specifically for you. I have only just wormed into this new gown and now you are demanding that I remove it."

Cale rolled off the bed like a lion rousing to his feet. With the silence of a stalking cat he closed the distance between them. As his shadow fell over her, his glistening silver eyes focused on her cupid's-bow lips. Cale ached to claim them, to lose himself in the sweet taste of her kiss—one that would be altogether different from the hasty peck she had planted on his lips during the wedding ceremony. What Cale had in mind was one of those sizzling kisses that could melt bone and muscle into a pool of liquid passion.

"Take it off, Ky," Cale rasped. "Or better yet, let me do it for you..."

His right hand glided between her breasts to tug at the elastic bodice. In less than a heartbeat the dainty pink gown fluttered to the floor. His arm circled the small indentation

377

of her waist, crushing her into his hard length. As his mouth slanted across hers, Mikyla felt the world narrow into a kaleidoscope of warm, giddy sensations. Eagerly, she gave herself up to the stormfire of emotions Cale had always instilled in her. Oh, how she adored this rough-edged cowboy who had become all things to her. Cale could make her feel every inch a woman. He had always been able to arouse her slumbering passions, to make her feel wildly feminine.

As her arms slid over his bare shoulders to toy with the crisp raven hair that capped his head, Mikyla felt the world tilting sideways. Her heart swelled with so much pleasure and contentment she feared it would burst before she could appease this gigantic craving Cale's kisses and caresses evoked.

"Lord, what you do to me should be labeled as a criminal offense," Cale growled when he finally came up for air.

"Arson?" Mikyla giggled as she tilted her head back to peer into his craggy features.

Cale broke into a roguish grin. "Arson," he concurred. "I'm burning up on the inside. If you don't put out the fire . . . and . . . quickly . . . I fear the excessive heat will cremate this confounded splint."

Mikyla's brow wore an expression of mock concern. Gently she led him to bed and urged him to stretch out on the sheets. "We certainly wouldn't want that to happen," she purred seductively. "Summoning a doctor on our wedding night might prove embarrassing."

When Mikyla set her hands upon him, Cale swore he dissolved into liquid fire. Her fingertips weaved a web of pleasure on his flesh, leaving him limp and pliant beneath her caresses. She touched him boldly and he responded. She plied him with tantalizing kisses and he lost touch with reality. And when her silky body slid over his, Cale swore he would burn alive before she eased the blazing need of longing.

"Ky, love me," Cale whispered before her soft lips melted like rose petals on his mouth.

"I can't remember when I didn't," Mikyla murmured with

378

genuine emotion. "And I can't imagine living a day without loving you. . . ."

Cale hooked his good arm around her hips, shifting so that she was beneath him. His eyes shimmered with longing . . . until the clatter on the front lawn shattered the moment like a rock colliding with a window pane.

"What the hell is that?" he groaned in frustration.

"A *charivari,* I suspect," Mikyla grumbled. Her voice crackled with longing and an undertone of disappointment.

Cursing the untimely interruption, Cale slid to the floor to retrieve his breeches and to toss Mikyla her robe. While they dressed, out of view of the window, a noisy, mock serenade wafted its way toward them. Friends and relatives had gathered beneath the window to beat their pots and pans, blow their horns, and make nuisances of themselves during the first hours of their honeymoon.

While he sat on the floor, Cale propped himself against the bed. His arms rested on his bent knees. He impatiently drummed his fingers and glared flaming arrows at the window. "How long are we to enjoy this orchestral clatter delivered by our so-called friends?" he questioned grouchily.

It was obvious that Cale was unfamiliar with the custom of the *charivari,* Mikyla thought to herself. She had witnessed two such goings-on in Kansas and had even joined in the celebration held for a newly married couple while they were in the Boomer camp. Mikyla was willing to bet Greta was responsible for this playful prank. The sentimental Swedish woman was a stickler for custom and tradition. No doubt, Greta would not consider the wedding proper without the *charivari.*

"They aren't going to go away and leave us in peace until we invite them in for refreshments," she informed Cale with an apologetic smile.

"What?" Cale croaked, staring frog-eyed at his lovely new wife, whom he had visions of holding in his arms all through the night. "Damn, this isn't at all what I had in mind."

Mikyla smoothed the frown from his rugged features. "A very wise man once told me that it is infinitely easier to accept one's fate than to fight it," she reminded with a wry smile "If you antagonize our guests they will only become more insistent."

"A party in the middle of a man's wedding night!" Cale grumbled sourly. "That's the most ridiculous tradition I ever heard. If ever there was a time when a man's friends should leave him alone *this* is the night!"

As Cale crouched to scamper toward the dresser to randomly grab a shirt and his boots, Mikyla crawled to the wardrobe to select a presentable gown. The amused chuckle from behind her caused Mikyla to swivel her head around. Cale was scrunched in a corner, wrestling to shrug on his shirt, watching her slink beneath the window to reach the closet.

"Our so-called friends have us creeping around like rodents," he snickered, his eyes lingering on the bare flesh exposed by Mikyla's gaping robe.

"Go open the confounded door and invite our guests into the parlor, Mr. Rat," Mikyla demanded as she dragged her dress over her head and smoothed it into place.

When Cale was fully clothed, he unfolded himself from the corner and strode toward the door. "You go fetch the refreshments, Mrs. Rat. This is going to be the shortest *charivari* in history. As soon as this mob has been fed, we are going to begin exactly where we left off!"

Mikyla drew herself up to full stature and sailed toward Cale. After planting a hasty kiss to his cheek, she breezed into the hall. "Perhaps we should start all over again," she threw over her shoulder. "I'm not sure I can remember *exactly* where we left off . . ."

Her impish smile and her titillating insinuation that he would be fully compensated for this inconvenience sweetened Cale's disposition considerably. He even managed a greeting grin when he opened the door to be swamped by the mob of guests who were led by Greta Ericcson and Belinda Grove.

As Emet Lassiter strode into the room, he cast Cale a meaningful glance. "This wasn't my idea," he hastily informed the groom whose shirt was improperly buttoned, giving evidence that the guests had indeed interrupted the newlyweds at an inopportune moment. "And if you dare pull such a stunt on my wedding night, I'll . . ."

Cale held up his hand to forestall Emet before he issued his threat. "You won't suffer this inconvenience. You have my word," he pledged sincerely.

Emet's shoulders slumped in relief and then he smiled a grateful smile. "Thanks, Cale. Thanks for everything . . ."

Cale nodded mutely as Belinda grasped Emet's arm, insisting that he accompany her on a tour of the house. Pasting on a smile, Cale accepted the congratulations of many of the neighbors he had met at Greta's socials. But after a half hour of pretending to be charming and gracious, Cale had enjoyed as much of the *charivari* as he could tolerate. His eyes met Mikyla's from across the sea of humanity that separated them. It was agonizing to see her idly chatting with a cluster of clucking hens while he was amidst a herd of roosters. Cale wanted Ky all to himself and he was tired of being a good sport.

Determined to rid his home of pests, Cale yanked open the front door and demanded that his guests evacuate the premises before each one was personally tossed out on his or her posterior part.

After several shocked gasps, mostly from those of the feminine persuasion, the pesky guests flooded out the door as hastily as they had swarmed in. Biting back an impish grin, Mikyla strode up beside Cale, who was guarding the portal like a resident dragon.

"That was terribly rude," Mikyla admonished, fighting to maintain a disapproving frown.

"This is our wedding night, for heaven's sake!" Cale snorted in self-defense. "I think *charivaris* should be outlawed as cruel and inhumane treatment . . ." His voice trailed off when the sound of approaching riders mingled with the hubbub of departing guests who were scrambling onto their horses and into their wagons. "Good Gawd, what now?"

An army patrol appeared as silhouettes in the moonlight and Cale muttered a few more choice words about the lack of privacy in Oklahoma country. When Brock Terrel swung from the saddle, Cale walked off the stoop to confront him. A muddled frown knitted Brock's brow as he surveyed the mob of guests.

"What is going on here?" he questioned curiously.

Cale managed the semblance of a smile. "Mikyla Lassiter and I were married this evening," he explained. "These . . . dear people . . ." he said for lack of a better description. ". . . were helping us celebrate the eve of our honeymoon with an annoying prank I have been told is customary."

Brock chuckled good-naturedly. "Well, it certainly must have caused quite a stir. One of the troopers in the area heard the whooping and hollering and presumed the Indians had gone on the warpath. He thundered back to our unit, spreading the alarm to all the homesteaders along the way. We thought we had a battle on our hands."

Cale's eyes soared heavenward. "All I wanted was a quiet evening alone with my wife," he grumbled.

"Then you shall have it, my friend," Brock guaranteed. "Compliments of the cavalry. We will escort your neighbors home and ensure that none of them return to harass you."

Brock wheeled around to march away, but suddenly he did an about-face and fished into his pocket. "I almost forgot," he mumbled as he strode back to Cale. "Morgan Hagerty asked me to deliver this message to you at my earliest convenience."

The pleasant expression on Cale's face disintegrated as he accepted the note. He waited until Brock had mounted his steed and ushered the guests on their way before he unfolded the letter. Employing the shaft of light that splintered from the parlor window, Cale squinted to read the message.

Despite your attempt to foil my plans, the townsite company turned a tidy profit.

"I'll bet it did," Cale muttered aloud. No doubt Morgan had found a way to dispose of his associates without being named as the murderer and now he was hoarding the profit for himself.

382

I have decided to seek out the sophistication of the city, San Francisco perhaps. You will understand if I say I hope we won't chance to meet again.

Morgan

Cale sagged in relief. He had assumed Morgan would become bored with the pioneer towns and venture on to bigger card games and the endless rabble of painted ladies, plying them with his eloquent flattery. The message had confirmed Cale's hope that Morgan would drift off before he got wind of the marriage . . .

"For a man who was impatient to rid his home of guests, you certainly don't appear the anxious groom," Mikyla taunted playfully.

Cale pivoted on his heels to see Mikyla garbed in her seductive negligee, her appetizing figure framed by the glow of lights in the foyer. Morgan's note fell from his fingertips as Cale moved swiftly toward the door.

"Now who seems overanxious?" Cale mocked, elevating a dark brow.

Her blue eyes sketched the muscular form that was suddenly looming over her. A mischievous grin touched her lips when she noticed Cale's shirt had been haphazardly buttoned. As her lashes fluttered upward, her wandering thoughts dispersed. Cale was staring down at her the way a starving man ogles a feast. He wanted her. It was in his eyes, in the way he clutched her to him. And she wanted him just as intensely.

"No more interruptions," Cale promised, and he meant it. He was prepared to shoot the next person who dared to disturb them. "Even if the sky comes tumbling down, ignore it."

Mikyla pushed up on tiptoe to press her lips to the full, sensuous curve of his mouth. "I have the feeling I will be far too distracted to notice if the sky is falling . . ."

With a flare of elegance Cale dropped into a sweeping bow and then offered Mikyla his arm. "Come along, Mrs. Brolin. I should like to see just how distracting *you* can be when you put your mind to it."

"A challenge, Mr. Brolin?" she inquired as she curled her hand around his proffered elbow. "Ah, I do love a dare. It allows one to prove what one is made of."

A roguish grin captured Cale's craggy features as he looked Mikyla from head to toe and all parts in between. "All night, madam?" he teased, loving the playful camaraderie they had shared since they had come to terms with their emotions.

Mikyla's answering smile was as rakish as his. "I think you will find me to be not only thorough but durable," she assured him confidently. "And time will determine *who* must wake *whom* to name the winner of this challenge, one which, I might add, I do not find the least bit distasteful or taxing. Need I remind you I am made of sturdy stuff, Mr. Brolin?"

"No, you need not," Cale countered as he strutted up the stairs with Mikyla on his arm. "I am well aware of your admirable qualities. Indeed, they are the reasons I married you."

Mikyla dropped her hand from his forearm before they crossed the threshold. Her chin tilted proudly. "You married me because I refuse to take no for an answer, because I would give out before I allowed myself to give up?" Her tone held the slightest hint of indignation.

The naughty smile on Cale's bronzed face alerted Mikyla to the fact that he had twisted her words to suit his own meaning. But she had no problem with that. His expression was a compliment of sorts and Mikyla accepted it as such. When it came to loving him she could indeed give out long before she gave up on him.

"You realize, of course, you are going to lose this bet," she assured him saucily.

Cale's arms encircled her, splint and all. "Even if I should lose, I ultimately win," he murmured provocatively. "I have found a woman who matches my passions and my zest for living. No man can want for more . . ."

His lips were poised above hers, his warm breath caressing her cheek. Mikyla felt very loved and wanted for the first time in years. And yet there was still a nagging concern that what they shared couldn't last forever, that it was almost too good to be true, just like the dream site she had lost. Yes, Cale confessed he loved her now. But what guarantee did she have that he wouldn't lose interest in six months or six years? Cale had a reputation with women and they flocked to him like flies buzzing around sugar.

The unsettling thought sent Mikyla out of his arms and into the proud, defiant stance Cale had come to know all too well. For a long moment he stared at her, wondering at her sudden change of mood. What the devil had he said to put her in a snit?

"Cale, are you still going to love me when I grow heavy with child, when my face is as wrinkled as a basset hound's?" she wanted to know that very minute.

A peal of incredulous laughter exploded from his lips. "What brought that on?" he questioned her question.

Mikyla stamped her foot. "Answer me, damn you. Are you going to love me while I'm young and thin and then go prancing off to seize and conquer another female who catches your eye?"

Cale couldn't believe they were having this conversation on their wedding night. But Mikyla had that determined look about her and she wasn't going to be content until she had received a satisfactory answer. "I loved you when you hated me, didn't I?"

"Because you saw me as a challenge," she argued. "Now there is no challenge, no conquest."

"Ah, but there is, you see," Cale pointed out as he swaggered toward her. His knuckles slid beneath her chin, lifting her gaze to his tender smile. "The challenge comes in *keeping* what I have already won, in proving myself worthy of the one woman I couldn't leave behind, even when I pointed myself toward Texas, vowing not to return until I recovered from my exasperating bout with love. The fact that I couldn't let go of the memories is proof of the potent hold you have over me, sweet witch. . . ." His lips grazed hers in an adoring kiss. "You once accused me of not knowing what love is. It is forever, Ky. I have thought I was in love once or twice in my life. Now I'm old enough to know what I want and what it takes to keep love alive."

A wry smile pursed his lips as he lifted his raven head. "It seems to me that *you* are the one who should be cross-examined. When we met, you were just a young thing who had virtually no experience with men. How do I know you won't search elsewhere for affection when *I'm* old and gray?"

Mikyla looped her arms around his shoulders and tossed him a sassy smile. "Because I am in love for the first time in my life," she confessed. "I have heard it said that one never truly forgets their first love." Her tapered finger traced the craggy lines of his face, smoothing away his skeptical frown. "And secondly, I perceive you as one of those rare, special men who could successfully seduce a woman, even when you are pushing eighty. I'm afraid I'm the jealous type. I have no intention of allowing another female to enjoy the pleasures we will spend a lifetime perfecting."

Suddenly Mikyla gave Cale a backward shove, sending him sprawling on the bed. "Now if you are quite through arguing with me, I would like to get on with this challenge."

"Arguing with *you*" Cale parroted. "You started it! I was being my usual, charming self and you . . ."

When Mikyla drew the flimsy gown over her head and tossed it toward the chair, Cale's brain collapsed. He could barely remember his name, much less what he had intended to say. His senses were filled with the alluring sight of the one woman who was strong enough to capture his heart and gentle enough to earn his love. It baffled him that Mikyla could have questioned his devotion, that she could think he would be lured form her silky arms by a lesser female.

This shapely blonde was in a class all of her own and she was way ahead of her time. Her reckless daring had always fascinated him, the passionate woman who had lurked beneath an armor of stubborn pride had always intrigued him. Mikyla was worrying for naught. Once he had the very best he wouldn't be satisfied with anything less.

"Come here, vixen," Cale rasped. "I need you. I'll always need you to make my life complete. And if I could command the world to stop spinning this night would be forty-eight hours long."

A confident smile rippled across Mikyla's lips as she eased down on the bed to press eagerly against him. "It will be," she assured him. "I only hope you have regained your stamina, Mr. Brolin. You are going to need it if you hope to win this wager."

But when she offered him a kiss laced with desire, energy was created from their mere physical contact. This wild, sweet angel was all the strength Cale needed to sustain him during his intimate flight among the stars. Even though he was hampered by his splint, he invented ways to pleasure Mikyla, ensuring that she could want no more than he could offer. Each caress was embroidered with gentleness. Each kiss was the soft, lingering whisper of love unfolding like a tender blossom opening to bask in the morning sun.

And even when passion had run its course, desire still lingered, appeased but never truly satiated. The feel of Mikyla lying in his arms aroused him each time he awoke. The need for her continued to gnaw at him, leaving him to wonder if he would ever fully satisfy this maddening desire for her. She had created a love that bubbled like an eternal spring. It fed upon itself until it filled to overflowing.

And this was one wager Cale didn't lose. He came away with his male pride and prowess intact. But as Cale had said the previous night—there was no such thing as a loser when the wager was mutual love. Mikyla wasn't the least bit disappointed that Cale had awakened her into a world of wondrous sensations just before the first light of dawn sprinkled across the heavens. Indeed, if she were to be roused each day by such tantalizing techniques she would have no complaint at all!

Chapter 27

The blazing August sun beat down, scorching the tender grasses. Hot winds tore across the prairie like the heat that radiates from a roaring fire. Mikyla mopped the perspiration from her brow and stared into the blistering south breeze. The past three weeks had been the longest twenty-one days of her life and the unbearable heat hadn't improved her disposition. Cale had ridden to Texas to inform his family of their marriage and to retrieve the brood mares he intended to give Mikyla as a wedding gift. He had decided it best to wait until cooler temperatures prevailed before taking his bride to Texas with him.

Mikyla had agreed that it was sensible to wait until early October for a visit and to trek Cale's herd of cattle north to their new pastures. But it had been agony to allow Cale to leave her so soon after their wedding. They had spent two glorious weeks together, decorating their new home, building fences during the day. And the nights . . .

A hot blush, one that had nothing to do with the suffocating heat, stained Mikyla's cheeks. Their nights of passion had been enough to melt the Indian moon and leave it dripping in the sky. And if Cale didn't hurry home Mikyla swore she would go mad with wanting!

Cale had promised to return home before Emet and Belinda's wedding. But if he dallied even a minute he would miss the ceremony. The wedding was to be held this very night and Mikyla had no wish to attend her father's marriage ceremony without Cale. Reuben Stubbs had accepted Cale's offer to reside at the ranch and to keep a watchful eye on Mikyla. Although Mikyla enjoyed the crusty character's company, she preferred attending the wedding on *Cale's* arm.

Miki tried not to think of all the disasters that might have detained Cale along the trail. But it was difficult not to fret when outlaws ran rampant in parts of Indian Territory. The horses Cale was bringing along with him would be an open invitation to the border ruffians who preyed upon innocent victims in Texas and then sneaked into Indian Territory to avoid the Rangers.

Attempting to ignore her worried thoughts, Mikyla focused on the patch of clouds that were billowing in the southwest. She knew her father would be disappointed if a brewing storm dampened his wedding, but the prairie could do with a thorough soaking. Although the spring had been unusually wet, the summer had become a scorching season of soaring temperatures and little rain. The settlers were struggling with their first crops and the pastures were brittle and dry, providing very little nourishment for the livestock. Even Sundance turned up his nose at grazing and impatiently waited for his ration of grain.

The distant rumble of thunder and the sweet, refreshing smell of rain brightened Mikyla's mood for all of a half-second. As much as Oklahoma needed rain, she knew Cale would never arrive on time if he were hampered by the storm. Cale refused to travel when lightning and thunder rippled across the sky. Even if Cale were as anxious to see her as she was to see him, he wouldn't risk his life or his herd. Nor did she want him to. It would be disappointing if he were late for the ceremony, but it was far better than not having him arrive at all, she reminded herself.

Heaving a weary sigh, Miki aimed herself toward the house to draw a welcome bath. The closing of the bunkhouse door drew her attention and Mikyla glanced back to see Reuben scurrying toward her.

"Aren't you ready yet, girl?" he questioned. His stubby finger indicated the boiling storm. "If we don't quicken our pace we might get caught in a cloudburst."

Mikyla knew Reuben was anxious to travel to Elreno. Now that Reuben was closer to civilization, he enjoyed his ventures into town. Although Reuben hadn't confided in her, she had the feeling there was a certain lady in Elreno who had caught his attention and that he intended to pay her a call before the wedding. Mikyla, on the other hand, was content to dally, hoping Cale would arrive in time to accompany her.

"Why don't you go on without me," Miki suggested as she grasped the water buckets to tote them into the house.

Reuben frowned. Cale wouldn't appreciate the fact that Miki was left to fend for herself. But Reuben had promised Doris Wells that he would take her to supper before the ceremony. "Cale ain't gonna like it if I ride off without you. One of the reasons he offered me this job was to keep a watchful eye on you while he was away."

When Reuben tugged the buckets from her hands and marched ahead of her, Mikyla smiled at his departing back. "I think both you and Cale have forgotten I have been taking care of myself for quite some time now. I doubt I will lose my way riding into Elreno."

Reuben swiveled his head around to peer at Miki's impish grin. She was such a dainty little thing that a man often forgot how capable Miki was. "Well, all right, if you're sure you don't mind my trotting off ahead of you," he relented with a defeated sigh. "But Cale ain't gonna like it, just the same."

"I'll handle Cale and you can concentrate on whoever it is that you can't wait to see in town," Miki teased with a sly wink.

Reuben actually blushed. "I . . . er . . . well . . . there is a . . ."

"Does she have a name?" Miki interrupted his stammering.

Reuben's face matched the shade of his wiry red hair that had been slicked back and arranged in the latest fashion. "Doris," he mumbled self-consciously.

"Then I suggest you and Doris enjoy yourselves and permit me to soak in a cool bath," Miki insisted, shooing

Reuben on his way.

Reuben resembled a wild creature that had just been released from captivity. He scampered out the door with his coattails flapping behind him. Mikyla giggled at his behavior. Reuben was a mite outspoken, but when it came to affairs of the heart he resembled a blushing schoolboy.

Another rumble of thunder resounded in the distance, spurring Mikyla into a swifter pace. From the look of the foreboding weather she would be traveling to Elreno alone. She certainly didn't expect her father to postpone his wedding, even when he had hoped Cale would arrive in time to stand as his best man. And if she didn't quicken *her* pace, she would be making her late-afternoon journey in a downpour.

After sinking into the cool water, Mikyla permitted herself a few moments of relaxation before she emerged from the tub. When she had toweled her hair dry she wormed into the pale yellow gown Belinda had created for the ceremony. Hurriedly she pinned her hair atop her head and secured the flowered headdress. The lace-and-satin hat added a sophisticated flair to the delicate satin ensemble. Mikyla thought she looked rather nice, even if she had to say so herself. And she did have to since Cale wasn't there to compliment her appearance. Confound it, where was that man? She had been anticipating his arrival for two days!

The sound of the front door opening and closing jostled Mikyla from her thoughts. Cale! He had arrived in the nick of time!

Her heart pounded in excitement. She could visualize his tanned face, the expression in those silver-studded eyes that could melt her into puddles. When she got her hands on that brawny mass of masculinity she was going to squeeze the stuffing out of him and then . . . Mikyla blushed at the direction her thoughts had taken. There wasn't time for "and then," not when they were due at Emet's wedding.

Sporting a smile as radiant as the summer sun, Mikyla sailed out of the bedroom. Lifting the front of her full skirt, she fairly ran down the hall. As she veered toward the steps, he very nearly stumbled over her own feet. There, leaning arrogantly against the balustrade was Morgan Hagerty. He looked rakishly handsome, but a satanic grin dangled from the corner of his mouth. His diabolical expression made the hair on the back of Miki's neck stand up. Her emotions swung like a pedulum. Mikyla was disappointed that it wasn't Cale who stood at the bottom of the steps. She was stunned to see Morgan and annoyed that he had barged into the house in such a rude manner.

What the devil was he doing back in Oklahoma? she wondered as she glared holes in Morgan's expensive waistcoat. Cale had informed her that they had seen the last of this snake who could shed his skin to reveal the true reptile who lurked beneath a veneer of sophistication. Obviously, Cale didn't know this serpent as well as he thought he did.

"I thought you were the epitome of proper manners," Mikyla sniffed, looking down her nose at Morgan. 'Apparently you have not been schooled in the more important social graces. It is polite to knock before barging in unannounced and *unwelcome.*"

Morgan raked her with a leer and Miki found herself wishing she had her pistol tucked in the folds of her gown. If she had known she was going to need it, she would have spared the time to retrieve her weapon before bursting out of the bedroom.

Her chin tilted to fling him an annoyed glare. "What do you want, Morgan? Don't tell me you have bought into another townsite company and have decided to locate on our ranch."

"I only wanted to congratulate you on your marriage," he informed her blandly.

"Now that I have been *properly* congratulated why don't you slither back into the river with the rest of the snakes," she suggested sarcastically.

"Tsk, tsk," Morgan clucked, undaunted by her attempt to oust him from the foyer. "Is that any way to speak to a member of the family?"

A wary frown knitted Mikyla's brow. "What are you

babbling about?"

"Cale didn't tell you?" His shoulder lifted in a carele
shrug. "No, I suppose he would prefer to forget he has
stepbrother, just as I would prefer to forget I spent half m
life standing in Cale's shadow, forced to live up to h
expectations."

The announcement very nearly knocked the props ou
from under her. Mikyla clutched the railing to preven
tumbling all the way down the staircase to land in a heap a
Morgan's feet. Morgan was Cale's stepbrother? Why hadn
he told her? Cale had mentioned his stepmother with fon
affection but he had said nothing about inheriting a broth
when his father remarried!

The stunned expression on Mikyla's face was all th
indication Morgan needed. The memories still haunte
Cale, Morgan predicted. If he had accepted what ha
happened, he would have told Mikyla the grisly story. Bu
obviously Cale preferred to carry the secret with him until h
was forced to admit to it.

The sound of thunder rolling overhead shook the window
panes and Miki jumped as if she had been stabbed in th
back. She didn't like the way Morgan was staring at her.
was unnerving. What he was thinking was anybody's gues
but he *looked* as if he were up to no good. A silent alarm ran
in her head and Mikyla gave way to impulse. As she pivote
to make her dash to the bedroom, she heard the deadly clic
of Morgan's Colt .45.

"Freeze, sweetheart," Morgan growled at her. "This tim
we have no eyewitnesses. You cannot know the temptation
face. Even if I have to shoot you in the back, I'm sure I ca
devise a believable alibi." His demonic laughter sent a snak
of apprehension coiling down her spine. "Indeed, mos
everyone thinks I left the territory . . ."

Mikyla glanced over her shoulder to see the pistol traine
on her, to note the malicious smile that claimed Morgan
features. "The same sort of alibi you concocted the nigl
Joseph Richards and his associate were murdered?" Sh
wrapped the spiteful words around her tongue and flun

them at him.

"I didn't say that," Morgan chuckled recklessly.

"You didn't have to," Mikyla countered more courageously than she actually felt. But if she were to die for whatever reason Morgan thought she should, she was going out in a blaze of glory and defiance.

Morgan was growing impatient with this sharp-tongued termagant. "Come down here," he barked brusquely.

Her chin tilted a notch higher. "I would prefer not to, thank you just the sa—"

The Colt cracked the silence, followed by a sharp peal of thunder. Shakily, Mikyla glanced at the shattered step just beneath her slippered feet.

A wicked grin displayed Morgan's gleaming teeth and Miki swore she could have counted them to determine if this maniac was blessed with a full set . . . if she had been inclined to do so. But at the moment she was more concerned about her future . . . or rather her lack of it.

"Make your choice," Morgan jeered. "You can work your way down the steps or I can work my way up with my pistol . . ."

Reluctantly, Mikyla descended the staircase. She glanced frantically about her, searching for an object to serve as her weapon of self-defense. Unfortunately, there was nothing at her disposal. She had scrubbed and cleaned the house to a polished shine in honor of Cale's homecoming—one she might not be around to enjoy if Morgan had his way—and it looked as though he were about to have it!

As she inched toward the bottom step, she suddenly came uncoiled to kick the pistol from Morgan's hand. But Morgan had dealt with this firebrand once too often not to be prepared. He jerked back before Mikyla's foot could connect with his arm. With one lithe move, Morgan hooked his arm around her neck and stuffed the pistol between her ribs.

Mikyla grimaced at her unsuccessful attempt and the feel of the Colt prying her ribs apart. "Why are you doing this?" she dared to ask. "You know Cale will hunt you down."

"That's what I'm counting on," Morgan snorted as he shepherded Mikyla toward the door, jabbing her with his pistol at regular intervals. "When Cale comes after me, I want him to be insanely furious. Naturally, I'll have to shoot him in self-defense."

"Why do you hate him so?" Mikyla burst out. "Wasn't it enough that you had Cale beat to a pulp?"

Morgan shoved Mikyla into the barn to saddle her stallion, which he fully intended to steal when Mikyla no longer had any need to ride . . . ever again. "Cale took the woman I loved away from me, as well as golden opportunity," he gritted out between clenched teeth.

His poisonous tone and the accompanying crack of thunder sent a shiver of dread down Miki's backbone. The hatred came pouring out and Morgan truly frightened her. He was hellbent on vengeance and she feared she was to become the weapon Morgan would use against Cale to satisfy this mysterious vendetta.

"If this lady loved you in return, I cannot imagine how you can hold Cale responsible," Mikyla taunted and then sorely wished she hadn't, for it only served to fuel Morgan's temper.

Morgan grabbed her by the hair of the head and swung her around to face him. "Jessica was coming to meet me. We were going to run away together, but Cale detested the fact that his precious little sister was in love with me," he hissed, lost in bitter memories. "Cale spent half his life trying to turn Jessica against me. But she loved me in spite of Cale's demands and threats. Cale told her I would only make her miserable, that I wasn't man enough to satisfy her." Morgan inhaled an angry breath and then plunged on. "Cale convinced my own mother to deny me my inheritance if I took Jessica with me. Since the time I was fifteen years old Cale has stood between me and everything I have ever wanted. His father constantly threw Cale in my face as if he were a shining example of what *I* should be, how *I* should behave. I was the outcast, the unwanted son, the troublesome brother."

Finally, Morgan got a grip on himself and released

Mikyla's hair before he yanked it out by the roots. Nudging her with the pistol, he silently demanded that she bridle the flighty stallion.

"Jessica was on her way to meet me so we could elope. But Cale overtook her during a storm." His voice crackled with venom and Mikyla felt sick inside. Intuition told her what Morgan intended to say long before he spat the words at her. "While Cale was leading Jessica home, a bolt of lightning struck the tree beside them. Jessica was killed and Cale was knocked unconscious." Morgan scowled as the horrible scene he had witnessed at a distance returned to torment him. "If Cale hadn't followed her, Jessica would have been safe within the shack where we had arranged to meet."

Mikyla shuddered uncontrollably when the bright flash of lightning illuminated the barn. She recalled the one time Cale had mentioned Jessica. His face had clouded with emotion before he could regain control. At the time, Mikyla had assumed Jessica was a lost love. But it seemed Cale was haunted by the tragic incident that had cost his sister her life. Now she understood why Cale had been lenient with Morgan after the brutal beating. Cale was plagued by self-guilt, held himself personally responsible for his sister's death. And Morgan probably held the disaster over Cale's head, never permitting him to forget what happened.

No wonder Cale had such respect for lightning. Each storm he endured triggered agonizing memories that he would have preferred to forget. But Morgan was determined to see vengeance served by sacrificing Mikyla, to repay Cale for something over which he had no control . . .

Before Mikyla could pursue the thought, Morgan grasped her arm, drawing her body into intimate contact with his. Mikyla strangled the gasp that crept to her throat. There was a demented look in Morgan's green eyes. The feel of his body pressed against hers was repulsive. Mikyla had referred to Morgan as a snake so often she could almost imagine herself held captive by a python.

Morgan broke into a wicked grin as his eyes raked Mikyla's comely figure. What he had originally planned for this blond witch and that bastard husband of hers would satisfy his craving for revenge. But now Morgan had stumbled upon another idea that would deal the crowning blow to his archrival.

"You once declared that I wasn't half the man Cale was," he chuckled fiendishly. "Before I dispose of you, I want to determine what there is about you that my stepbrother finds so fascinating. And you will have the opportunity to see which one of us is the better lover . . ."

Mikyla's heart leaped to her throat when Morgan's mouth took hers hostage in a possessive kiss. She knew he would probably turn his pistol on her if she fought him, but his touch was a torture worse than death. What Morgan had in mind for her was humiliating degradation, one he would later flaunt in Cale's face, she mused bitterly.

Refusing to submit, Mikyla braced her hands on Morgan's chest and shoved for all she was worth. Unfortunately, his fall was blocked by the wooden stall. In panic, Mikyla wheeled to find protection, but Morgan sprung at her before she had taken two steps in the opposite direction.

"You feisty little bitch," he growled as he forced her into the straw. "What you've always needed is a man who knows how to handle a spitfire like you!"

When Morgan grabbed her shoulder to fling her to her back, the gown gave way, baring her flesh. Instinctively, Mikyla covered herself and glowered mutinously at the man who had planted himself on her belly. "You can never be half the man Cale is," she spat into Morgan's flushed face. "I would prefer to die than have you touch me!"

A menacing snarl swallowed Morgan's handsome features. "Your fate is to endure both," he assured her harshly. "I can think of nothing more gratifying than pleasuring myself with Cale's whore!"

Mikyla fought like a wildcat when Morgan tugged at the hem of her gown and wedged his knee between her thighs. Before his lips slanted across hers, Mikyla screamed Cale's name at the top of her lungs, wishing he would miraculously appear to protect her from this brutal assault. But to her

398

dismay, all she heard was Sundance's snort and the stomp of hooves in the straw. Yet, the stallion's commotion, so close beside them, was enough to give Morgan a start. He raised his head to see Sundance, with ears laid back and nostrils flaring, backing toward the corner of the barn. Fearing he was about to be kicked senseless, Morgan rolled away to grope for the pistol he had discarded.

Mikyla vaulted to her feet the instant Morgan granted her freedom. During that critical second when Morgan was fumbling to retrieve his Colt, Mikyla scrambled under Sundance's belly. With a sharp bark to her fidgety steed, Mikyla grasped the pommel of the saddle and stuffed her foot in the stirrup. The steed trotted toward the barn door while Mikyla fought the hampering skirts to seat herself in the saddle.

Muttering a string of unprintable curses, Morgan leaped on to his horse to apprehend his runaway victim before she could reach the exit of the barn. When Morgan's outthrust arm circled through the air to knock her off balance, Miki sprawled on top of Sundance's back and hung on for dear life. Morgan found himself holding nothing but an armful of air, and he had overextended himself so completely that he very nearly toppled from the saddle. While he was uprighting himself and untangling his pistol from the reins, Miki gouged her stallion in the flanks. Accompanied by the abrupt crack of thunder, Sundance exploded into his swiftest pace. Mikyla pressed herself against the winged steed as they sailed across the pasture and away from impending doom.

Swearing vehemently, Morgan charged after her with fiend-ridden haste. "Stop that horse or I'll shoot him out from under you!" Morgan bellowed in rage.

The thought of this spitfire escaping him unscathed infuriated Morgan. He had meticulously plotted his revenge for weeks, praying for a storm, waiting to bring Cale hell on earth. The possibility of failure incensed Morgan to the point of demented fury. Mikyla had already managed to ward off his sexual assault and he was not about to permit her to escape the ironic death he had planned for her.

When Mikyla refused to heed his command, Morgan took aim and fired. The bullet lodged in Sundance's hip, causing him to stumble. The steed was flying at such swift speed that he was thrown off balance. All Mikyla could remember, as she was ejected from the saddle, was the crack of the pistol and the stallion's shrill whinny. And then she was tumbling pell-mell into a bottomless ocean of black . . .

With a pained grunt, Sundance struggled back to his feet. Favoring his hind leg, he trotted off. His wild eyes flickered in the blinding flash of lightning that seared the heavens and his piercing scream mingled with the boom of thunder as the ominous clouds swallowed the countryside.

Morgan skidded to a halt beside Mikyla's lifeless body. It was a pity he hadn't thought of knocking this crafty bitch unconscious to begin with. He could have saved himself considerable time and energy.

After hoisting Mikyla's unresisting form over his steed, Morgan reseated himself. Riding southwest, Morgan approached the site he had prepared for just such a stormy night.

A satanic smile rippled across his lips when he spied the tall metal pole with the lightning rod attached to it. He had erected this towering monument two weeks earlier anxiously awaiting the opportunity to satisfy his demented vendetta against Cale. When Cale came upon his missing wife he would know exactly who was responsible for her demise. And very soon, Morgan and Cale would square off. They would resolve this feud that had tormented Morgan for years. At long last, Cale would be dead and Morgan would finally be satisfied!

Hastily, Morgan dragged Mikyla's unconscious body to the ground and tied her to the pole. His gaze swung skyward as he wound the rope to hold Mikyla upright. The last thing he wanted was to have his hands on the rod when lightning struck. He was taking a dangerous risk, but his method of vengeance was too appropriate to disregard. Morgan had never forgotten the night Jessica was lightning struck because of Cale's intervention. And now Cale's precious wife would meet her demise the same way Jessica had met hers.

An eye for an eye, Morgan reminded himself with a wicked cackle. Finding Mikyla fried alive would leave Cale's soul to bleed. And then Morgan would put the bastard out of his misery, once and for all. Cale could join his love in hell. And even *that* was more than they deserved! Morgan thought spitefully. If he had his way these two lost souls would spend eternity searching for each other . . . with no success.

Chapter 28

Cale scowled at the threatening sky. He had very nearly ridden his horse into the ground in attempt to reach the ranch as he had promised. Rustlers had been lying in wait just across the border. Their attack had cost Cale precious time. Stringing his herd in front of him like a shield, Cale had run right over the top of the desperados. But with all the shooting and commotion, the mares had broken loose and scattered in all directions. It had taken Cale two days to round them up. It had not been easy to ward off the three men, especially with his arm in this blasted splint. But Cale had accomplished the feat and escaped unscathed . . . Well, except for the bullet that had lodged in his splint, he amended with a wry smile. It was the first time he actually appreciated the hampering blocks of wood that encased his arm. Without them, he might have lost half his blood and all his horses . . .

A shrill whinny interrupted his pensive musings. Cale glanced up from the dry arroyo where he had hobbled the horses to wait out the storm. The icy fingers of dread flew down his spine when he saw Sundance limping onto the hill above them. There was no mistaking the magnificent stallion with the flaxen mane and tail and Cale was instantly aware that something was amiss. Sundance was saddled and Mikyla was nowhere to be seen. She had always pampered Sundance as if he were a newborn child and she never neglected him.

Impatiently waiting for the roar of thunder to die in the wind, Cale whistled at Sundance. The stallion tossed his head and glanced toward the sound. Cautiously, he limped down the steep slope of the gully. When Cale spied the bloody wound on Sundance's hip, he let loose with a string of curses that would have burned the ears off a priest.

Morgan! The name, and the face attached to it, blazed across Cale's tormented mind. Morgan had returned. Cale could sense it. The words his stepbrother had uttered so long ago came back at Cale like a howling specter of the night. Morgan had sworn he would repay Cale for what had happened. Damnation, Cale should have had more sense than to leave Ky in Oklahoma, even under Reuben's protection.

A jagged bolt of lightning tore gashes in the threatening black clouds. Rain poured down in sheets and Cale sat there, dazed, immobilized by a fear that rivaled nothing he had ever experienced. He had been out of his mind with worry when he saw Mikyla in the flooding river. But it didn't compare to what he was feeling now. What diabolical end had Morgan planned for Ky? Cale shuddered to hazard a guess. Knowing the demented working of Morgan's mind, he would attempt to re-create . . .

Cale was like a man deprived of oxygen. He couldn't breathe for a full sixty seconds. Sweet mercy, Morgan wouldn't dare . . . Before Cale could complete the thought, he knew he was deluding himself to believe Morgan would spare Ky such a horrible death.

Struggling to gather his wits, Cale glanced wildly about him. He had to move. He had to locate Ky before . . .

With a growl that sounded more like a tormented animal than a human, Cale loosed the horses and leaped onto his steed, spurring him up the steep walls of the arroyo. Cale rode at breakneck speed, following the general direction Sundance had come. Damn, he should have settled with Morgan long before now, Cale scolded himself. But he felt Morgan deserved to vent his hatred. After all, Cale had it coming. But this was different, Ky had nothing to do with what happened to Jessica. Ky was an innocent victim, the pawn Morgan had played to appease his crazed need for revenge.

For the first time in three years Cale paid little heed to the raging storm. Although he practically lay down atop his horse to lessen the risk of being struck, his thoughts centered on Mikyla's safety, not his own. He could see her enchanting face before him, those wide, expressive blue eyes that could grow dark with passion or flare with anger. He could see that silver-gold mane of hair whipping about her exquisite features, taste those soft sweet lips . . .

If Morgan took Ky away from him, Cale swore he would annihilate his vicious stepbrother. Ky had come to mean all things to Cale. He could not imagine the world without her in it. His life would become as gloomy as this storm. The days would be plagued by perpetual rains that drowned his grieving soul.

A wave of terror splashed over Cale's body when he came upon the ridge to see the towering pole that scraped the low-hanging clouds. God! Morgan was so poisoned with hatred that he had gone stark raving mad. What sane man would carry his vengeance to such cruel extremes? No doubt Morgan hadn't left the area at all. His note had been a ploy. Morgan had been waiting, living for this moment of deranged retribution.

Morgan glanced behind him when he heard the clatter of hooves. Scowling, he snatched up his pistol. Cale wasn't supposed to arrive just yet. He was to come only after Mikyla had been sacrificed!

Firing a rapid round of shots, Morgan dashed toward his mount. Cale was charging toward him like an enraged bull and Morgan decided it wise to run for his life.

The murderous look on Cale's face would have crumbled a marble statue. His teeth were clenched with unrestrained fury. His eyes were spewing silver fire. Cale moved in perfect rhythm with his steed as he gobbled up the distance that separated them. Morgan winced in fearful apprehension when he heard the creak of leather, when he noted the powerful gait of the centaur who thundered across the prairie like an avenging god. Morgan felt as if he were moving in slow motion, as if he were fumbling in the face of imminent disaster. To complicate his woes, his contrary horse kept prancing away each time Morgan attempted to step into the stirrup.

Although Cale was itching to get his hands on Morgan, his first concern was Mikyla. To partially satisfy his frustrated fury, he swerved his steed toward Morgan and collided with his stepbrother broadside on his way to rescue Mikyla. Morgan was left spinning like a top before he collapsed on the ground with a pained grunt. Dazed, Morgan clambered to his feet and glanced around, blurry-eyed, to retrieve the pistol that had flown from his hand when Cale very nearly ran him down.

Cale knew he had only a few moments to release Mikyla and drag her to safety before Morgan got his bearings and located his pistol. But time was shorter than Cale anticipated. The instant after Morgan's pistol discharged, the bullet struck the pole just inches above Cale's head. Using his steed as a shield, Cale pulled Mikyla's limp body to safety. Then, and only then, did Cale focus his murdering gaze on Morgan.

"She deserves to die," Morgan screeched, furious that Cale had reached Mikyla before lightning struck the rod. "You took Jessica from me. It's only fitting that I take your wife from you!"

Cale grimaced at the peculiar tone of Morgan's voice. It was shrill and blistered with fury. "You didn't love Jessie," Cale growled back at him. "If I had believed that for a minute, I wouldn't have gone after her."

Morgan poked his head above his horse's back to glower at Cale who was employing the same tactic for protection. "I loved her!" he roared in contradiction. "But you didn't *want* to believe it. You spited me every day since my mother married your father. You even convinced my mother to disown me so you could inherit my wealth."

Cale swore under his breath. It was time Morgan heard the truth. Cale had spared Morgan until now. But the maniac needed to know what had really happened. "Even your own mother disapproved of the marriage," he growled

406

hatefully. "Jessica had gone to Patricia, hoping she would understand and offer her blessing. Your own mother denied Jessica's request and begged her not to go with you. But even Patricia's pleas didn't stop Jessie. Your mother sent me after the two of you." Cale glowered at the shadowed face beneath the black felt hat. "Patricia was ashamed to call you her son. You whined and complained from the moment you arrived at the ranch. Work was beneath you. Never in your life have you earned an honest day's wage. That was why Patricia disinherited you. My father and I had nothing to do with it. You brought your troubles on yourself."

Cale watched the explanation soak into Morgan's face before it became a mask of killing fury. When Morgan tried to interrupt, Cale hurried on. "Patricia hoped you would make something of yourself if you were forced out on your own. But you turned to Jessica, knowing you could charm her into loving you, knowing you could live off *her* inheritance like the leech you are. Your *own* mother, your flesh and blood, betrayed Jessica's secret, Morgan. I knew nothing of your scheme until Patricia begged me to bring Jessie back and send you on your way!"

"You lying bastard!" Morgan hissed venomously. "It was you who poisoned my mother against me. You saw to it that I was deprived of my inheritance. And then you killed Jessica, your own sister, just to spite me!"

"If Jessie hadn't died that night you would have killed her," Cale flung at him, his voice harsh with accusation. "She was young and foolish. She fell for your charismatic charm. But you would have taken her money and left her in some dusty cowtown while you drifted off to find another lover, a new saloon, and steeper stakes. Patricia didn't want that kind of heartache for Jessie. She betrayed you to save a young, innocent girl from a life of hell . . ."

And then it came, the deafening crash Cale had heard before. Sparks flew like an array of fireworks when lightning struck the rod. Brilliant, white-hot light exploded in unison with the ear-shattering clash of thunder. Horses screamed in terror and darted blindly toward safety. The ground shook as if it had been besieged by an earthquake. Rain pounded down around them as if the sky had collapsed like the crumbling wall of a dam.

Although Cale had been knocked to his knees and his entire body tingled as if pins had been inserted under his skin, he struggled to regain his feet. Like an exploding cannon ball, Cale leaped on Morgan. But Morgan came up fighting for his life. Fists flew from all directions at once and flesh cracked against flesh. Cale had his hand full—the one that wasn't hampered by the splint. Morgan was a man driven by vengeful demons. He cursed Cale's lies with every blow he delivered. He was determined to beat Cale to bloody shreds and dispose of Mikyla.

Cale was numb to his old wounds and to the new round of pain that was inflicted on him. Adrenaline shot through his bloodstream, providing him with superhuman strength. Ducking away from another oncoming punch, Cale uncoiled like a tightly wound spring. Using the wooden splint as a weapon, he backhanded Morgan across the cheek. His worthy opponent staggered back, dazed by the punishing blow to the side of his head.

"Admit it, damn you," Cale growled as he stalked toward Morgan. "What you wanted from Jessie had nothing to do with love. She was your meal ticket, your way out."

Morgan's wild laughter split the damp air. "You want the truth? Then you shall have it," he sneered. "Of course I didn't love that naive little chit. She was too much like her older brother—a Brolin through and through. I would have gotten to you by using and discarding her when her supply of money ran out. I would have had my revenge on *all* of you to compensate for the years I suffered with your despicable arrogance, your unreasonable demands. You wanted me to become your hired hand, doing all the dirty work that was beneath *you* . . ."

His last word erupted in a menacing growl. Morgan threw himself at Cale. But Cale was braced and ready for the wild attack. He came uncoiled like a raven-haired snake. His fist caught Morgan on the chin, uplifting him from the ground, leaving him dangling in midair for a split second. Although Morgan landed in a tangled heap, he refused to admit defeat.

He was fighting for all the years he had been forced to bow to Cale's superiority, his unrivaled abilities. He was battling to prove to himself and to Cale that Morgan Hagerty was the better man.

"I'll go to my grave hating you," Morgan gritted out the side of his mouth that wasn't swollen and tender from the devastating blows Cale had delivered. "I despised you long before I could turn my charms on that lovesick little sister of yours. I detested your arrogance. I wanted to repay you for all the miserable years you barked your orders and I was *forced* to obey my older stepbrother—bastard that he was and always will be . . ."

Cale jerked Morgan up by the collar of his muddy shirt. Their eyes clashed—tarnished silver boring into frothy green. "And you'll never change," he sneered contemptuously. "You always wanted to think you were being ostracized and cheated, that I pressured you. But the fact is Patricia wanted to make a man out of you instead of the sniveling, whining brat who didn't know how to toil and sweat for what he wanted. Patricia asked me to take you under my wing, to teach you to become a man who could face a *man's* responsibilities. She even told me the greatest cross she had to bear was raising a son who wasn't worthy to carry his father's name. All I felt for you was pity. But you aren't worthy of anyone's emotion or concern, little brother. You are a lost cause and I have wasted my last thought on you!"

When Morgan retaliated by kneeing Cale in the groin, it only served to infuriate the man who possessed the strength of two good men. Cale reacted spontaneously. As he buckled beneath the breathtaking blow, his left arm crashed against Morgan's skull, felling him like a tree beneath a lumberjack's ax. Cale's splint had become an effective weapon that coldcocked Morgan, toppling him into a lifeless heap.

There was no pity or remorse on Cale's battered features when he stared down at his stepbrother's motionless form. Morgan lived for spite alone. He had spent his life devising schemes to cut Cale down, one way or another. Morgan had always plotted to acquire easy money by lying, conniving, and cheating. The closest he had come to an honest day's work was when he strutted *past* a man at labor.

While Cale was studying Morgan's bloody face, he pensively reflected on the night Patricia had bared her soul to Cale and his father. Through a sea of tears Patricia confessed that she was ashamed of her son, appalled by his selfish attitude and humiliated by his total lack of respect for his new family. More than anything, she wanted Morgan to make something of himself, cease his grumbling, and bury his ill-founded resentment. She wanted to make him realize he was wasting his life by expecting to be handed wealth on a silver platter.

But Morgan made no attempt to become a productive, integral part of the family. He refused to do his share of the work. He had been a constant thorn and he continually proclaimed that common labor was beneath a man who had blue blood flowing through his veins.

And then, to satisfy his revenge for being disinherited, Morgan sought to tear the family apart by persuading Jessica to run away with him. Morgan would never change, but Cale no longer felt responsible for his stepbrother. Morgan deserved no more consideration. He was so self-centered that he couldn't see that his family had spent years trying to help him, not hurt and humiliate him.

Inhaling a ragged breath, Cale turned his back on his stepbrother once and for all. Let Morgan crawl away like the disgusting serpent he was, Cale thought as he strode toward Mikyla. If Morgan didn't have sense enough to abandon the territory the moment he regained consciousness, Cale would show him no mercy the next time they met . . .

A disgusted scowl claimed Cale's chiseled features when he noticed Mikyla's torn gown and the scratches on her shoulder. His murderous gaze flew back to Morgan's motionless form. Cale could guess how and why Mikyla's dress had been torn away. The man had gone utterly mad, Cale decided. Not only had Morgan intended to murder Mikyla, but he had raped her. The thought made Cale's blood run cold. The ultimate insult, Cale mused furiously. No doubt Morgan had intended to flaunt that in Cale's face.

He shuddered to think what a dreadful nightmare Miki had endured at Morgan's hand. His stepbrother would have been rough and abusive. He would have purposely hurt Miki, knowing he was indirectly hurting Cale.

And it did hurt. It hurt like hell. The vision of Morgan pawing at Ky, touching her intimately . . . Cale's heart twisted in his chest. He ached to kiss and caress away Morgan's abusive touch, to reassure her that he was nothing like his vicious stepbrother.

Warm kisses intermingled with the cold rain that tapped against Mikyla's bruised cheek. Slowly, she fought her way through the dizzy haze and lifted heavy eyelids. There was a face above hers, but she couldn't identify it. The terrifying memories came rushing back and Mikyla instinctively shrank away with a choked whimper.

"It's me, Ky," Cale whispered tenderly as he drew her onto his lap.

"Cale? Mikyla strained to see his craggy features through a blurry cloud of gray. She wondered if this was another of Morgan's deceitful ploys, if she were about to endure another terrifying nightmare.

"Can you stand up, love?" Cale questioned in concern. His gentle fingers smoothed the renegade strands from her grimy face, waiting for her to recognize him.

"I . . . I don't know," Mikyla stuttered dazedly.

When Cale steadied her on her feet, her right leg folded up beneath her and pain streaked across her knee. Mikyla clutched Cale's wet shirt to prevent collapsing on the ground. Her wide eyes searched his rugged features. "Sundance? Is he all right?"

Cale rolled his eyes skyward, only to be slapped in the face by a gigantic raindrop. Mikyla had been sexually abused. She could barely identify her own husband and yet here she was, demanding to know what became of her precious stallion.

"Sundance has a bullet in his rump, but he will be fine when we have tended him. Morgan is out cold." Cale

411

expelled a frustrated breath. He had been to hell and back and he needed consolation, no matter how small it was. He needed to know that Miki's horrifying experience with Morgan hadn't soured her toward all men, that she wasn't afraid of her husband's touch. "And if you don't mind, I would appreciate a greeting kiss, my neglectful wife! It's been one helluva day, if you want to know."

Cale's gruff voice soaked into her soggy brain and she finally smiled at him, even if his face still appeared a fuzzy shade of gray. "You're late," she chided before granting him the kiss he demanded of her.

"I thought I arrived in the nick of time," Cale contradicted just before he captured her wet lips in another savoring kiss. Lord, he wanted to crush her to him, to drive away the painful memories. He ached to lose himself in her silky arms, but he kept reminding himself that Mikyla needed comforting and compassion after her tormenting ordeal.

His remark made them both realize how close they had come to losing each other forever. Mikyla squeezed him so hard she feared she would leave another set of bruises. And Cale had to control himself for fear he would crack Mikyla's ribs, if they weren't cracked already.

The fact that Cale held her so gingerly disappointed Mikyla. She wouldn't have cared if Cale had hugged the stuffing out of her, but for some unexplainable reason he embraced her as if she were a fragile china doll.

Her bruised face tilted upward to study his face, which was a mask of carefully guarded emotion. "Is that the best you can do after a three-week absence?" she sniffed disappointedly.

Cale shifted uneasily from one foot to the other. "I was afraid that . . . after . . ." Damn, how did a man delicately broach this subject? How could he reassure her that nothing had changed between them? He had selfishly demanded a greeting kiss, but he was apprehensive about forcing Ky to cope with intimate embraces so soon after she had been attacked by that madman of a stepbrother-in-law. "I . . . didn't want to subject . . . you to . . ." His pained gaze fell to the drooping sleeve of her gown and the claw marks on her

412

shoulder. "I'm sorry, Ky."

Finally, she understood why Cale was stuttering and stammering. Her hand lifted to smooth away his concerned frown. "Morgan tried to assault me in the barn," she told him quietly, and then smiled an impish smile. "But you know how offended Sundance becomes when men dare to come too close. Sundance was prepared to kick in Morgan's skull, and he would have if that horrible brute hadn't dived to safety."

Mikyla felt Cale's taut body sag in relief. She had dissolved his worst fears and allowed him a small degree of inner peace.

Ever so slowly, Cale bent his head to brush his lips over her soft mouth. "Remind me to express my gratitude to Sundance. For once, I appreciate his protective attitude toward you." His good arm enfolded her, giving her a loving squeeze. "Let's go home, Ky," he whispered as he scooped her up in his arms.

Casting Morgan one last glance, Cale helped Mikyla onto his stepbrother's horse. Her eyes fell to Morgan, but she spoke not one word. The man deserved to lie there for all eternity after his fiendish attempt to molest her and then cook her alive.

After Cale escorted Mikyla home, he fully intended to return to retrieve Morgan and haul him off to jail if he hadn't slithered away on his own accord. But Belinda, Emet, Reuben, and his new lady were at the ranch, frantic to learn what had become of the Brolins.

Belinda's mother-hen instincts took control the moment she spied Mikyla and Cale's battered condition. She scurried about, determined to practice her nursing skills. Cale found himself shuffled upstairs and into bed before he caught the grippe. Mikyla's head and leg were securely bandaged. With those ministrations accomplished, Belinda saw to it that Mikyla was dumped in bed beside Cale. Not that Cale minded, but he felt like a caged baboon with the foursome scuttling around the bed, trying to make their patients comfortable.

The older couples stood over them, wagging their fingers

413

and firing instructions like a barrage of bullets. Once Miki and Cale promised to rest, the brood of hens swept out like a misdirected cyclone.

"We spoiled Papa's wedding," Mikyla remarked, staring at the door that had slammed shut behind their departing guests.

Cale's shoulder lifted and dropped in a lackadaisical shrug. "They didn't seem too disappointed about postponing the ceremony until tomorrow."

A wry smile pursed Mikyla's lips as she tossed Cale a sidelong glance. "I would have been upset if *I* had been forced to wait another day."

Cale returned her impish smile. "Eager little thing, weren't you?" he teased playfully.

"I still am," she confessed unrepentantly. Her arms glided over his shoulders as she wriggled to make tantalizing contact with his solid strength. "And I missed you terribly. . . ."

She had that look about her, the one that spoke volumes without the use of a single word. Cale removed her arms and folded them in her own lap. "Do you realize how many miles I've covered today, madame? Not to mention the fact that you took a nasty fall that might have landed you a concussion. And let's not forget that you wrenched your leg out of its socket." When Miki sidled closer, despite his attempt to hold her at bay, Cale frowned disapprovingly. "If you have no regard for your own haggard condition, at least consider mine! I have a bullet hole in my splint from a near brush with disaster and I have just gone a round with my stepbrother, which came dangerously close to costing both of us our lives. Besides, Belinda made us promise to rest and recuperate."

Mikyla's bottom lip jutted out in an exaggerated pout. "It's been a long three weeks," she grumbled resentfully.

"And I'm trying to be sensible," Cale muttered as he wormed beneath the sheet to glare at the ceiling. "We both need the rest."

"I don't want to be sensible," Mikyla declared rebelliously. Her hand dived beneath the sheet to make timulating contact with his hair-roughened flesh.

"I have a broken arm and you have a lame leg, for Pete's ake!" Cale insisted, removing her wandering hand. "Go to leep."

In flagrant disregard of his order, Mikyla slid her leg etween his thighs and pulled upon his chest. The smile on er bewitching features caused her eyes to sparkle like olished sapphires. "Fine," she said airily. "You be the ensible one. But I'm going to indulge my whims, lame leg or o . . ." Her lips feathered over his, tempting and taunting im with seductive techniques she had acquired from the naster himself. Her soft breasts caressed his chest, sending is heart into full gallop, lighting a torch in his blood.

"If you love me, you will . . ." she murmured provoca-ively.

"I love you, but I won't," Cale declared with an rrepressible chuckle. Then he choked on his breath when Mikyla's straying hands migrated over his sensitive flesh, :rumbling the last barriers of his self-control.

"Wanna bet?" she purred softly.

Cale ran out of resistance. Her arousing kisses and :aresses sent sensibility flying right out the window. "No," he eplied hoarsely. "I have the feeling I'm about to lose . . ."

His prediction proved correct. Mikyla proceeded to erase he miles he had traveled and to block out the terrifying ncident that had come dangerously close to claiming her ife. Cale forgot about Morgan, the interrupted wedding olans, the herd of mares that were probably scattered to kingdom come. He forgot everything except the sweet, oewitching angel in his arms.

Lord, how could one woman's love completely turn a nan's life around? he wondered. Would he always feel his neart leap into triple time when this enchanting temptress ouched him? Would her soft, throaty voice always whisper across the miles that occasionally separated them and :ontinually lure him back to her arms? Would her face al-ways form the dimensions of his dreams?

As Cale returned her worshiping caresses and surrendered o unrestrained passion, a voice deep inside him answered

415

yes. Mikyla was a special breed of woman whose wild spirit transformed his life into one long, lively adventure. This love affair had been a whirlwind—constantly changing directions, churning his emotions into chaos. Mikyla was one of those rare individuals who simply made things happen. She was the vortex of a storm that generated swirling tempests. She was stormfire. Cale mused as the blaze burned hotter, searing him inside and out. Mikyla was wind and flame and Cale felt like a defenseless leaf being scorched and flung hither and yon.

As the world spun crazily, Cale was besieged by this witch's magical power. Cale asked himself why he had bothered being sensible in the first place. This blue-eyed sorceress would always have her way with him. And he didn't mind a bit. In fact, he really didn't mind at all.

"Mmm . . . do that again," Cale rasped as he roused from sleep to find honeyed lips playing softly on his. Mikyla's exploring hands had lifted him from the depths of drowsiness, leaving him bobbing just beyond reality's shore.

Are you the same man who told me to be sensible last night?" she mocked as she nibbled at his full lips.

"You reformed me," Cal assured her as he rolled above her.

Her eyes glistened with unmistakable pleasure. Lovingly she raked her fingers through his thick raven hair. "I rather thought it was the other way around." Her hand glided to his cheek and her lips quivered with tender emotion. "I love you, Cale . . . with all my heart."

Her expression melted him into sentimental mush. Love was staring him in the face—a face that was embedded with enormous blue eyes, a face that was surrounded by thick rich strands of silver-gold, a face that was blessed with the most kissable cupid's-bow lips he had ever encountered. "Tell me you love me to the end of my days, Ky. I'll never grow tired of hearing the words."

"I'll never tire of saying them," she whispered softly.

The thud of hooves clomping in the mud interrupted what

had every indication of becoming a very satisfying moment of mutual admiration and affection.

"What the bloody hell is it now!" Cale scowled in annoyance. "I swear we're going to pack up and move to the Antarctic! Maybe in that barren land of ice we can enjoy a little privacy!"

Still muttering, Cale dragged himself away from his tempting wife to peer out the window. A curious frown plowed his brow when he recognized Brock Terrel leading the cavalry patrol.

As Cale scooped up his clothes and climbed into them on the run, Mikyla wormed into her gown. "What do you suppose they want at this hour of the morning?"

"Unfortunately, there is only one way to find out," Cale declared, giving Ky a loving pat on the derriere as he sailed out the door. "Whatever it is, I resent Terrel's poor sense of timing."

Smiling to herself, Mikyla followed Cale downstairs with the use of a makeshift cane Emet had designed for her. "Shall we finish our discussion later?" she questioned.

"I'll be counting the moments," Cale assured her as his booted foot hit the hall floor, taking him swiftly toward the door.

Brock Terrel assessed the newlyweds with a befuddled frown. Mikyla was a mass of bruises and scrapes and she was leaning heavily on an improvised cane. Cale looked not one bit better with his broken arm and discolored cheek. It wasn't too difficult to tell they had engaged in some sort of battle, and Brock knew with whom.

"It appears the two of you met with disaster," he said grimly.

Cale nodded affirmatively as he gestured for Brock to join them for a cup of coffee. "Morgan Hagerty kidnapped Miki and came within an inch of killing her last night," he growled bitterly.

Brock sank down at the table. His expression was somber as he peered into Cale's scowling features. "Morgan Hagerty is dead," he said quietly. "We came across his body several miles from here. He was lying facedown in the mud."

"Dead?" Mikyla and Cale chirped in unison. Mikyla hobbled over to set the coffee pot on the table and then collapsed into a chair. "Are you sure?"

Brock nodded positively. "Tell me it was self-defense, Cale, and I will accept your testimony, no questions asked. I knew there was trouble brewing between the two of you. When I questioned Morgan about the death of his associates, he was bitter where you were concerned." He paused to inhale a deep breath and slowly expelled it. "I will see to the necessary arrangements. All you have to do is tell me what happened and I will take care of everything."

"It *was* self-defense," Cale declared emphatically. "The man was crazed with vengeance. But I didn't think Morgan was dead when I brought Ky home to treat her wounds!"

Brock shrugged. "Well, he was certainly dead when I came upon him while we were riding patrol. He looked as if he had received a severe blow to the head." His eyes fell to the splint that encased Cale's left arm, wondering how imposing the wooden blocks would be if they were employed as a weapon.

Cale's face was alive with unguarded emotion—relief intermingled with regret and confusion. "Morgan was trying to kill my wife to repay me for something that happened long ago. If I had arrived ten minutes later, Morgan would have seen to it that Mikyla became a human lightning rod."

Brock sipped his coffee. "If I have your word, it's good enough. I'm sorry about this. I have had one or two occasions to speak with Hagerty. I never could understand his animosity toward you, but I was aware of it. He made several spiteful remarks the night Emily . . ." His voice trailed off as he unfolded himself from his chair. "I won't detain you. You both have suffered from the unpleasant incident and I will see to the matter for you."

When Brock made his exit, Mikyla slipped her hand into Cale's. "I'm sorry. I know there was dissension between you and Morgan. He told me his version of the story before he . . ."

Cale's hand drifted away from hers and so did his thoughts. He needed to be alone to cope with the death of his stepbrother. Cale had told himself he didn't care what happened to Morgan. But they had grown up together and Cale was having difficulty accepting what had happened, wondering if he were indeed responsible for delivering the fatal blow. "I need to retrieve Sundance and the mares," he said as he strode out the door.

Mikyla's sympathetic gaze followed Cale until he disappeared from sight. She knew it was painful for Cale to learn he had killed his stepbrother. It was going to be even more uncomfortable for him to relay the news to his family. Cale was undoubtedly wrestling with his emotions, hating himself and yet attempting to defend his actions.

She had indeed read Cale's mind. The previous night, Cale had been consumed with murdering fury, just as Morgan had been. But Cale could have sworn Morgan was alive when they left him. Had the blow to the head . . .

Cale grumbled under his breath. He was justified in taking Morgan's life. With malice and forethought, Morgan had set about to fry Mikyla alive! Dammit, Morgan didn't deserve to live. So why was Cale mourning his passing? Because he had spent fifteen years of his life trying to transform Morgan into a productive citizen. Even as a boy Morgan had felt slighted and abused, Cale told himself ruefully. Perhaps if Cale had been more understanding, more aware . . . Well, it was too late to undo the damages he might have done. Morgan had always resented him. He disliked Cale's father and he had caused dissension since the day he set foot on the ranch.

Heaving a frustrated sigh, Cale gouged his mount and flew like the wind. He wanted to outrun his troubled contemplations, to forget the previous night existed. He should be thanking his lucky stars that Mikyla was alive and reasonably well. If Morgan would have been allowed to have his way, Mikyla would be only a haunting memory that would torment Cale the rest of his life.

As long as Morgan had lived, Cale would have been hounded by the nagging fear that his stepbrother would be watching and waiting to destroy their happiness. In the beginning, Cale had been overly cautious of his affection for Ky, hoping to protect her from his vindictive stepbrother.

But he couldn't hide his love for that feisty sprite forever. And just as Cale had anticipated, Morgan had plotted to take Mikyla's life. In Morgan's bitter, demented estimation, Cale was due to pay tormenting penance for what had happened three years ago.

Cale shuddered at the horrifying method Morgan had devised—the ultimate revenge. Yes, he lamented Morgan's death. But deep down inside, Cale knew one or the other of them would have had to die to end this long-standing feud.

Determinedly, Cale flung aside his musings. It was over and done. He had a new home and a new life. He had Mikyla's love . . . A wry smile pursed his lips, which soon gave way to a broad grin and finally to a deep skirl of laughter. He could see that lovely nymph bending over him as she had the previous night. My, but she had become an inventive, aggressive lover. Cale thought he knew all there was to know about passion. But with the right woman, there was absolutely no comparison. That blond-haired seductress could arouse him to the limits of sanity, forcing him to abandon common sense. And what a splendorous night it had been, every wild, breathless moment of it . . .

Chapter 29

Wearing a contented smile, Mikyla hobbled out to the barn to attend Sundance. Cale had doctored the wound her stallion had sustained the previous week and Sundance was mending nicely. *We are a matched pair,* Mikyla thought as she limped toward the stables. Both she and Sundance were favoring one leg, but Mikyla wasn't about to complain. She was enjoying a marriage made in heaven. Her father had wed Belinda (and without a *charivari*, as Emet requested). And Reuben had shown himself to be a good friend and an excellent assistant on the ranch. Ah, life was grand, Mikyla mused with a cheerful sigh.

The crack of a rifle suddenly split the morning air. The bullet sailed so close to Mikyla's ear that her heart leaped into her throat, practically strangling her. Instinctively, Mikyla dived to the ground, using the water trough to protect her from her mysterious assailant. What had she said about life being so grand? Sweet mercy, someone was trying to kill her!

The abrupt sound of the rifle and Mikyla's startled yelp brought Reuben and Cale to the door of the barn. Their stunned gazes landed on the shiny silver-gold hair that slowly rose from the far side of the water trough.

"What the hell is . . ."

Cale was interrupted by the exploding weapon. He jerked his head in the direction of the sound. Who the devil was taking pot shots at Ky now? His stormy eyes flew to Mikyla, who had slowly begun to rise from her hiding place. The bullet had missed her hand by a fraction of an inch. It had ricocheted off the trough and clanked against the leg of the windmill that supplied the power to pump the well that Cale and Reuben had erected the previous afternoon.

Cale jumped as if *he* had been shot when he noticed the shocked expression on Mikyla's face. She had shrunk away from the oncoming bullet, but her blue eyes were wide and frantic as they swung to Cale, who stood frozen like a block of ice.

Her unspoken plea spurred Cale into action. He spun around and grabbed the halter of the nearest horse. Using the animal as his protection, Cale started out of the barn, only to be unexpectedly yanked backward.

"What are you trying to do, get yourself shot?" Reuben snapped in annoyance. "You just got that doggone splint off your arm and now you're looking to have the doctor cut a bullet out of you!"

"Miki is out there, for God's sake," Cale snorted as he wrestled his arm from Reuben's grasp.

"I ain't blind," Reuben sniffed sarcastically. "I know where she is. But that's no reason to get yourself killed!"

Another well-aimed bullet whistled through the air, lodging in the wood just above Mikyla's head.

"Stay down, dammit!" Cale's sharp words sent Mikyla sprawling on the ground. "Where's my rifle when I need it?" he asked himself irritably.

After several tense minutes, no other shots broke the silence. Despite Reuben's protest, Cale led the mare outside, keeping her between himself and the direction from which the barrage of bullets had come. But the sniper, whoever he or she was, had abandoned the attempt to dispose of Mikyla.

Cale scooped Miki up off the ground and held her in his arms until he was certain she was still in one piece. "I didn't realize you had made so many enemies," he muttered sourly. His narrowed gaze scanned the clump of tall sunflowers and goldenrods that had served as the assassin's protective cover. But for the life of him, Cale couldn't imagine why Mikyla had become a sniper's target. All those who had reason to

422

dispose of her were dead. "I think perhaps you should stay in town with your father." His tone brooked no argument, but he found himself in the middle of one just the same.

"I most certainly will not!" Mikyla countered, her chin jutting out stubbornly. "My father is a newlywed and I'm not about to impose on his privacy."

"Maybe she could stay at the trading post," Reuben suggested as he strode up beside them. "I'm sure the man you found to replace me wouldn't mind . . ."

Cale gave his head a negative shake. "It's a long ride to the post and there are too many sites suitable for an ambush."

"Well, perhaps she could . . ."

"I'm staying right here," she told both men firmly. "This is my home and I will not be frightened off our property again!"

"You nearly got yourself shot!" Cale's voice rose to an exasperated roar. "We are not taking any chances."

"You needn't shout!" Mikyla yelled in the same booming tone.

"I may be lame, but I am not deaf."

"No, but sometimes I wonder if you have the good sense God gave a mule!" Cale snorted, but without excessive volume. "You have already proven you are by far the stubbornest female on the planet. You needn't try for the title of *stubbornest creature in the galaxy!*"

This was the first stalemate they had reached since their wedding day and suddenly Cale had reverted to his annoying tactic of ordering her around and crowing like an over-protective rooster. Mikyla knew he was upset, but she did not appreciate being raked over the coals with Reuben as witness.

"You can insult me until you are blue in the face, but I am not leaving!" She punctuated the statement with a rebellious glare.

Muttering, Cale paced back and forth for a full minute. He pivoted to stare at Reuben, whose eyes were swinging from Mikyla's unyielding stance to Cale's scowling face. "You talk some sense into her, Reuben," he demanded.

Squaring his shoulders, Reuben opened his mouth to

second Cale's opinion that Miki needed protection. Mikyla's delicately arched brows lifted, daring him to lecture her. Reuben closed his mouth and threw up his hands in a gesture of futility. "I'm not sticking my nose in the middle of this domestic quarrel," he declared before stomping back to the barn with the mare in tow. "The two of you can fight it out. That's supposed to be one of the luxuries of wedlock."

Cale crossed his arms over his chest and stared at his independent wife for a long, thoughtful moment. "You think I'm being ridiculous, don't you?"

"I do," she confirmed.

His silver eyes probed into hers for another pensive moment. "I think I love you *too much*," Cale confessed suddenly.

Mikyla did a double take.

A tender smile bordered Cale's lips as he slipped his arm around her waist and ushered her toward the house. "That has been my main concern since I found myself way in over my head. I didn't want you to make the Run because I was afraid you might get yourself hurt. Since you wouldn't come to Texas with me, I wanted to be there with you when you staked your claim. I wanted to be there to pick you up on your way down, to protect you from the inevitable."

Cale let his breath out in a rush as he kicked the front door shut with his boot heel. "Even in the beginning I was afraid I would smother you with too much affection, afraid I would cling too tightly and drive you away. You are too strong-willed and independent to tolerate being loved to the point of suffocation," he analyzed. "But for the first time in my life I find myself overly possessive. I know you can't tolerate being coddled and protected as if you were made of fragile crystal. It goes against your grain after you have spent so many years fending for yourself." He drew Mikyla into his protective embrace, nuzzling his face in the sweet-smelling strands of silver gold. "I have to fight to keep from trying to dominate you, from hovering over you like a mother hen. But when you're hurt, it wounds me. When you're frightened it scares the hell out of me. I don't want to lose you, Ky," he murmured softly.

424

Mikyla was touched by his words, but before she could wedge a comment in edgewise, Cale rushed on. "Promise me you'll stay in the house for a few days, just until we determine who is out to get you and for what reason."

"Very well," she relented. "I will honor your request." She leaned back as far as his encircling arms would allow to toss him a provocative smile. "But when I get that fenced-in feeling, I hope you won't mind distracting me . . ."

Cale's grin was as wide as the South Canadian River. "I'll drop whatever I'm doing and come running," he chortled softly. "Between the two of us, surely we can invent some pastime that will prevent you from feeling so trapped." His calloused hand lifted to settle on her forehead and he frowned in mock concern. "It appears you're coming down with the first symptoms of fenced-in fever already. I think I better put you to bed . . . immediately."

Mikyla had no qualms with that. As a matter of fact, she had no complaint about being confined to the house. She found herself on the most fantastic of journeys without ever leaving the magical circle of his arms . . .

Mikyla was true to her word for the first two days. And since Cale had spotted no one sneaking around their ranch, she considered it safe to venture outside. Whoever had attempted to dispose of her had obviously decided against the fiendish plan. While Reuben and Cale were erecting fences, Mikyla seized the opportunity to sneak out to exercise Sundance. A few minutes of riding couldn't hurt either of them, Mikyla rationalized.

Mikyla couldn't believe her rotten luck! She had only been in the saddle for ten minutes when the crack of a rifle shattered the air. Her wild eyes swung toward the sound as she flattened on Sundance's back. Although instinct prompted her to urge the stallion into his fastest gait and thunder toward the house, Mikyla wouldn't risk injuring her steed while he was mending from his wound. She kept the stallion at a trot, but she refused to push him. After the second bullet zinged past them, Mikyla spied Reuben and

Cale galloping over the rise.

Cale glanced at her the way a hunter glares at a tiger on h[is] way to shoot a bear. After flinging her an I'll-deal-with-you later glower, Cale sailed toward the row of cedar trees an[d] sunflowers that rimmed the small, natural pond.

Deciding it best to return home and allow Cale the chanc[e] to cool off before she confronted him, Mikyla aimed herse[lf] toward the barn. When Sundance was safely in his stal[l,] Mikyla headed to the house, only to be cut off by Cale wh[o] loomed over her from his lofty position on his horse.

Swinging from the saddle, Cale stomped toward h[is] contrary wife. "You gave me your word you would stay i[n] the house. The minute my back was turned you did as yo[u] damned well pleased," he snapped furiously.

"I did promise, but . . ." Mikyla was ready with he[r] excuse. However, Cale was in no mood for an argument.

With Mikyla's arm in a vise grip, Cale spun around t[o] bark an order to Reuben before he could dismount. "Ride t[o] Elreno and fetch the sheriff and ask him to organize a poss[e.] I'm not about to live with this threat for another day[.] Someone wants Ky dead and I can't keep her caged lon[g] enough to determine who!"

When Reuben had galloped away, Cale glared holes i[n] Mikyla's sheepish smile. "Woman, you are absolute[ly] impossible!" he bit off. His arm shot toward the hous[e] indicating that she should lock herself in it. "I found no on[e] hiding in the cover of the underbrush and wild flowers. An[d] until we locate your would-be assassin, you are to keep ou[t] of sight. Do . . . you . . . understand?" He dragged out th[e] words, emphasizing each syllable.

The sound of yet another rifle discharging in the distanc[e] caused both Cale and Mikyla to glance south. Withou[t] another word, Cale leaped onto his steed in a single boun[d] and aimed himself toward the creek from which the shot ha[d] come. Mikyla chewed indecisively on her lip. If she wen[t] thundering after Cale he would be irate. And if she didn't sh[e] would worry herself sick until he returned. Mikyla instantl[y] decided she would prefer to endure Cale's bellowing tirade[.] In swift, precise strides, she marched to the barn to saddl[e]

one of the mares. She intended to follow after Cale at high
speed and she did not wish to risk Sundance. The stallion
had had enough exercise for one day.

Cautiously Cale made his way through the brush that
lined the creek. When he heard hooves resounding behind
him, he swiveled in the saddle to train his pistol on the
unknown rider. To his dismay, Mikyla's wild mane of hair
appeared on the rise. Damnation, what did it take to make
that woman listen to reason, Cale asked himself in exasperation. He should have tied her in bed!

"Confound it, woman, if you have no concern for your
own safety, at least consider my feelings," Cale snapped
none too gently when Mikyla skidded to a halt beside him.
"Call me sentimental, if you wish, but I have grown accustomed to having you around. If you get yourself killed
I'm going to hold it over you for the rest of your life!"

Mikyla giggled at his remark. He was so irritated with her
that he wasn't making sense. And *never* had she considered
calling this powerful mass of brawn and muscle sentimental.
But it was his best effort at confessing that she had become
a habit he didn't want to unlearn. Cale was taking a terrible
risk by tracking the would-be assassin and Miki didn't want
to lose him. She felt the compulsive need to lend an extra
weapon, should he meet with trouble.

"I'm here because I love you," she murmured into his
condemning frown.

Cale finally understood the exasperation Mikyla had
experienced when he had made such confessions at improper
moments. The anger drained from his chiseled features. Try
as he might, Cale couldn't suppress the smile that rose to his
lips as he stared into the sparkling blue eyes that dominated
her lovely face.

"Did I ever tell you that you are worth your weight in
trouble?" he grumbled, but his voice was too soft and husky
to sound insulting.

An impish grin captured her exquisite features. Mikyla
tossed her head, sending her lustrous blond hair cascading

over her shoulder. "I do believe you have hinted at it once or twice."

Cale released his breath in a deflated groan. "Come along, minx. But stay behind me. I have no intention of employing you as a decoy."

After they crept along the natural fence of thick underbrush, Cale noticed someone or some*thing* lying near the creek bank. A wary frown furrowed his brow as he laid his index finger to his lips, requesting Mikyla's silence. Cale and Mikyla clutched their pistols. Silently they edged toward the creek, hoping to catch the assailant off guard.

A strange tingle trickled down Cale's spine when he squinted through the maze of underbrush. A man lay facedown in the creek, an open satchel clutched in one motionless hand. The other arm was bent and his limp hand lay against his forehead in an odd manner—a most unusual position for what appeared to be a dead man.

As they approached the corpse, Mikyla's breath stuck in her throat. "Oh, my God. It can't be . . ." she gasped, clutching Cale for support. She recognized the man but she couldn't believe her eyes. "I thought Morgan was supposed to be dead!"

Cale shoved his Colt into its holster and squatted down on his haunches. "He is," Cale murmured absently. "For the second time . . ."

Giving his stepbrother a gentle shove, Cale rolled him to his back to see the bullet wound near the heart. Mikyla felt her stomach churning in revulsion. Hastily, she presented her back to gulp down the lump that had collected in her throat.

"Do you suppose it was Morgan who tried to kill me after he was presumed dead?" she choked out.

"I'd bet on it," Cale scowled, unfolding himself. His troubled gaze scanned the damp ground along the bank, noting the two sets of tracks that pointed northwest. "Who would have suspected a ghost of returning from the dead to haunt you?"

"Who could have done this?" Mikyla mused aloud. "Do you suppose someone saw Morgan taking shots at me and decided to put an end to him?"

Cale considered her speculation but he voiced no comment. Something was very wrong. This befuddling puzzle was missing one crucial piece. A logical explanation was there, just beyond his grasp. But dammit, Cale couldn't quite fit all the information into place to make sense of it. Who would want to see Morgan dead? And how could Morgan have pretended death when Brock and his patrol came upon him? And if Morgan had been so near death to be *presumed* dead, how could he have been sneaking about, taking shots at Ky? And if the missing corpse *had* gotten up and strolled off before Brock and his men returned to fetch it, why hadn't Brock informed him? Had Brock been trying to spare Cale the anguish of reporting that he had lost his stepbrother's body? Or had someone else come along to collect Morgan before Brock returned to the scene? And what had been in the open satchel Morgan had been carrying? Who had been with Morgan when he died the second time?

Lord, he was going to drive himself crazy trying to determine what really had happened to Morgan. Muttering in frustration, Cale stomped toward his horse. But an eerie sensation commanded him to wheel back around to stare at his stepbrother. Cale half-expected Morgan to pull himself off the ground and charge at his enemy. But this time, Morgan was going nowhere, Cale assured himself. He knew *dead* when he saw it.

As Cale and Mikyla rode silently toward the house, the questions whirled through Cale's mind. And then suddenly, a picture flashed across Cale's mind. It was the odd position of Morgan's right hand, the one that had rested on his brow while he lay facedown in the creek.

"Damn!" Cale burst out suddenly.

His explosive tone and the unsettling incident they had encountered caused Miki to shoot straight out of her saddle. Her wide, questioning eyes landed on Cale's dark frown. "Now what's wrong?"

"Where is the sack I was stuffed into the night I was beaten and dumped in your camp?" he demanded to know.

She stared incredulously at Cale. What did that have to do with anything? And how did he know about the oversize bag? The night Cale had been brutally assaulted, Mikyla had stuffed the sack in with her supplies. She had been so concerned about Cale that she had neglected to mention that he had arrived in a bag . . . hadn't she? And so much had happened since that night, even Miki had forgotten that minor detail.

"I don't recall ever mentioning that you arrived in a bag," she informed him shakily. Something was terribly wrong. Mikyla could sense it!

"You never did," Cale assured her grimly. "That's what worries me. Where is it, Ky? I want to see it."

Frantically, Mikyla racked her brain. What had she done with the sack? "I'm . . . I'm not sure. Perhaps it's in the barn with the folded tent. I can't remember if . . ."

Cale took off like a shooting star blazing across the pasture. Mikyla stared, dumbfounded, as she surveyed his departing back. Muttering at Cale's refusal to explain what he was thinking, Mikyla followed in his wake. But by the time she reached the barn her curiosity had transformed into dread. Cale had bounded out of the saddle and dashed inside, only to find they had an uninvited guest.

"Climb down off that horse and come inside before I put a hole through your dear husband's chest . . ."

Mikyla cursed herself for thundering after Cale without thinking. But then she consoled herself for her impulsive reaction. She had no way of knowing Morgan's killer was awaiting their return. In fact, she wasn't sure who it was . . . as of yet. And when she did discover the knowledge, it was going to be too late to do her or Cale any good.

As Mikyla begrudgingly tossed her pistol aside and walked into the shadows of the barn, Cale glared mutinously at Morgan's assassin. "What was in the satchel?" he questioned boldly. "Was it the profit you and your associates made from selling town lots on Mikyla's property?"

Brock Terrel broke into a sinister smile, but his attention remained fixed on Cale. Cautiously, he trained his Winchester rifle on Cale's broad chest. "How did you guess I was nvolved with the townsite company?" he questioned, sparing Mikyla a quick glance.

"Morgan told me," Cale informed him in a gritted growl.

The news caused Brock to flinch. How could Morgan have told his stepbrother when Brock was reasonably certain his associate was dead before abandoning the scene of the crime? Yes, it had been Brock's idea for Morgan to pretend death. But that double-crossing scoundrel didn't truly possess the nine lives of a cat . . . did he? The unnerving thought provoked Brock to glance expectantly toward the barn door, wondering if he were about to see Morgan appear from the dead for the third time.

"When we found Morgan's body he was frozen in what must have been a *salute*. It was his way of naming his murderer," Cale snorted at his nemesis.

Brock chuckled lightly, relieved that he would not be forced to confront Morgan again. "A rather creative attempt on Morgan's part," he congratulated. "But, unfortunately, Morgan won't be around to have his satisfaction, and neither will you. Your stepbrother was a fool. We had him pronounced dead and he was free to leave the area. But he was hellbent on disposing of Mikyla and taking all the profit for himself. He forced me to kill him." His eyes took on a deadly glow. "And now I am forced to dispose of the two of you as well. By the time anyone happens along, I will have dragged Morgan's body into the barn. It will appear the three of you were engaged in a gun fight from which none of you emerged alive."

Mikyla blinked bewilderedly. She still couldn't understand how and why Brock Terrel had become involved. Was he still carrying a grudge against Cale because of Emily? Had Brock only pretended to forgive Cale? Was Brock trying to throw suspicion on Morgan so no one would guess the major was involved with the fraudulent land company? Was his pretended friendship with Cale a ruse? Was Brock the mastermind behind the company? Had he been giving the orders to harass Miki until she sold her property?

"Why?" she chirped curiously. "If I am about to die, I would at least like to know why?"

431

"For the money, of course," Brock said blandly. "An officer's salary provides prestige, but very little profit. I was in the perfect position to make arrangements with the railroad and interested investors for a townsite company. I had traveled the Unassigned Lands extensively and it wasn't difficult to help the railroad determine sites for communities and logical crossings for their rails." A dark scowl puckered his tanned features. "But Joseph and his friend became greedy and demanding. They wanted more than the share we originally agreed upon. Morgan and I decided to split the profit in half rather than fourths, so we disposed of our greedy partners."

"It wasn't Morgan who had me beaten, was it, Brock?" Cale growled contemptuously. "You let us believe my stepbrother was responsible in order to throw us off track and keep your part in the company a secret. You were the one who hired henchmen to pistol-whip me, and then you had me dumped in an *army surplus* sack to frighten Mikyla off her property and to repay me for that unfortunate fiasco with Emily."

The comment caught Brock off guard. "I suppose that was a careless mistake on my part. I assumed you and your stubborn paramour would be too rattled by the threat to notice the army surplus sack that might link me to the conspiracy." His gaze shifted to Miki, flinging her an annoyed glare. "And when this minx wounded me in the arm the night we dumped you in camp I had to take particular care not to let anyone know I had been injured. If she had known I was the man she shot, I feared you would make the connection. That was why I decided to befriend you after you dallied with Em. I didn't think you would link me with your problems if you thought I was on your side."

A hateful sneer curled Cale's lips. "Actually, it was you who gave yourself away, even when you schemed to portray the honest, compassionate enforcer of law and order. You were the one who commented about my being dumped in a sack when you arrived in camp the day Ky lost her land. At the time I was too preoccupied with my injuries and Mikyla's forced removal from her claim to puzzle out how *you* knew

432

about the bag. Mikyla hadn't bothered to mention it to me and it struck me odd that you would know about the small detail." An intimidating smile thinned Cale's lips. "It seems you were too clever for your own good, Brock."

Brock laughed humorlessly. "It's all academic now, Brolin. The information will be of no use to you. My only regret is that I have had to tolerate you these past few years. Each time you swaggered into the fort, Emily was reminded of her fascination with you," he spat bitterly. "Don't think I didn't know about your affair with her. I knew and I detested you because of it. "I couldn't even enjoy the pleasure of defeating you on the racetrack, much less in my own bedroom." Another peal of icy laughter shook the silence. "But I no longer find myself in competition with your prowess, your horsemanship, or your wealth. Once I am rid of you and your troublesome wife, I will enjoy all the pleasures money can buy. I intend to resign my command and become a land speculator."

The muddled frown on Mikyla's face provoked Brock to grin haughtily. "Haven't you heard, my dear Mrs. Brolin? There are to be two more land runs in the next few years. First the Cherokee reserve will be opened to settlers and then the Cheyenne-Arapaho land will be offered to homesteaders. With my knowledge of the territory and my connection with the railroads, I will enjoy dozens of opportunities to turn a handsome profit. And when Emily realizes I am every bit the man you are, she will come back to me. I'll adorn her with riches and you will be out of our lives, once and for all." His eyes glittered spitefully as he focused on Cale. "It's a pity you won't be around to see me sitting in the lap of luxury. Perhaps you would have envied me for a change."

Brock had expected to rattle Cale with his insinuations, but to his disgust, Cale was still sporting a taunting smile. Even when all odds were against him, Cale refused to admit defeat and that rankled Brock to no end.

"It seems to me that you have overlooked one major detail," Cale commented flippantly.

"I cannot imagine what it might be," Brock scoffed at him.

"I have been painstakingly thorough. No one knows of my involvement in the townsite company . . . except the two of you. And that is only a temporary inconvenience."

"The detail to which I refer is your exit and escape from the barn," Cale informed him all too calmly. "Just how do you propose to walk out of here alive?"

Although Cale's voice had a deadly ring to it, Brock burst into a supercilious snicker. It was obvious Brolin was attempting to bluff his way out of trouble. But Brock intended to call the bluff. Cale and his troublesome wife had interfered in Brock's plans once too often. They wouldn't live to do it again.

"I think you have that backward, Brolin," he parried arrogantly. "*I* am the one who is armed with a rifle. You and your wife are the ones who won't be coming out of here alive."

Cale's stormy silver eyes glistened menacingly. "I may die," he conceded. "But rest assured, I'm taking you with me . . ."

Mikyla's frantic gaze darted back and forth between Cale and Brock. Had Cale lost his mind? How could he stand there defying a man who kept a Winchester trained on his heart? Damn, Cale was going to get himself killed quicker than Brock intended! Was Cale stalling until Reuben arrived with the sheriff?

And suddenly Mikyla understood Cale's intentions. When his sharp whistle split the silence, everyone moved in accelerated motion. Sundance burst through his stall in the rear of the barn to answer the call. Boards shattered and flew in all directions as a thousand pounds of solid horse flesh crashed through the restraining wall. Instinctively, Brock swung toward the sound and then realized his blunder of turning his back on Cale. Although the wild-eyed stallion was charging toward him, Brock was more concerned about the man who was now *behind* him, not the best position for an opponent.

With his trigger finger poised, Brock whirled around. But the split second Brock had granted Cale was all that was necessary to even the odds. While Brock was pivoting about to refocus on his challenger, Cale had lunged into the straw to retrieve his discarded weapon. To his chagrin, Brock found himself staring into the stormy gray eyes of the man who was holding a Colt .45.

What happened next was a simultaneous chain of events that occurred so quickly it left Brock's head spinning. Brock attempted to blow Cale to smithereens before Cale could accomplish the same feat—in reverse. But Sundance plowed into Brock's backside, misdirecting the bullet. Cale's accurate shot seared through Brock's hand, causing him to drop his weapon. Sundance, who had been startled by the fast exchange of gunfire, trampled over the top of Brock on his way out of the barn. Before Brock could regain his feet and run for his life, Mikyla pounced on him, scratching his face to bloody shreds.

By the time Brock's head cleared he found himself staring at the toes of Cale's dusty boots. And to make matters worse, Mikyla kicked Brock in the shoulder once more for good measure, even after the stallion had left footprints all over his back.

"Get up, Terrel," Cale growled venomously. When Brock didn't immediately obey, Cale grabbed him by the nape of his jacket and yanked him to his feet. "It looks as if you are going to remain in the cavalry a mite longer than you originally anticipated—in Fort Reno Stockade to be precise," he added with a sarcastic snort.

Mikyla peered up into the chiseled features of the man who had come to mean all things to her. Cale had been staring death in the face, but he hadn't allowed impending doom to rattle him. Even with a Winchester rifle aimed at his chest, Cale had emerged victoriously.

Only now did she realize what Cale meant when he said he always had been expressing his love for her without actually voicing the words. He had been there for her, standing as sentinel. He had been protecting and keeping a constant vigil over her, allowing her the space to follow her heart and grasp at her obsessive dream.

He could have *physically* bent her to his will any time he felt inclined. But Cale had permitted Mikyla to indulge herself in her fleeting hopes, to grasp those few precious moments, without forcing her to do his bidding. He had made it possible for her to enjoy her dream site before it was snatched out from under her. And, stubborn though she had always been, she would have been no match for Cale if he had decided to force her off her claim or subtly guide her away from her hopeless battle. He had indulged her childish whim because he loved her enough to permit her to experience what she thought would make her happy—her dream of land. And through all her trials and struggles, Mikyla had come to realize that it was Cale who could make her happy, whether they wandered the plains like vagabonds or built a ranch that boasted champion race horses.

Pride shone in her eyes as she assessed this lion of a man. He had become a perfect friend, she realized. Cale was sensitive to all her needs, responsive to her many moods. He was her tower of strength and her gentle lover. That pretty much said it all, Miki mused with an adoring smile. What more could a woman want than a man who loved her enough to allow her to be herself? Cale was the domineering, forceful type, and yet he had come to respect Miki's individuality, to grant her a small glimpse of her coveted dream.

As Cale escorted Brock outside, he glanced down at the human scarecrow who had shafts of straw jutting from her hair, from the sleeves of her shirt, and from the leg of her breeches. When Ky stared at him with such an odd mixture of emotion Cale frowned puzzledly.

"Are you all right, Ky?" he questioned in concern.

A wry smile blossomed on her lips as she curled her hand around his free arm. "I'm better than all right," she murmured confidentially. "I just fell in love with you all over again. And for the third time, might I add." Her blue eyes sparkled with mischief. "According to Ozark superstition, the third time is a charm. Later, I intend to show you the full extent of loving the same man the third time around . . ."

Cale would have melted beneath her affectionate smile if the clatter of hooves hadn't distracted him. He was forced to squelch his lusty inclinations toward his wife until he presented Brock to the approaching posse led by Reuben Stubbs.

A bewildered gasp gushed from Reuben's lips when he recognized the military officer. He stood with his jaw swinging while Cale handed his prisoner over to the sheriff and watched the procession ride away.

"I don't understand what Terrel had to do with this," Reuben sighed. "Why did he want Miki dead?"

"He didn't," Cale mumbled. Painstakingly, he plucked the straw from Miki's tangled hair while Miki stared up into his tanned face, memorizing every chiseled feature, every fascinating expression.

Reuben wore a confused frown. "If Brock Terrel didn't want to dispose of Miki, why was he taking shots at her?"

"He wasn't," Cale replied, heedless of Reuben's mounting frustration.

The old man raised his arms in exasperation and then let them drop loosely to his sides. "Then who the devil was trying to kill her and what was the ruckus with Brock Terrel all about?"

Cale's gaze was still intently focused on his bewitching wife. "I'll explain it all to you later, Reuben," he promised absently.

"Later?" Reuben hooted like a screech owl. "I don't think I can wait until later!"

"Neither can I," Cale murmured. He tossed the old man a sly wink as he steered Mikyla toward the house.

Reuben expelled the breath he had been holding. It was obvious that he was going to learn nothing about the fiasco until Cale had satisfied his insatiable craving for the feisty blonde. "Does that mean we're finished building fence for the day?" he asked with a teasing grin.

Cale and Mikyla both glanced over their shoulders to grace him with mischievous smiles. "Why don't you take the rest of the day and put it to good use," Mikyla suggested. "I'm sure Doris would be delighted if you paid her an unexpected call."

"You're trying to get rid of me," Reuben accused,

although his voice was vibrating with too much inner laughter to sound insulted.

"I always did say Reuben was astute," Cale remarked as he escorted Mikyla to the house.

"You're darn right I am," he exclaimed with a self-righteous snort. "Hell, I'm the one who said you were in way over your head before you would admit that Mikyla was the first woman who . . ."

"*Good-bye,* Reuben," Cale interrupted before the old man's tongue ran away with itself. "And . . . since I'm feeling so generous this afternoon, why don't you take two days off instead of one . . . "

As the chummy couple closed the door behind them, Reuben pivoted on his heel to spruce himself up before he galloped back to town. Ah, the energy of youth, he mused with a snicker. Cale had been trailing after that curvaceous beauty like a lovesick schoolboy for months. He probably wouldn't emerge from his bedroom until the following evening. It was a good thing Cale Brolin possessed the strength of two men, Reuben decided as he ran a quick comb through his hair and shrugged on a clean shirt. Reuben suspected that high-spirited vixen who had taken hold of Cale's heart was going to prove to be an exhausting pastime. And Reuben, being the astute old man that he was, proved to be absolutely right!

Chapter 30

Cale pried one eye open when he heard the unidentified clank at the foot of the bed. A muddled frown plowed his brow when he spied Mikyla standing before him, dressed in her tight-fitting jeans and thin shirt that exposed the generous swells beneath. Clasped in one hand was the reed basket she had carried to the box supper. But today the basket was decorated with ribbons and an array of colorful wildflowers.

A disappointed groan erupted from Cale's chest. "Don't tell me Greta has been by to invite us to another of her socials. We have already erected a church and a school. Now what does she intend to build at the expense of her charitable neighbors?"

Mikyla tossed Cale his breeches, along with an impish smile. "This is an intimate social affair . . . just for us," she declared. "Reuben found your strawberry roan gelding stashed in the stables at Fort Reno. After we retrieve him we are going to picnic at Blue Lake."

One thick brow elevated as Cale raked Mikyla with a roguish glance. "Are there sentimental reasons for this journey?" he wanted to know.

Mikyla peeked at him from beneath a fringe of long curly lashes. "I thought perhaps Sundance would appreciate a swim. He loves the water as much as I do."

Like a rousing tiger, Cale unfolded himself from bed and stepped into his jeans. "Then, by all means, let's not dally another minute," he exclaimed caustically. "Why not completely spoil that nag! He has already been pastured with two dozen brood mares. I cannot imagine how a stallion could want for more. But if Sundance told you he needed a swim, let's make certain that pampered nag is granted his every whim."

When Cale reached the barn to see that Miki had already saddled Sundance and one of the mares, he glared at the stallion. "Shall I fetch a bucket of oats to take with us, in case you feel the craving for your ration of grain before we return home, Your Highness?"

Mikyla suppressed a giggle when Sundance indignantly threw back his head and stamped outside. By the time they rode to Fort Reno to retrieve the roan, Cale's disposition had sweetened considerably. Although he claimed to have no perverted attachment to the animal, he seemed pleased to be riding the muscular gelding whose speed was only second to Sundance's. Cale constantly teased Miki about her misdirected affection for her stallion, but it was obvious he was partial to the strawberry roan.

The moment they arrived at Blue Lake, Cale sat himself down to watch Mikyla and her half-human stallion amuse themselves with their aquatic antics. But he was not prepared for the scene that immediately filled his senses to overflowing. Mikyla peeled off her clothes in a most provocative manner, taking Cale's all-consuming gaze on a most arousing flight across her creamy skin. Looking every bit like Lady Godiva, with her long blond hair flooding over her bare flesh like a seductive cloak, Mikyla rode the stallion into the water.

When she slid from the saddle to drift like a swan, Cale felt himself melt into his boots. The tantalizing scene reminded him of their first encounter at Blue Lake. Yet it was far more titillating for Mikyla had become a proficient seductress who could arouse a man with her sylphlike poise and graceful movements. As she arched backward, the sun beamed down on her skin like a spotlight fixed on her alluring curves and swells.

"Are you trying to seduce me?" Cale croaked, shocked

that his voice would have sounded more appropriate if it had erupted from a bullfrog.

Mikyla rolled over in the water to grasp the saddle horn as Sundance swam by. With lithe grace she pulled onto the stallion's back. Leaning back, she braced her hands on his rump and propped her shapely legs against his shoulders. "It certainly took you long enough to notice," she replied with a pixielike smile.

Lord, she was breathtaking sitting there—the profile of exquisite beauty. Cale quickly reduced himself to a cloud of steam. He didn't remember peeling off his clothes, but he supposed he must have since he waded into the lake as naked as the day he was born. Either that or the internal heat of passion had burned his garments to a crisp, causing them to disintegrate, he decided as he stretched out to follow in the wake of the magnificent stallion and his enchanting mistress.

His outstretched hand folded around Mikyla's elbow, pulling her from her perch and into his waiting arms. His steamy gaze left her luscious figure momentarily to bark a command at the stallion who appeared none too pleased to have his rider snatched from his back.

"Go take a swim," he ordered. "The lady and I have better things to do."

Mikyla curled her arms and legs around Cale as he walked through the water . . . or on it. Both of them were too engrossed in each other to know for certain. "What are we going to do?" Mikyla inquired throatily. "What did you have in mind? Sampling the goodies in the lunch basket, perhaps?"

"Don't play naive, little nymph," Cale growled seductively. The rumbling purr of his voice sent a herd of goose bumps galloping across Mikyla's skin. "They don't package what I want in reed baskets."

Mikyla's hands began to weave intricate patterns on his chest as she set her feet to the sandy shore. "I really didn't come here to satisfy Sundance," she confessed as her lips skimmed his muscled flesh, turning it into melted butter. "I wanted to determine if this secluded wonderland was as magical as I remembered it."

Cale's body shuddered when it came into arousing contact with Mikyla's velvet skin. "And is it?" he queried huskily.

Mikyla gave her head a negative shake, causing the damp strands to ripple like the waves upon the crystal-clear water. "*You* provide the magic," she whispered as she drew him down with her to the sand.

His hands possessed a will of their own. They glided over her soft flesh, starting fires that inflamed her soul. Moist kisses splayed across her skin, setting her heart ablaze. Mikyla remembered the first time Cale had made love to her, the incredible patience and tenderness he had shown. And even now, he worshipped her, cherished her as if she were his treasured gift.

Her trembling fingertips scaled the breadth of his bronzed shoulders and drifted over the accelerated thud of his heart. Her lashes swept up to see the liquid silver of his eyes. The intensity of his stare had always been able to hold her spellbound. Every ounce of feminine reserve melted beneath his warm regard. Cale was wearing a look of love, and her pulse leapfrogged in response to his potent gaze.

Her palm flitted across the dark matting of hair that covered his chest. Her caress wandered over the lean muscles of his belly, feeling him tense and then relax beneath her intimate explorations. She watched his reaction to her adventurous caresses, marveling at the power she held over this invincible mass of brawn and muscle.

Cale groaned in sweet torment as the hot, consuming fires began to burn back on top of each other. The flames leaped across his skin and boiled in his blood. It amazed him that he could still feel this wild, mindless craving when Mikyla had not denied him passion even once since they spoke the vows. Once a day wasn't enough to appease the ache she created within him. Even every day for the rest of his life would not suffice, Cale mused as her hands and lips whispered her desire, her affection for him.

For pity's sake, how could he feel like her champion when she made him her slave? If Ky had requested the moon he would have flown off to fetch it for her. He had spoiled her and yet he couldn't seem to give her enough. Miki had spent years scratching and clawing to survive. She had carried the lion's share of responsibility. Cale longed to compensate for all her woes, for the heartaches and disappointments she had endured. He wanted to place the world at her feet and yet he wanted her to want *him* more than all else. He loved her, totally and completely. And yet he couldn't seem to express all the wild, ineffable emotions that were churning inside him.

Cale was certain his brain had been burned around the edges. Why else would he be stung by such contradicting thoughts? Mikyla's wandering kisses and caresses had fried his sanity to a crisp. He could make no sense of these violent sensations that erupted within him. They were every bit as explosive as they had been the first time they had come to Blue Lake. The trembling anticipation was still there, just as vivid as he remembered. All the erupting emotions were bubbling within, awaiting sweet release.

Again Cale found himself wondering if he didn't love this spirited vixen too much. She could touch each and every one of his emotions when they gushed forth, and then she touched them again when they receded. Mikyla could set him to swirling with her unrivaled passion. And when the maelstrom of sensations ebbed she caressed each one with love. This vivacious nymph stirred him, coming and going, he realized with a tremulous sigh. When the lovemaking was over the loving began. The tender afterglow lingered like smoldering coals until the fires billowed in the ever-constant draft of passion. And then the entire process began again . . .

His pensive thoughts took flight when Mikyla, murmuring her love, drew him to her. Cale responded without restraint, aching to satisfy the craving she instilled in him even when he knew the gnawing hunger would come again and again. His sinewy arms enfolded her as he strived for unattainable depths of intimacy. The fierce feelings of passion, entwined with love, encompassed him. At long last, Cale was assured that he was man enough to tame Mikyla's wild heart. She was his—not his possession but his equal. She was that special part of him that satisfied his restless spirit. She gave his life purpose and blessed him with that rare, unique brand of love that would last eternity.

As they soared across the heavens on love's most intimate of journeys, Cale knew for certain he had discovered the kind of happiness that would endure forever. "Lord, how I love you," he breathed as he bent to place a fleeting kiss to her soft lips. "Too much . . ."

An adoring smile curved her mouth upward as she reached up to rearrange the tousled raven hair that lay across his forehead. "I'm not sure too much will be enough," she whispered with genuine emotion.

"Nevertheless, I . . ." Cale's voice trailed off when he realized Sundance was breathing down his neck. Damn that nag! Sundance could never seem to tolerate Cale's affection toward Mikyla. Slowly, he swiveled his head to glare into the stallion's big brown eyes. "I rode all the way to Texas to present you with your own harem and still you deny me the only woman I've ever wanted," he snorted in irritation.

Sundance laid back his ears and stamped his hoof—all too close to Cale's hip. Then he nudged Cale's shoulder. Cale was knocked off balance and left to sprawl on top of Mikyla, who was giggling in impish delight.

"I think that means Sundance approves," she speculated as she wrapped her arms around Cale's neck to keep him where Sundance had put him.

"All I have ever wanted was that horse's blessing," Cale said in a tone that implied he couldn't have cared less.

"We shouldn't disappoint him," Mikyla tittered, flashing Cale a come-hither glance.

Mikyla might have trusted that feisty stallion enough to turn her back, but Cale wasn't at all confident that he wouldn't be trampled. Sensing Cale's wariness, Sundance laid the soft muzzle of his nose to one bare shoulder, shoving Cale down immediately after he had levered himself back up.

"I can take it from here . . . without your assistance, thanks just the same," Cale grumbled as he glared into Sundance's wide face.

"While the two of you are trying to settle your feud, I'm

dying for the want of another kiss," Mikyla confessed as she brushed wantonly against Cale's hair-roughened flesh. "But if you would prefer to carry on a conversation with a horse I suppose I could substitute my craving with a leg of chicken and a slice of fresh baked bread . . ."

Against his better judgment, Cale ignored the stallion and presented Mikyla with a half-hearted kiss. But his eyes shifted slightly to monitor the movement of those powerful hooves. To his surprise, Sundance gracefully bowed out, permitting Cale to concentrate on a kiss that was slowly towing him into the depths of desire.

As he lifted his head, Cale peered down into those beguiling blue eyes that mirrored her deep affection. His heart hammered in double time, knowing he was the reason for her radiant smile. His all-encompassing gaze drifted to the glorious mane of hair that was the mystical combination of sunlight and moonbeams. Reverently, he traced the sensuous curve of her lips with his index finger.

Just staring at this bewitching beauty evoked a myriad of tingling sensations within him. He wondered if he would always find himself engulfed in stormfire each time he took Mikyla in his arms. The faintest hint of a smile rippled across his lips. With this lively free spirit, each time would be just as wild and wondrous as the first, Cale assured himself.

His smile broadened into a roguish grin as he poised his mouth only a hairbreadth above her cupid's-bow lips. "You can forget about the chicken . . ."

And she did . . . the moment Cale came to her, loving her in all the unique ways they had created to express their affection for each other. This remarkable man, this rare combination of overpowering strength and amazing gentleness had taught her the meaning of love. She had just begun to explore the limitless boundaries of Cale's affection and Mikyla valued her precious treasure with her heart and soul. Now that she had Cale's love she had it all. His gift of love made all the difference . . .

EXPERIENCE THE SENSUOUS MAGIC
OF JANELLE TAYLOR!